A HISTORY

OF

WILD PLACES

ALSO BY SHEA ERNSHAW

Winterwood

The Wicked Deep

A HISTORY

OF

WILD PLACES

– A NOVEL –

SHEA ERNSHAW

ATRIA BOOKS

NEW YORK   LONDON   TORONTO   SYDNEY   NEW DELHI

An Imprint of Simon & Schuster, Inc.
1230 Avenue of the Americas
New York, NY 10020

First Atria Books hardcover edition December 2021

ATRIA B O O K S and colophon are trademarks of Simon & Schuster, Inc.

For information about special discounts for bulk purchases, please contact Simon & Schuster Special Sales at 1-866-506-1949 or business@simonandschuster.com.

The Simon & Schuster Speakers Bureau can bring authors to your live event. For more information or to book an event, contact the Simon & Schuster Speakers Bureau at 1-866-248-3049 or visit our website at www.simonspeakers.com.

Interior design by Jill Putorti

Manufactured in the United States of America

1 3 5 7 9 10 8 6 4 2

Library of Congress Cataloging-in-Publication Data

Names: Ernshaw, Shea, author.
Title: A history of wild places : a novel / Shea Ernshaw.
Description: First Atria Books hardcover edition. | New York : Atria Books, 2021.
Identifiers: LCCN 2021012842 (print) | LCCN 2021012843 (ebook) |
ISBN 9781982164805 (hardcover) | ISBN 9781982164829 (ebook)
Subjects: LCSH: Communal living--Fiction. | Missing persons--Fiction. |
Psychological fiction. | GSAFD: Suspense fiction.
Classification: LCC PS3605.R73 H57 2021 (print) |
LCC PS3605.R73 (ebook) | DDC 813/.6--dc23
LC record available at https://lccn.loc.gov/2021012842
LC ebook record available at https://lccn.loc.gov/2021012843

ISBN 978-1-9821-6480-5
ISBN 978-1-9821-6482-9 (ebook)

For Jess, my agent

There is always danger for those who are afraid.

—GEORGE BERNARD SHAW

A HISTORY

OF

WILD PLACES

FOXES AND MUSEUMS

Excerpt from Book One in the Eloise and the Foxtail series

The green eyes of a riddle fox peered into Eloise's bedroom window.

It was a Wednesday, and the sun had long since dipped beyond the whispering evergreens. Eloise should have been asleep, but she kept thinking about the woods, about the lean-to fort she and her little brother had made at the base of a pine tree, and if it was strong enough to withstand the winter storms.

It was surely a dream—those eyes that stared at her through the glass, snow whirling and catching against the wool of its pointed face. Riddle foxes were rare this deep in the mountains. But dreams were nearly just as rare. Eloise never saw images when she slept anymore. They were fanciful and indulgent. The world wouldn't allow for dreams.

Even nightmares were scarce.

PART ONE

THE BARN

D eath has a way of leaving breadcrumbs, little particles of the past that catch and settle and stain. A single strand of copper-brown hair, the follicle ripped from a skull, snagged by a door hinge or cold, clenched fingers. Drops of blood and broken skin, carelessly left at the bottom of a bathroom sink when they should have been scrubbed away.

Objects leave hints too: a bracelet broken at the clasp, dropped in the red-clay dirt; a shoe kicked off during a struggle, wedged behind a rear truck tire; a contact lens, popped free when the person screamed for help in some deep, dark part of a backwoods lot where no one could hear.

These things, these artifacts, tell me where a person has been. The last steps they took.

But not in the way you might think.

The past sputters through me, images reflected against my corneas, revealing the strained, awful looks carved into the faces of those who've gone missing. Who've vanished and never returned home.

I see them in a sort of slideshow staccato, like the old black-and-white nickel films. It's a terrible talent to hold an object and see the likeness of the person it once belonged to, their final moments shivering and jerking through me as if I were right there. Witnessing the grim, monstrous ends of a person's life.

But such things—such abilities—can't be given back.

Snow blows against the truck windshield, icing it over, creating a thin filigree effect—like delicate lacework. The heater stopped working three days back, and my hands shake in my coat pockets as I peer through the glass at the Timber Creek Gas & Grocery, a tiny, neon-lit storefront at the edge of a mountain town without a name. Through the gusting snow, I can just make out a collection of homes sunk back in the lodgepole pines, and several businesses long since boarded up. Only the small firehouse, a tow truck service, and the gas station are still up and running. A stack of cut firewood sits outside the gas station with a sign that reads: $5 A BUNDLE, SELF-SERVE. And in smaller print: BEST PRICE ON MOUNTAIN.

This town is merely a husk, easily wiped off the map with a good wind or an unstoppable wildfire.

I push open the truck door, rusted hinges moaning in the cold, and step out into the starless night. My boots leave deep prints in the fresh two inches of snowfall, and I cross the parking lot to the front doors of the gas station, sharp winter air numbing my ears and nostrils, my breath a frosty cloud of white.

But when I pull open the gas station door, a tidal wave of warm, stagnant air folds over me—thick with the scent of motor oil and burnt corn dogs—and for a moment I feel light-headed. My eyes flick across the store: the shelves have a vacant, apocalyptic feel. Dust molders on every surface, while a few solitary items—starchy white bread, Pop-Tarts, and tiny boxes of travel-size cereal—seem almost like movie-set props from another era, their logos sun-bleached and outdated. At the back wall of the store sits a droning cooler lined with beer, cartons of milk, and energy drinks.

This place isn't haunted—not in the way I'm accustomed to—it's paralyzed in time.

At the front counter, a woman with feathered gray hair and even grayer skin sits perched on a stool under the headache-inducing florescent lights. She's tapping her fingers against the wood countertop as if she's tapping a pack of cigarettes, and I move across the store toward her.

To the left of the cash register sits a coffee maker coated in a heavy layer of dust—I'm tempted to reach for one of the stacked paper cups and fill it with whatever stagnant, lukewarm liquid is waiting inside, but I suspect it will taste just as it looks: like oily truck tires. So I let my gaze fall back to the woman, my hands clenching inside my coat pockets, feeling the burn of blood flowing back into my fingertips.

The woman eyes me with a nervy-impatience, and a hint of suspicion. I know this look: She doesn't like me at the onset. The beard I've been cultivating for the last month doesn't rest well on the features of my face, it makes me look ten years older, mangy like a stray dog. Even after a shower I still look wild, undomesticated, like someone you shouldn't trust.

I smile at the woman, trying to seem acquiescent, harmless, as though a glimpse of my teeth will somehow reassure her. It does not. Her sour expression tugs even tighter.

"Evening," I begin, but my voice has a roughness to it, a grating unease—the lack of sleep giving me away. The woman says nothing, only keeps her paled eyes squarely on me, like she's waiting for me to demand all the money in the register. "Have you heard of a woman named Maggie St. James?" I ask. I used to have a knack for this: for convincing people to trust me, to give up details they've never even told the police, to reveal that small memory they've been holding on to until now. But that talent is long gone, sunk like flood waters into a damp basement.

The woman makes a half-interested snort, the scent of cigarette smoke puffing out from her pores—a salty, ashen smell that reminds me of a case I took out in Ohio three years back, searching for a missing kid who had been holed up inside an abandoned two-story house out behind a run-down RV park, where the walls had the same stench—salt and smoke—like it had been scrubbed into the daffodil and fern wallpaper.

"Everyone around here's heard of Maggie St. James," the woman answers with a gruff snort, wrinkling her stubby nose and looking up at me from the nicotine-yellow whites of her eyes. "You from a newspaper?"

I shake my head.

"A cop?"

I shake my head again.

But she doesn't seem to care. Either way, cop or reporter, she keeps talking. "A woman goes missing and this place turns into a damn spectacle, like a made-for-TV movie—helicopters and search dogs were swarming up in those woods, found a whole heap of nothing. Searched through folks' garbage cans and garages, asking questions like the whole community was in on something, like we knew what happened to that missing woman but weren't saying." She crosses her arms—all bony angles and loose, puckered skin, like a snake slowly shedding her useless outer layer from her skeleton. "We're honest people 'round here, tell ya what we think even if you don't ask. Those police made people paranoid, creeping around at night with their flashlights, peeking into decent folks' windows. Most of us didn't leave our homes for weeks; cops had us believing there was a murderer out there, snatching people up. But it was all for nothing. They never turned up a damn thing. And all for some woman who we didn't even know." At this she nods her head, lips pursed together, as if to punctuate the point.

The locals in this town might not have known who Maggie St. James was when she turned up in their community then promptly vanished, but a lot of people outside of here did. Maggie St. James had gained notoriety some ten years ago when she wrote a children's book titled *Eloise and the Foxtail: Foxes and Museums*. What followed were four more books, and some fierce public backlash that her stories were too dark, too grisly and sinister, and that they were inspiring kids to run away from home and venture into nearby woodlands and forests, searching for something called the *underground*—a fictional location she wrote about in the series. The *underground* was supposed to turn ordinary kids into something unnatural—a dark, villainous creature. One quote in particular from a noted literary journal said, *St. James's take on the modern fairy tale is more nightmares than dreams, stories to make your children fear not just the dark, but the daylight, too. I wouldn't read this to a serial killer, let alone to my child.*

Shortly after her fifth book was published, a fourteen-year-old boy named Markus Sorenson ventured deep into the Alaskan wilderness in search of this *underground* and died from hypothermia. His body was found seven days later. I remember the case because I got a call from a detective up in Anchorage, asking if I might come up and see if I could assist in finding the boy. But they found him at the entrance to a small rocky cave the following day, skin whiter than the surrounding snowfall. I wondered if in those final moments, when the delirium of cold began to make him hallucinate, did he think he had found the *underground*?

After the boy's death, Maggie St. James just sort of slipped into obscurity—with good reason. According to Wikipedia, there was a planned sixth book in the Eloise and the Foxtail series. A book that would never be written, because the author, Maggie St. James, vanished.

"Do you remember her stopping here?" I ask the woman, whose pale blue veins are tightening beneath the waxy skin of her throat.

She raises an eyebrow at me, as if I've offended her in suggesting that she might *not* remember such a thing after five years. I know Maggie St. James stopped at the Timber Creek Gas & Grocery because it was in the police report, as well as a statement from a cashier who was not named. "She was unmemorable at best," the woman answers, what's left of her thinning eyelashes fluttering closed then open again, dark mascara clotting at the corners. "But lucky for the police, and you, I remember everyone." She glances to the oily storefront windows—snow spiraling against the glass—as if the memory were still there, just within reach. "She got gas and bought a pack of strawberry bubble gum, tore open the package and started chewing it right there, before she'd even paid for it. Then she asked about a red barn. Asked if I knew where she could find one around here. Of course, I told her about the old Kettering place a few miles on up the road. Said it was nearly collapsed, a place kids go to drink, and hadn't been properly used in twenty years. I asked her what she wanted with that old place, but she wouldn't say. She left without even a thanks, then drove off. They found her car the next morning, abandoned." She snuffs, turning her face back to the windows, and I get the sense she wants to make some comment about how rude city folk can be, but catches herself just in case *I* might be city folk. Even though I'm not. And from what I knew of Maggie St. James, she wasn't either.

I clear my throat, hoping there might be more beneath the surface of her memory if I can ask the right question and pry it loose. "Have you heard anyone talk about her in the years since?" I ask, tiptoeing around the thing I really want to ask. "Someone who saw her, who remembers something?"

"Someone who remembers killing her, you mean?" She unfolds her arms, mouth tugging strangely to one side.

I doubt there's a serial killer in the area—there'd be reports of other disappearances—but perhaps there's someone who keeps to themselves, lives alone up in these woods, someone who maybe hadn't killed before, but only because he had never encountered the right opportunity—until Maggie drove into town. Someone out hunting deer or rabbit, and a stray shot tore through a woman with short, cropped blond hair—a woman whose body now needed to be disposed of, burned or buried. Accidents can turn people into grave diggers.

"I can't say for sure that some folks around here don't have a bolt untightened from the mind, a few cobwebs strung between the earlobes, but they aren't killers." The woman shakes her head. "And they certainly can't keep their mouths shut. If someone killed that girl, they'd've talked about it by now. And soon enough, the whole town would know of it. We're not much for keeping secrets for long."

I look away from her, eyeing the coffee machine again, the stack of paper cups. *Should I risk it?* But the woman speaks again, one eyebrow raised like a pointed toothpick, as if she's about to let me in on a secret. "Maybe she wanted to get herself lost, start a new life; no crime in that." Her eyes flick to the pack of cigarettes sitting beside the cash register, a purple lighter resting on top. She needs a smoke.

I nod, because she might be right about Maggie. People did sometimes vanish, not because they'd been taken or killed, but simply because they *wanted* to disappear. And Maggie had reason to escape her life, to slip into the void of endless highways and small towns and places where most don't go looking.

Maybe I'm chasing a woman who doesn't want to be found.

Behind the cash register, the woman finally reaches for the pack of cigarettes, sliding it across the counter so it's resting on the very edge. "Maybe it's best to just let her be, let a woman go missing if that's what she wants."

For a moment, she and I stare at one another—as if we've reached some understanding between us, a knowing that we've felt that same itch at the back of our throats at least once in our lives: that desire to be *lost*.

But then her expression changes: the skin around her mouth wrinkling like dried apricots, and a shiver of something untrusting settles behind her eyes, like she's suddenly wary of who I am—who I *really* am—and why I've come asking questions after all these years. "You a private detective?" she asks, taking the pack of smokes in her hand and tapping out a single cigarette.

"No." I scratch at my beard, along the jaw. It's starting to feel too warm inside the little store—humid, boxed-in.

"Then why'd you come all the way out here in the middle of winter, asking about that woman? You a boyfriend or something?"

I shake my head, a staticky hum settling behind my eyes—that well-known ache trying to draw me into the past. I'm getting closer to Maggie, I can feel it.

The woman's mouth makes a severe line, like she can see the discomfort in my eyes, and I take a quick step back from the counter before she can ask me what's wrong. "Thank you for your time," I tell her, nodding. Her mouth hangs open, like the maw of some wild animal waiting to be fed, and she watches as I retreat to the front doors and duck out into the night.

The sudden rush of cold air is an odd relief. Snow and wind against my overheated flesh.

But my head still thumps with the heavy need for coffee, for sleep—but also with the grinding certainty that I'm getting close. This gas station was the last place Maggie St. James was seen before she vanished, and my ears buzz with the knowing.

I climb back into the truck and press a hand to my temple.

I could use a handful of aspirin, a soft bed that doesn't smell like industrial-grade motel detergent, the warmth of anything familiar. I crave things I've forgotten how to get. An old life, maybe. That's what it really is: a need for something I've lost long ago. A life that's good and decent and void of the bone-breaking pain that lives inside me now.

The truck tires spin on the ice, windshield wipers clacking back and forth, and I swerve out of the gas station parking lot back onto the road. I glance in the rearview mirror and see the woman watching me from the window of the little store, her face a strange neon-blue glow under the shivering lights.

And I wonder: Did Maggie St. James see that same face as she sped away five years ago? Did the same chill skip down her spine to her tailbone?

Did she know she was about to vanish?

―――――

The truck headlights break through the dark only a few yards ahead, illuminating the icy pavement like a black, moonless river, and casting ribbons of yellow-white through the snow-weighted trees that sag and drip like wet arms.

I drive for an hour up the same road that Maggie St. James followed, passing only one car going in the opposite direction, and a scattering of small, moss-covered homes.

Until at last, through the tall sentinel pines and sideways snow, a red barn appears.

What's left of it.

The woman at the gas station had been right, the entire left side is caved in, a heap of splintered wood and old nails now buried in snow. But a metal weathervane still sits perched at the highest peak, the moving pieces locked in place by the cold or rust. It's the same barn I saw in a police photograph that Maggie's parents showed me. But in the photo, parked in the foreground, was a pale green, four-door, newer model Volvo: Maggie's car. She had parked here alongside the road, gotten out of the driver's seat, took her purse and her cell phone, then vanished.

I ease off the gas pedal and pull the truck onto the shoulder of the road, stopping in the very same place where she did.

It was midsummer when Maggie was here, the leaves on the trees a healthy, verdant green, the sun crisp and blinding overhead, and it must have warmed the inside of her car. Perhaps she had the windows rolled down, smelled the sweet scent of green manzanita and wildflowers growing up from the ditch beside the road. Perhaps she closed her eyes for a moment while she sat in her car, considering her options. Perhaps she even thought back on all the things that led her here: the faraway moments, the fragmented pieces of her life that only come into focus in times like this.

She was building a story in her mind, just like the fairy tales she wrote, but this story was her own—the ending not yet written. Or an ending only she foresaw.

Ahead of me, the mountain road makes a sharp left turn and a small solitary house—the only one for miles—sits tucked back in the pines, a porch light on, illuminating the gray front door. Mr. and Mrs. Alexander live there. They've lived in the squat, single-story home for forty-three years—most of their lives—and they were there when Maggie's car was found. The police spent quite a bit of time interviewing the Alexanders. From the report, it's obvious the detectives had their suspicions about Mr. Alexander, and they even dug up parts of the Alexander's backyard, searching for remains: a thighbone, an earring, any clues that Maggie might have met her fate inside the Alexander's home. One of the detective's theories was that Maggie's car may have broken down—even though it started right up when the tow truck came to haul it away—and maybe she wandered over to the Alexanders' hoping for refuge, for help. But perhaps instead Mr. Alexander dragged her into his garage and bludgeoned her to death before burying her out back. They found a hammer in his garage with blood splatter marks on it, that was later determined to be rodent blood. He had used the hammer to end the suffering of a mouse caught in a trap. But that didn't detour the police from keeping Mr. Alexander as their main—*and only-* suspect.

There weren't many leads in the St. James case, and the local police found themselves pacing this length of road with little to go on. Cases go cold this way. They grow stagnant, lose momentum. Without a body, without any blood or sign of a struggle, Maggie St. James might have simply wanted to vanish—just like the woman at the gas station suggested. *No crime in that.*

I reach into the backpack on the seat beside me and pull out the tiny silver charm. My ears begin to buzz. The charm is shaped like a small book, with thin metal pages and a narrow spine, and it's no bigger than my pinky nail.

When Maggie's parents gave it to me, they explained that the charm once hung from a necklace that Maggie always wore. There were five charms on the necklace—five tiny silver books—one for every book in the *Foxtail* series. And each one had a number engraved on the front.

The one I hold in my hand is number *three.*

The charm was found by police a few feet from the trunk of Maggie's car. Which was the only indication that there might have been a struggle: someone who pulled Maggie from the driver's seat, kicking and clawing, and during the fray, the charm was torn free from her necklace and fell to the gravel beside the road. But there were no hair fibers found, no broken fingernails, no other clues to support this theory.

I close my eyes and clench my hand around the charm, feeling its sharp corners, its delicate weight in my palm—imagining it suspended at the end of a silver chain, against the warmth of Maggie's chest, pressed between four other identical charms. The air pulses around me: cotton in my ears, a tightness in my throat, and I imagine sitting in Maggie's green Volvo, just as she did, the idle summer breeze through the open window. The radio is on, playing an old country song, Waylon Jennings: *"She's a good-hearted woman in love with a good-timin' man. She loves him in spite of his ways that she don't understand."* The music rattles from the speakers, sailing out the open windows—like a memory plucked from the trenches of my mind. Except this memory doesn't belong to me. It's a slideshow, distorted and marred with tiny holes, like an old film through a sputtering projector.

I open the truck door and step out into the snow.

And even as the cold folds itself over me, I feel the warm afternoon sun against my skin, the hot pavement rising up beneath my boots. I feel what Maggie felt.

It's been five years since she was here, but the memory replays itself across my mind as if I were standing beside her on that quiet afternoon. We all leave markers behind—dead or alive—vibrations that trail behind us through all the places we've been. And if you know how to see them, the imprints of a person can be found—and followed.

But like all things, they fade with time, become less clear, until finally they are washed over with new memories, new people who have passed through here.

I squeeze my fist, knuckles cracked and dry in the cold, drawing out the memory of Maggie from the small charm. *She* has brought me here. Dust and fluttering eyelashes beneath the midday sun. Memories shake through me, and I walk several paces up the road, to the exact place where she stood. A bird chatters from a nearby pine, bouncing from limb to limb, back to its nest. But when I open my eyes, the bird is gone—the trees covered in snow. No nests. No roosting jays and finches. All gone farther south for the winter months.

I glance back up the road—my truck parked in the snow just off the shoulder. There are no other cars, no logging trucks wheeling up into the forest. But in summer, surely there was more traffic. A family heading into the mountains for a weekend camping trip at one of the remote lakes, locals driving into town to fill up on gas and beer.

Yet, no one saw a woman slip from her car. No one saw a thing. Or if they did, they aren't saying. Silence can hold a thousand untold stories.

The Alexanders' porch light winks against the snow that has collected on the railing and front steps—the house itself giving the impression of sinking into the earth, doing its best not to collapse completely. I can hear Maggie breathing, the beat of her heart beneath her ribs—she wasn't panicked or afraid. Her car didn't break down like the police report had suggested. She stood on the side of the road and stretched her arms overhead, like she had merely stopped to work the tension from her joints after a long drive. Her eyes blinked against the sun and she drew in a deep breath, tilting her face to the sky.

She wanted to be here; she came with a purpose. But she didn't turn for the Alexander's house. She may have peeked at it briefly, observed it in the same way I do now, but then she shifted her focus toward the barn. Walking to the edge of the road to stare up at it.

Yet, the barn was not her destination either, it was only a clue. *She was on the right path. She was close.*

I mirror her footsteps, letting the memory pull me back to her car where she opened the trunk, metal hinges creaking as she bent to look inside. She hoisted out a backpack from the trunk and stuffed it with two bottles of water, a hooded sweatshirt, and a fresh pair of socks. In her front pocket was the pack of strawberry gum she purchased back at the store, and her cell phone.

Around her neck, she wore the silver necklace—five charms clinking together.

She slung the pack over her shoulders and locked the car, taking her keys with her. *She planned on coming back.* She wasn't running away, not for good. She believed she would return to the car.

I watch as the memory of her takes several steps toward the side of the road, and when her hand brushed at her hair. . . it catches on something. Maybe the straps of her backpack snagged the silver charm, or just her fingertips, but it breaks free from the chain and falls to the gravel at her feet. She didn't notice, didn't hear it fall, and she strode on.

It wasn't a struggle or a fight with an attacker that caused her to lose the charm: it came free on its own.

I watch her image walk down the embankment toward the barn, her pace assured, easy.

She only had enough supplies for a day's hike. No sleeping bag, no tent, no dehydrated food to be reheated over a camp stove. She didn't mean to vanish. Or she anticipated she'd have shelter and food wherever she was going.

She anticipated something other than what happened to her.

————

A little over a month ago, I was sitting in a truck stop parking lot on the northern border of Montana, considering crossing over into Canada and seeing how far north I could travel before the roads ended and there was nothing but permafrost and a sea of evergreens, when my cell phone rang.

An annoying little *chirp, chirp, chiiirp.*

I rarely answered it anymore—*it rarely rang.* The battery was perpetually low and I'd only ever charge it enough to keep it from dying, in case of emergencies. In case I got a flat tire. In case I wanted to call someone—which I never did.

But when I picked it up from the dashboard, I saw the name light up on the screen: Ben Takayama, my roommate from college, the guy I once drank a whole bottle of vintage bourbon with then drove all night to Reno only to sleep in the bed of his dinky Toyota truck, sweating under the midday sun as the alcohol seeped from our pores, then vomited in the bushes that lined a shady, neon-lit casino. No one even batted an eye at us. Not even the security guards. Ben and I had shared countless stupid, half-brained adventures together, most of which ended badly—with our wallets stolen, our dignity facedown in an alley gutter, our flesh bruised and sliced open. He was notably one of the few people who I still called a friend. And probably the only person whose call I would have answered in that moment, longing for a homemade meal and something familiar. Anything. Even a call from Ben.

"Travis?" he said on the other end when I answered, but I just sat there, mute. *How long has it been since I talked to someone from the old days? How long have I been on the road, driving across state lines, heading east and then north? Two months? Three?*

I cleared my throat. "Hey."

"No one's heard from you in a while." His voice was strange, concerned—unusual for him. And I didn't like the way it made me feel—like he was trying to peer beneath the shadow I had been hiding under. He exhaled, as if he knew I didn't want his sympathy. I wanted the old days, before it all went to shit. Cheap beer and Friday nights in our dorm room, bad breakups and failed economics classes. I missed those days in the way most people miss their college years, even though at the time you don't realize you're living smack in the middle of the years you will tell stories about later. The years when you're so damn broke you have to steal rolls of toilet paper from the restroom of a dive bar two blocks from campus that serves a weekly happy hour special: a beer and a slice of pie for four dollars.

You miss those years, but you also wouldn't go back.

They were also the years when I drank because it dulled the effects of my ability. When I was drunk, and even hungover, I could touch objects and not feel a thing. No flashes of memory. No seizing images of the past. When my mind was clouded over with booze, I felt almost nothing. I made it through college this way. And sometimes, I still drink just to escape the things I don't want to see—*don't want to remember*.

"I like that you've gone all Jack Kerouac and abandoned social norms," he began, "living on the road like a fucking heathen. But you need to check in every once in a while."

On the dashboard sat a half-eaten pile of French fries that had begun to soak through the thin cardboard tray. I was hungry, but I couldn't stomach to finish it.

"Tell me where you're at; maybe I can take a long weekend and come join you." He sounded earnest, a shiver in his voice, like he longed to escape the normalcy of his perfect, sterile life. Two kids and a corgi named Scotch and a wife who bakes sugar cookies in the shapes of trees and hearts every damn Thursday. *Every goddamned Thursday*, he told me once. Like he both loved and loathed it. He longed for dirty hotel rooms and shitty roadside diner food and smoky bars and smoky girls who all have the same names. Who all think you're a better man than what you really are.

Ben wanted what I had.

But Ben's *average* life had something mine didn't: a home. Shelter. A place you went after a long day that folded you into its center and held you there, safe, protected from everything that lurked beyond your front door. Instead, I had an old truck that wheezed and choked every time I started it, and a quarter tank of gas. And that was about it.

But I didn't deserve a safe, average life. Those things were given to good, decent people. I was not good or decent.

I was destruction and missed chances and moments I couldn't take back.

"You don't want to come here," I said into the phone. "Trust me. Jack Kerouac wouldn't be sitting in a truck stop parking lot eating day-old fries and considering how far I might get into Canada before I run out of money." I sounded morose, desperate, and I didn't like the feeling.

"You're right, Kerouac would be drinking his dinner," Ben said. "Maybe that's your problem."

"Maybe." I smiled.

Silence cut through the phone and I could hear Ben breathing. He didn't just call to check up on me, make sure I wasn't dead. He called for something else. "I've got something you might be interested in."

I swallowed and turned my gaze to the truck stop diner a good distance across the parking lot. Two men were walking through the double doors, and I could make out a long bar inside with metal stools that ran the length of the diner and several booths set beneath the windows with sad, olive-green upholstery. Most of the stools and booths were occupied. The place was meant to be brightly lit, to serve coffee all night, to keep drivers awake for whatever long stretch of road they faced ahead.

"What's that?" I asked Ben.

"A job."

"I don't do that anymore."

He exhaled into the phone. "I know, but it might be good for you. Give you something to focus on." So he didn't truly think the Jack Kerouac life was the one I should be pursuing after all: He was trying to lure me back to my old life. Ben was a detective now. After eight years as a cop he finally got promoted, but now he spends most of his time behind a desk, and he hates being sedentary. *A slow fucking death*, he once said. Over the years, he'd sent cases my way, referred families to me when they started to lose hope. And I knew how this call would go, he would try to convince me to take one more job. One more missing person. Like he thought it might bring me back.

"I can't," I said. *My work was the very thing I was trying to escape.*

Again, he made a sound, drawing in a deep breath, like he was trying to think of the right words that might convince me. "You'd be doing me a favor," he added. So, he would use guilt, a favor for an old friend. Only an asshole refuses that.

"How's that?" I asked cautiously.

"They're friends of my family. I've known them my whole life. Their daughter disappeared."

My heart began to pound inside my chest. *A missing daughter.* A string of words I've heard too many times over the years—the most common type of disappearance. Also, the kind of disappearance that now makes my skin break into a sweat. Regret and grief and sickening dread wove itself through me, suffocating me with a wave of memories that I had been working so hard to forget.

"You might have heard of her," he continued. "Her name is Maggie St. James. She's a writer. She vanished five years ago, police have stopped searching, and the family's desperate."

Desperate family. Another common phrase. That's when they track me down, that's when someone suggests they call Travis Wren: *He might be able to help.* I'm the last resort.

"Five years is a long time," I said. Even though I knew it wasn't. I once found a kid who had been abducted seventeen years earlier when he was only six months old. And I found him, alive, living with a family up in Rhode Island. Not his real family—but the family who kidnapped him. They wanted a baby so bad that they stole one from a stroller in a Kroger parking lot while his real mother was loading bags of produce and dog food into the back of her silver Honda.

"Not for you," Ben said. He knew about most of my cases. But he probably also knew I was looking for an excuse, any reason to say *no* to what he was about to ask. "They need your help," he said then. "Do me this favor, Travis. I wouldn't ask if I didn't know the family; they live in the same neighborhood as my parents. You remember Aster Heights, with that old Rotting Hill Cemetery at the east end?"

Its real name is Rooster Hill Cemetery, but we always called it *Rotting Hill*, for obvious reasons. It was also the cemetery where my sister was buried, set down into the earth much too soon, eyes wide and blue beneath her closed lashes, as if searching, *searching*. Waiting for me.

I'm not sure if Ben remembered it was where Ruth had been buried, but hearing him mention the cemetery caused memories to coil tight inside my mind, painful and blunt-edged, like being struck on the back of the head with a hammer.

If it weren't for this single thing, if he hadn't brought up Rotting Hill, I might have flat-out said no. But instead I sat, watching the sky turn a muddy, washed-up gray as rain began to fall in oversized drops against the windshield.

"At least go talk to the parents before you say no," Ben urged. "Hear the details of the case. I think it's one you might want to take."

I breathed into the phone and stared out at the truck stop parking lot, at the dark line of trees beyond. A good place to leave a body. To hide the things you'd like to forget. I know these kinds of places, I've found missing people in tree lines just like this one, half buried, pine needles woven into knotted hair, leaves pressed damply over the eyes. Dried blood under fingernails.

"Okay," I said.

––––––––

I stand at the side of a mountain road facing a decaying red barn, soft, lazy snowflakes tumbling down from a milk-white sky, turning everything noir-film quiet.

I curl my fingers around the silver book-charm, trying to squeeze memories from it like juice from an overripe lemon. After locking her car, Maggie St. James strode down the sloped side of the road toward the old barn. Her cropped blond hair, smelling of freshly cut flowers, lilacs, and vanilla. She was more bone than anything else, not unhealthy, but a woman who didn't seem suited to long treks into the wilderness. She was a coffee-shop and gluten-free-croissant kind of woman, leisurely strolls through a city park maybe, but certainly not this.

There were a few stories online theorizing that Maggie's disappearance was merely a publicity stunt for the final book in the Foxtail series. And watching the afterimage of her striding away from her car, casually surveying the landscape before her, I wonder if they might have been right.

Perhaps she was mimicking the very thing that happened to the kids who read her books and ran away—she wanted to vanish.

And perhaps this is why her disappearance was never taken seriously, not even by the police.

But after five years, could she really just be in hiding, awaiting the perfect moment to reappear? *Poof*, and Maggie St. James magically strolls out of these backwoods, ready to reveal the sixth and final book in her series, all orchestrated by her clever publicist. Or did something else happen to her?

Maggie was twenty-six when she went missing. She'd be thirty-two now, if she's still alive. Just another missing woman.

The words form and scatter my thoughts: *just another missing woman*. Like too many others. Like the one that keeps me up at night, the one I can't shake—*her* eyelids gone still, pupils black and glacial and refusing to blink.

I take a step closer to the abrupt edge of the road, the wind creaking through the trees, whipping across the icy surface of the road, reminding me that I'm still standing at the edge of a winter forest. The memory of Maggie blinks in and out, fading with time, but then I see her—the *afterimage*—veering around the side of the barn, following a hidden driveway deeper into the trees, narrow and rutted and easily missed if you weren't looking for it. If you didn't already know it was there. But Maggie St. James walks down the little road with purpose.

She knew where she was going.

I stomp back to my truck and climb inside, melted snow dripping onto the rubber floor mat.

I won't follow her on foot, not in this deep snow.

The truck heaves once before the engine turns over and I pop it into gear, steering off the shoulder of the road and down onto the snow-covered driveway. A gate that once blocked the drive when Maggie passed through here now sits bent and partially swung open, resting in the snowbank. The truck squeezes through the gate opening—just barely—the passenger side mirror scraping against the metal post, but it doesn't sheer off. The truck tires sink into hidden ruts, and the driveway leads around what's left of the old red barn, through the trees, to an open plot of land not visible from the road. Ahead of me, sits the remains of a house, only a chimney now rising up into the thick night sky—a solitary symbol of what once had been.

I put the truck in park, and walk through the snow to the chimney, the headlights gleaming over the carcass. I place my hand against the brick.

The chimney is cool to the touch, and I glimpse the vibrating image of a porch swing and a little girl in army-green rain boots pumping her legs into the summer wind, sending herself up higher and higher. The next burst of memories is of someone screaming, a woman wailing from an upstairs bedroom while tears spilled down her strawberry cheeks. She died in childbirth, left her daughter motherless. A quick slideshow flashes through me, decades of time in half a blink: a man waving goodbye to someone on the porch, his hands work-worn and trembling; a curtain flapping from a kitchen window where a girl is crying softly, writing a letter at the dining table; a boy with autumn-brown hair and deep-set eyes, jumping from the roof and breaking his arm at the elbow when he hit the ground. He never wrote his name right after that, never could bend the arm without causing pain.

Several families, several lives existed within this house.

Click click click, and then it's finished.

I yank my hand away. I don't want to muddy my focus, to chase these images deeper and deeper until I know the details of all these lives. I wheel my eyes away from the crumbling chimney and look to the trees beyond the house. Maggie didn't stop here, she didn't encounter some villain in the shadows like in her fairy tales, who snuck out from the dark and choked the life from her, silent and still. She isn't buried beneath the rocks and soil and soot that clot the area around the chimney.

She kept going.

She slipped through the trees. Deeper, *deeper*, into the woods.

At this point, I would usually call Maggie's family. Let them know that I might have a lead. That their daughter had not wandered over to the Alexanders' place like the police report had surmised. She came here intentionally, to this old barn, this burnt-out house in the Three Rivers Mountains of northern California. And second, she brought a backpack and supplies with her, then locked her car and strode off the road into the forest. She knew where she was going—she had a plan.

Rarely do I phone the local police—I let the family who hired me make that call, if they want to convince the nearest jurisdiction that I'm worth listening to, that they should come out and take a look, follow me into the forest in the middle of the night. Only if I find hard evidence do I call it in. I don't want my prints on anything. Don't want to give anyone cause to suspect the only reason I found this evidence is because I put it there myself.

Keep your hands clean, Ben told me some years ago. And I've stuck to it.

But I don't call Maggie's family. Or the police. Because my cell hasn't had a signal since I left Highway 86 a few hours back. And I haven't found any hard evidence, no stray boot tossed into the hollowed-out house— a size seven, same as Maggie's. No clump of hair yanked from her pale white skull. No solid clues that Maggie came this way. Only the memory of her I can see in my mind—a woman who slipped into the trees and disappeared.

No proof of anything yet.

When I took this case, I told myself it was a favor to Ben. And I needed the money. Maggie St. James's father wrote me a personal check for 50 percent up front—standard with all my cases. The remainder due only if I find Maggie, *dead or alive*.

But there is another reason I took this case.

My sister.

A nagging in my solar plexus, a black rotting pit in the deepest hollow of my stomach. If I can find Maggie St. James, maybe it will be like rescuing my sister, the one I didn't get to in time. Maybe it will fill the hole that's been trying to swallow me up, and I'll be able to sleep without seeing her pale arms, palms to the ceiling, mouth slightly open, as if she tried to say something at the end but ran out of time. Finding Maggie will be like finding Ruth.

It will set something right.

When I took this job, I also told myself if I found nothing, if there were no remnants of Maggie St. James along this stretch of road, I'd call Ben like a coward and tell him to notify her parents that it was a dead end. I wouldn't have the courage to do it myself—to admit that I failed. And then I'd resume my own disappearing act, I'd continue north into Canada and then Alaska. I'd vanish and maybe I wouldn't come back.

Back in the truck, I peer out at the line of trees, trying to steady my focus on Maggie. But out in the dark . . . my eyes catch on something, and I lean forward against the steering wheel, headlights illuminating the trunk of a tall fir tree.

Three straight gashes are cut vertically into the bark.

Maybe they were made by an animal, a bear tearing away the fleshy surface of the evergreen, yet they look oddly clean and straight. Slit into the wood by the sharp blade of a knife.

A marker, a sign—a *warning*.

The scent of lilacs fills my nostrils again. This is where Maggie entered the forest, rot and green and black interior. After five years, she might still be alive, somewhere within this mountainous terrain. Or I might discover her body coiled and stiff at the base of a tree, having gotten lost, knees drawn up, autumn leaves and a thick layer of snow her only burial. Eyes frozen open.

But I've found worse.

I steer the truck closer to the mark cut into the tree, snow falling in sheets now against the windshield, and discover another half-hidden road—an old logging road maybe, back when this mountainside was clear-cut for timber—and it winds up into the forest. I feel another itch at my spine. An uncertainty. A need.

Redemption.

I'm going to see this through.

I'm going to find Maggie St. James.

———

My talent might be considered a disease, a thing suffered among generations, passed down through a family tree.

There were always stories about my ancestors, about Aunt Myrtle who wore long abalone shell earrings that touched her shoulders, and had a habit of lighting matches at the dinner table to rid the room of *nosy, lingering ghosts who should have moved on by now*. Aunt Myrtle saw things in the objects she touched. Just like her uncle Floyd before her, and a great-great grandmother who immigrated from Dundalk, Ireland.

We were a family of uncommons.

When I was nine or ten, I thought I was seeing flashes of the dead, pale shifting forms, effigies, traces of those who were long buried in the earth. It frightened me, the threat of seeing ghostly apparitions in any-thing I touched. But my dad—always efficient with his words, and having seen the quiet, distant look in my eyes in the months previous, the way I paused whenever I touched objects around the house—patted me on the shoulder one morning while I sat over a bowl of frosted cornflakes and said, "You have the gift, kid. Tough luck. My advice would be to ignore it, don't go making a show of it or people will think you odd. Better to stuff it down."

So I did for a time, careful not to touch anything that didn't belong to me—I was a hands-in-pockets kind of kid—but there were slip-ups, unintended moments when my fingers found themselves retrieving some item that wasn't mine: a unicorn barrette slipped free from the honey hair of a girl seated in front of me in history class, my father's reading glasses left on the kitchen counter that he asked me to retrieve.

In these brief errors, I glimpsed the jerking, shuddering moments from a past that belonged to someone else: the golden-haired girl brushing her hair that morning before school, carefully clipping the barrette into place while her parents argued downstairs, their voices rattling up the hallways, making the girl wince. Or my father, removing his eyeglasses and plac-ing them on an olive-green tiled kitchen counter that wasn't our own. A woman that was not my mother, round hips and freckled skin, standing before him, her lips on his.

I saw things I didn't want to see. It was a talent I didn't want, an ability I didn't ask for. But it was one I couldn't give back.

It wasn't until years later I learned to focus this skill, to use it to find things that had been lost—*to find people*. If I knew what I was looking for, if I had the image of someone I needed to find, I could locate the town or street corner where they last boarded a bus or got into a stranger's car. I could see the argument they had with a spouse, the knife they slipped out from a kitchen drawer. I could see the things they had done, even if they were still alive. Even if they weren't dead yet.

In college, Ben worked as a private detective, and he hired me on the side to help him with a few cases: stolen pets and stolen lovers and a few stolen credit cards. It was shit work. Driving around at night, rooting through people's garbage, snapping dark, out-of-focus photos.

But after we graduated, he referred me to someone he knew at the Seattle PD and they asked me to come in and help with a missing person's case. At first, they didn't tell me much—they didn't trust me, and I couldn't blame them. I was in my early twenties, and looked like I could just as easily commit the crimes they were in the business of preventing. But when I found a fourteen-year-old kid who had vanished from his home a week earlier, camped out in a tent in the woods behind his school—a runaway—the police asked me to look at a few other cold cases.

Within a year, I was getting calls from weeping, anxious, distressed families who had heard I could find their missing whoever: a brother vanished from a Quick-E-Mart parking lot under the glaring eye of the midday sun; a daughter slipped from her second-story bedroom in a cookie-cutter neighborhood with the window still open, rain soaking the caramel-tan carpet; or a niece gone out for a jog along the rocky shoreline near Port Ludlow but never returned home. Her laced running shoes found a day later bobbing in the foamy water, brought in with the tide.

I became a finder of the missing. But I didn't always find them alive.

———

The old logging road is narrow, overgrown, and hasn't been traveled down in a decade at least. I steer the truck through a low gully—probably a dried creek bed now buried in several feet of snowfall—and the tires threaten to sink into the deep sloppy layer.

When Maggie passed through here, she bounded from one rock to the next over the creek, cold water splashing up her legs—I can hear the memory of water, and the soft tune Maggie hummed while she walked, a nursery rhyme I think, meant for bedtimes, but it's one I don't recognize. Maybe she wanted to soothe herself, to feel not so alone as she trekked deeper into these woods.

The truck headlights bounce among the trees. Snow continues to fall from the sky. And the windshield wipers wheeze back and forth across the glass, barely keeping up, while the heater sputters out lukewarm air. But after three hours, I lose the afterimage of Maggie.

She fades in with the evergreens, with the falling snow, and flickers out.

She might have turned into the trees somewhere and I missed it. She might have slumped down into a layer of pine needles to rest and never woke.

Perhaps she turned back.

Or maybe I'm just too tired, my eyes unable to focus, to keep her after-image steady in my mind. I reach an intersection where another razor-thin dirt road intersects the one I'm on, and I ease the truck to a stop. I need to consider turning around—that maybe I've lost Maggie's image for good, maybe I've reached a dead end.

I squeeze the tiny book-shaped charm in my left hand, trying to draw up any last flickering memories. If Maggie reached this intersection, if she kept going, she had to make a decision of which route she'd take. But when I stare out at the snow-laden terrain, at the crossroads, there is no sign of her—only the dark between the trees and the beams of light cutting faintly into the forest ahead of me.

I have to turn around. Go back the three hours to the old chimney and the collapsed barn. Maybe I can try again in the morning, once the sun is up. Or I can backtrack all the way out to Highway 89, turn north, and keep going until I cross over the Canadian border. *I tried to find her, didn't I?* I drove way the hell out here into these woods, and now the trail has gone cold. The after-image of Maggie blotted out or faded with time. Either way, I have no way of knowing which way she might have gone from here. Which road she took.

That old familiar ache thuds at the base of my neck, the doubt always there: *It's probably too late. The odds aren't good, not after five years. She's probably already dead.*

I put the truck in reverse and the tires spin briefly before finding traction. The truck lurches backward, the rear bumper nudging against a small tree, and when I crank the wheel, the headlights swing wide, illuminating the tall pines.

. . . there's something there.

My foot slams the brake, and I squint through the falling snow. Etched into the bark, are three gashes. The same ones I saw back at the burnt-out house. A marker, a roadmap. Maggie turned left here. She followed the marks on the trees: This is how she knew where she was going.

I put the truck back in gear and fishtail up this new, narrower road. Five more times I come to a fork in the road or an intersecting route—a decision to be made. And each time, I find the three marks.

Maggie didn't wander aimlessly into this dark forest, just out for an afternoon hike, she followed marks made by someone else.

I travel like this for another two hours—cresting the top of steep hills, then inching through a maze of low-hanging branches—until I reach an abrupt end: a mammoth pine tree fallen across the path, limbs splintered and broken, blocking the road. But there is a thin opening through the trees to the left, and I steer the truck toward the gap.

The engine whines as I accelerate, the truck bounces over something— a large rock or a tree stump—and then I hear the sound: the squeal of the engine, followed by the *whoosh* of tires spinning in the snow.

I'm stuck.

I climb out of the truck, and after several attempts at packing down the snow in front of each tire, then trying to accelerate slowly out of the deep snow, but listening to the tires just spin in place, I realize the entire truck is high-centered, resting atop the packed snow.

Without a winch or a tow truck, I'm fully fucked.

I kill the engine and the headlights fall dark. I check my cell phone, but there's not even a blip of a signal, no way to call Ben, or that little tow truck company I passed back in town. I'm too deep into the wilderness now. *I'm on my own.* I grab the backpack on the seat beside me, filled with mostly convenience store snacks, a flashlight, and a notebook for jotting down the things I will relay to the family or police later. I cinch the pack closed, slip the small silver book-charm into my pocket, along with the truck keys, and step out into the snow.

I will follow Maggie on foot.

And in some strange way, walking away from this shitty old truck feels like the full demise of my life. Rock bottom.

I have nothing more to lose.

———

Tree limbs sag overhead like carcasses of the dead. But the snow has stopped falling and the clouds have separated enough to see the quarter moon. *Space*

Donut Hole, my sister Ruth called it when we were little. She'd pretend to reach up into the sky and pluck it down with her grubby, lollipop-sticky fingertips, then pantomime taking a big bite out of it while rolling her eyes in exaggerated delight. My little sister loved to make me laugh.

This is the memory of Ruth I prefer.

Not the one that came later.

When I found her crumpled in the corner of a shitty motel room outside Duluth, Minnesota, right along the shore of Lake Superior. She'd been missing for a month when I finally decided to go look for her. *A whole wasted month.* But she'd gone missing before—chasing bad boyfriends and dead-end jobs serving drinks at dusty, cigarette-clouded bars. She'd call every few months, promise that she was fine, then slip off the map again. The last time I saw her before she vanished, she looked strung out, on more than just booze, and I was worried about her. A ticking in my ears that wouldn't go away, telling me that something wasn't right this time—that she was worse than usual.

I don't know where things went wrong for my sister. She'd always been tough, thick-skinned and thick-skulled, even as a kid. And after our parents died only a few months apart—colon cancer, then lung cancer—she decided everything was fucked anyway. She was only twenty when they passed away, and my sister became a don't-piss-her-off-or-she'll-pop-you-right-in-the-face kind of girl. It's also what I loved about her. Her sturdiness—she was built to last. Her I-can-take-care-of-myself attitude. But it also made it difficult for her to ask for help, to admit when she needed her big brother.

I tracked her afterimage for a week and a half, using a broken seashell I found in the box of her belongings she'd asked to keep at my apartment months earlier. When I dug through the cardboard box, looking for something of hers to use, I recognized the shell from a trip we took to Pacific City, Oregon, when I was twelve and she was seven. She'd held on to it after all those years—tucked away in that box. A piece of our childhood. Broken, just like she was.

I had the shell clutched in my hand when I tracked her to that motel room and pushed open the door, left ajar. It was four in the morning, and when I saw her, I stood stock-still in that doorway. I knew the slack look on her face, the drooped shoulders, the strange half-closed eyelids. I'd seen the look before.

I knew my sister was gone.

I crossed the room and knelt beside her and held her in my arms like she was seven years old again. Like when we were kids and she'd wake from a nightmare and crawl into my bed. I wept, too, an awful heaving of my rib cage, like some brittle place inside me was trying to crack open. It was the cold, hard realization that I'd found her too late. My parents were long buried in the ground, and now my only sister was dead too. I was painfully, sickeningly alone.

The police said she died sometime in the night, in the early hours before I found her. The front desk clerk at the motel said Ruth checked in around ten in the evening. Another guest, whose right jawline twitched when she spoke and her eyes were unable to focus on anything for longer than a few seconds, said she saw no one enter or leave Ruth's room.

This wasn't a homicide; her death was exactly what it looked like: suicide.

The empty bottle of prescription pills beside the sink told the story that her toxicology report would verify—overdose. Oxycodone, to be exact, with a dash of muscle relaxers. And she hadn't taken just four or five, she'd taken roughly twenty. Enough to finish the job.

The detective on the scene suggested that it might have been an accident. Maybe she didn't mean to take as many as she did. *She didn't intend to end her life.*

But I knew that wasn't true, because I saw the afterimage of my sister standing at the bathroom sink, with its butterscotch linoleum floor and cracked mirror—like some previous guest had punched it, sending a web of fractures out from the point of impact. I saw how she tipped the prescription bottle to her lips, swallowing whatever was left inside—not even bothering to count them. She then tilted her head to the sink and drank water straight from the tap. Quick and efficient. There weren't even glasses in that stale-smelling motel room for her to pour herself a cup of water—that stuck with me, the inhumane nature of it, that she wasn't even able to take her last drink from a proper glass.

I knew my sister had been depressed, a slow unwinding in recent years, but I didn't know how bad it had gotten. I didn't know how deep into the hole she had tumbled—headfirst like Alice down the rabbit hole. *I should have seen, should have recognized the already half-gone slant of her eyes.* She didn't even leave a note, just pills down the throat and then lights out. Maybe she knew I would come find her, maybe she knew I would see her afterimage and know what she'd done—a note was unnecessary. Redundant. She knew her big brother would see it all once he arrived, a sputtering slideshow of awful images. Maybe it's why after she took the drink from the faucet, she looked into that broken mirror and winked. She did it for me: a parting gesture, a last goodbye.

See ya later, big brother.

She knew I'd witness it all.

But that's not the part that keeps me up at night.

It's the moments, the hours, that separated finding her alive and finding her dead.

If I'd driven faster, if I hadn't stopped a few miles back at some crappy roadside bar that served black coffee, if I hadn't pulled off the road and slept for four hours the morning before at the south Dakota border, I would have gotten to the motel just as she checked in. I would have found her in her room, switching through channels on the TV, unpacking her duffle bag. I would have caught her before she found the bottle of pills, tucked between sandals and unwashed T-shirts. I would have taken her by the hand and pulled her from the room, then driven her to the twenty-four-hour diner I passed up the road. WORLD FAMOUS PANCAKES, the sign declared. We would have eaten two heaping, butter-drenched stacks of apple pancakes. We would have drunk cup after cup of burnt, artificially sweetened coffee, and I would have shown her the shell that led me to her, and we would have laughed about that day at the beach and I would have said, *Let's go back there. Let's drive to Pacific City.* She would have shaken her head and called me crazy but we would have gone anyway. Gotten into my truck and driven all night into the next day until we reached the wide, glittering Pacific coastline. My sister and I would have stood on that shore, salty air against our faces, in our hair, tired but happy, and she'd still be alive.

I would have saved her.

I could have.

But instead, I arrived a couple hours too late. I stood in the doorway and watched them fold my little sister into a black body bag and hoist her out into the morning sun. *Ain't life fucked.*

This. *This* is why I dropped out of existence. Why I stopped answering my phone, why I started sleeping in truck stop parking lots. Why I had been thinking of going to Canada and getting as far away from my sister's death as my truck would take me. I'd been running from it for a year.

Guilt is a beast. And it might just kill you, if you let it.

But now, out on this snow-covered road—with this feeling, this burden sunk like a half-ton weight inside me—I force my legs to move forward. Because maybe this is also how I save myself. Redemption is somewhere out there in this dark, cold forest.

I just need to find it.

If I can rescue *this* woman in time. Bring her back to her parents and her old life. Then maybe it'll fill the ravine that split me wide open when I walked through that motel doorway.

Maybe.

I haven't gone far from the truck, it's still visible behind me, when I see the flicker of her: Maggie St. James plods ahead of me up the road, her backpack sagging low against her waist. Her legs are moving slowly now, tired. Shoulders slumped from the weight of her pack.

Her chin lifts as she rounds a bend in the road, and she stops walking.

I stop too, trying not to lose the flickering memory of her. Trying to hold on to it. But my eyes begin to blur and a cold spot blooms in my chest.

Maggie sees something ahead.

And then I see it too: a wood fence, bordered by rocks. But there are no sagging or broken boards, the fence is well maintained. A sign is nailed crookedly to one of the posts: PRIVATE PROPERTY.

Out here, in the middle of nowhere, seven hours deep into the woods— the sunrise surely close—I have come upon signs of life.

Something is out here after all.

———

A chill scuttles through me, that itchy needles-against-your-skin-before-you-walk-down-into-a-basement feeling. I've felt it before—many times— it means I'm close.

Maggie's afterimage flickers on the road ahead of me, only a few steps from the fence, and for the first time, she looks back over her shoulder: ice-blue eyes and flushed cheeks, sunlight winking through the tree branches against her freckled nose. My heart stalls against my ribs. It feels like she's looking right at me, a dead unmistakable stare, and for a half second, her gaze seems unsure—like she's considering something. She's wondering if this is a bad idea, if she shouldn't have come so far into these woods on her own. *I've seen this look before.* That moment when something doesn't feel quite right, when she could have turned around, saved herself. But Maggie blinks, shakes her head—as if shaking away the creeping sensation that had settled against the back of her throat—then says aloud to herself, "No turning back now."

Maggie's stare reminds me of her mother's—cool and precise—a woman I met two weeks ago when I took the ferry across Puget Sound to Whidbey Island, off the mainland of Washington State. Maggie's childhood home had that damp wool smell, rain shedding over the roof, and I sat on the overly cushioned couch while Mr. St. James recounted the facts of his missing daughter's case—the police reports, the news coverage, the items left in her car. He was a likeable man, with warm, sad eyes, and when he reached into his pocket and pulled out the small, silver book-charm the police had found outside Maggie's abandoned car, his voice broke.

But his wife, Mrs. St. James, watched me dubiously. I knew she didn't want me there, this was her husband's idea—hiring someone like me instead of a real PI. They hadn't agreed on this. But at the end of our meeting, Mr. St. James stood and shook my hand, handing me a check for half my payment, and a photograph of Maggie—the hard lines of Maggie's face just like her mother's.

I left the St. Jameses' home and drove the ten minutes back to the ferry station, parking my car in the short line of vehicles waiting to board the next ferry service that would arrive in half an hour. I had time to kill, so I walked to the edge of the wharf overlooking the bay. Across the channel, I could see the mainland, a gray fog settled over the row of waterfront homes.

I was feeling that old tug against my ribs, the pain wanting to settle back in, telling me I didn't need to take this case, I should just go north once

I was off the ferry and slip back into the darkness of my own thoughts, when a voice spoke behind me, as if summoned up from the cold sea. "Mr. Wren."

I turned, and she was standing a few paces behind me, now wearing a long gray wool coat and a checkered scarf in deep greens and Prussian blues. Yet Mrs. St. James looked just as displeased to see me here as she did in her home, and I wondered if her husband knew where she'd gone when she left the house and came after me. Or if she lied and said she was running to the market to pick up a few things for dinner. A bottle of wine maybe. A quick, easy lie.

Her hands were deep in her pockets, shoulders set. "My husband hired you, not me," she said sharply, like she needed to get it out of the way.

My first instinct was that she'd come to ask for the check back, and tell me they no longer needed my services.

"I know it can be hard to believe in what I do," I said. Because I understood her misgivings—most people were reticent at first, skeptical, until I found their loved one and made the call to let them know, their grateful sobs gasping on the other end. "But you don't need to believe in what I do for me to find your daughter."

Mrs. St. James cast her gaze out over the water, seagulls spinning above us, looking for scraps of fish on the docks left behind by fishing boats. "Maybe she doesn't want to be found," Mrs. St. James said, keeping her eyes averted from mine, watching the fog settle and then part as boats passed through.

I'd found countless missing family members—husbands, wives, brothers—who boarded a bus or a plane or just walked out of their old lives and into a new one. People sometimes vanished and constructed better, untarnished lives: new bank account, new dog, new six-hundred-thread-count cotton sheets, and a monthly water bill under a fake name. It's what my sister tried to do many times until the last time.

So I knew it happened.

"Do you not want me to find Maggie?" I asked.

She shrugged, an odd gesture, like she wasn't sure what she thought. "Some things should remain hidden." A wind stirred up from the water, coiling over the wharf. It caught Mrs. St. James's scarf and pulled it free from her neck, carrying it softly away from her toward the water. She reached for it but missed, and it tangled itself around the wharf railing. I unwrapped the scarf from the wood post and held it briefly in my hand—a quick glimpse of Mrs. St. James shuddering through me. They were distant, broken images: she was much younger, pregnant with Maggie, and she was standing in a kitchen that was not the one I had seen in her home a half hour earlier.

"You lived somewhere else when you were pregnant with Maggie," I said aloud.

Her eyes went wide and she took a step closer to me, snatching the scarf from my hand. She coiled it back around her neck and crossed her arms. But she peered at me differently, not warily, but with interest.

"Do you know where Maggie is?" I asked her directly.

She shook her head, but again her eyes swayed out to the bay, like there was something she came to say, but had forgotten how. She had built a wall inside herself, a fortress of hard cheekbones and stiff gazes to protect herself from the grief she'd felt the last five years. It wasn't uncommon— *hell, I did the same thing after Ruth's death.*

"If you know where she is," I pressed. "You could save your husband a lot of agony."

"I've never been close with my daughter—" Her voice had taken on a plaintive tone, the same airy quality as the fog, not quite solid, flimsy even, like it might collapse under too much weight. "We were two different people. And I won't pretend I was a good mother. But now she's gone and I—"

I tried to pick apart the root of what she was trying to say. If I could have touched her scarf again, held it in my palm, I might have been able to steal a glimpse of the truth, of her real past. "If you're certain your daughter is safe, if you know she doesn't want to be found, then I won't go looking for her."

She winced, a tiny motion, and she uncrossed her arms. "I'm not sure anymore," she admitted, and it felt like the first truly honest thing she'd said. Not guised in misdirection.

I stepped closer to her and her eyes flinched back to mine. "If any part of you thinks she might be in trouble after all these years, then tell me how to find her. At the very least, I'll go make sure she's safe. And if she is, I'll leave her alone and I won't bring her back."

Mrs. St. James's eyes vibrated, like a tremor was working its way up her spine, vertebrae by vertebrae, uprooting her from where she stood.

"Pastoral," she finally said. A single word.

At that, she pushed her hands into her coat pockets, lifted her shoulders as if she could escape the damp wind, and turned away from me, walking back to her silver sedan parked at the curb.

She drove away and never looked back.

———

I sat in my car on the ferry and pulled out the silver book-charm from the plastic bag and held it in my palm. I closed my eyes and felt the lolling teeter of the ferry as it surged forward across the bay. Flashes of Maggie stuttered through me, broken images: she was driving her car, tall evergreens whirring by out the windows, while the radio thumped loudly from the speakers. Maggie was singing along, belting out the tunes. But then the images splintered apart—I was too far away from her.

I needed to get closer: to the place where the police found her abandoned car.

I slid the silver charm back into the plastic bag and pulled out my cell phone. I typed *Pastoral* into the web browser and got pages and pages of disjointed links: *Pastoral Pizza in Boston, Pastoral Winery in southern Italy, Pastoral Greeting Cards: now hiring.* I scrolled the Wikipedia page for pastoral: *a lifestyle of shepherds herding livestock around open areas of land according to seasons. It lends its name to a genre of literature, art, and music that depicts such life in an idealized manner.* I narrowed down my search to the Klamath National Forest where Maggie's car was found. I dug through layers of blogger sites and pages that led me nowhere—a deep, unending hole of research. Until I hit on something in a genealogical website for a man named Henry Watson, and his wife, Lily Mae Watson. They had disappeared sometime during 1972, and among the scant information about the Watsons was a newspaper article written on September 5, 1973 in the *Sage River Review: a weekly paper for local folks.*

The newspaper article was old, had been scanned-in at some point, and the heading for the article was smeared and a little off-center, as if the paper had been folded in several places. It read: *Commune Buys Land in Three Rivers Mountains.*

Not far from where Maggie's abandoned car had been found was a small town and a local paper—that after another quick search, I discovered was no longer in business—but it had printed an article about a community that called themselves Pastoral, who had purchased a plot of unwanted land somewhere in the nearby mountains.

The article explained that previously, in 1902, a group of German immigrants occupied the section of wilderness. The immigrants had been gold miners, following riverbeds and creeks north through California. There was talk of a railroad being laid through this stretch of forest, so the group settled in an area deep in the mountains, hoping the railroad would come straight through their plot of land. But only a few short years later, when the railroad never came, they abandoned their settlement and left behind homes and pastures and several livestock barns. Decades passed, and most locals forgot the settlement even existed. Until, in 1972, a group of *beatniks and hippies and undesirables* (the reporter lamented) drove an old school bus up into the remote backwoods, and purchased the forgotten land.

They called it Pastoral and claimed they were part of a movement *seeking purpose and a reinvented way of life*, the reporter quoted. But one interview with a local man named Bert Allington called Pastoral a cult, a place of *wild, reckless depravity*. But to the reporter's credit, she went on to say that the group had *fled the social norms of society and came deep into the wilderness to live off the land and start a commune that was built from the simple principles of shared living. Their burdens would be spread over many, so as never to be too much for one.* The article ended with the reporter leaving a few words to her readers: *It's easy to fear what we do not know. But perhaps these newcomers only wish for the same as the rest of us, a place to call home.*

I read the article twice. Then I searched the same newspaper for more articles about Pastoral, but there was nothing. No other mention of it. Either the community broke apart in the years after, its members scattering back to their old lives, or something else happened.

When Maggie abandoned her car out on the road, she must have believed she had found the hidden location of this place. She must have thought she was close.

Maybe she was wrong.

Or maybe not.

———

The wood fence stretches along the left side of the road, straight and low, with snowdrifts against each post. I scan the trees, the length of road, but there are no signs of a house or a mailbox or lights in the distance.

Maggie's afterimage loses its density, fading in with the snow. But I keep walking, following the road where it rises up over a small hill and the trees begin to thin, a clearing opening up on the other side of the fence. A field. A pasture in warmer months, where animals graze, ripping up the tall meadow grass. Horses or cattle or sheep maybe.

My gate hitches slightly as I move faster through the snow, the cold making my joints stiff. But I know I'm closer to Maggie than I've been; I can feel it in the hum at the back of my teeth, a grinding pulse in my eardrums.

I swing one foot in front of the other, moving quickly up the slope.

And then I see something ahead through the snow, blocking the road.

A gate.

A small outbuilding also sits on the right side of the road, with a single window at the front. The structure is just large enough for a guard to sit inside, his gaze turned out to the road. A checkpoint.

I take a few cautious steps closer—my heart ratcheting up in my chest, pounding like a fist.

I haven't been invited.

Yet, chances are, way out here, this deep in the woods in the middle of the night, the hut will be deserted. A remnant of something: a compound, a logging site. It's obvious no vehicles have passed up this road in a long time—the snow hasn't been packed down—and with no visitors venturing this far up into the mountains, there's no need to post someone at the hut to keep watch.

But when I'm within a few yards, I see movement inside.

A tall, lank figure steps out from the little building, a hand over his eyes as if to block the moonlight, to see me better, and his expression seems just as startled as my own.

Behind him, a piece of wood is nailed to the front of the gate, with letters carved slantways into the grain. They are shallowly carved, weather-worn, and barely legible, but I can make them out. Each one proof of where I am.

I've found it, a community forgotten, hidden for the last fifty years. A myth deep in the woods.

Carved into the sign is a word, a welcome for those who have made it this far: PASTORAL.

Yet the man standing before me looks anything but pleased by my arrival. He looks terrified.

FOXES AND MUSEUMS

Excerpt from Book One in the Eloise and the Foxtail series

Eloise crawled from beneath the sunflower-embroidered blankets of her wood-framed bed, and tiptoed across the floor. The fox spooked at her movement and its face vanished from the other side of the window.

But she caught sight of it again, darting through the backyard, past the crooked swing set her father had built two summers ago, to the border of the woods. It paused at the spiky line of trees, beckoning her, its eyes just as wild and vibrant under the moon as they were at the window.

She glanced at her cherry-red rain boots beside the bedroom door, feeling the pull to chase after it, but when she looked back into the yard, the fox was gone.

Slipped into the dusk and dark.

PART TWO

THE FARMHOUSE

THEO

I like the way her head looks resting on the pillow.

A hard, white shell with a cascade of auburn hair draped over her sun-kissed shoulders. When she sleeps, sometimes I don't recognize her: She is a stranger in the bed beside me, breathing softly, her chest expanding like a bird pressing against its cage. She is a curiosity, a woman who feels like an endangered creature—a thing I don't deserve.

A summer wind blows through the open windows of the old farmhouse, and in the distance, I see the line of broad oak trees that border the community—a line we do not cross.

Calla wakes, a dimple drawing inward on her left cheek, eyes pearly and clear in the morning light, drawing to mind the images I've seen of the ocean: specks of light winking across the roiling surface. I curl my toes, as if digging them into wet sand—a sensation I've only ever imagined.

"You couldn't sleep again last night?" Calla asks, running her fingers through my hair. She moves with the slow gentleness of a wife who can't see the thoughts strumming inside my skull—the ideas I would never say aloud, the places I sometimes imagine beyond the walls of Pastoral.

"I was thinking about winter. About the snow," I answer, a strange little lie. But my wife doesn't like it when I talk about the *outside*. It irritates her—her ears drawing down, the line between her eyebrows puckering close. So a lie is easier, as lies usually are.

"Winter won't come for another few months," she says softly. *Plenty of time to prepare firewood and stock the cellar for the cold months ahead.*

"I know."

She slips free from the sheets and walks to the closet, the old wood floor moaning against even her softest footsteps. She is pretty in this light, younger-seeming than her true age. She pulls on a pair of jean cutoffs with holes worn in the pockets from too many washings, and a thin cotton T-shirt. Our clothes are in endless need of mending, of stitching, an ongoing effort to make everything last for one more season.

Whatever we have is all there will ever be.

Calla looks out the window at the fields beyond the farmhouse, the chores to be done, fruit trees to be harvested, laundry on the line to be brought inside. She places her hands on her hips then turns, crossing the room back to the bed—her movements slight and easy. She is comfortable in this house, inside these walls. I peer up at my wife and at first her expression is flat, giving nothing away, but then a little smile curls across her upper lip, as if she's forgiven me for my silence. Forgiven me for whatever wandering thoughts were flitting around inside my head. She kisses me full on the lips, tracing her finger up my temple, coiling it in my dark hair. "I love you still," she says, a reminder.

At times, in the long hours of late afternoon, it feels as if we are living a life we have agreed to share but we can't remember why. A sentiment I suspect many married couples feel after the years have worn thin. But now, in these early dawn moments, my wife feels familiar in a way that makes my heart ache just a little. A soft pain that's hard to describe. "I love you still," I answer in return.

"I'm meeting Bee in the orchard," she says, lowering her hand from my face and walking to the bedroom door.

I nod.

Perhaps we are like two old people who have lived together too long, a lifetime, a hundred years or more. The cobwebs of tiny mistruths, little papercut deceptions, rooted in our joints and slung between rib bones. We've built ourselves on these microscopic lies, so small we can't recall what they were. But they're there all the same, binding us to one another. But also ripping us apart.

I hear Calla move down the stairs and pull on her mud boots before she leaves through the back door, the screen slapping back into place behind her. The scent of her leaves too, lilacs and basil, soil and devotion. I would do anything for her. She is more than I deserve. Yet, there is something in her movements, in the way she looks at me from across the room. Something that lives inside her: a thought, a clattering idea that she won't let me see.

Much like my own.

She loves me, I know. But she's also keeping something from me—secrets under her fingernails. Deceit in the creases of her eyelids.

My wife is a liar.

CALLA

My sister is a nocturnal creature.

She has always preferred the night, even as a child, hiding in dark closet corners and beneath the creaking boards of the stairwell, cobwebs gathering in her uncombed hair the color of maple syrup, slightly burnt. She preferred the weight of shadows over the bright warmth of the sun.

But now she cannot escape the dark.

"He doesn't seem like himself," I tell Bee. My sister and I kneel beneath the hazelnut trees that line the creek, the air softened by the sound of water spilling over rocks and tugging at the shore. Methodically, Bee and I gather the hazelnuts that have fallen to the ground in the night, and I watch her with a fascination I've always felt for my younger sister. Even now, all grown up, she is still a marvel to me—the ease with which her strong, sun-stained hands sweep the ground, deftly picking out the round nuts from the leaves and twigs and underbrush. A tactile skill, feeling for what she cannot see.

She was only nineteen when she lost her sight. I barely remember it now, but she still talks about it sometimes: how it happened strangely, how at first she saw liminal waves of sunlight and then bright bursts of color and odd, shifting shadows, before complete blindness took hold and it all went black. A sweeping darkness that never receded.

Perhaps, if we had lived *out there*, beyond the border, she could have gone to a doctor. A specialist who would have peered into her cloud-gray eyes and declared some medicine or surgery that might have saved her vision. But I try not to think about it: how things might have been different.

Because in the end, there was nothing to be done.

My sister has adapted, made use of her limitations, and maybe it's even made her someone she might not have been otherwise.

"The seasons are changing," Bee answers. "He always gets moody this time of year." She rubs at her neck with the back of her hand, beads of sweat rising against her summer-browned skin. The three of us—my husband, my sister, and I—have lived together in the old farmhouse since Theo and I married. The same house where Bee and I grew up. And although Bee likes to tease Theo—making jabs at him during breakfast about how he's too tall to fit through doorways, and his only real use to us is retrieving things from the top kitchen cupboards—he's been like a big brother to her.

"This is different," I say. There is a gnawing at the back of my teeth, an ache when he looks at me, like he's thinking of things far away from here. There has always existed a strange sort of alchemy between us, two people who cannot live without the other—an earnest, unmistakable kind of love. And sometimes this well-deep feeling frightens me. The fragile devotion nested in my solar plexus, the desperation I feel for my husband, and the unconscious fear that I might lose him someday.

I place my palm flat against the soil. "At night sometimes," I continue, "I wake and he's standing at the window, looking out at the trees."

Bee lifts her head, pale eyelids fluttering. "We all look to the trees."

"But he doesn't seem afraid. It's like he's looking *for* something."

She lowers her hands again to the ground and finds another round nut, the shell still a pale brown, uncracked. A good one. She drops it into the basket. "It's not dangerous if he stays on this side. And he's probably just looking for signs of the rot in the trees." Her voice is measured, unemotional. And I want to believe her.

I touch the thin copper ring on my finger: the wedding band Theo gave me two years ago when he asked me to marry him. I've known him my whole life, we both grew up inside the boundary of Pastoral, and yet I had never truly noticed him—not in the way I should have—until the afternoon I was foraging for wild morels near the creek, and he appeared on the path. "You found my secret spot," he said, giving me a weighing look.

His dark hair slid across his eyelashes, in need of a haircut, and we sat on the shore, side by side, until the sun had set, telling made-up stories about the land and its history, and I wondered why we had never talked like that before. How it was that we knew so little about each other? It was as if we had slipped by one another unnoticed for our entire lives, until that day beside the creek.

It was only a few months later when he asked me to marry him in that same spot, the sun hovering beyond the trees and the sky a burnt autumn shade. I nodded and he kissed me and I was sure I would never be as happy as I was right then.

"Theo's not dumb," Bee says, drops of sweat gathering on her upper lip. She seems always overheated lately, like the mothers in Pastoral when they're carrying a child, the little thrumming heart inside their bellies like a fire. "He won't go over the boundary."

I nod weakly, and we spend the next few minutes working in silence, filling the basket near to the brim, until Bee's palm stalls against the ground, eyelids closed, as if she could feel the tree roots beneath us winding through the soil in desperate woven patterns—in search of water far below. "The trees sound sick this year," she says, breathy and low.

I peer up through the branches. Soon the tree will be a galaxy of ripe hazelnuts, but for now we gather what we can from the earth. "It's still early in the season," I say. "There will be more to harvest later."

She rocks back on her heels, feeling for the edge of the round basket with her fingertips, then dropping a handful of nuts inside. She smiles softly, like she thinks no one's watching, and reveals the slightly crooked tooth on the upper right side, in an otherwise perfect row of teeth.

I wish I could hear what she hears: the far-off hum of honeybee wings across the meadow, the subtle shift when the summer air changes directions, a rainstorm in the distance. Once she told me she could smell a hint of salt from the Pacific Ocean, blowing in from the west a hundred miles away. She feels what I cannot—my eyesight an impediment to truly absorbing the world whirling and clicking around me.

Bee pushes herself to standing, reaching out a hand for the trunk of the hazelnut tree to orient herself. "Do you think he wants to leave?"

The question cuts through me, unexpected, and I shake my head. "No," I answer quickly, before the idea can embed itself into my skin. But I look out at the border trees to the west, surveying the landscape, the pond with its calm surface, the slow-moving creek, the farmhouse at the low end of the meadow, and I wonder if my husband has considered leaving this all behind. A wooden fence runs along the road in front of the farmhouse, and if you turn south, the road will lead you to the gate where Theo stands guard most nights. But if you turn north, the road takes you into the heart of Pastoral, dead-ending at a small parking area where two dozen cars sit rusted and pillaged, weeds growing up around their flattened tires, some with hoods propped up, their parts stripped clean, others are missing doors. Even an old school bus sits on its rims: the same bus that the founders drove into these woods and never drove back out. It's a cemetery of bent metal and steering wheels and spark plugs long corroded. Mementoes of old lives. Useless machines now.

I brush my hair back from my forehead, the wind pulling it loose from my braid, while my sister's golden-red hair swirls about her like a firestorm, long and unruly—easily tangled and set into knots. She is a rare, wild creature—as lovely as the blooms beside the pond, as gentle as the trees that sigh in the evening breeze. But she is also reckless: often venturing too close to the border, where the pox threatens to sink into her flesh and rot her from the inside out.

The wind unsettles the leaves above us like a million scraps of paper under the blue summer sky, and I know she can hear it: the changing seasons, the buoyancy in the air, the fragile quality.

"A storm," she says, turning her sightless gaze to the west. "Lightning. I can feel it."

In the distance, a bulkhead of clouds is drawing close.

I lift the basket into my arms and stand up. A spire of electricity snaps across the dark clouds and a second later, thunder shakes the ground beneath us. "We should get inside," I say. But she hesitates, tilting her chin upward, as if she could already feel the rain against her forehead. "Bee," I say more sharply.

It isn't safe out here, in the open, with the rain drawing close. We need to get indoors.

Finally, she nods, and we hurry back toward the farmhouse, cutting through the far field where the tall grass shivers like a golden sea, waves heaving beneath a bruise-black sky. Bee's summer dress flaps around her knees as we run, the little white flowers stitched into the hem shivering as if they sense the storm. Thunder shakes the air and our bare feet leave footprints in the dark earth.

We reach the garden, edged by a low fence, the green tomatoes and ripe strawberries shivering in the sudden hard gust of wind. The chickens who live within the protected plot scramble back to their henhouse at the back corner, clucking nervously. Just to the south of the farmhouse, the windmill churns quickly, metal blades spinning, drawing water up from the well deep within the earth.

At the house, we scramble through the screen door just as the rain reaches the edge of the porch. I drop the basket of hazelnuts onto the dining room table—nuts that will later be ground down into a butter, to be spread on toast and eaten by the spoonful. A second later, the *ping ping ping* of raindrops on the metal roof echoes through the house. "We stayed too long in the field," I say, out of breath.

Bee walks to the kitchen sink and turns on the tap, fresh well-water spilling over her dirt-crusted hands. "We got to the house in time."

Some in the community don't think we should fear the rain, that it couldn't possibly bring the rot over our borders, but even a molecule of sickness carried in by a storm—a drop of infected rain against the skin—could be enough to force the lungs to stop breathing. Many years ago, Liam Garza was out repairing fence posts along the eastern edge of the crop fields, it was autumn—the harvest finished—when a late season rainstorm blew over the valley. But Liam didn't gather his tools and hurry inside, he stayed out in the rain for another hour, finishing the last of his work. Two days later, he became sick, confined to his bed: a deep, awful cough and pale skin and eyes turning an acrid black. He was dead in a week.

After that, the community decided it wasn't worth the risk. Maybe it was the rain that brought the illness over the border, maybe he was out in it for too long—allowing it to soak into his skin, drops catching on his tongue, breathing it into his lungs—or maybe Liam had slipped over the boundary into the trees but refused to admit it. Either way, we now move indoors when the rains come. Just to be sure.

Bee turns off the faucet and I can feel her stormy gray-blue eyes on me—even though she can't truly see me. Another crack of lightning splinters the air and the walls tremor around us, the weathervane atop the house spinning wildly—the barometric pressure dropping. The magnolia trees beside the back door quiver, leaves opening wide as if in prayer, awaiting the rain, and I think how I wouldn't want to live anywhere else. Unlike my sister and my husband, this place has always been enough.

"I think Theo's keeping something from me," I say at last, the words swallowed up by the darkening sky.

Bee turns her gaze to the window, thunder rolling across the horizon, a deep belly of fury and rainwater and electricity. "All men lie."

BEE

My sister is afraid of the dark: of the trees at our border, the moon hanging too low in the sky, the stars pinwheeling down to crush us. She scurries indoors when it rains, while I stand in the open and beckon down the sky.

We are originals—Calla and I. We were born in Pastoral.

Our parents came in the autumn of 1972, when all mad, wild, enraged hippies were fleeing the war and the draft. They retreated across borders and into remote lands where they couldn't be tracked down.

Our mom had been an out-of-work elementary school teacher and our father repaired refrigerators. Both skills, as it turned out, served them well in Pastoral. Mom taught all levels of education to the children of Pastoral, while my father kept things running: well pumps and windmills and wood-burning stoves. When mom was still alive, she told me how they gave up everything they knew—neighbors and family and the local market only two blocks from their home—to come live here in these woods, and they made a life in Pastoral, a good one.

She gave birth to me within these forest walls, without doctors or drugs.

People say you can't remember your birth, but I do. I was born in this farmhouse, on the second floor, with the windows open to let in the breeze—curtains brushing against the wood floor. I can recall the feel of the sunset glimmering across my newborn body, the smell of the air so sweet for the first time, the magnolia trees in bloom. The midwife, who had long, braided gray hair, held me against her heart, and I can still recall the beating of it against my tiny shell-shaped ear. I never cried as a baby.

I looked around the world with curiosity, as if I knew it wouldn't last, that someday it would all be taken from me.

Now I navigate the farmhouse halls easily, knowing the divots in the wood floor, the slanted walls and the angles of each doorway by heart. I smelled the rain in the air as we ran from the orchard, I felt the dampness against my skin before a single drop fell from the sky. I absorb the world like a bird navigates, a memory imprinted in hollow bones, flying south season after season. The scent of poppies beside the back porch have colors that brand into my memory, the lemon trees that line the pond smell like bright, sunlight-yellow, much richer and sharper than the actual color of a lemon I recall from my childhood. The world comes to me in ravenous hues and disjointed shapes. A thing that is hard to describe.

After my sister and I retreat to our rooms, rain sheds over the house like a great weeping, slow and doldrum. Sometimes, on evenings like this, it reminds me of when Calla and I were younger—after our parents died—and it was just her and me in the old farmhouse.

But Calla doesn't like to talk about before—the memories hurt too much. *Remember how Mom would hide our stuffed animals under our blankets at the foot of our beds, so when we climbed beneath the sheets at night, we'd find them by wiggling our toes?*

No, Calla would answer, shrugging off the memory. *I don't remember things like you do.* As if we had a different childhood, as if she's blotted out the years we shared with our parents before they passed. I think she's angry at them for dying too young and leaving us alone. Instead she'd rather forget them completely than carry the hurt around inside her like a rotting piece of wood. Maybe she feels betrayed by me, too, because I've refused to let them go, and sometimes the divide between us feels so big I worry it will break us both.

After an hour, I leave my bedroom and walk out into the hall, unable to sleep.

My footsteps are the only sound; even the wind outside has softened, the rain reduced to only a few scattered drops. The room my sister shares with Theo is two doors down on the right, past the white-tiled bathroom with the cracked clawfoot tub we rarely use. In summer, we bathe in the pond or in the metal basin beside the back door, and after, we let the sun bake dry our skin.

I walk to the stairs and down into the living room. A hallway stretches back from the kitchen to the mudroom, where a crooked, unwieldy door opens up into overgrown grasses, mangy shrubs, and several honey locust trees that press their thorny barbs against the siding of the house, scratching away the old paint.

We rarely use this back end of the house; it feels dark and closed off, from another time.

But a small room juts off the hall, down a series of low steps.

It was once a sunroom, where tall windows let in the southern light, and herbs and root vegetables were grown late into the season. But half the windows have been boarded up, the others draped with heavy linen curtains.

I touch the cold door handle, feeling the stale draft coming out from beneath the door. When I was little, the converted sunroom was used for outsiders, a place where new arrivals who had found their way through the woods to Pastoral would stay, awaiting the ceremony to initiate them into the community. I remember the wearied faces of strangers when they shuffled up our front porch steps, tired and hungry, their eyes wide with a different kind of thirst.

Sometimes they stayed in the sunroom for only a couple days, sometimes weeks, while it was decided whether they could remain—if they were a good fit for Pastoral. But rarely was anyone ever turned away.

It's hard to imagine now: strangers in the house. It's been over ten years since anyone new has wandered up the road to Pastoral. And just as long since anyone left.

I open the door and step inside the darkened sunroom—the rich scent of soil filling my nostrils, left over from the room's previous life. Moss and stubby shards of grass poke at the bottoms of my bare feet from where they grow up through the floorboards, the wood planks set down directly onto the earth. The room feels like stepping outside, with its thin shell of glass walls. Some years ago, after a storm, we found one of the windows broken—a limb from a honey locust tree must have forced its way through the glass—and we nailed wood planks across the opening. But it was a hasty job, and now I can feel the breeze hissing through the wood boards, a wisteria vine weaving its way through the gap, reaching up for the ceiling.

I find the metal bed frame pushed up against one wall, the mattress bare, and I run my hand across the dusty footboard. A white dresser stands at the opposite wall, although I imagine its color has faded, turned dull and layered with several years of dirt. I walk to the windows over-looking the meadow and orchard trees, and I press my fingers to the glass, imagining the scenery before me: the dark, starlit sky, the moon pouring down over the tall summer grass that moves in waves with the wind from the southeast.

A memory slips over me.

Of this stale room. Of a stranger standing at this same window.

He smelled of pine.

But the memory feels wrong and far too recent. Hearing his heart in-side his chest, *beating beating beating.* He sounded like a fox, quick and panicked, a heartbeat that wanted to find a safe place to hide. To run.

I turn and rub my palms up my arms, chilled suddenly.

I can't remember his face, his name, but he was here. Only a season or two ago. A man.

A stranger.

THEO

By evening, the rainstorm has passed, and the moon makes long, angular shapes through the trees as I walk up the road to the guard hut.

Through the dusty window, I can see Parker seated inside: narrow shoulders and close-set eyes, like a young deer, watchful of anything twitching around him. He nods at me when I step through the doorway of the small hut, picking up his coffee mug—handmade by someone in the community with a handle like a tree trunk. On the desk, the pitcher of coffee looks like it's still warm, steam rising from the top, and there's enough left to get me through the night.

Parker sidles past me in the doorway, tossing whatever's left in his mug out into the grass beside the road. His mom makes the coffee fresh every morning and afternoon, then brings it out to Parker, and he leaves whatever he doesn't drink for me. It's ashy, gritty stuff, but it's drinkable. And most of the others in the community would trade just about anything for a cup of it. Tea leaves are grown in abundance, while the few coffee plants produce far less—so I drink it gratefully.

"Fucking exhausted," Parker comments, scraping his hand through his dirty-blond hair.

"You see anything tonight?" I ask.

"Sure did." He pivots to lean against the doorway while I take a seat in the only chair inside the guard hut, looking out through the smudged window at the road. "Three UFOs and a bigfoot. That sucker could run though, I chased him for ten miles before he dove into a river and sunk to the bottom. It might have been a girl bigfoot though, hard to tell in the dark." He winks at me and smiles so wide I can see all of his mangled teeth. Parker can be a little shit sometimes, and he taps a finger against the revolver strapped at his waist. *Tap tap tap.* As if it gives him more authority than anyone else within the compound—more authority than me. And maybe it does. I don't know why Levi allows Parker to keep it. He's more likely to shoot himself than anything out on that road.

I pour myself a cup of coffee then lean back in the old, repurposed office chair, adjusting the lever to lower the seat down. Parker is tall and lanky, like most twenty-one-year-olds, but he's still shorter than me and he can't see out the window when the chair is too low.

The summer wind blows through the doorway and Parker straightens up, as if the breeze were ushering him home. His shift over. "See you in the morning," he says with the sudden gravel of a man twice his age, the long hours wearing on him, aging him quicker than it should.

"Hey," I say, before he steps out of sight. "How far have you ever been down the road?"

An itchy maw of silence congeals between us and I wonder if he's heard me. His jaw sticks out and his dark, sleepy eyes flatten. "Outside of Pastoral?"

"Yeah," I answer, trying to sound like I have nothing to hide. I sip my coffee then wince at the bitterness.

"Shit, man, I don't know, not far."

In all the years we've worked the guard hut—the passing conversation when I arrive in the evening for the night shift, and then again in the morning when he appears after sunup for the day shift—we've never discussed this. Both of us have spent hours staring out at that long dirt road, where it slopes up and down over low hills before vanishing into the trees. A road that leads out into a world where both of us were born. Parker lived in Sacramento with his single mom before they moved here when he was only three years old. *We got lucky*, he told me once. *Somehow my mom found this place.*

But I don't remember anything beyond Pastoral—I was only an infant when I was dropped off at the guard hut: abandoned, cared for by several of the older women in Pastoral, raised by the community. But whoever left me here thought this place was better than *out there*.

"I chased my dog down the road once," Parker says, his mouth finding a strange flatness, like he's fighting a warning in his head, telling him not to talk about it. "He was a collie, I think. Black and white. A good dog, shit at hunting, but he was loyal. Until that day." Parker's eyes blink rapidly, as if the memory were passing through him by rote, fingers twitching against the handle of the gun. "I was probably only twelve or thirteen when it happened. He was chasing something down the road, a rabbit, I think. I followed him for a bit, a good mile maybe, hard to tell when you're that age, but he was too fast. The road got pretty narrow, intersected with other roads, and I wasn't sure which way he went." He shakes his head, shaking away the memory, and draws his shoulders back. "Never saw that dog again."

I lean forward in the chair. *Parker went past the gate, past the boundary.* "You didn't get sick?" I ask.

"Guess not. I never told anyone what I did."

He was only a kid when it happened; maybe he didn't go as far as he thinks. Maybe he only took a few steps over the border.

"Did you see anything else out on the road?" I ask.

"Like what?"

"You know what."

His eyes drop and he kicks at the dirt just outside the doorway, like he knows he's said too much. "Didn't see anything," he answers. We both know the penalty for going beyond the perimeter, the panic it would cause among the community, the ritual he would face: packed dirt and blood and bound wrists. He didn't just risk his life by walking past the boundary, he risked it by returning, and now by telling me.

"I won't say anything," I say now, to reassure him.

He nods, eyes half-lidded like drowsy moons. We've known each other a long time, and maybe that's why he's told me this story. Or maybe he's just tired—let it slip without meaning to.

A moment of quiet falls between us and the chair settles as I shift my weight back, taking another long gulp of the coffee, the liquid less bitter now—my taste buds already familiar with the grit and ash of it.

"Why you asking about the road?"

The jittery pulse of caffeine begins to thrum through me. "Just curious," I say.

"You know you can't go out there," Parker warns now, raising a blond eyebrow at me, as if it were a pointed finger. "You can't go past the boundary."

No shit, I think. At every weekly gathering, we're reminded of the dangers waiting inside the woods. And our job—our post at the gate—is meant to keep any outsiders who might wander up the road from getting in. From bringing the rot over our borders. We keep watch. We protect. But in all the years I've sat inside the hut, I've never seen a single person striding up the road to Pastoral.

I shoot Parker a look, a half smirk, like my question was only a joke. "Don't worry, I'm not going anywhere." And I settle back into the chair, making myself look perfectly content to stay put, ignoring the lump rooted in my stomach. The lie so easily told.

He eyes me a moment longer, like he doesn't believe my gesture of ease, as if he senses something stirring along my thoughts, a thing I've been thinking for far too long: *What if I could make it down the road? What if I could make it through the trees to the outside? To the world that lies beyond?*

Parker lets out a low, deep breath. "Okay, I'm heading back, need to get some sleep." He tips his head. "Keep watch for Olive and Pike's chickens, they've been burrowing out of their coop the last few days. Coyotes might get 'em if they wander past the perimeter."

I nod. "Our job as community security is never done."

Parker waves a hand dismissively then turns in the doorway, stepping out onto the road. I listen to the sound of his feet thumping sleepily against the dirt, making the half-mile walk up the road into the heart of Pastoral, until they fade in with the dark and are gone completely.

My thumb traces the edge of the mug.

I peer out at the road, at the path that leads away from Pastoral to a world I've never seen.

I leave the mug on the desk and stand up, walking through the doorway onto the road. The gate beside the hut is rusted and locked in place— it's been too long since someone new has arrived safely to Pastoral.

I breathe in the mild night air, the scent of lilacs blooming in the ditch beside the road, and stare out into the dark. Into the nothing beyond the road.

I take a step past the gate. Then another.

I push my hands into my pockets and think about Parker's story, about chasing his dog past the boundary. Calla would be furious if she knew what I have been thinking for too long now, the notions crackling along synapses, the idea I can't shake—that's tugged at me for the last year. Maybe longer.

But she hides things from me too—buried thoughts beyond her water-deep eyes. A part of my wife she keeps hidden, a feeling I can't put words to, but I sense it there all the same.

I look back at the gate, the tiny, cramped guard hut where I've sat nearly every night for too many years, too many seasons—snow and biting autumn winds and the heat of summer when not even a breeze slips through the doorway to cool my overheated flesh. How many hours have I spent in that room, drinking the same ash-coffee, staring out at this stretch of road, wondering.

I walk to the edge of the road and find a small stone in the tall reeds. I pick it up; my heart already beginning to batter my rib cage. With the stone held in my right hand, I walk away from the guard hut, down the dirt road, careful that my boots are quiet against the dirt.

I walk away from my post.

I leave Pastoral.

————

The border of Pastoral is marked by a wood fence along the right side of the road, and nailed to the last post is a hand-painted sign that reads: PRIVATE PROPERTY.

The sign is pointless—no one has come this way in over ten years. No one has made it through the dense forest. And if they did, they'd surely be sick with rot, and we couldn't allow them through anyway. It's not safe like it used to be. Still, I step across the boundary, and into the land that exists outside Pastoral: the place we do not cross.

But this is not the first time.

I walk five paces and stop at the misshapen rock placed on the road. The first time I set the rock here—over a year ago now—I remember my heart beating wildly and my breathing so loud I feared someone from the community would hear me. I crouched down and quietly placed the rock on the dirt road—marking how far I had made it—then I sprinted back to the safety of the gate and the hut. I didn't go down the road for a week after that—I was too terrified. Instead, I would stare in the bathroom mirror each morning and lean close to the glass, examining my eyes, looking for something that wasn't right: for the black of my pupils to expand like mud seeping up from the earth. I was looking for signs of the disease.

But it never came.

A week later, under a nearly full moon, I gathered enough courage to walk back down the road—my eyes darting into the woods, listening for the sounds of trees splitting open, bark peeling back—and when I reached the palm-size stone, I walked five paces past it, placing another stone in the dirt at my feet.

I've repeated this every night for the last year: walking five more paces up the road, then leaving another stone to mark my progress. I've been risking my life for something I'm not sure of, just to see a little farther, to know what lies beyond the next rise in the road.

And tonight, when I reach the last stone in the line, I look back at the gate, the little hut, both still visible in the dark. But ahead of me, the road makes an abrupt left turn, and I've never been able to see what's beyond it. I squeeze the rock I plucked from the tall grass, and silently count off my paces. *One, two, three, four* . . . I swallow down a breath. *Five.* I'm not quite around the bend in the road, I can't quite see what's beyond it, but I set the stone on the ground at my feet—my heart a drum. *I'm so close.* In the trees, I hear a cracking sound, like someone running a hooked claw down the rough bark of a tree, peeling it away to reveal the soft white center inside. Like flesh. Like the parts of a tree you shouldn't see.

The trees are separating themselves.

But I don't run, I don't turn back. I take another step forward, beyond the last stone.

Curiosity does this: It prods at the gut; it pushes fear aside and causes smart men to do stupid things.

I look back at the gate as it slips from view, and I round the bend in the road, my mind no longer counting my paces—my legs carrying me forward, one after the other—and then I see something ahead. Resting just off the side of the road.

A vehicle.

A truck.

———

There's a feeling sometimes, when you wake up from a deep, deep sleep and your eyes flash open and for the briefest half moment you can't remember where you are—the room and the movement of the curtains against the open window all feel foreign in that distant, not quite lucid way. Like you might still be asleep.

That's how it feels, looking upon the truck.

A felled tree is lying across the road, limbs shattered and broken apart, effectively blocking the path. The truck is parked askew, between an opening in the trees, as if the driver had tried to steer off the road then gotten stuck—in deep spring mud or even deeper winter snow.

I move closer, ignoring the fear clamping down inside my chest. *I shouldn't be here.*

The windshield and hood are covered in golden leaves and rotting pine needles, a couple seasons' worth. *The truck hasn't been here long.* The two driver's-side tires are sunk into the earth, buried. Stuck. I touch the door handle and a shiver of northern wind passes over my neck, a quick gust, and then it's gone.

I pull open the door and take a step back, expecting something to lunge out at me, or to find a calcified body slumped against the floorboards—frozen or starved or *rotted* to death. But there's no corpse. No scent of decaying flesh.

The truck looks generally undisturbed. A layer of dust covers the bench seat, the dashboard, the radio dials, the steering wheel. The kind of dry summer dust that seeps through cracks in windows and doors and floorboards.

There's not much inside, no obvious clues about why the truck is here, and when I flip down the visor, several papers drift down around me: insurance card, three years expired; a coupon for a discount oil change at Freddy's Oil & Lube in Seattle, also expired. I pick up a truck registration card and scan the details: The vehicle is registered to Travis Wren, a name that falls flat in my mind.

I reach across the bench seat to open the glove box. Inside, I find a wool cap with MERLE'S TREE FARM printed on the front, a few wadded dollar bills, a toothbrush, a pocket knife—the blade dull—a road map of the West Coast (Washington, Oregon, California), and a photograph.

A crease runs through the center of the photo, like it had been folded in half at one time, and most of the image has been obscured, damaged by water that must have leaked into the truck during wetter seasons, the colors of the photograph now puckered and warped.

I straighten, holding the picture toward the moonlight and running a thumb over the partial face I can still make out, staring up at the camera. The water has distorted all but the woman's left eye, a cheek partly turned away—like she was uninterested in having her photo taken—and her cropped, sunflower-blond hair. I can't tell much from the image, but there is a starkness to her, a seriousness you can only see in the lidded eye.

I run my thumb over her face, and a throbbing pulses above my left ear, an itch beneath the scalp. I flip the photograph over, where a name has been scrawled in hasty letters, as if written while the person was driving. Bumping over potholes, trying to keep from driving off the road.

The name is Maggie St. James.

CALLA

I'm standing in Bee's bedroom doorway, the morning sun diluted through the curtains, watching her nostrils swell with each dreamy exhale. Her knees are drawn to her chest atop the threadbare quilt, like a pale-skinned nautilus shell. I have a memory of us when we were little, when we would sleep in the same bed, hands clasped, afraid of ghosts hiding in the closet, monsters beneath the bed frame, forest goblins at the window. But it's a watercolor memory: nebulous, faded with age, hardly there at all.

Pink spots dot Bee's cheeks in the sunlight, but she doesn't wake, doesn't feel my gaze on her. The rain has let up outside, and the air in her room feels stagnant, in need of an open window.

But I don't step into the room, I stay like the ghosts we used to fear, pressed to the doorframe, while a sinking feeling finds weight inside my chest. There is an ocean that swells and heaves between my sister and me, a vast sea that neither one of us will cross. She prefers to remember the past, pick apart the moments from our childhood, while I keep it stuffed down where it won't hurt me.

And when I look into my sister's eyes, there is something there I don't understand—the woman she's become is a stranger to me.

Downstairs, the front door slams shut, the vibration rattling the walls of the house, followed by the sound of footsteps across the living room floor. Theo is home.

I close Bee's bedroom door, letting her sleep, and descend the stairs.

Theo is standing at the sink in the kitchen, looking down at something in his hands, and he's still wearing his boots—a trail of dirt across the hardwood floor. I stop short at the bottom step. His posture is strange, shoulders rounded forward, back rigid. And a spider-crawling-across-flesh sort of unease rises up into my chest.

"Theo?" I ask.

He turns quickly, nearly dropping the thing in his hand. But he doesn't try to hide it from me—to tuck it away behind his back—instead he holds it between his fingers, and his face sags with an odd trace of confusion. Like he's unsure what he's holding.

"What is it?" I ask.

"A photograph."

I cross into the kitchen and my eyes flick to his, suddenly unsure if I want to look—want to see what has caused this unnatural discomfort in his eyes. "Of what?"

"A woman."

My gaze skims the photo, catching a glimpse of blond hair and a sharp blue eye peering up from drawn, hard features. The rest of the image is damaged, waterlogged. "Who is she?"

"Her name is Maggie St. James." Theo stares at me like he's looking for clues, like I might know who she is. "Have you heard of her?"

"No." The floorboards above us creak softly—Bee has risen from bed, and she walks across the hall to the bathroom. A moment later, the sound of water rattles up through the pipes in the walls, taking a moment to reach the upstairs sink. "Where did you find it?"

There are only a few photographs within the community, brought to Pastoral by the founders who wanted to remember those they left behind in the outside. Grandparents, old friends, Roona even has a photo of her dog, Popeye, who died before she moved to Pastoral.

"In a truck," he answers.

"What truck?"

He won't look at me; his eyes are all wrong. "Out on the road."

"What do you mean?" I take a step back, away from him.

"I went past the boundary," he admits, his mouth slack, his fingers running across the photograph.

The air leaves my lungs, little sparks flaring across my vision. "Theo," I hiss, and glance to the door, as if someone might be there, someone who might hear. "What the hell are you talking about?"

"I just wanted to see what was out there."

My hands begin to shake, and I take another step away from him—my heart a club against my eardrums. "Death is out there," I answer, my eyes tracing the features of his face now, looking for cracks, for any hint that he's changed.

That he's brought something back with him.

My husband has done the very thing he should not do: He went over the border. *Over the border.* Where dark things live. Where no one comes back alive—at least not for long.

"I feel fine," he says quickly, eyebrows sloping downward, mouth mirroring the same shape.

But I take another step back from him and my heels hit one of the dining room chairs. It scrapes across the wood floor and stops at the edge of the table. Knots form inside my chest, and my fingers reach out for the table to brace myself. "It takes a day or two for the symptoms to show," I answer.

I shouldn't be here in the house with him. *I should run, call to Bee, warn the others.*

"I'm not sick," he insists, and he raises his palms to me, as if I could see some proof in the work-worn surface of his hands. "I don't have it."

"You can't know that." I inch around the end of the table, my eyes locked on his. The back door is only a few steps away, I could dart out through the screen door and be in the meadow in less than a minute. I could run up the path to Pastoral and leave my husband behind. My husband who might be infected. *Sickness coiling itself along his tissues, his marrow, a ticking clock he won't survive.*

But I don't, because I'm afraid what it'll mean if I do. I'm afraid of what will come next. So I stay rooted to the floor, a roaring, clacking dread thumping at my temples.

He moves closer to me, but not enough to touch me, not close enough to pass whatever might be inside him onto me: he senses the fear screaming down my veins, pumping blood to my limbs, ready to bolt. "I promise I'm not sick," he says again. He clears his throat and drops his hands to his sides. "It wasn't the first time I went down the road."

My eyebrows screw together, my heart pumps faster.

"I've done it before," he says, a cool, calm slant to each word. As if they hardly mean anything at all.

I release my hold on the table. "You went down the road before last night?"

His eyes slip to the floor, his hands worrying against the photograph he still holds. "Every night." His gaze lifts back to mine and there is a burden in them, a heavy kind of remorse that he's been carrying for much too long. "I've been going down the road every night for the last year, a little farther each time. But I've never gotten sick, Calla. I've gone past the boundary hundreds of times, and I've never caught it."

This is the thing he's been keeping from me, hidden from view, but always there just the same. A lie I sensed, felt in his palms every time he touched me, masked behind half-closed eyes, where he thought I wouldn't see.

"Maybe I'm immune," he continues. "Maybe I can't get it." He seems alight suddenly, eyes widened, like he's been holding this in all this time, and now he can't wait to get it out. "I've never seen anything out on the road, not until last night. It was just sitting there—a *truck*—and I don't think it's been there long. A few years at most. There were only a couple seasons worth of dead leaves on the hood."

The roar in my ears grows louder, fear mixed with hurt: Theo has lied, and worse than that, he has risked his own life.

"Someone just left it there," he adds, eyebrows drawn upward. "Someone named Travis Wren."

"I don't care about the truck."

"He didn't just vanish," he goes on, ignoring the hurt rising in my voice. "He either went back down the road, or he came to Pastoral."

I look to the door, biting my bottom lip, terror ebbing in my mind, making it difficult to think clearly. "There's no one named Travis in the community," I say. We shouldn't even be talking about this. He shouldn't have gone over the boundary, shouldn't have risked everything, only to find some worthless old truck and a photograph.

He scratches at the back of his head. "I know." More footsteps creak upstairs, Bee moving down the hall to the stairs. I should shout up to her to stay put, to not come any closer, because Theo might be infected, but her footsteps stop. Maybe she's retreated back into her room.

"No one new has come to Pastoral in over ten years," I tell him. Not since our borders became unsafe. When the rot edged so close to our community that we had to mark a line around Pastoral that we would never cross, or risk getting sick.

"Maybe he came and we didn't know," Theo suggests, his voice tremulous, unsteady, like he doesn't quite believe his own words.

"If a man came wandering up the road, you or Parker would have seen him at the gate."

Theo's mouth turns down.

"If someone new came," I continue, hardly taking a breath. "We'd have a community gathering, we'd perform the ritual. We'd have to know if he was sick."

"I know," Theo answers, looking down at the photo again.

"You risked your life, you risked everything by going past the boundary," I tell him, tears wetting my eyelids, the floorboards feeling as if they're swaying beneath my feet. To imagine him stepping over the boundary, his heart beating in his chest, lungs gulping in the night air, forces a spike of nausea into my stomach. I can't even walk within a few feet of the boundary without fear rapping at my rib cage: a dark hole of unease widening inside me. We have been taught to fear the trees, but this fear feels as if it were born inside me, taken root long before the first stories of an illness began sweeping through the community. I fear what lies beyond our boundary as though it already lives within my dreams, always there, trying to draw me out into the dark.

Yet my husband has walked over the boundary every night for a year—a whole year. As if it were nothing. As if he wasn't afraid.

"Whoever that man was," I begin again, "he probably left his car and walked back down the road, away from here. And maybe that photograph was his wife, or his girlfriend; it doesn't matter." My voice sounds weak, splintered, and I wipe the tears from my cheeks.

Theo looks to the window over the kitchen sink, but he doesn't speak—as if all the words he had planned to say, to justify what he's done, are now trapped in the attic of his mind. And I wonder if the rot might already be inside him, making holes in his lungs, turning his blood the color of a black winter sky. I wonder if it's already too late.

I turn away from him, knocking over a dining room chair, before I push open the screen door and step out into the dawn light. I descend the porch steps, past the garden, now fragrant with basil and chamomile and lavender, where the hens peck at the ground, plucking worms and seeds from the rows.

I hurry away from the house, toward the pond, the morning birds singing from the trees and a chorus of frogs erupting from the shallows.

I think I hear Theo say my name behind me. I think maybe he's stepped out from the house onto the porch, coming after me.

But when I glance back, he's not there.

BEE

I heard them arguing.

My sister's razor-edged voice bouncing along the high walls of the old house. The timbre of each word like a blackbird screeching from the pines in the heat of afternoon. While Theo's words seemed to stall in the air, as if he was unsure of them. Like he was saying things even he didn't quite understand.

Theo went past the boundary.

He walked up the road and found a truck abandoned in the forest. And he may have come back with illness tiptoeing down his spine, into the deepest part of his bones.

Disease. A word that lingers in the throat after you've said it. A word spoken too often within the community. A threat that's always close: blood in the stomach and lungs and sometimes in the eyes. Weeping, *weeping.* But the blood is not crimson, cut-from-the-flesh red. It's black—rotting, virulent. Thick like soil after it rains, an awful sight. A memory you can't shake once you've seen it.

We call it a *disease,* but its true scientific classification is unknown: spores or virus or bacteria, we have no idea. But it rots away your insides. It begins in the trees, turning the leaves spotted and decayed, then the bark begins to peel away, revealing pale white centers, sap weeping down their sides: a last cry for help, wounds that will never heal. The disease hangs in the air from these open wounds, waiting to be breathed into lungs, to touch bare skin, to be passed from one organism to another.

It's a kind of blight that the founders had never seen before in the

outside. Something new—anomalous. And it has infected the forest surrounding Pastoral. A barrier we cannot pass through.

Elm Pox, we call it. But we also whisper another name, a simpler name: *rot*.

The younger kids sometimes play a game, chasing one another through
the crop fields, shouting, "Rot, rot, you'll soon die of the pox!" They tag
one another, as if they were passing the pox onto the next person, and the
game continues this way, endlessly. Until one of the older women tells the
children to hush, dragging them indoors.

The rot burrows into the skin, absorbs through the lungs, and kills
a person within a week or two. Unless we can treat them before it's too
late—before it spreads to others. But we've rarely succeeded in ridding the
body of the illness once it's taken root.

When I stood at the top of the stairs, listening, I could hear Theo's
heartbeat pulsing at his neck—a gift of losing my eyesight, the ability to
hear the tiniest of sounds, the beating of moth wings and the heavy exhale
of lungs. But Theo didn't sound sick. No illness throbbing through his
organs, swimming down his spinal cord, eating away at soft tissue like the
blight that's been known to ravage the green oak leaves in early autumn.

He doesn't have the rot.

Instead, what I heard were my own memories, cool and quick, like dip-
ping my toes into the creek in early spring, when the water has only just
thawed from the glacial snow higher up in the mountains.

Theo said a name I've heard before.

Not the woman's name—not the person in the photograph.

The other name: Travis Wren.

It binds itself to a memory: the sound of foreign footsteps across the
hardwood floor, a man sleeping in the converted sunroom at the back of
the house, whose heart fluttered rapidly. *He didn't want to be here.*

He slept in that room and I snuck inside, listening to his heartbeat,
trying to decide if it was fear that made it thunder inside his chest. Or
something else.

Trying to decide if I could trust him.

The man whose truck Theo found out in the woods—a man named
Travis Wren—slept here in our house not long ago.

He was *here*.

CALLA

I want to believe that he's not sick.

I strip from my green tulip sundress and leave it in a heap beside the oak tree. I kick free from my sandals and walk down the slope to the pond, sinking into the cool, shallow water—my body turning weightless. The cold pricks my flesh and I drift onto my back, rings of water echoing out around me then unfurling against the shore.

But my heart feels knitted, pinched too tightly together, knowing what Theo has done. This man I love has risked everything, and I'm terrified I might lose him—that it might already be too late.

I stare up through the branches of the lemon trees, not even a breeze stirring their boat-shaped leaves. The fruit will be ready to harvest soon: the sun browning our shoulders while we perch on ladders, lemon skins under our fingernails, plucking the ripe yellow orbs that will glow like the sun on the kitchen counter when we cut them open. In the fall we will begin the canning, making a syrup with lemon juice, wild blackberries, and currants in dozens of glass jars—the urgency of autumn always prodding at us. Yet, when the temperature drops and the first few flakes catch on windowsills, when the ground hardens and the sky turns gray, we can't help but wonder what else we could have done to prepare. *Will we have enough? Will we survive this season? Will we have a winter like last year, when the mice got into the sacks of cornmeal in the cellar and spoiled nearly half of it?*

There is hardship here, but there is also a slow contentment: the way the sun sweeps through the trees in the morning, the broad-billed hummingbirds' methodical pulsing among the wildflowers beside the porch, gathering the first nectar of the day. And yet, my husband found it so easy to stride down the road, past the border trees, as if he could leave it all behind. As if all of this means nothing. Our home, this land. *Me.*

Watching him in the kitchen, he showed no signs of illness, no inky spots at the rims of his eyes, no darkened fingernails. But it makes no sense: How could he walk down the road, breathe in the damp moldering air of the forest, and not bring back the rot?

Unless he's right—*and he is immune.*

But if it's true, shouldn't we tell the others? Shouldn't they know that he can pass through the woods untouched by disease, while everyone else who's dared cross the boundary has returned sick and died shortly after?

Yet I also know admitting what he's done to the group would mean admitting that he's broken our rules. Not just once, but hundreds of times. He's gone down the road and risked bringing back the pox, he has betrayed all of us. And for what? To find an old abandoned truck and a meaningless photograph?

A soft breeze ripples over the surface of the pond, my skin briefly pricked with gooseflesh, and a memory comes with it: of Rose and Linden, their deaths still so razor-edged in my mind. Their bodies left to rot in the woods, visible from the border—limp, unmoving. They knew what could happen, but they risked it anyway: sneaking past the perimeter. Just like the story of the young wheat farmer's daughter who lived in the valley back when the town was first built—before the members of Pastoral bought the land. She was only nine or ten when she snuck from her room after dark and went into the forest. Seven days passed before she was seen again, wandering beyond the border trees looking wild and mangy, like a forest creature covered in rotted elm leaves. It was the first time the early settlers started to suspect the trees might contain an illness—something they should fear. They abandoned the town shortly after, frightened of what might live in these woods.

It's why I fear what my husband has done.

And yet, I will keep his secret, I will protect his lie—*I am a good wife,* I think. I am a wife who won't say a word, because he would do the same for me, he would form a wall around me to keep me safe—he loves me in this way, deeply, no matter what.

I stay in the pond and the sun climbs up from the east, unsteady and fat. In the distance, I can see the silhouette of my husband inside the house, visible through the kitchen window above the sink. He's looking down at something again, probably the photograph. *He won't let it go.*

I move closer to the shore, keeping my eyes on him.

A roar pulses in my ears.

Another figure appears at the window: my sister. She's leaning slightly, a hand on the counter to orient herself, and Theo lifts his head to look at her. They aren't close, but near enough to talk softly so their voices won't carry out the open windows into the meadow. To the pond where I float, watching them.

My legs wade up toward the shore, feet sinking into the mud, and I see Travis's head flick toward the window, as if to see if I'm close, if I might walk through the screen door and catch them.

The meadow grass pricks the soles of my feet, the air is slightly cool against my flesh, pond water dripping from my hair down my back, but I turn my ear toward the farmhouse, straining to hear. A knot tightens in my stomach. They're much too far away for me to hear the words being muttered between them.

But it doesn't feel right, the clandestine way Theo leans close to Bee, his eyes flashing to the window.

Some secret thing is being shared between them.

Words meant only for their ears.

BEE

"He was here," I whisper, standing at the kitchen counter, my chin tilted upward. Theo, my brother-in-law, is a tall man and I don't want to speak to his chest, his throat, so I lift my face, hoping my clouded eyes have met with his.

Maybe I'm stupid to be this close to a man who went over the boundary and into the trees. But when I calm my own breathing and listen again to the slow cascade of blood through his veins, at his temples, his throat, it still sounds clean, unfettered. No illness streaming through him.

"Who?" Theo asks, swiveling to face me, a tremor of something in his voice. My sister is still out in the pond, floating in the cool water. Theo and I are alone in the house.

Still, I speak softly so only he will hear.

"The name you said earlier when you were arguing with Calla."

"We weren't arguing," he replies quickly, as if I'm the younger sister he must pacify, prove that he is being a good husband—a man who never raises his voice.

"I don't care about that," I say, my ears trained to the open window for sounds of Calla walking through the field from the pond. But it's quiet, too quiet. Only a lazy breeze tickling the tips of the alpine meadow grass. "Travis Wren," I say softly. "The truck you found."

Theo's breathing changes and I think he even leans in close, his skin radiating heat. "What about it?"

"I think he was here, Travis Wren, in the house. He was in the sunroom at the back."

A wind brushes through the screen door and with it comes the sound of Calla rising from the pond, water dripping from her skin onto the blades of grass at her feet. It's far off, but I can hear her movements. "Why do you say that?" he asks.

"I remember him."

Theo makes a strange sound, a clearing of his throat, like he doesn't believe me. "When was he here?"

Calla is moving toward the house now, getting closer.

"A year ago, maybe. Could have been longer."

Theo swallows, and his voice dips low, like he too doesn't want Calla to catch us talking. "How could he have been in the sunroom? We would have known." His words trail away like he's looking to the door.

I shake my head, my own sightless eyes flicking to the back door, knowing Calla is close. *Quickly. Quickly.* Her pace is almost a run. "I don't know," I answer.

A second passes. Calla is almost to the back porch, her footsteps loud against the earth. I think Theo must see her because I hear him stiffen, shifting something away that was in his hand—the photograph maybe. He's tucked it into a pocket so Calla won't see. "Why are you telling me this?" he asks. What he means is: why am I telling him and not my own sister.

"Because I knew you would believe me. And she wouldn't." I swallow down the guilt and take another step back, toward the living room. "She doesn't want to know about anything *out there.*" I nod toward the front of the house, the road, the gate in the distance and the forest beyond that. "But you do." I touch the stair railing, my heart climbing up my windpipe, scraping me open.

He might nod, but he doesn't get a chance to speak, because the screen door swings open and the scent of my sister, of green-golden lemons and silty pondwater, enters the house in a burst of fragrance and wind. I turn and hurry up the stairs before my face can give anything away.

"What are you doing?" I hear my sister ask Theo, her voice a coil drawn tight.

The faucet turns on at the kitchen sink, the clank of old pipes, of water rising up from the well before it splashes into the basin. "Washing my hands," Theo answers—the lie oddly believable.

"Where's Bee?" Her voice is strained, a scratch at the back of the throat, unusual for her. She knows something's wrong. Maybe she saw me talking to Theo, or she just senses it—when you live in a house with three people, secrets are rarely kept for long, everything is found out eventually.

"Upstairs, I think," Theo answers, his tone perfectly dull, a man who is only half listening to her line of questions. *A man who is used to lying.*

Calla blows out a breath and moves across the house, across the living room rug that mutes her footsteps, until she reaches the stairwell. I sink back into my bedroom before she can see me. Another moment passes and then her voice echoes back across the house, directed at Theo, "Tonight's the gathering."

The water in the kitchen sink turns off. "I know," he answers. Voice still flat, insipid. Maybe even a little annoyed.

The gathering. Tonight we will walk to the center of Pastoral.

Tonight, I will see Levi.

PART THREE

THE GATHERING

CALLA

The weekly gathering begins at sunset.

Theo and I walk up the path to the center of Pastoral, the sky teeming with evening birds, the air smelling like lilac blossoms, bitter crab apple trees, and cooked corn on the cob from the bonfire near the gathering circle.

There are twenty-two dwellings within the confines of Pastoral: several homes like ours, a community lodge, a dormitory with a dozen smaller bunkrooms, a large kitchen and dining hall, a woodshop, and a birthing hut set back in the trees to the west. Cooper, our founder, purchased the land and all its structures from a bank some fifty years ago. He got it cheap, because no one wanted to buy a remote outpost in the woods that had sat abandoned for seventy years—the structures sinking into the earth, the forest taking back the land. And most people didn't even know it was here.

Our farmhouse, where Bee and I grew up, sits at the southernmost border of the community, and closest to the guard hut. To the north of Pastoral are the wheat and cornfields, just visible in the waning light. The eastern boundary runs along a shallow ridgeline, where Henry and Lily Mae's home sits nestled in the dense pines, their goats often foraging along the border trees. And the path that runs along the creek—where Theo and I walked tonight, from the farmhouse to the heart of Pastoral—is the western line.

Pastoral is ninety-some acres: ninety acres that provide us shelter and keep us safe.

Members have already begun to find their seats in the gathering circle—constructed in the open stretch of flat land behind the dining hall, and between the massive gardens—and they're talking in small groups. This is where we gather each week, sitting shoulder-to-shoulder on the split-log benches that form a semicircle around a low wood stage, where we discuss harvests and weather and how to keep the community safe. It's a place where we also celebrate birthdays and weddings and mourn those we've lost. Every December, we sing songs the elders remember from the outside, about mistletoe and gifts wrapped in colorful ribbons. We drink muddled apple wine and light candles around the Mabon tree. We have brought customs from the outside into the woods with us, but we have also created some of our own.

But now, Theo and I stand just outside the circle—outside the ring of light from the bonfire—both of us afraid to speak to the others. Fearful that our mouths might betray our minds.

Theo went past the boundary.

Down the road.

And he might have the pox.

Still, when I peer at his skin, the sharpness of his eyes when they glance at me, there are no threads of dark in them.

Night bugs descend down from the trees, and Ava's three young girls—all tightly wound coils of long black hair and big crescent eyes just like their mother—run figure eights around the adults' legs, then loop over to the Mabon tree at the center of the circle. In spring, we tie ribbons to the branches of the old oak to celebrate the planting season, and again in the fall to celebrate harvest. And sometimes, the tree is used for other, darker things: to determine if illness resides in a body.

Now, the girls dart around the trunk of the tree, shrieking, "Rot, rot, you'll soon die of the pox. Rot, rot, they'll bury you in a coffin box." Then they sprint out into the rows of corn before anyone can yell after them.

Theo clears his throat, his eyes on the stage, waiting for Levi—he looks as if he's barely keeping the lie hidden at the base of his throat—and I think of Bee, standing so close to him inside the kitchen, whispering words I couldn't make out. But when I strode up from the pond and entered the house, Bee was gone, and Theo stood at the sink pretending he had nothing to hide. *He thinks I don't see.*

There are trenches in my mind, diverging lines of betrayal and confusion, but mostly fear. I want to trust that he won't go past the border again. But something in his eyes reveals the curiosity that lives there still.

From our left, Ash and his wife Colette—seven months pregnant—move toward the gathering. For weeks, Ash has been doting on his wife as if she might break, as if the child inside her were a fragile piece of glass. They pause near us, surveying the open benches for a place to sit, and Ash rubs a hand along Colette's neck. She closes her eyes briefly, tilting her head forward. I can see the weariness in her curved posture—her pregnancy has been difficult, plagued by morning sickness and bouts of dizziness, and she rarely leaves their home at the north side of Pastoral, except for the gatherings.

"Evening," Ash says softly, giving Theo and me an exhausted look.

"Evening," Theo responds in kind, nodding. "How are you feeling?" He directs the questions to Colette, keeping up the pretense of normalcy.

Colette turns only slightly, her rounded stomach limiting her movements, eyelids swollen at the edges. She is a slight woman, short in stature and small-boned—even in pregnancy—with glossy brown hair that drapes to her tailbone, and a gentle, uncomplicated way about her. Every movement feels as if she's gliding through water.

"Well enough," she replies, circling a hand around the globe of her stomach. "It already feels like I've been pregnant a whole year."

I've always liked Colette, and I feel the need to say something comforting, to assure her that *it'll all be worth it once you hold your baby in your arms*, or *I'm sure most women feel the same as you*. But I would also like to avoid any further conversation, any risk that she or Ash might see the secret tucked neatly behind my eyes.

"Let us know if we can do anything to help," my husband replies, but I can hear the strain in his voice—he wants this conversation to end as quickly as I do.

Thankfully Ash nods and they walk toward the circle, finding a place to sit near the back, talking softly between them—of baby names perhaps, of the crib that Ash has been building, or if they'd prefer a boy over a girl.

We just need to get this over with, I think. Avoid eye contact, keep our heads down, and we won't have to lie to anyone. But from the corner of my vision, I see Birdie edging her way toward me.

She does it slowly—no loud greetings or outstretched arms to draw me to her. Instead it's a clandestine effort, and when she reaches me, her head is low. "Warm night," she says, her flat, terse lips drawn down. Birdie and I have an easy, quiet kind of friendship. She's taught me how to stitch Theo's old shirts into sacks for storing flour and grain, the best way to layer compost, and how to can wild blueberries in lemon juice so they don't turn into lumpy syrup. It's a friendship of little burden or necessity.

But now, something seems off, and Birdie's eyes skip around the gathering circle to those standing near us, then touches the old scar on her left elbow, like she could worry it away—some years ago, she sliced it on a metal scythe during the wheat harvest and it healed jagged, a serrated uneven line of pink flesh.

"Yes, it is," I answer, hoping she will wander away to find a seat, and not ask me why Theo seems so stiff beside me. But instead she releases her hand from her elbow and touches my arm. "I need to speak to you." She looks at me slantwise, her skin like the surface of a walnut, cracked and worn down.

Before I can ask what's wrong, she tugs me several paces away from Theo, back into the shadow of the elms behind us, where our voices won't be heard.

"How is your garden?" she asks, her eyes too white at the edges. This question isn't merely a common inquiry into the health of my summer garden—she needs something.

"It's fine."

"Is the yarrow ready to harvest?"

"Almost." Some in the community hang fresh yarrow—immediately after it's been plucked from the soil—from the highest point of their ceilings. It's said to keep away illness, and when drunk in tea, it can cleanse a common winter flu from the body. "It should be ready in a week," I tell her.

Her right eye twitches, and she starts rubbing the scar again. I wish she'd stop. It's making me edgy, a nervous ache already twisting at my joints. "Has something happened?" I ask.

Several yards away, Theo turns his head, glancing back into the trees at Birdie and me. He's pretending not to listen, but I'm sure he's able to pick up a word or two.

Birdie's mouth sinks into a frown, and for a moment she looks like she's going to stride away without saying anything—lost her nerve. But then she clears her throat. "Three days ago, Arwen got too close to the edge." She looks out into the crowd not yet seated, and her eyes find her son, Arwen, standing beside her husband. Arwen is only ten years old, and has always been a crouched-in-the-corner, rather-be-reading-a-book kind of child. Timid and quiet, thoughtful. "He didn't mean to, he was hanging laundry on the line when one of my kitchen rags caught in the wind and blew into the trees." She sucks in a shaky breath. "I yelled to him just as he reached an arm across the boundary. I told him to leave the rag, and he did, but his arm still went past the border trees."

I reach out and squeeze her hand. "It was only an arm, Birdie, I'm sure he's fine."

She nods quickly, manically, and in lieu of jittering her leg, she begins chewing on the side of her cheek. She's lived here most of her life, came in the early years, then had her son in Pastoral. She knows the risks. She knows what could happen if Arwen brought the sickness back with him. "Our house is so close to the border," she continues. "I can see it from our bedroom window." She stops fidgeting and looks me dead in the eyes. "Lately, the trees at the boundary have been splitting open."

My breathing stalls in my throat. We've gone months without seeing the border trees peel open, and at times it feels as if the sickness might have left our woods, and perhaps our forest might be safe. But then, always, the bark begins to crack open again, sap leeching down their trunks, and we know the *rot* is still there. Always close. I want to turn and look at Theo, to see if he's listening, if he's heard, but I keep my gaze on Birdie. "It doesn't mean Arwen is sick," I assure her, but a thread of ice runs down to my tailbone. "How has he seemed?" I ask softly, leaning closer to her.

"We haven't noticed anything yet. No signs of it."

He shouldn't be here, I think. *Among the others. He should be at home, in his room, kept separate until we know for sure.*

But my husband is here, isn't he? A man who has done far worse—who willingly, defiantly, stepped over the boundary each night, countless times. For a whole year he has lied, but he has also survived. Never showing any hints of illness.

"Have you told Levi?" I ask.

She looks down at her hands. "I told him about the trees breaking open. But not about Arwen." Her eyes lift. "I don't want to alarm anyone if it's nothing."

I squeeze her hand, understanding all too well why she doesn't want to say anything to the group. No point causing panic if it's unnecessary.

"We've told him to stay away from the border so many times." She shakes her head and I worry tears might be about to break over her eyelids. "At night, we even tell him the story of the wheat farmer's daughter."

I smile at her, knowing she is a good mother, she does everything she can. "The yarrow won't cure him of the illness if he already has it," I explain, still holding Birdie's hand. Yarrow is only used for mild sickness, an upset stomach, a lingering fever. But I can see that she's desperate, willing to reveal what's happened to Arwen in hopes I might be able to help. But there is only one possible remedy for *elm pox*, and I know she won't want to do it. So instead, I offer her something benign, something to ease her mind, but in truth, won't save her son if he's infected with the rot. "Come to my house tomorrow and I'll give you a bit of fresh ginger root. You can give Arwen a warm bath steeped with the ginger, and it might leech any remnants of the illness from his skin."

This is a lie, and maybe she knows it, but she manages a tiny smile. "Thank you," she gulps out, her gaze skipping over the gathering circle, where almost everyone has found a seat, then she adds, "Please don't say anything."

I nod at her. "I won't."

She releases my hand and steps out from the shadowed trees, working her way through the group to find her husband and son.

My own husband is silent as we find a seat at the very back of the circle on one of the last open benches. I know he heard our conversation—at least some of it—but he won't look at me. Maybe he can see the tension tugging at my temples, the emotion I'm trying to hide. Birdie's son made a foolish mistake, he reached an arm through the line of border trees. While my husband willingly crossed the boundary night after night, as I slept in our bed, thinking he was safe.

But this isn't only what bothers me. It's the other thing Birdie said.

The trees have been splitting open.

The elm pox is close. Right at our borders, inching along our valley.

I swivel around, scanning the crowd for my sister, but she's not in the group.

She's still with Levi, in his house at the far end of the compound. They often meet before gatherings—she offers him guidance and direction. But only I know she gives him more than just acuity.

She gives herself.

BEE

Levi's house at the eastern edge of the compound smells of damp pine, moss embedded in the roof, and linens freshly washed by one of the women who regularly cleans and cares for his home—a task he is not burdened with as the leader of our community.

He lives in one of the larger homes in Pastoral: an original homestead built when settlers first arrived in these woods, before they fled and never came back.

I sit on the couch, running my palms across the woven fabric, a square pattern repeated over and over. I've felt this fabric against my bare skin many times before—my shoulder blades, my hipbones, making raw marks across my flesh. My own kind of pattern. Levi has peeled away my clothes and kissed me on this couch. He's whispered things no one else would believe.

My love for him is almost painful: desperate, needy. Tears on the floor, deep, heartsick kind of love.

He was with me the day my sight left me: lying on our backs in the meadow, toes just barely touching the edge of the pond, while Levi ran his thumb across my palm, whispering a story I can't recall now. The trees above us began to quiver and I remember laughing, thinking the shimmery prisms of light were some trick of the summer sun. That the sky had gone a little mad. But then I blinked and a deep wave of panic shook through me, like the ground was heaving, and I was drifting away on a great wide river where I couldn't reach the shore. It was all being ripped away—so quickly I didn't even have time to take one last look. "I can't see," I said aloud, the terror rattling my voice.

But I felt Levi's hand tighten around mine, squeezing. "I'm right here," he said, and my heartbeat calmed, my breathing slowed. "I've got you."

I knew my vision wouldn't return after that day. I felt the absoluteness of it.

I was nineteen, and I was blind.

But Levi was always there, never allowing me to feel alone in that immeasurable darkness. I loved him for it, for not letting go of my hand that day, for promising to stay with me—no matter what.

The following year, Cooper—our founder—died, and Levi became the leader of Pastoral.

He had been raised by Cooper after Levi's mother—one of the originals to arrive in Pastoral—died in childbirth. He was brought up as if he were Cooper's own son, groomed to lead, to take over once Cooper had passed away. And I knew he would embrace his role as if he were meant for it. Because he was.

I hear footsteps on the stairs, a hand against the railing, and then his voice. "Bee," he says. "You came early." There is a gentle smile between each word, his heartbeat growing louder as he crosses the living room to sit beside me. He is warmth and the familiar weight of his eyes on me, needing, seeing me in a way no one else ever could, and I know there are things I should say to him—about Theo and the truck, and other secrets I've kept—but I keep my mouth shut. For now.

Instead, I think of nights when his hands razed my flesh, pulling me to him like he would die if I didn't promise to stay his forever. "I've missed you," he says now, sliding his hand over mine, his voice like wax dripping from a candle.

"It's only been a couple days," I answer, barely able to speak past the lies lodged inside me.

Sometimes I try to picture Levi when we were younger, the curve of his river-green eyes, the half-grin he sometimes offered up, only one side of his mouth rising as he held back a laugh. He was handsome. Bold in a way that was sometimes unsettling, as if he could do no wrong. A man who hid his flaws well, who seemed beyond fault or measure. But I know his weakness: me.

His fingers slide across the middle of my palm, like he's reading my fate, tracing the lines with the tip of his finger. "Are you okay?" he asks gently.

I nod, reaching out for him—needing the anchor of him—and I touch his collarbone, my fingers traveling up the slope of his neck to his jaw.

"What is it?"

"Nothing." I give him a tiny smile, a convincing little lie.

"How are the others?" he asks, tucking a strand of hair behind my ear, his breathing slow and rhythmic. I know the sound of his lungs, of his beating heart—even during the gathering, among the pattering heartbeats of so many others—I can always pick out the measured rhythm of his. Because it belongs to me. I know it as well as my own.

"They're fine," I answer.

"Anything to report from the gate? Has Theo said anything?"

Before the start of our weekly gathering, he likes to discuss the business of the community, if I've heard anything—conversations muttered in the community kitchen, speculations passed from ear to ear while members wander the corn rows in the evening—things only I can hear when no one knows I'm listening.

I also feel the shifts in the weather, the approaching cold as winter nears or a storm drawing close during the night. I know when the crops are unhealthy or when a woman is pregnant. I know when there is a quarrel and when two people are in love: little things that help Levi to govern, an assurance that he *sees* and *knows* all things happening within the community.

But right now, I only want to press myself close to him and let the sound of his heart drown out my thoughts.

"You could ask him yourself," I answer.

"Yes," he agrees, lowering his hand from my hair. "But you're the only one I trust to tell me the truth."

Levi and I have spent most of our lives side by side, even when we were kids. Levi would stand in the cold creek up to his knees, holding a net made of wire and string we constructed ourselves, and I'd wade upstream, hands in the water, ushering the quick, glistening fish toward him. Together we'd hoist the wriggling things up to the shore and wait for their last gulping breaths to leave their lungs.

We've always needed each other—as if we'd never be as strong alone as we were together.

Levi breathes softly, and I know his mind is churning over something. "Do you think the others are starting to forget why we're here?" he asks, his voice slipping away like water from steep rooftops. He often worries the members of the community are growing restless, he worries our borders aren't safe, and he worries everything we've built here will break apart with the autumn winds.

I hear him lean forward, resting his elbows on his knees, hands folded together. I touch his shoulder. "The others are content," I assure him. "Nothing's changed."

And for the most part, this is true. Aside from the rare desire for medicine or packaged food or a good bottle of brandy, most never speak of the outside. Many have never even seen it. The rest barely remember it.

Yet I now know Theo has gone down the road past the boundary. He has broken our most vital rule. But I don't say a word to Levi—because there is a kernel of doubt growing like a seed inside me. Something I don't yet understand, a memory I can't explain, even though the burden of saying nothing is already starting to swell at the back of my throat.

I pick at the edge of the couch, finding a loose thread. It will need to be mended—a constant battle to keep our small life within these woods from unraveling. What little we have must last: stitch and thread, mud and nails. Keeping the forest from taking back the land, the homes, and us trying to live within it.

"They pretend," Levi answers. His gaze is looking elsewhere, not at me.

"They're only afraid," I say. "The trees have been breaking open along the boundary again."

Levi is quiet for some time, his thoughts toiling over this, before he finally says, "If we stay on our side, if we don't cross the perimeter, we'll be fine."

Protected, safe, eyes shut against the dark.

But if Theo is infected, the rot could spread through the community in a matter of days. And in a few more, there would be no one left. He was stupid to do what he did.

I reach forward and touch Levi's knee. The heat of him soothes me, and he relaxes beneath my hand. "They trust you," I assure him. "They've always listened to you."

This is his other constant worry, the paranoia tunneling through him: He fears the others don't trust him like they trusted Cooper, that someday they'll mutiny and decide he isn't fit to lead. Cooper was loved, he was the one they followed into these woods all those years ago with promises of a different life. He built this community, kept them safe, and they all loved him for it. When Levi took over, it was not because he had won their loyalty or trust, it was because Cooper chose him to lead the group once he was gone. And for many of them, Cooper's belief in Levi has been enough.

Yet, Levi still feels the burden of the role he's been given, a battle with his own self-doubt. And I've often wondered if power does this to a man: unravels him slowly over time, doubt itching beneath his flesh until it's all that's left.

He reaches forward finally, stroking his cool fingers across my skin, tracing a line from my earlobe to my lips. In the dark of my mind, I see him. I know the curve of his mouth, the lazy shape of his eyes, as if he were always squinting away from the sun. When we were younger, when my eyesight was starting to fade, I tried to memorize his face—brand it into my mind. I would place my lips to his and hold on to those moments for as long as I could. I was terrified I would forget him someday, that he would become only a gray, indefinite outline in my mind.

"You're the only thing that makes sense," he whispers. I coil my fingers through his hair and he turns, drawing me to him like an old familiar ritual we know by heart. I peel away his shirt, one button at a time. I let his fingers slide beneath the thin cotton of my dress, finding curves and sharp angles, hips and elbows.

He kisses my neck, and in the heated breath of his exhale, I hear him say, "I love you."

He pulls apart the threads of my mind that keep me tied together. My bones become heavy like river stones. My eyes flutter closed, and I hear a change in the air, like the ice splintering along the edge of the pond in winter, thin and delicate. *I* am the ice: sharp, deadly. I will break if Levi isn't careful. I will slice him open if my edges are exposed.

Our heartbeats rattle against one another. And with his hands braced against me, I wonder if we will tear each other apart someday.

If love like this—deep and painful and reckless—can last.

————

The gathering begins.

Calla and Theo are seated near the back of the circle—I can hear their raised heartbeats, Calla's fidgeting hands in her lap. My sister is easy to find in a crowd, she smells like yellow, like sunlight, and sometimes I imagine there is a chestnut-size glow burning out from inside her, always shimmering, even on winter-dark days.

But I don't go sit beside them. I stand near the corner of the dining hall, listening as Levi takes the stage and the community falls silent.

I feel Levi's eyes survey the group as though he's taking a tally or attendance. "Good evening," he begins, his voice deep and steady, well beyond his thirty-two years. "I know many of you have seen the trees opening up in recent days, and many of you are afraid, but we need to be cautious right now, and stay clear of our borders. If we respect the forest as we always have, then we have nothing to fear." He moves across the stage, slow and practiced—he feels comfortable up there; it's where he belongs—and he stops at the far side, taking a moment before he continues. "We have lived by three rules in Pastoral"—he begins the gathering as he always has, with the three pillars—the basis of everything—"the first rule is privacy. Not just from the outside world, but within this compound. We should each be afforded to live our own lives, singular among the whole of the group." He breathes, letting this first rule settle in our minds, giving us time to nod our heads. "The second rule is community—we value it more than anything. It's what keeps us together, keeps us safe. We are stronger as a whole than if we were separate." There are murmurs among the group, an agreement we have all made in living here together, and even after all these years, it's still what binds us. "The third rule is trust." His voice dips lower, reminding me of his breath against my ears, telling me he loves me. "Without trust," he adds. "We are fractured."

A sickening wave of betrayal worms its way along my gut—I have lied to Levi. And still, he believes I'm the only person he can trust.

"I know at times we all feel frightened," Levi continues, taking two more steps to the front of the stage. "But I assure you, if we do not breech the barrier, we will not risk bringing the illness back onto our side."

The group falls into a long, stale hush. Feet no longer shift in the dirt, bodies do not adjust in their seats. Even I feel the tug of Levi's words, leaning forward to absorb whatever he will say next, each word like cool water on skin. "We will burn sage along the perimeter again, just as we have before, and push the illness back into the trees."

Several women near the front of the circle whisper softly, and I can picture their nodding heads, their lips pinched in agreement. Levi's always been a good storyteller—even when we were teenagers, he'd tell long, meandering tales to the younger kids—and there was something about the way he spoke, the lilt that hung against each word, the magnetic, enchanting gleam of his eyes drawing you in. He's even better at it now, more skilled. He's had practice.

But I don't stay to listen to the rest of Levi's speech.

I push away from the corner of the building and count my steps back to the edge of the woods, where the path leads away from Pastoral to the farmhouse. I've heard all the stories before, the warnings: how several of the first settlers back in the early 1900s became sick, how they fled the woods soon after, abandoning everything they had built here.

And when Cooper bought this settlement fifty years ago, the founders of Pastoral didn't believe in the old stories—not at first. They didn't believe there was an illness in our woods. They passed freely through the forest, they visited the outside towns, and new arrivals were welcomed. It was a community with open borders.

But we stirred something loose in the trees. We awoke a disease that had been asleep.

And now we live in fear of something we can't even see.

Levi will tell this story tonight; he will remind us of what's at stake.

But my own mind rattles with other thoughts, with a memory: Travis Wren—whose truck Theo found down the road. He came through the forest, past the boundary, and he arrived at Pastoral. It wasn't long ago, a year, two at most. He was in our home, secretly, hiding in the old sunroom, curtains drawn and grass growing up beneath the floorboards. A ghost we didn't know we had.

And then he simply vanished.

Maybe he was sick. Maybe he brought it past our walls and then died. Maybe something else happened. Something I can't pinpoint—something I can't quite remember. And the not remembering is what's unhinging the gears and cogs of my mind. Shaking me apart. Making my skin itch and burn, a piece of charcoal sizzling inside my rib cage.

I can feel the hole where the memories should be, gaping, bottomless.

I move quickly down the path, forcing my legs to move faster, tree limbs catching the strands of my hair, tugging at the blue-stitched hem of my dress. My hands wave out in front of me to keep myself on the path, to keep from veering off into the trees and getting lost.

Night creatures stir in the underbrush along the trail, woken by my footsteps, while an owl swoops low over the ground in search of prey, of rodents scampering across the moonlit soil. I can hear its wings, the slicing of air, the intensity of its eyes scanning the dark.

I hear it all.

But beyond this sound, in the distance, I hear something else—a biting, gnawing ache. I can hear the trees cracking, fissures twisting up their trunks, splintering apart. They are sick, bloated with disease.

The sound echoes over our valley, a warning that we are not safe: The rot is looking for a way in.

My legs break into a run.

I sprint all the way back to the farmhouse, panicked, feeling my way up to the porch and yanking open the screen door. Clumsy and hot with sweat, I dart up the stairs, taking them two at a time, my hands skimming along the wall until I find my room. I stumble inside and crawl into bed, pulling the thin summer blankets up over my head.

I am a little girl again. Afraid of the dark.

Afraid of the forest.

Of the things I can't quite remember.

FOXES AND MUSEUMS

Excerpt from Book One in the Eloise and the Foxtail series

Eloise lies awake for three nights in a row, waiting for the fox to return.

And when it does, peering in through her bedroom window, Eloise is ready. She springs from her big-girl bed, already in her red rain boots, and rushes out into the night. She chases the fox past the border of the lawn and into the trees beyond her family's home.

But the fox is quick, disappearing into hollowed-out logs and through patches of wild boar nettles. Several times Eloise loses sight of him, but always catches a flash of his scarlet fur. She chases him over a river, where she sees her wild reflection staring back, hair a nest of knots and leaves. She follows him through a gully where bright yellow poppies have bloomed all at once, to a stump coated in pale blue snails, crawling and slithering over the dead wood.

Finally, she stops and shouts after the fox, "Why do you show me pointless things?"

The fox stares back at her, tail swishing in the air.

"I want to see the darkness that lives in these woods," Eloise demands. She knows the fox is keeping secrets, refusing to show her what truly resides in the trees. The hidden passageways, the holes in the ground that lead to other lands. "Please?" she begs.

But the fox looks back at her and snarls, as if she is the thing to fear. And it scampers away through a thicket of willows. Leaving her alone in the trees, leaving her to find her own way home.

THEO

I promised Calla I would let it go.

But I sit at the edge of the bed, hands worrying the fabric of the bedspread, and my mind keeps straying over the memory of the truck parked at the edge of the road. Tires sagging, doors unlocked. Travis Wren walked away from it and never went back.

Beside me, Calla sleeps with her face pressed into the pillow, soft, sun-browned skin and dandelion fluff eyelashes—I love her, I'd do anything not to lose her, and yet . . . my mind won't stop coiling and uncoiling, stuttering over the things that don't make sense. *Let it go*, I repeat to myself.

Calla reaches across the sheets as if she's reaching for me in her dreams, lulled by the sound of the wind against the walls of the house. I should leave and head to the gate, relieve Parker of his shift, but from my coat pocket, I pull out the photograph: the distorted image of a woman I see even when I close my eyes, even when I try to force it from my thoughts. I trace her forehead with my index finger, her cropped hair, a summer-blond. Someone you'd notice if you passed her out in the real world, someone you'd remember, not because she's pretty, but because there is a darkness about her, a sadness.

Maggie St. James.

It's a deceit, holding the photograph while my wife sleeps a foot away. It's a deceit to the entire community, slipping well past our borders to find it. This truth welled like a bruise in my chest when Levi spoke of *trust* and *community* and how we're *stronger together*. I have defied the very framework of our way of life. And for what? Because of an itching curiosity, because of a boredom I can't explain, but is always there. *Scratch scratch scratch*. Like little mice clawing at my bones.

A feeling that only disappears when I take those few cautious steps down the road.

I hold the photograph closer, squinting down at it. This belonged to an outsider.

He was here, Bee said to me in the kitchen. *Travis Wren*.

Could he have arrived in Pastoral without us knowing, snuck in through the back door of the farmhouse, then slept in the sunroom? Folded himself onto the old, dusty mattress while the dark fell through the windows onto the floor, then crept back out in the morning before any of us were awake?

The house comes alive at night, creaks and pops with the rising sun, walls breathing like wooden lungs, the roof finding its own weight more and more troublesome as the years wear on. A man could easily live within these walls, couldn't he? Take up residence at the back of the house and not be known for some time, his footsteps blending in with the settling floorboards.

But why would he do it? Why would he sleep in our house and not just make himself known? This stranger.

It doesn't make sense.

The creak of a door opening draws my attention to the hallway.

Bee is up.

Her bare feet are soft against each wood stair, and then I hear the click of the back door shutting into place. I stand from the bed and move to the window, watching her shadow scurry up through the meadow, past the pond, to the path that leads to the community.

BEE

The worn record wobbles around the player.

Joni Mitchell sings her sad, woeful songs about rivers and desperate love. The stack of old records, brought here by the originals when they came into these woods to build a different life, sits below my bedroom window. I found them in the attic long ago, and I prefer the slow, steady thrum of music at night when I'm trying to sleep over the creaky silence of the old house.

I find the small dictionary resting on the windowsill and thumb through the pages until I find the only one I care about: where the daffodil—dried and pressed flat—is resting inside. I run my fingers up the stem, remembering when it was first plucked from the ground, and the heady way its cool spring scent made me feel.

I think of *him*. Like a god unsettling the stars, reconfiguring the galaxies, his touch alters the arrangement of my cells. He destroys me then pieces me back together. But sloppily. I always feel a little more off-balance after I'm with him, seams tugging apart, my skin reddened in places. And still I keep going back.

I was sixteen when he pulled the daffodil from the meadow and placed it in my hand, then kissed me for the first time under the far-leaning magnolia tree near the pond, my back pressed against the smooth bark, my fingertips touching the arches of his collarbones. He told me I was the most starry-lit thing he'd ever seen, and I absorbed his words like rain against dry summer soil—thirsty for the sound of his voice.

My eyes started fading later that year, bursts of shadowy orbs flashing across my retinas, and slowly Levi became only a gray vestige. But I knew him even in the dark; he smelled like pine and freshly chopped wood meant for the fire. I could feel him approaching even when he tiptoed up behind me, his hands sliding carefully through mine, across my ribs, over the thin fabric of my summer dress. Our devotion grew into something neither of us truly understood at that age. We needed each other. Greedy hands and sweat beading along spines and blades of grass caught in muddy hair.

As my eyesight failed, he led me through the community, helping me to trace a path I could remember, feeling for doorways and fence posts and rocks I might tumble over, counting the steps from one building to another. He loved me. And I knew my dream of leaving Pastoral someday, to escape the closeness of all these trees, had faded with my vision.

Long ago, I would imagine myself walking the streets of New York City like Holden Caulfield in *The Catcher in the Rye*, renting a room atop a hotel high-rise in SoHo, ordering room service after midnight, and waiting for the knock at the door. How easily food could be summoned. It was a fanciful, indulgent daydream, but I craved things beyond these forest walls—things I've never known. The feel of carpet underfoot, sidewalks and sunrises against an ocean, or the chatter of strangers' voices on a subway. It was a desire that Levi said was born from reading too many books and spending too many afternoons caught in my own mind instead of living directly in the present moment where I belonged.

But when my sight left me, these daydreams slipped away with it.

I would remain in Pastoral.

Right where Levi assured me that I belonged.

The record slows to a stop, the music growing quiet—the old mechanical player needing to be re-cranked. But the curtain over my bedroom window blows inward, a slow curling that sounds like waves against sand, followed by a slow, languid silence.

But there's something else: a thing between the quiet.

I place the dried daffodil back inside the dictionary and remove the record from the player. Out in the hall, I let the railing guide me down the stairs—the old wood floor cold and grooved in places, marks left by the people who lived here once, long before us. My mind ebbs back to our mother: her bare feet striding across the floor into the kitchen in the early morning hours, making tea and oats before the rest of us had woken. In the darkness of my eyes, I can recall faint flashes of her long chestnut hair, the side of her face as she washed dishes in the sink, her voice calling to me from the screen door. She died not long after my vision failed. Pneumonia—the community thought. It took her quick.

But now, outside on the back porch, I can still hear it: low labored breathing, a heartbeat—tiny and small in the distance.

In my bare feet, I leave the safety of the porch and walk out into the field, listening.

I hear the cry of a woman.

I wash my hands in the white basin sink outside the birthing hut, a bar of homemade tea tree oil soap foaming between my fingers, dirt sloughing off down the drain. The scent of the soap reminds me of all the births I've witnessed over the years: counted fingers and toes, *ten and ten*, wailing cries and lungs sucking in their first breath, followed by exhausted sighs of relief from the mothers.

A baby is about to be born in Pastoral.

I enter the circular birthing room encased with windows, the morning sun just beginning to peek through the tree line, warming my face. The skylights overhead have been propped open and the sounds of the forest—birds beginning to chitter, leaves brushing together—filter in. The circular hut was constructed beyond the main row of homes and buildings of Pastoral, away from the commotion of community life. It rests beside the creek, tucked among the trees—a quiet, restful place where mothers can feel calmed by the sounds of the forest.

"She's almost fully dilated," Netta informs me quietly when I enter the room, then her footsteps move swiftly away from me, toward the far wall, her left heel dragging across the wood floor. I've never *seen* Netta—she came to the community later than most, after I lost my eyesight. But I know her by her walk, her odd labored steps, as if one leg is bent wrongly outward from the other. She is a short, narrow, wisp of a woman, and she always smells of basil and a little of something sweet, like wild bearberries.

On the bed, in the center of the room, is Colette Lau; I can hear her throaty moans. And seated on a wooden stool at the end of the bed is Faye—Pastoral's resident midwife.

Netta, Faye's assistant, mutters something at the far side of the room, like maybe she dropped something. Cursing her clumsiness.

"Baby's coming fast," Faye says to me when I reach the bed, my fingers finding the white cotton sheet and then Colette's hand, seized into a fist.

Too soon, I want to say in response. *The baby is coming too soon.* But everyone in the room already knows this: Colette still has another eight weeks to go. *Too soon.*

I hear the faucet turn on at the little sink inside the room. Netta is preparing cotton rags, heating water, busying herself with tasks. *Idle hands . . .*

I lay a palm on Colette's shoulder. "Bee," she says, her voice breathy, strained. "Is the baby okay?"

I do not come to the deliveries to assist in the process. I have no interest in midwifery. I am here to listen, to feel for the baby's heartbeat, to sense if anything changes inside the womb: if anything feels wrong.

I slide my small hands over Colette's stomach, swollen and shifting like an ocean tide, the baby inside is anxious—ready. "She sounds good," I tell Colette. "Strong. Ready to be born." A little lie to reassure her. *The lies come so easily these days.*

Three months back, I had been sitting next to Colette at the gathering when I felt the baby's heartbeat thrumming rhythmically inside my ears. A distant pumping of blood, the rush of a heart pattering against not yet fully formed ribs. She was a girl, with tiny nub fingers and toes that curled together. I told Colette she would give birth to a girl, and she cried, clutching her stomach. Colette came to Pastoral twelve years ago, just before everything changed, before the forest was unsafe and the borders could not be crossed. But she's never talked about her life before, in the outside—only that she lived in southern California and was living a life that didn't feel like her own. So she fled north to Pastoral.

I wonder if Ash—her husband, and one of the community builders— knows that she's in labor. Two years ago, they fell in love swiftly during the heat of midsummer, and soon after, they stood beneath the Mabon tree in the gathering circle while Levi bound their wrists together with yellow yarn, a symbol of their union. I felt envious—a pit sprouting thorns in my stomach—listening to the words Levi spoke, how their love could not be severed after that day.

Levi and I have never bound ourselves to one another, never stood side by side and promised to only love the other in front of the whole community. He insists we keep our devotion a secret. *A quiet love*, he called it once. But I've always sensed a hesitation within him, reasons he won't share with me. And in truth, a part of me likes the idea of it—a secret love—a thing meant only for us. But there are other times when I want a loud love: screaming, lungs burning, moon-deep kind of love.

Colette claps her hand over mine and squeezes, her expression wincing away from the pain. The contractions are coming swiftly now.

The baby is close.

"Slow your breathing," Faye instructs, standing up from the stool. Faye never delivered babies in the outside world. She was a therapist before she came to Pastoral, counseling families and children in a small town in Washington State. But when the community's midwife passed away, Faye took up the responsibility and read every book we had about childbirth. "Your body knows what to do," Faye assures. "We just need to listen to it."

I don't say aloud what I also feel inside Colette's belly, the strange sputter, the uneven fidget. The baby is anxious, wants to come out, but something isn't quite right.

Colette grips my hand as the delivery begins in earnest now.

Faye coaxes her to push with each wave of contractions, while Netta brings damp washcloths, draping them over Colette's forehead, cooing softly and stroking the hair from Colette's eyes. Netta is well-practiced, and someday she will take over as Pastoral's midwife when Faye's hands begin to tremble too badly for deliveries, when her eyes can no longer focus and her stamina wanes.

The sky through the windows grows brighter as the sun washes over the valley. Netta opens more windows to let in the morning breeze and Colette's moans turn into hisses and then a puffing sound she makes with full cheeks. Morning becomes midday, hours of pain and moments of strange calm.

In the heat of afternoon, I settle my hands on her stomach and feel the baby's stammering heart rate, the slowing pulse, the struggle to be free of the womb. "She needs to be born now," I say aloud, a little too urgent. I feel Colette's heart rate quicken.

There is no response, but I know Faye understands. The heart isn't as strong as it should be. *Too small, too weak.*

Faye urges Colette to drink a warm mixture of crushed herbs—raspberry leaf, black cohosh, and primrose—most of which were grown in my sister's garden. The tonic will speed the delivery, urge the baby into the world, and Colette chokes it down with eyes pinched closed, drops slipping down her chin that Netta wipes away.

The minutes move swiftly now, the contractions coming in bursts. Netta scurries around the bed, making adjustments, bringing water, *always water*, to soothe and quench and clean away sweat mixed with tears. Colette holds in her breath, a tightened sound as she bears down—the strength of countless women before her who gave birth in this same way shivering through her—her body knows the rhythm, the task to be performed. And finally, as the sunlight begins to dip to the west, the air growing cooler against my skin, she pushes the baby forth.

A little girl wails into the soft dusk light, startling an owl who had been roosting near the birthing hut. I listen to its wings thumping out into the dark.

The air smells of salt, and a strange silence sinks over the room.

"Is she okay?" Colette asks, her voice fevered, out of breath. But the baby has fallen silent; no more cries.

Faye swaddles her in a clean cloth, then places her onto Colette's chest. But I feel the air change, the fear rising in all our throats. I rest a hand on the baby's small back—the size of a large potato, not yet ripe but plucked from the soil all the same—feeling its warmth, its smooth waxen skin and soft center. Babies always remind me of something forged up from the garden, the mothers like the tender soil, bodies weak and worn out after delivery, in need of a long cold winter to rest.

It's too soon, I think again. There is a hitch and flutter beneath its birdlike rib cage. Heart wobbling, something amiss.

I feel Faye at my side, and Netta wipes again at Colette's forehead, cooing over the baby, trying to distract Colette. "She's beautiful," Netta says, her voice filled with warmth, a smile on her lips, the reassuring tone of a midwife's assistant.

Faye and I walk to the door of the birthing hut and step out into the twilight.

I feel exhausted suddenly, eyelids heavy, all the scents of the forest hitting me at once. Pine and dew on moss. "What did you feel?" Faye asks.

"Her heart isn't beating right," I answer. "She came too soon."

"It might be PDA," Faye mutters. "A heart vessel not closing properly. It happens in premature births, but I've never seen it, only read about it." Faye crosses her arms. "If it is, the baby will need a hospital, real doctors. More than just us."

She blows out a shallow breath, her feet shifting in the dirt, knowing the fate of the baby as well as me. Because there are no hospitals, no doctors, and no way to reach them.

Faye touches my shoulder, lingering a moment, and I nod. A shared understanding: We know how this will likely end. She steps back into the birthing hut, but I don't follow. I can't. Instead, I find the path through the forest.

The woods are silent, the night animals not yet awake, and as I walk, I touch my own belly.

I whisper names that have no meaning yet, that might never exist.

But there is weight and substance beneath my palm. A thing growing inside. And it will change everything.

CALLA

I stand at the back of the garden, a hand over my eyes, and look out at the meadow for any sign of Bee returning from the birthing hut. She's been gone a full day and night—but sometimes she likes to walk alone after a birth, her mind a tight coil needing unwinding. Still, I'm anxious for any word about the baby.

My mind feels anxious, unquiet, so I move through the garden, pulling up weeds that will sap moisture from the ground—the rhythm of it like a familiar friend, the garden a place where I feel safe. I pluck a sage leaf and rub it between my thumb and forefinger until it releases its earthy scent. I pull away a few dead leaves from the St. John's wort—used for bruises and inflammation—the yellow flowers nearly ready to be gathered and ground into a paste. This is how I contribute to the community: the herbs I grow, the calendula tinctures, poppy essence, and wild arnica tonic, are used as medicine. Faye, our midwife, visits my garden every two weeks, and together we fill our aprons with green, fragrant herbs, then boil them down and steep them in sunflower oil to preserve them for future use.

I didn't always know my way around a garden; my knowledge came from books, and from seasons spent out here in the soil.

On hands and knees, I move down the row of rosebushes, their buds growing heavy on the stalks, morning dew shimmering along the peach-hued petals. The rain that fell two nights ago has made everything green and sodden. The same rain we fear also keeps the garden blooming. A strange dichotomy.

My hands stall against the earth, and a feeling twitches through me—the haunting sense of déjà vu—the kind of memory that's marrow-deep. I press my palm to the ground and clear away a layer of fallen leaves, sweat beading at my spine, eyes watering, then yank up a clump of knapweed.

But something else comes up with it, caught in the veiny roots.

I sit back on my heels and pluck the thing free from the dirt—holding it in my palm. It's small, silver, not earthen-made. Carefully, I blow at its edges, and bits of soil and loam scatter, revealing a number on the small thing: 3.

My eyes refocus, holding the thing close, and I finally understand its shape: it's a tiny silver book, no larger than my fingernail, with a small broken clasp.

Perhaps it was a child's toy, dropped in the garden a century ago by the first settlers. But it doesn't seem that old, the silver still has a shine to it. I run my thumb over it, trying to see if there are any other markings, a way to identify it, but there is only the number three—as if there were others like it. One and two, at least. Part of a collection.

But how did it find its way into the garden, buried beneath the wild roses?

I wipe the sweat from my eyes, glancing beyond the garden fence, when I see her: a flash of long auburn hair, hues of red shivering in the morning light.

Bee is moving swiftly down through the field, past the pond, toward the house—her stride is a pinwheel, every movement rounded and fluid. The world gives way for her, spreads open, clears a path.

I tuck the small book into the pocket of my apron and stand up, squinting through the slanted rays of sunlight.

"How is the baby?" I ask when she reaches the garden gate. A few nervous chickens scatter away from her, moving farther back into the garden to hunt for earthworms in the damp soil.

Bee shakes her head. "Not well."

"Will she survive?"

My sister seems to look past me at the house, at the peeling blue walls, and the second-floor windows. But I know it's just her eyes straying, not focused on anything in particular. A crease forms between her eyebrows. "Not without medicine or a doctor."

She moves past me, up the porch steps, and into the house. Not wanting to discuss it further.

But I leave the garden and follow her. "There must be something you can do?" I ask, closing the screen door softly behind me.

Giving birth within the community is a tenuous act—a thin thread separates life from death, survival from a slow, often painful letting go. Death is not dignified out here, it's often bloody and full of long, wretched moans, pleading for relief we have no way to give.

Bee stops at the sink and washes her hands, scrubbing at her fingernails roughly, like she could scrub away the skin. "No," she answers, a cold bite to the word. She turns off the sink faucet and exhales, looking exhausted. But she doesn't make a move to grab the towel on the counter, she lets the water drip from her fingertips onto the floor, standing like a doll whose cotton stuffing has been torn free from the cavity of its chest, and now it's forgotten how to move, how to swing its arms with its insides now gone. "She needs a hospital," Bee says at last.

I shake my head even though she can't see me, and my heart makes a little twisting ache in my chest.

"Faye will talk to Levi," she explains. "There will likely be a gathering tonight to discuss it."

I rest a hand against the kitchen counter, needing to feel something solid. "It won't change anything," I say softly, knowing all too well from other such gatherings where requests have been made, desperation for some *outside* thing: a dentist, a visit to see an aging family member. They are never granted—it's too dangerous.

While my heart throbs with the thought of Colette losing her baby— a life so quickly lost after taking its first fragile breath—the other pang sparking in my chest is louder, the screaming fear: *We can't go past the trees; we can't go down the road.*

We can't go for help.

Bee doesn't respond, but I can see the pained lines forming on her face, drawing the smooth skin of her forehead together, making her look older than she is. She leaves the kitchen and walks to the stairs.

"It's not your fault," I say after her. But I don't think she hears. Or cares. She's already walking up the stairs and down the hall to her room. I hear her collapse onto her bed, the springs giving way. She will sleep until tonight, until the gathering. She needs rest.

Whatever decision is made, not everyone will agree.

A child is sick.

Some will want to go for help, for a doctor. For medicine we can't make ourselves.

Some . . . will want to go past the boundary.

———

The members of Pastoral are seated in the half-circle facing the stage—the wind gusting from the north, shaking the oak leaves of the Mabon tree, rain threatening to fill the skies. But the group does not sit quietly or talk in hushed tones as is usual—they are speaking in a fervor, some are even arguing, red-faced, talking with their hands to punctuate a point.

Theo and I sit at the back, my own hands working together, my body strangely uncomfortable. I feel fidgety and nervous. This gathering won't be like the others, and I have the sense—a tiny imperceptible itch—that nothing will be the same after today.

I look for Bee perched beside a nearby tree—she doesn't like to sit among us, she prefers to be separate, where she can listen from afar and avoid the messy noise of too many voices, too many heartbeats. *When there's too much sound,* she told me once, *I can't pick out a single voice, because the crush of them all becomes like mud.*

But she's not standing at the tree line or at the corner of the kitchen building where I usually see her. She must be somewhere else.

Levi appears from the fence line that borders the crop fields—as if he's been wandering the rows, thinking—and he climbs the short steps and walks to the center of the stage, his hands in the pockets of his jeans, head bowed slightly, like he's carefully considering the words he will speak, sensing the restless state of his people.

I do not envy what he must do—decide the fate of Colette's child.

A hush sinks over the group, faces tilted upward and bodies leaned forward, anxious to hear about the baby—the too-small newborn with a too-small heart. It's been years since one of our members was this gravely ill, aside from the few elders whose time it was to pass on anyway.

I lean forward, hands in my lap.

"I know everyone has their own opinions about what should be done," Levi begins, eyes cast down at the stage, a sign of his humility, a show of his reverence for his people. His eyebrows are sloped together, and he has the look of a man burdened with something none of us could imagine. "But we have more than one life to consider here. We have an entire community." He finally looks up, his soft gaze passing over the crowd, and any lingering side conversations fall quiet. A wind stirs over the group, brushing through our hair, chilling our skin, and I catch Levi's eyes straying on me, then flicking out beyond the circle—he's searching for Bee, for the comfort and assurance she provides. He needs her, but she has slipped away somewhere out of sight.

"As most of you know," he continues, eyes clicking back to the front row of the gathering circle, "our newest arrival was born into Pastoral last night. But she was born early, *too early*, and she is unwell."

Someone coughs, shifting in their seat, and the wood bench creaks beneath them.

Someone else, seated near the front, speaks up—her voice like a sharp stab in the air. "We can't let the child die." It looks like Birdie, her nest of curly gray hair pinned at the nape of her neck. She asked me for yarrow at the last gathering, her nerves on edge, fearful that her son Arwen might be sick. But she never came to the house for a bit of fresh ginger from the garden. Perhaps she was afraid the others might see her—and they might wonder if something had happened. Or maybe she realized it was a worthless remedy anyway. I only offered it as comfort.

Several heads in the group nod, but others grumble their dissent.

Levi's posture changes, but it doesn't stiffen, he seems to relax, settle in. "I know some of you believe we should go into town, get medicine or help. But I assure you that Faye is working tirelessly to save the child."

The group slips into low conversations, questions that congeal in the air, becoming thick and suffocating. I twirl my wedding band around my finger, a nervousness I can't shake, then look across the crowd, searching again for my sister, just as Levi did moments ago.

But a voice rises above the group, cutting through the chatter. "The baby needs a doctor."

I know the voice, could pick it out anywhere: Bee. And when I turn, this time I do find her, leaning against one of the skinny aspen trees just outside the circle. Her arms are crossed and she doesn't make a move to step closer to the group. Instead, her gray eyes are focused solely on Levi, even if she can't see him.

Levi raises a hand as if he could calm the nerves rattling up inside everyone's throats. "We don't yet know how severe her condition is."

"I do," Bee replies, oddly defiant. Lines of confusion tug across Levi's forehead—Bee doesn't normally speak to him like this, certainly not in front of the others at the gathering. This birth, this child, has upset Bee more than usual, and I'm not sure why. She uncrosses her arms. "The baby needs medicine, possibly surgery," she adds. "Or she'll die."

"We should take the child into town," Birdie interjects, swiveling around to face Levi.

More heads nod, severe and quick.

"There is nothing to decide," a male voice says now. "We will go get help." A different kind of silence falls over the group. It's Ash who's spoken up—Colette's husband and the baby's father. He's been quiet this whole time, listening, but now he stands up from his seat and everyone turns to face him. He is a tall, broad man, but he is also soft-spoken, careful with his words. "No one's traveled the road in years," he appeals, his voice sounding like it might break, close to giving out completely. "Maybe someone could pass through safely without getting sick."

A chatter of yesses and motions of agreement stir like a spring breeze, calm at first, but a storm could easily be brewing deep within.

"We should try," Roona—the community cook—says.

"Poor Colette," Olive chimes in—one of the guardians who teaches lessons to the younger children.

The group often makes decisions on matters like this together, through vote or simply by beginning a project in earnest (i.e. the building of a new storage shed, the tearing down of a dying tree). We operate collectively. But we also defer to Levi when a decision cannot be made. His opinions are final, and are not questioned.

A moment passes and Levi holds his palms up to the group, asking them to quiet so he may speak. It's not a forceful gesture—it's patient, reverent, and again, I think how difficult this must be for him, to see his people desperate to save a life while also bearing the responsibility of protecting us all. "We should not be foolish in thinking the road is clear or safe. Many of you have seen the trees breaking open along the boundary in recent days, and we cannot risk more lives for the life of one. The safety of our community is most important."

I feel in my pocket for the small silver token I found in the garden. I grip the miniature book in my palm, grains of dirt still stuck to the edges. It's a peculiar object, one I don't understand, yet I keep it secret in my pocket so Theo won't see. A thing only meant for me.

My eyes find Henry—seated near the front of the circle, his white-gray hair trimmed closely along the nape of his neck, shoulders bent forward, old bones unable to find a posture that doesn't hurt on the hard wood benches. Henry is one of the oldest members in Pastoral—he arrived on the yellow school bus with the other founders. He's seen the hardest winters and known every decision our community has made over the years. He's also mended and repaired and built many things within the community: dining chairs, windchimes, spoons, garden gates, and doorknobs. Theo even had him craft the wedding band I wear on my ring finger, forged from an old bit of scrap metal. I trust Henry, and I wait for him to speak up, to share some knowledge he's gathered from all his years inside Pastoral, about what should be done. But instead, he merely tilts his gaze up to the trees, as if he's recalling something, a time that's slipped from his grasp.

"We are grateful for this new life Colette has brought into the world," Levi says now, walking from one side of the stage to the other, keeping our focus on him. "But we should not get carried away with ideas that could endanger our community or our lives. Our solitude is what has allowed us to endure." All eyes meet with Levi's. A toddler makes a soft sputtering sound to my right, fussing in his mom's arms. "We should not make a foolish mistake; we should not risk our safety by venturing down the road. We should not risk more lives."

A mix of words are passed down the rows. Members deciding for themselves if they agree with Levi's assessment, or if it's worth going past the border . . . and leaving Pastoral.

"We could take one of the cars," someone suggests softly, meekly. "Maybe one of them still runs."

The collection of cars sitting abandoned in the dirt lot just south of the community haven't been started in years. Most have been picked apart, tires taken off, motors repurposed, fuel siphoned. The odds of one of their engines actually turning over seem unlikely.

"Please," Levi says, shaking his head. "I understand why you all feel so strongly about this. It is a life that we want to protect—a new life—and we value this life more than anything. It is precious and vital to our existence—to our survival. But we have made a decision in living here, separating ourselves from the outside. And we cannot risk the whole of the community for one life." He walks to the side of the stage, the group following his movements with the turn of their heads. "And yes, perhaps we could provide Colette's baby with medicines and care inside a hospital, with the help of doctors, but is that what we really want? To sacrifice our way of life, to not let nature decide for us if she should live? Isn't this what we have dedicated ourselves to: trusting the land to provide for us, to give what it can, and sometimes take away as well." He breathes and clasps his hands together. He knows the group has fallen still—rapt in their attention, focused solely on him. "Isn't this the cycle we have agreed upon? We cannot be so selfish to think we can change the course of what is meant to be. This baby was a gift, and not all gifts are meant to be kept."

A few people fidget in their seats, someone clears their throat just to my right but they do not speak.

Levi lifts his head, looking tired suddenly, as if each word were stripping away a part of him. "Yes, it is a life. But we have lost lives before, dealt with death and grief, even in ones as young as Colette's baby. This is not a first for us."

A cool, eerie quiet sinks over the group, as if each of us is recalling some loss: those we have buried in the earth at the edge of the community.

"I know it's tempting to think perhaps the road is safe after so long, but we have all seen the border trees weeping. The illness still resides in our woods." He points at the forest to the west, the boundary not far from where we all sit gathered together.

More hush, not even a whisper.

Theo's back is rigid beside me, hands on his knees, not so much as a flinch while Levi speaks—no recognition that he has done the very thing Levi is imploring us to avoid. And yet, my husband feels warm and alive beside me, not a man with rot inside him.

"Do not judge each day by the harvest you reap, but by the seeds that you plant," Levi continues. He walks to the front of the stage, eyes wide and bright now. I understand why Bee loves him, why she is drawn to him—his words feel like cold spring water on sunburnt skin. A remedy we all need. "Haven't we planted seeds here, set roots in the ground for a different way of life? Do we want to go backward now? Rip the plants from the soil and destroy what we have cultivated?"

I find myself leaning forward in my chair. *Yes*, I think. *We have built something here. Something beautiful, and we should not give this up. We should not risk more lives just for one.*

There is a long, heavy pause, and I can almost hear the brushing of eyelids opening and closing—the breath weighted in our lungs.

"We cannot risk sending anyone through the woods." His eyes lower, then lift again. "I am your leader, and I am protecting you now by deciding that we shall not take Colette's baby down the road, through the forest. I am bearing this burden so none of you have to. Her small, precious life is my responsibility. And I choose to protect the group, protect our life here—this is the sacrifice I make for you all, to take her tiny life into my hands." He breathes deeply again and brings a hand to his heart, eyebrows curved down, a look of sincere sadness in his dark, unflinching gaze. "Tomorrow night, we will burn sage along the boundary and the smoke will push the disease back into the trees. We will be safe. We will endure as we always have. We will survive."

A few members whisper softly under their breath, but each word is careful, easily lost to the night air—there are no more arguments of dissent—we understand why Levi has made his decision; we know the burden he bears.

"If you have questions you want to discuss about the safety of our community," Levi continues, nodding slowly while he surveys the crowd of faces, as if assessing who agrees with him, and who still might not. "I ask that you come speak to me in private, so as not to upset the group." He lowers his hand from his heart. "For now," he adds, "let's keep Colette's baby in our thoughts and hope that she strengthens in these next few days."

I feel Theo turn to look at me, but I keep my gaze leveled ahead.

"Now, let us talk of the crops and the summer harvest," Levi continues, his shoulders dropping, eyebrows lifted. "Henry has some thoughts on the construction of the new drying shed he would like to discuss with everyone."

How swiftly the topic has shifted: We've moved on to other things, the daily workings of life within the community, the changing seasons, the harvest, the effort just to stay alive.

But my heart is beating a hole through my rib cage. A knowing rising like bile, a ticking in my eardrums: My husband *could* be immune. And if he is, he could save Colette's child.

But first, he'd have to confess to what he's done.

And face the ritual.

THEO

The sky turns dark, a mantle of clouds swallowing up the evening stars and laying its weight over the trees. We are still seated around the gathering circle when the first snap of lightning tears apart the horizon and turns everything briefly white-blue.

Someone shrieks; a baby starts to cry.

"Move quickly," Levi says, his voice booming over the thunder. "We need to get indoors."

The gathering has not yet ended—there was still talk of the harvest and a new drying shed to be discussed—but the weather has descended over us without warning, air shivering with electricity, wind gusting through the crop fields, and the group scatters.

The rain imminent now.

I grab Calla's hand, and I pull her toward the trees.

"No, Theo," she shouts at me. "It's too far to the house. We need to find shelter here, closer." I ignore her and lead her on, to the path that winds along the stream, back to the farmhouse. "Theo!" she cries, tugging against my hand, her eyes flashing to the sky. "The rain is almost here."

But still I don't answer, my gaze is focused on the route through the dark, listening as the sky cracks and splinters—a summer storm upon us. I know my wife is afraid, but I feel an almost mechanical need to get back to the house, to flee the heart of Pastoral and the others. To get my wife safely inside.

We're nearly to the back porch of the house when the first raindrops fall. And they're not light, half-hearted droplets—it's a full downpour. A deluge of water from the sky.

Rain explodes against our skin, absorbing into our scalps, our cheek-bones, and our too-thin clothing. Calla lets out a small, terrified sound, and I yank her up the porch and through the back door. I only release her hand once we're inside, and she stands in the doorway, arms hanging like wet sacks of corn flour, hair dripping over her face, a puddle collecting at her feet.

Her eyes lift to mine, the whites taking up too much space.

"Theo—" her voice trembles, "the rain. I'm—" She looks down at her arms, her hands, like she's afraid to wipe away the water, to rub the sick-ness into her skin. Her jaw begins to tremble.

I move toward her. "We have to get you out of those clothes."

She nods mutely and strips her shirt over her head, followed by her jean shorts. We leave them in a heap beside the back door and climb the stairs. Naked, she steps into the bathtub, and I turn on the tap, cupping my hands beneath the cold well-water and pouring it quickly over my wife's shoulders, her hair, her pale, *pale* face. She wipes at her skin with her hands, the panic rising inside her—rubbing at her flesh, clawing at it, turning it red.

"Calla," I say, when her skin is the color of a cardinal's wings, and I grab her left hand, holding it in place. "You're okay. There's no rot on your skin. You don't have it."

"You can't be sure. We shouldn't have tried to outrun it." She shakes her head and I can see the tears cresting her eyelids now, the panic in her breathing like she's going into shock. "Why did you do that?" she asks now. "Why did you drag me through the rain?"

I release her hand. "It's okay," I assure her again, but I have no reason to believe this—it's a certainty I feel without real merit, without proof. "You're not sick."

"You don't know that," she spits. "You've been over the border, you've been down the road, but I haven't. You might not be able to catch it, but I could. We should have stayed in Pastoral."

I rock back onto my heels, the rainwater on my own clothes dripping onto the aquamarine tiles of the bathroom floor.

"You pulled me through the rain," she repeats, every part of her body shaking. "The rot might already be inside me."

Her words land like a club against my skull.

"Calla." I reach out to touch her, but she winces back so violently that I drop my hand.

"Please get out," she whispers through trembling lips.

"I didn't mean to—"

"Theo—" She shakes her head, rubbing water up her arms. "Please, just leave me alone."

My legs push me up and I move into the doorway. I open my mouth to apologize, to tell her how sorry I am, but the tight line of her jaw, the cold cast of her gaze, tells me there's nothing more I can say.

I leave the bathroom and walk back down the stairs. But I don't stop in the living room, I exit the house and step out into the rain—the very thing Calla fears—and slog through the downpour to the path, back to the center of Pastoral.

———

The community is quiet—the rain has forced everyone inside.

I slink past the gathering circle and kitchen building, down the row of homes lit by candlelight, curtains drawn. The night is somber, hushed, and I think: We have agreed to let a child die. To do nothing.

I walk to Levi's home and up to the porch, turning the doorknob and letting myself inside, out of the downpour. The house is mildly warm, candles throwing soft, palliative light against the wood walls.

"Whiskey?" Levi asks from the shadowed dark to my right. I jerk toward his voice, and realize he's standing not far from me—in the doorway that leads into his office—and he must have seen me entering his home uninvited.

But he doesn't say anything about my intrusion, or that I'm soaked from the rain, instead he walks across the living room to a narrow table just below the stairs.

There are only a handful of real bottles of booze left within the compound—bottles from the outside, brought here by new arrivals. Mostly we drink a harsh, white alcohol that Agnes makes from a still in the back corner of his shed. *Moonshine*, he calls it. We also use it to clean wounds and polish silverware. But Levi pulls out a half-full bottle of whiskey from a cupboard inside the table—the label a shimmering gold with black lettering. It's a bottle he keeps hidden, all to himself. "It was Cooper's," he tells me.

He pours the dark liquid into two glasses, measuring them carefully, not a drop to be wasted. If this bottle really did belong to Cooper, then it's at least ten years old, a remnant from when our founder was still alive.

He hands me a glass, and takes a quick swig from his own. "You walked here through the rain?" He nods down at my clothes, one eyebrow lifted.

"It's starting to let up," I say, which we both know is a lie. The rain is thrumming loudly against the roof.

But Levi's expression falls strangely flat, neither worried nor fearful nor angry at my recklessness. "You need to be more careful," he answers simply, raising his glass to his lips and taking another drink.

I stare down at my glass, at the dark amber liquid, the words I need to say lodged like bricks in my throat. Levi and I have become friends in recent years, a genial friendship that requires little of the other. In the evenings, we often play a slow game of chess on his front porch, rarely finishing a match, and sometimes we sit and drink Agnes's moonshine well into the night, talking of the coming seasons, of crops to be planted. He's always seemed relaxed with me in a way that he's not with the others. And yet, I've also known there are things he won't share, a burden he carries as the leader of our community, a responsibility that is mightier than anyone else could understand. These things, I suspect, he shares only with Bee.

"You don't agree with my decision about Colette's baby?" he asks, pinpointing the reason I've come. Why I'm really here.

"I wanted to offer—" I catch myself, searching my mind for the right way to explain. "I could go down the road into town. I could bring back a doctor."

Levi takes another hard swig of the whiskey, eyes closing, savoring the taste. And when his eyes blink open again, they are glassy and unfocused. "It isn't safe," he answers, each vowel gone slack from the booze. This is a conversation he doesn't want to be having right now, but one he also knows is necessary.

"But perhaps if I move quickly," I say. "I can make it through the trees without—" My voice breaks off. *Without getting sick. Without bringing back the thing we fear.* "No one has to know," I amend. "I could go tonight, while everyone sleeps."

I consider saying aloud the thing I've done: admitting that I have already been over the perimeter countless times. That I've not gotten sick. That perhaps I am the only one who can do it safely.

But I keep my mouth shut. Because there are other things I would have to explain: the abandoned truck, the photograph I still keep in my pocket.

Levi lowers the glass of whiskey, holding it loosely at his side, and his expression pulls tight. Maybe he sees something in my face—the thing I'm trying to hide. "And when you don't return, what should I tell the others?" he asks. "What should I tell your wife? Or worse, if you do return, what then?"

I know what he means.

If I leave and come back, they will think I have brought the illness back with me. They will assume I am sick. And they will fear I might infect others.

"You can separate me from the community," I say. "And watch for symptoms." I don't offer the other thing: the way to rid rot from the body. The old way, the cruelest way. "Someone should at least try."

He exhales through his nostrils and walks across the room to the old fireplace, black, half-burnt logs resting at the bottom, leftovers from the last fire that warmed the house—months ago now. "You would risk your life for that child?" he asks, placing a hand on the mantel.

"Yes."

He takes another drink and stares down at the dark fireplace, candlelight throwing strange, dancing shapes along the back of his head. "Because I don't think you'd be doing it for the child," he says. "You'd be doing it for yourself." He nods but doesn't lift his gaze. "You want to know what's at the end of that road, don't you? It's your curiosity that begs you to volunteer your life."

"No," I answer, but there is a tightness in my voice, because in truth, it's a little of both. If Levi gave his permission, I could travel farther down the road than I ever have, and I might find more clues about Travis Wren. I could also go to the nearest town and bring back medicine to save the child. And then, maybe, I'd know for sure if I'm really immune.

Levi raises his eyes, brows sloped together, but his gaze is not angry, it's edged in worry. "I understand why you might feel this way," he continues, like he hadn't heard my response. "Staring out at that road every night, questions stirring inside you. I've thought the same things from time to time." He raises an eyebrow. "It's the question we all have, the need to know what's out there."

A river of tension slips along my jaw. *A truck*, I want to answer.

"We're friends, Theo. I want you to be honest with me." He takes another drink of the whiskey, finishing it. "Have you ever gone past the boundary?" He's circling around a truth he's getting closer to. His eyes cut over to me, narrowed, but I can see fear in him—not just fear for me, but for the whole community. He worries about us more than we know. He worries we are always on the brink of extinction—our entire community could be wiped out by a single spore set loose from the trees, a disease that could kill us all within weeks. Or maybe all but one: *all but me*.

"No," I croak in response, and finally, I take a sip of the whiskey, letting the amber warmth slide down my throat. I could tell him the truth— admit to what I've done. Perhaps my admission will help him to see that I can travel safely beyond our boundaries, that I could go for help. But the look in his eyes, the terrified, feral glint of a man who is weighted by too much responsibility, who worries his own friend has betrayed him by going past the boundary, forces my mouth shut.

He taps a finger against the edge of his empty glass and I find my eyes staring at it, unable to look away.

"My job is to protect the border," I add, keeping my voice level. "Not go past it."

He nods approvingly, jaw softening. "This is a difficult time," he says, walking across the room to the table, where he pours himself another half-glass of whiskey. He swirls the glass in his hand and the brown liquid rises up along the sides in a cyclone. "But we have faced difficulties before, harsh winters and deaths we weren't expecting. It's part of our sacrifice in living here. I know you understand this better than most." He brings the glass to his mouth but doesn't drink, his mind stirring against a thought. "Did you know that when Cooper bought this land, and all these buildings, he used to walk the border at night, listening into the trees, to see if the rumors were true." His eyes blink slowly, the alcohol settling into his joints and muscles—mechanical eyes controlled by a lever. *On the count of three, the eyes will lift.* "He thought the stories about the early farmers who feared the woods were just that: stories. But he was wrong." He drinks all the whiskey in his glass in one gulp. "This land has always been unforgiving, cruel. But it wasn't until after Cooper died that we saw the disease for ourselves, and how bad it could be."

I finish my own whiskey but I don't dare ask for more, even though the soft buzzing in my ears relaxes me, makes me want to sink onto the couch and fade into an alcohol-induced sleep. I know the story of the wheat farmer's daughter, of course, but he's never spoken about what Cooper knew before he died, or if he suspected the woods held a sickness that might trap us within its boundary.

"There are too many risks in allowing you, or anyone, to go beyond our community. I hope you understand that." He clears his throat. "Your leaving would only make things worse."

My mind flicks back to the truck. To the photograph. Did Travis Wren make it to the community, as Bee said, or did he die out in those woods, illness rotting his body from the inside? His corpse somewhere in those trees, his grave unmarked, becoming part of the land.

Levi reaches out and takes the empty glass from my hand, placing it beside the bottle of whiskey. For a moment I think he's going to refill both our glasses, and I watch intently. But then he speaks without turning around. "Cooper used to say that people on the outside crave something they can't describe, a thing they have no words for: a forgotten taste at the back of the throat, the feel of a westerly breeze without the grit of pollution. They long for something they don't know how to find. But we have found it here, within these walls. We pay a price for it certainly, we sacrifice something, but it's worth it . . . don't you think?" He turns around, leaving the glasses on the table. "This way of life gives us more than it takes. And we'd be stupid to give it up."

I nod at him, a wave of guilt sliding along my spine for all the times I went down the road.

"And the truth is—" he continues. "We don't know how far the illness has spread, if it's gone beyond our forest."

I swallow tightly. "What?"

"There might not be anything left, Theo." His eyes cut slantwise to the front window. "There might not be anything out there."

I feel myself wanting to step closer to him, as if I've misheard.

"Even if you made it through the trees," he goes on before I can ask what he means, "even if you made it out to the main road, there might not be any help to be found. No medicine. No doctors. Nothing."

"You think the disease—" I catch myself, swallowing the words, choking on them.

The few who remember the *outside*, who've been there, have often talked of what they left behind: cities and wide oceans and electricity so abundant you never run out. I've always assumed it was still there, all of it, just waiting for us—for the day when it might be safe to move beyond our walls back into the world. I had always believed that if I made it through the forest, to the world beyond, there would be nothing out there to fear.

Maybe I was wrong.

"We can't know for sure," he continues, mouth pulled flat. "And I don't want to frighten the others, but we have to protect what we have built here, just in case."

I feel the room tilt slightly, the candlelight flickering in spasmodic patterns. I reach out and grip the edge of a chair.

"If you see anyone try to sneak past the gate," Levi says now, his tone lowered, like he doesn't want anyone beyond the walls of his house to hear. "I want you to stop them."

I swallow, and release my hold on the chair.

"If anyone tries to leave, I want you to do whatever you have to." His eyes settle on mine. "Do you understand?"

If Levi is right, and there's nothing beyond our valley after all, then even if I'm immune, even if I made it through the trees, there might be no help to bring back. "I understand," I say, a nagging ache tugging just above my left ear, like a scab not yet healed.

He steps forward and claps me weakly on the shoulder, and in his eyes I see the weariness of a man who hasn't slept. Whose hair is beginning to gray at the temples. A man worn down by the strain of too many burdens within a community he's trying to protect.

I feel sorry for him suddenly, and also like I don't really know him at all.

He releases his grip on me and turns back to the cabinet and the wait-ing bottle of booze.

I walk unsteadily to the door, and when I glance back, he's reaching for the bottle—he's going to have a glass or two before he sinks into sleep, maybe he'll finish it, pass out with the bottle tipped over beside him on the couch. He has the look of someone who's venturing too close to madness.

I yank open the door and let myself out, breathing in the damp night air.

I thought I was hiding things.

But Levi has kept secrets too—a deep ravine of them.

BEE

It's raining.

I hide under the eaves of the garden shed, waiting for it to let up.

The others have fled into their homes, tiny lives folded into fortress walls, as if nothing could hurt them while they slept in their beds, candles illuminating only the shallowest places, never revealing what hides in dark corners and within the raindrops spilling down their roofs and windowpanes.

The sky becomes a mournful gray, and I cross my arms, huddled against the cold, listening as others sink into their mattresses and pillows, the heavy breathing of deep sleep, the twitch of fingers and toes as they drift off.

But I also hear something else.

A figure is moving through the downpour, feet slapping against the muddy earth, his breathing an unsteady metronome.

It's Theo.

My brother-in-law is unafraid of the rain—he makes his way up the center of Pastoral, wet droplets beating over him, soaking into his hair, until he clomps up the steps of Levi's porch and enters without knocking.

I strain to hear their voices inside, their conversation, but it's too far away and the rain is a steady thrum in my ears. So I stay tucked under the garden shed eave, and I wait.

Trees moan along the boundary, rain beats against the earth, and I listen for the sound of oak and elm and aspen trunks cracking open, the rot breaking them apart. And in that silence, in the waiting, an old feeling begins to prick at me: that thorny, too-tight sensation of being caged, stuck inside Pastoral, a gnawing beneath my shoulder blades that has only worsened over the years. Some mornings, when the air is calm and milky, I think I can hear the ocean a hundred or so miles away to the west, and I feel the pressing urge to reach a hand through the border trees and touch the foaming sea with my flattened palms. To stretch my fingertips as far as they will go through the dense woods, until I feel something other than the prick of pine needles and moss. I long to sleepwalk through the trees and let my legs carry me somewhere in the distance—a needle-sharp desire that has rested inside me my whole life.

I want to leave this place.

But this feeling vanishes with the sound of a door thudding closed, followed by the quick descent of footsteps down Levi's porch. Theo has emerged, and he's moving quicker now, out through the rain toward the farmhouse. He's heading home.

I lift my hand, palm to the sky, and consider sliding it out beyond the eave of the roofline, until little explosions of rainwater speckle my skin. But I close my hand into a fist, too afraid. Theo might be immune, but that doesn't mean I am.

I wait for the rain to recede, and after another few minutes the storm pushes east, moving out over the treetops, and soon the last of the rain sheds down from the roof above me and the air falls still—a silent, dark dripping over the valley.

I step out into the open and walk to Levi's house.

Blood pulses between my ears—the words I need to say already clawing at my insides, wanting to sputter free.

When I reach his porch, I touch the frame of the front door, imagining tiny hands reaching out for the knob, tiny feet running across the hardwood floors, laughter like a bell always chiming. This house could be made into a home. A place where a family could live. Children always stirring, fingerprints on the windows, garden dirt on the rugs. Levi and I could make something in this house, a life sturdier than the ones we live separate from each other. We could be happy.

I imagine it so clearly that when I turn the knob and enter his home, I feel as if I belong here, a purpose greater than the sum of the words I'm about to say to Levi.

I hear his heart beating as soon as I enter—quickened in his chest, the blood hot in his veins.

"Bee?" he says, his voice thin. He sets something on the cabinet near the stairs, probably the bottle of booze he keeps hidden there.

"I need to talk to you," I say. I know he's surely upset with me for speaking against him at the gathering—for saying that the baby needed a doctor—but I need to tell him the thing that's been roaring inside me for too long. The secret I can no longer keep.

He staggers toward me, and I know he's been drinking. I can smell it on his skin: sickly sweet and salty skin. It's been months since he's been into the bottle of whiskey, since last winter, when a heavy snow sunk over the community and we all started to feel a little desperate. Levi feared winter was growing too long, that spring would come too late to plant crops, and the community might not have enough food to last through another year. But the snow thawed and spring came quick, almost overnight.

He drinks when he's worried. When a thought begins to wear at him like a river against soft wood.

"You think Colette's baby won't survive?" he asks, his voice cold, grating against my ears.

"She needs a doctor," I echo what I said at the gathering. "Her heartbeat is weak. I don't think she'll last much longer."

He moves closer to me, then sinks onto the couch—I can hear the depression of the cushions—and he scrapes his hands through his hair, pulling tightly. "We should prepare a ceremony," he says. "I'll have one of the men construct a coffin, and we should mark a space in the cemetery. Let it be done quickly, so the community can mourn and then move on."

A wall of air builds inside my throat. "She's not even gone yet."

"You know there's nothing we can do."

"We could try."

He makes a sound through his exhale—a tired irritation. A weariness I don't fully understand.

"We can't just do nothing," I press, easing onto the couch beside him.

He shifts, leaning forward, his breath bitter and hot. "This isn't nothing," he says, words like sharpened blades. "This is surviving. This is keeping our community alive."

"Everyone except Colette's baby."

"Yes." He's stopped pretending now. He's given up trying to smooth over the ugliness of his words. "I will sacrifice the one for the many. I do this for you. For all of them." A hand waves in front of him, I can hear the *shush* of the air. "You know this better than anyone."

I press my palms against my knees, wanting to push away the hurt welling up behind my eyes. I need something I don't know how to ask for. I need him to reach out and touch me, soothe the scraping thoughts racking at my skin, but he might as well be a hundred yards away from me. I can hear the distance in his voice.

"It's still out there," he continues. "Beyond our valley. You can hear the trees separating, can't you? The wood peeling away. It will kill anyone who tries to leave."

I know he can see the answer in my face—*I have heard the trees*. In the deepest hours of night, they crack themselves apart, trying to rid themselves of disease. The sound echoes over the valley and it keeps me up, unable to sleep.

"It isn't safe, Bee." He reaches out now, for the first time, and touches my hand gently, like he's afraid I might pull away. I close my eyes and absorb the warmth from his touch. We sit like this for a while, in the quiet of our own thoughts, until he says, "I feel like I'm losing control." There it is, the idea always nagging at him: the one that never leaves him alone, a ticking inside his rib cage like a beetle looking for a way out. He fears the community doesn't trust him like they trusted Cooper. He fears his role as our leader won't last, that in time they will see that he was never as good as Cooper—the man who they followed into these mountains. The man they trusted with their lives.

I worry his paranoia will be the thing to finally tear him wide open for all to see—a festering wound he's been carrying all this time.

He releases my hand and pushes up from the couch, and my heart breaks a little.

"You're not losing control," I offer. I feel the urge to stand as well, to press my lips to his, to comfort him in that way. But I resist. *Not yet*. "They just want to believe the child could be saved somehow. They're afraid."

He paces to the fireplace and back, footsteps heavy against the floor. "They should be afraid." I imagine him shaking his head, his gaze sinking to the floor, his mouth turned down. I imagine a darkness in his eyes and an uncertainty leveled across his brow. "They *should* fear what's out there, they should know fucking death is waiting for us in those trees, waiting for someone stupid enough to cross the perimeter and bring back an illness that would destroy us all. And still, they talk of leaving, of going in search of a doctor, as if they've forgotten." He stops pacing and I can hear his heart banging irregularly against his ribs. He's looking at me. "Still," he says, the breath tight against his teeth, "they want to defy our rules."

"It's not defiance," I answer. "It's hope. Because next time it might be one of them who needs a doctor. And they would want us to risk everything to save them."

"It's just a child," he says coolly. "Just one life."

I stand up from the couch—the stone I've kept stuffed inside me is too heavy, the burden unbearable. I need to tell him the truth. I hope my gaze is centered on him, spearing him straight through, but my fingers tremble at my side and I grab the loose fabric of my dress to quiet them. I need to force the words out. I can't keep them locked in the cage of my chest any longer; it hurts too bad. Especially now, hearing him talk of *a child*. Of *just one life*. My heartbeat pounds against my ears. "I'm pregnant."

The room feels like it swells outward, and I listen for the sound of Levi moving closer, reaching out to touch me. But he stays where he is. "You're certain?" he asks. I can't read anything in his voice, but his heart betrays him, rising in cadence, hammering from the inside out.

My legs quiver, and I wish he would cross the space between us and pull me to him. Tell me that he loves me. Really *loves me*. Not just when our flesh is bared and we're pressed to each other, but that he loves me in a way that makes him feel sick when we're apart, that he would do anything for me. But when he doesn't, I swallow and say, "I can hear its heart beating inside me." I smile a little, a warmth in my chest. "I've felt so many heartbeats inside the bellies of other women, and still . . . I wasn't expecting how it would feel to hear a second heartbeat inside my own body. The pulse like a tiny fluttering fish." I touch my stomach lightly, feeling for the sensation beneath the fabric of my dress. The roundness of my belly is still slight, barely there, but I press my fingers against it, hoping to feel something. "It's our baby," I say at last.

Levi remains perfectly, sickeningly still. This isn't how I wanted it to happen. I wanted him to kneel down and press a palm over mine to feel the life tucked inside the hollow of my belly, I wanted to hear his words against my skin as he promised to keep me safe, to do whatever it takes. But this is the opposite. *This* is me breaking.

"Levi?" I say. But he doesn't reply, and it feels as if I'm suddenly all alone in the cavern of his house. Just me and his baby. I can feel all the words he wants to say but won't, hanging in the air. He wants this to all go away, to disappear like dew on prairie grass when the sun first rises. Evaporating into nothing. He wants me to become air and dissolve before his eyes.

And right now, I want it too.

"We're going to have a baby," I try, blinking, holding back the tears. "You always say how important new life is, that it assures the community will continue. This baby is ours, it—" I swallow down the hurt pooling inside me. "I thought you would want this," I say. "To have a child of your own."

"I do," he answers finally, and he sounds suddenly sober, a tightness in his throat, the world snapping back into solemn focus.

In the stretch of silence that follows, a bright spark of clarity flashes through me: *He just doesn't want a child with me.*

I wipe at my eyes, trying to keep the tears from surfacing—*stupid fucking tears.*

"I *do* want to have children, to commit myself to someone," he says, rubbing a hand over his face, obscuring his words.

My body feels too heavy, stones in my gut, and I think: *If I slid into the pond right now, I'd sink straight to the bottom like an anchor.* I wouldn't fight it either. "But not with me," I say for him, the words he wants to speak but won't.

"I love you, Bee," he says, his voice settling into a tone I recognize, the one he uses at the gathering circle, the one that lures and seduces and can convince you of almost anything. "I always have. You are important to me and to the community."

"I don't give a fuck about the community." My hands tighten into fists. "I'm carrying your baby."

"Bee," he says gently, and I can feel him take a step closer to me. He wants to touch me, but now I don't want his hands on me, fingertips smudged in hurt. "We've always understood one another. We've made this place what it is together. I couldn't have done it without you."

"But you don't love me enough to have a child with me."

"No." His hand grazes my arm but I flinch back. "It's not that."

I brush a palm over both my eyes, my traitorous body upheaving the pain I'm trying to hide. I won't let him hurt me this way, break me apart. *I am stronger than anything he could do to me.*

He clears his throat. "But you're not the only one I love."

Little spasms erupt along my spine and tears finally streak past my cheeks, catching on my chin before falling to the floor. I need to reach out for something, my legs suddenly weak beneath me, but Levi is the nearest thing and I refuse to touch him. "Who?" I ask.

"Alice Weaver and I have been close for some time."

Alice. Alice. Alice fucking Weaver. Alice who works in the community kitchen and always smells of flour and fresh honey, a few years younger than me, her laugh like a quick tolling bell, gentle, easy. I've always liked her: *sweet, mild Alice.* But now I might hate her. Alice Weaver, who he loves more than me. *A decent wife.* One befitting the leader of Pastoral.

You do not marry the blind girl—the one others speak about in whispers, who hears too much, who always stands apart at the gatherings, who sneaks into Levi's house when no one's looking, *a strange girl indeed.* You marry the girl who bakes bread loaves on Wednesdays and Sundays, who laughs brightly when you run your fingers through her hair.

A good, predictable wife.

I've been so dumb. *Dumb.* I didn't see what this was, what *he* thought it was. I am the girl he sleeps with in secret, who he's known most of his life, the girl he trusts.

But Alice. She is simple and uncomplicated: *a perfect wife.* She will stand on the stage with him during weekly gatherings and smile and talk about the crops and the preservation of our way of life. She will be obedient. She will never defy him—as I have.

Alice will be his. And I will be . . .

"Bee?" Levi says, and I tilt my head, unsure if I've spoken any of my thoughts aloud. But I don't give a shit if I have. *Alice Weaver. Alice Weaver.* Her name won't stop clacking against the walls of my mind, carved there now, etched in good. Fucking permanent. "I was never sure if you really loved me anyway. If you wanted to be my wife."

"What?" I hear myself say, although I'm certain I'm no longer in control of my vocal cords.

"You've always talked of the outside, of leaving. I never thought you really wanted to be here, with me."

He's full of shit. He knows this isn't true. I've always loved him; since we were kids, I've done everything for him. I built my life around him, *waiting,* waiting for him.

But—

Maybe I never told him this.

Maybe he's right, and I kept this reckless devotion for him tucked safely inside myself where it couldn't be seen. Maybe he never knew how I truly felt: how much I needed him. How my love was making me mad. *Maybe this is my fault.* My knees begin to shake and the darkness beyond my eyes starts to toss and teeter.

"You can still have this baby," he says in the dark of my mind, drawing me back. "Do you hear me? You should have the baby." As if I need his permission. As if I care anymore what he thinks. "But someone else needs to be the father."

I'm shaking my head, a reflex. *I might be sick.* Right here on his living room floor, where little feet will run and skip and summersault. Where knees will be skinned and late nights spent curled up on the rug beside the fire. A life that won't be mine.

How did I not know after all this time, not hear the waver in his voice, the omission of truth?

Surely others in the community have known. Surely he has not kept Alice a secret from everyone. But I didn't see. Because love is madness and blindness and deception.

I reach forward and my fingertips find his chest, the slow rise and fall—I need to feel him one last time. One last goodbye. I trace a line up his throat to his chin, feeling the small scar cut vertically into his flesh. Most don't know it's there, but I do. When we were eleven, we climbed one of the hazelnut trees beyond the pond, and a branch broke beneath him and he fell to the ground, cutting his chin on a limb. I remember how frightened I was—in my child-mind, I was certain he was dead. I scrambled down the tree and pressed a thumb to the cut, absorbing his blood. He smiled up at me, and I knew he was still alive—I knew he meant more to me than anything else, and I couldn't lose him.

I lower my hand, pressing it to my side. Because now I *am* losing him.

"You will marry her?" I ask.

A slow beat of silence, and then, "Yes."

I wish he had lied, kept this from me a little while longer. But instead, my heart becomes a stone, hardening in my chest, no longer pumping blood. He will live in this house with her. Swollen belly and swollen toes that he will rub and kiss and make better. While I will grow in size in a farmhouse down the road with only my sister to care for me. I will be alone. And a baby will be born with an unknown father who I will not name.

He tries to touch me again, his fingers trailing over my palm, but the heat inside my chest boils, bubbles over. "Don't fucking touch me," I snap, turning away. I can't be here, in the house where I believed someday I would live. With this man who . . . this man who I can no longer allow myself to love.

My legs carrying me to the door, hand cutting through the air in front of me so I don't stumble over the wood chair that sits near the entryway.

"I didn't want to tell you like this," he says behind me, and his voice actually sounds weak, filled with regret. But I don't need his regret. It doesn't change what he's done, what he's *doing*.

I yank open the front door.

"Please," he says. "Don't go."

I step out into the night, imagining the bright moonlight against my skin as it breaks over the trees. He moves through the doorway behind me, following me. But the heat of him is unbearable. I think of the tiny dried daffodil pressed between a dictionary in my room, kept after all these years—a stupid, childish thing. I thought it meant he loved me, that I was his and he was mine and nothing would ever change that.

But now I march down the steps before he can touch me again or say another word, and I break into a run. My legs need to feel it, the ground pounding beneath me, the wind against my cheeks, the darkness rushing past my ears: the blurring of all sound, all feeling. Not even the trees can wrestle me from silence.

I don't want to hear a thing.

CALLA

We tie strings around bundles of dried sage, hang them from the lowest limbs of the boundary trees, then light them with golden-yellow beeswax candles, the flames catching quickly.

The sun has long set, and in the dark, the burning sage looks like floating orbs along the perimeter: an eerie midnight conjuring, spells cast into the woods. But these aren't spells, this is survival.

Theo moves farther down the border, lighting the next bundle, but I stay, watching the smoke spiral up through the branches and drift away deep into the forest. The sage will rid the trees of their illness, clotting the sap that oozes down their trunks, deadening the rot and keeping it from spreading. It's been several months since we've lit the sage, since we last saw signs of the illness moving closer into our valley.

He's several paces away when his eyes lift, a cool darkness in them that for a moment I think might be the sickness, the rot spreading along the whites of his eyes, but then he tilts his gaze and the candlelight reveals his pupils are clear and undamaged. No blood pooling in them. We stare at one another for some time, the acidic blue moonlight making broken patterns across the ground, and I wonder if the things we keep from one another will break us apart. I wonder if the things we don't say are worse than the lies we do. Like the illness, they will rot us from the inside out.

"I'm sorry," he says across the open space between us, his left hand fidgeting at his side while his right holds a candle, wax dripping onto the ground at his feet, making a small syrupy puddle between blades of grass. "I shouldn't have pulled you through the rain last night; I was stupid."

The thick smoke stirs higher into the treetops, creating a veil of gray that begins to blur out the stars. "Ever since you found that truck—" A cold nip of fear tickles the hair on my arms—I hate being this close to the boundary, the shadows reaching long across the ground, the echoey stillness of the trees. This forest could kill us all, if we let it. "—you haven't been yourself," I confess. "You're reckless."

Theo rubs at the back of his neck. He traded shifts with Parker today so he could help me light the sage along the southern border—while the others are hanging bundles along the remainder of our boundary. I can even see spots of light farther up into Pastoral, waves of smoke and the scent of green and musk gathering over us.

"I know," he agrees, but offers no explanation why, makes no promises that he'll stop going down the road or peering at the photograph when he thinks I can't see.

I move closer to him. "Where did you go last night?" I ask. "After you left the house?" It was still raining, and he should have waited for the storm to pass.

"Levi's."

A sourceless, indefinable prick of worry nudges at my thoughts. "What did you tell him?"

"Nothing." Sparks from a nearby sage pinwheel down to the ground, smoldering a few feet from Theo. He steps forward and presses the toe of his boot into the embers, suffocating them so they won't catch on the grass several feet behind us. "I offered to go get help for the baby."

My stomach turns. "You would go over the border again?"

"Levi won't allow it. I'm not going anywhere."

"But if Levi had said yes, you would have left?" He looks at me but doesn't answer, and I let out a breath, a furnace roaring inside me—but it isn't anger, it's fear. I'm terrified of what my husband might do, terrified of the thoughts strumming through him. "Remember Linden and Rose?" I ask. But I don't need him to answer, I know he remembers. "They left. And it killed them." Linden and Rose were founders, originals. Linden worked at the guard hut with Theo and Parker, and Rose did laundry for some of the members, including Levi. We often spent evenings on our back porch, the four of us, sharing stories and listening to them recount memories from the outside. I can still picture Rose's warm, pinked face, wide toothy smile, and soft coiled hair that was beginning to gray at the roots. She used to talk of her brother, of family who lived out in Colorado who she hadn't seen in years. They knew the dangers if they tried to leave, but they did it anyway—about a year ago. Rose didn't say a word to me. They snuck from their home just before dawn, walked through the clot of swaying oak trees behind their house, and stepped past the boundary. They didn't take the road, instead they followed the creek for a mile, right along the edge of the boundary—as if they might change their minds and step back over the threshold into the safety of Pastoral. But they kept going.

Yet, they never made it out of the woods.

Their bodies were found, spotted from the edge of the border, down a low gully near the creek. It was discussed for many days if we should venture past the boundary to retrieve their bodies so they could be properly buried in the community cemetery. But it was decided the risk couldn't be taken.

It was only a couple days more when their bodies were no longer visible from the perimeter. They had been dragged away, deeper into the trees by some wild animal. Some said it was a mercy, that we didn't have to watch their corpses slowly rot over the next few seasons.

We held a ceremony the following afternoon, placing stones in the graveyard without bodies to bury. "We should not speak their names after this day," Levi said. "They risked all of our safety by trying to leave. They deserted us. And so we will desert their memory."

And now they are the nameless. Those who chose the unknown over the community that sheltered and protected them. It hurts to speak their names aloud now, the silent grief, a wound left untended.

"They lost their lives going past the boundary," I say, my voice wavering. "They knew the risks, but they did it anyway." I want him to see, to understand: Death is all that waits for him out there. Even if he thinks he's immune, we can't be sure. It's possible he's just been lucky, evaded getting sick each time, until the *next* time when he returns with rot inside his lungs and eyes and fingernails. "I know what you're thinking," I say, pressing my teeth together at the back. "You want to go down the road anyway, even though Levi told you not to, you want to find a way to help Colette's baby."

His temples contract. "You don't?"

"I don't want to lose anyone else." I feel the hot prick of tears behind my eyes. "I won't lose you." I'll do whatever it takes to keep him here with me, on this side of darkness.

My husband's shoulders draw back, and he breathes in the thick, gray air.

"Please," I beg. "Forget about the road, the truck. Promise me you won't leave. There's nothing out there."

He nods like he understands, but his eyes stare into the trees, over our border, and for a moment his expression is stark and pale in the moonlight, inhuman almost. A man with too many things secreted away inside him, things he won't let me see. And for the first time, I think perhaps I don't know him at all: this man I married, who lies beside me each night smelling of the forest, our breathing taking on the same sleepy rhythm, who sometimes looks at me as if he doesn't know me either. As if I'm a moving puppet with disjointed arms and legs, words muttered from my wooden mouth.

A puppet wife.

His eyes lift, watery and bloodshot from the smoke, and he says, "I can't."

THEO

The white farmhouse with its mockingbird-gray shutters and tall, crumbling chimney, looks like a ghost ship set adrift among a sea of shadowed summer grass. A place where people wait out bad storms, protected from an illness they don't quite understand.

We are those people.

But Calla doesn't feel the gut-ache inside her like I do. The *need* that's been etching ravines through my flesh. *If I made it past the boundary once, and survived, could I do it again? Could I make it on my own?*

The screen door creaks then *thumps* shut behind me, and I hear my wife upstairs, walking across our bedroom floor, from the doorway to the closet, bare feet, shedding her clothes and letting them fall to the floor. I stop at the bottom of the stairs, holding tightly to the wood railing. If I go to her now, if I whisper into her ear that I'm sorry: *I'm sorry, little rabbit*—a nickname I gave her shortly after we were married because she reminds me of a rabbit always in the garden, pulling up herbs and fresh carrots from the soil. Maybe if I climb the stairs and find her in our room, she will incline her head, enough space for me to kiss the soft, pale skin behind her ear. She will let my hands rove up her back, her spine, into her long dark hair, beginning to turn auburn from the summer sun. I will promise her anything, everything, just to hear her say that she forgives me.

I will prove to her that I will never leave.

And if I'm lucky, she'll believe me this time.

But even as this thought skips across my mind, my legs carry me away from the stairs, past the kitchen, and down the far back hallway to where it ends. I stand facing the closed door on the left—the room that was a sunroom once, and then a guestroom for outsiders. But it has sat unused for years, for as long as I can remember.

I turn the knob and step inside.

A metal bed sits against one wall, coated in dust. The floor bends away from my feet as I cross the room, grass poking up between the boards, cobwebs spanning much of the ceiling, a vine from a half-dead wisteria growing through the broken window, inching its way up the wall—dried purple flowers scattered beneath it from the last time it bloomed and shed its petals onto the floor.

One of the heavy curtains has been drawn back from a window, revealing a slant of moonlight. Perhaps it was Bee, the last time she was in here, her small footsteps visible in the layer of dust along the floorboards.

Years ago, when Cooper was still alive and outsiders arrived from time to time—appearing from the distant curve in the road—this room housed exhausted travelers. They slept here for weeks or months until it was decided if they could remain in Pastoral. And then they were given a job; a place to stay within the community. This was the halfway house. An in-between.

With slow, deliberate steps, I walk to the bed where a pillow and a blanket the color of oatmeal sit folded at the end, awaiting a new arrival who will never come. But I wonder: Did Travis Wren somehow sleep in this bed without us knowing? Did he shake the dust from the old blanket and rest beneath a canopy of cobwebs, a nightly breeze hissing through the broken window?

My hand trails across the metal bed frame to the mattress. *He stayed here*, Bee told me, eyes watering, lashes fluttering like small, frightened wings. But if he was here—a stranger asleep in our house—where is he now? What happened to him?

I slide my palm along the edge of the mattress—instinct buzzing at the ends of my fingertips—between the box springs, feeling for something. *Something.* Forgotten things, left-behind things. Something that could be hidden here by a man who once slept in this bed and then vanished.

There is nothing. Only a dead beetle; a clot of dried leaves.

But then. . . my fingers touch something else. I yank my hand out, startled by the solid nature of it. *There's something there.* I inch my hand back between the mattresses, and feel the hard corner of a book. Of paper.

It takes some effort to dislodge it, as if it's imprinted itself in the mattress, molded, been here too long. But finally, I yank it free and it comes out with a puff of fine dust.

My eyes blink in the dim light, holding a small book with a blank cover, no markings on the front. Carefully, I open it and see that it's a journal, with someone's blunt, crisp handwriting scribbled across the pages.

His.

I snap it closed. And my heart makes a sudden dip into my stomach.

I back away from the bed, holding the book clamped shut in my hand, feeling like a thief. Like the ghosts of this room might see what I've taken and start rattling the walls of the house, shrieking for me to put it back.

I slip out into the hall, closing the door behind me, and move quickly to the back door, escaping outside. Crickets sing in the far field, happy little chirps, a song to call out the night insects. And soon the frogs begin their bellow from the banks of the pond—a summer tune that folds over me, familiar, but also an echo in my ears that feels too close. Conspiring. Everything awake and alive and *watching*.

I hurry down the porch steps, past Calla's garden that smells of green tomatoes and night jasmine, and continue through the grove of elms at the south side of the house, beyond the windmill turning slowly high above, until I can't see anything but trees and stars. Until the house vanishes from sight behind me.

I stand in a shaft of pale gummy moonlight, looking down at the notebook.

This is another deceit. Another secret I will keep from my wife.

My fucking treacherous heart.

I turn through the pages quickly at first, as if I need to hurry, absorb as much as I can before Calla discovers me in the trees—catches me with a notebook written by the man whose truck I found days earlier.

But as I skim the pages, I find my gaze softening, slowing down, reading every word as if I were starving for them. A story unfolds within the pages, events and roadmaps and snowy mountain roads that led to the night—the moment—the notebook was stashed beneath the mattress. But there are also pages missing, torn free. Lost or discarded.

When I reach the end, I close the book and blink through the trees in the direction of the house. All this time, the house has concealed a secret, held it captive, hidden.

Bee was right: Travis Wren was in our home.

He came looking for a woman named Maggie St. James.

And now, both have disappeared.

BEE

There is a place beyond the pond, in the high meadow, where the ground feels oddly hollow, a cavity in the earth where sound travels easily—a place I often come. I lie down between the blades of grass and clover, and press my ear to the soil.

I listen to the tiny thump inside my stomach—the little burst of life, the delicate, wondrous growing of cells—that Levi doesn't want.

Tears fall sideways across my cheeks, then spill to the ground and soak in. I am comforted by the earth beneath me—the mass so much larger than my own body, a great revolving orb that I cling to. And then I hear the back door of the farmhouse open, the quick, fettered pace of Theo's heartbeat emerging into the night, his gate strange, unbalanced—rushed even. He moves away from the house into the grove of elms. He is quiet there, standing, and when I strain my ears I can almost hear the rasp of his breathing. Broken gulps of air. *What is he doing?*

But then my focus is drawn away, to another sound in the opposite direction.

The ground aches beneath me, twigs snap, leaves fall in slow measure—lazy and truant—followed by the faint preternatural hiss of trees cracking apart, limbs opening up, and disease spilling out.

I snap my head away from the ground.

THEO

"The dogs have been barking," Parker tells me when I reach the guard hut.

He finishes the last of his coffee then places it on the table. He looks like he got a haircut from one of the women in the community—the sides of his hair trimmed too close to the scalp, an honest but uneven effort. Some of the men in Pastoral call him the *kid*, and in recent months he's tried to rid himself of the title by growing a mustache which is now just a few scattered blond wisps.

He stands up from the chair and edges past me to the open doorway, our routine well practiced. "Oh?" I ask. The sun has long set, and I shift the notebook I found the night before under my arm so he won't see.

"It's Henry's dogs," Parker says. "They won't shut up."

"What do you think's got them worked up?"

He lifts his bony shoulders to his small ears. "Dogs can be stupid," he says, but I can't tell if he means it, or if something's spooked him and he's trying to shrug it off. "Or maybe they hear the trees splitting open at the border."

"We lit the sage," I say, sinking into the chair. "The smoke should push the sickness away."

Parker makes a sound, turning in the doorway to peer down the road, a peculiar look of doubt cut into his face.

I glance at the notebook wedged between the arm of the chair and my leg, and a thought begins to jab at me—it's an idea that's started to gain substance since I discovered the truck and the photograph, and now this notebook that once belonged to Travis Wren. "Have you ever thought it's strange that we guard the gate at all?" I ask Parker. "Since no one ever comes up the road anymore?"

His frown dips even deeper, showing the ash-blond stubble along his jawline. "We keep Pastoral safe," he says, as if he repeats this phrase to himself every morning, a reminder of why he sits inside this little hut through the long, arctic cold of January winters, and the drowsy, unbearable heat of summer.

"Was there ever anyone who came up the road when you were working?" I ask. "A man maybe, someone named Travis Wren?"

Parker laughs and leans his shoulder blade against the doorframe, as if working out a knot from sitting all day. "Sure," he says, thick with sarcasm. "I just forgot to mention it to you. But people have been strolling up the road all year."

"Or a woman maybe?" I try.

He raises an eyebrow at me, starting to realize that I'm not joking. "What are you talking about?"

"A woman with short blond hair?"

The smirk falls from his lips. "I haven't seen a man, a woman, or anyone walking up that road, ever. Blond hair or not. Did you sleep at all today? You need me to cover the night shift? You're sounding a little sideways."

I lean back in the chair and turn my gaze away from him, to the window. "I'm good. Just thinking about things, I guess."

"No thinking required in this job," he says. "That's why I like it. Best job in the whole community. You start thinking too much and Levi will think you want his job."

"I don't want Levi's job," I answer flatly.

"Me neither. Crap thing, to be responsible for all this. For everyone. I'd rather sit out here where it's quiet. Drink my coffee and read a book."

Parker prefers the quiet solitude of his position. He has no interest in anything else, anything beyond this little guard hut. He'll probably die right here in this chair.

And the next thought that lands in my mind, makes me wince: *So will I.*

"I'm gonna head home," Parker says with an absent wave of his hand. "My mom made apple jam yesterday. I might eat the whole jar."

Even at twenty-one, Parker still seems so young—sleeping in the same room he grew up in, inside his mother's home. Just a kid, really. For a moment, my eyes survey his soft, freckled face, looking for something he might be hiding. If he did see Travis Wren walking up the road, would he have reason to lie about it? Would he go tell Levi but keep it from me? Would he be able to look at me with a straight face and say nothing? Maybe there's more hidden behind his lazy blue eyes than I know.

But Parker turns in the doorway and disappears into the dark, heading up to Pastoral.

For some time, I stare through the dust-coated window, filaments of moonlight sliding across the road, making the landscape look wrinkled like an unwashed quilt. A familiar tingle prods at me just above my left ear, a pain that's been growing in recent days.

I pour myself the last cup of coffee, and when I'm certain it's late enough, when I know Parker is good and gone, I open the notebook and sit back in the chair. I need to read it again, thoroughly. I need to understand.

The first few pages are filled with dull, tedious notes about mile markers and hotels where Travis Wren spent the night. A few expenses are scribbled in the margins: *breakfast at Salt Creek Motor Lodge, $14.78. Gas at Fairfax, $62.19.* The notes are inconsistent, and some are more detailed than others. Several merely state the cost, but not what it's for. He was sloppy, but he was hoping to be reimbursed.

He was on the hunt for Maggie St. James.

Her parents hired Travis to find her, and after his meeting with them, he wrote a single word on a page: *Pastoral?*

Eventually, he tracked her all the way here, following marks cut into the trees, carrying a small *charm* he mentions a few times: a charm shaped like a book with the number *three* etched into the surface.

And then, he arrived in Pastoral.

They fear something in the woods, the notebook reads. *Herbs tied with string hang from the trees, marking the boundary they do not cross. I'm starting to question whether it was a mistake coming here without notifying someone.*

I skim through the notes quickly to where they stop—only half the notebook filled. But there are also missing pages, ripped out near the end.

His last notation at the bottom of a page is carefully written, not in haste.

I found her. Maggie St. James is here.

CALLA

I don't feel sick.

I don't feel the rot carving tunnels along my bones, intricate designs like snowflakes on glass. Each morning, I run my fingers down my forearms, searching for places where the delicate blue veins have begun to turn black. I peer at my eyes in the mirror over the bathroom sink, looking for tiny, needle-prick spots of blood, but so far, I show no symptoms. No sign of the rot.

Perhaps I got into the bath in time after Theo pulled me through the rain, scrubbed my skin raw before the illness could soak into my flesh. Maybe I'm okay.

But there is still an edginess inside me, a slippery, nearly-there-and-then-gone feeling. Something in my periphery I can't quite see, a rustling disquiet that I have no word for.

I open the shallow drawer of the bedside table, pulling out the silver book I found in the garden. My fingers feel the impression of the number *three* stamped onto the front. Whether by accident or on purpose, it was buried in the garden beneath the wild roses. I would like to show it to Bee, let her hold it in her palm, and maybe she will have some memory of it. Of who it once belonged to in Pastoral.

But I haven't seen her since the gathering.

Yesterday evening, I thought I spotted her kneeling down beside the pond, but when I stepped out onto the porch, a hand over my eyes to block the waves of setting sunlight, she slipped away into the grove of lemon trees. Thin as paper. She knows how to stay hidden, how not to be found—she can hear my footsteps from a mile or two off, the vibration against the ground.

I check her bed to see if she snuck in during the night to sleep, but the sheets are still tucked neatly under her mattress. Something's wrong, and I worry she might be straying too close to the perimeter—where the sage smoke has hopefully pushed the rot farther back into the trees, but we can't be sure.

I stand at the window and watch the morning sunlight whirl and leap across the meadow grass. I watch for my sister.

But she doesn't appear.

Two days pass. Theo returns home late in the mornings after his shift, wandering in, heavy boots dragging across the floor as if he took the long way home—strolling along the creek, past the hazelnut grove—before finally shuffling through the front door and up the stairs to collapse in bed. Without a word. One afternoon, I found him standing at the end of the back hallway, staring at the door into the old decaying sunroom—a part of the house we have left to rot over the years.

When I look at my husband, I see a man who's already half-gone, like he's still out on that road, his steps moving quicker with each mile he puts between him and Pastoral. He is a man who has already left me behind.

Tonight, after he leaves for his shift at the gate, I don't climb the stairs to our room; the bed will feel too empty, the house too hollow-boned and vacant.

Instead, I walk out to the garden, searching for something.

The chickens sleep restlessly in the small wood structure at the back corner of the garden—Theo built it some years ago, a slanted ramp leading up to their roost, safe from night predators. But they've never laid eggs inside their hen house—for reasons I don't understand—instead they drop their small, oat-brown eggs throughout the garden, along the paths where they might be stepped on and flattened, they roll into divots and collect along the fence line. Lazy chickens, I've always thought. Careless.

A curiosity tickles at my fingertips, and I crouch down beside the wild rosebush, pressing my palm to the earth at the place where I found the small silver book. *How did it get here?* I brush the dirt away—remembering the glint of silver when it blinked up at me—and begin to dig a new hole beneath the rosebush. Drawn by a sourceless need. My fingernails pack with dirt, my back aches with the work, but I keep going—as if I might find meaning deeper in the soil. I pull dirt from the hole, uncovering sleeping earthworms, roots coiling outward from the rosebush, but find no more tiny silver books.

My eyes water in the cool night, but I keep scratching at the ground, desperate . . . when at last, I feel something.

A sharp, distinct corner.

There's something else buried here.

I scoop away another layer of dirt, clawing now. The thing is larger than the small silver book I found in this same spot—*much* larger. It fills up most of the hole, substantial in size and heft.

My heartbeat clamors up into my temples, and finally, I wedge the thing free from the soil—from a tangle of rose roots that had started to tighten like knobby fists around it—and I slump it into my lap.

It's a book.

A real book. Big and thickly bound and heavy. I sink back onto my heels and wipe the dirt from the cover. Its surface is no longer smooth, warped and distorted from rainwater, but I can still make out the silver lettering on the black cover: *Eloise and the Foxtail, Book One.*

Was the tiny silver book merely a marker for what really lay beneath—a hint to keep digging?

I hoist the larger book under my arm, and scramble up to the porch, into the house, sinking into the chair beside the unlit fireplace. I read the cover again, my index finger tracing each letter, each loop and line: *Eloise and the Foxtail, Book One.* But there is no author's name on the front cover, no indication of who wrote it. The dust jacket is missing, only the hard cover remains.

A nagging creeps up the rungs of my ribs.

If it were a community garden, a place where others tend to the plants and stride among the rows, it might not seem so unusual to find foreign things in the dirt, items dropped or left behind. But I am the only one who enters through the small gate and kneels among the lemon balm and basil and tulsi. Not even Bee steps foot within that plot of land.

My fingers tremble, drawing back the mass of pages, and I open it somewhere in the middle. The paper is stiff, hardened by rain and wet soil, and many of the pages are stuck together. But inside, my eyes absorb not just words and sentences, but illustrations as well. The smudged char-coal drawings fill nearly every page, broken and gritty, the ink bled into the margins in places; they depict trees and bony limbs, a girl in a pinafore wandering through the dark, and sometimes there are eyes peering out from the black line of trees, slanted and low. Something watching her.

I slap the book closed and press my palms to the cover.

It's a children's book. A fairy tale maybe. But a dark one—meant to be read late at night when the wind howls against doorways. Meant to frighten.

I breathe for a moment, letting my heart rate settle, then I open it again and read the words written there. To prove to myself there's nothing to fear.

FOXES AND MUSEUMS

Excerpt from Book One in the Eloise and the Foxtail series

The fox had lied to Eloise before.

Leading her to plain, ordinary places within the forest.

But this time she knew it would lead her somewhere else, somewhere new—it would take her to the underground museum, the place where all forgotten artifacts were kept. She followed it to a stone well in a high meadow near the sea. And when it leapt over the edge and down into the deep, hollow well, Eloise did the same.

She climbed atop the stone well and took a step into the dark, into the nothing. Without fear, she fell into the well that seemed to have no end. For hours, days, she plummeted, the fox only a few feet below, *falling falling falling.* Until at last, she splashed into a pool of water that was not water at all. It was a syrupy mud, black and slick like oil. And when Eloise pushed herself up and looked around, she was in the museum of forgotten artifacts.

But she wasn't alone. Eyes peered at her from all sides.

Eyes that watered with thirst in them, eyes that would not let her leave alive.

CALLA

I close the book and dig my fingernails into the edge of the chair.

I do not like this story. I do not like the eyes or the well or the underground museum. It feels too familiar, too much like the forest surrounding the farmhouse.

But I do not toss the book aside, I press it to my chest and close my eyes. And when I open it again, this time to the title page at the front—the place where publishers list their legal notations about copyrights and publication dates—I find the author's name for the first time: Maggie St. James.

Maggie. The name of the woman in the photograph that my husband found in the abandoned truck. The photograph I know he still keeps in his back pocket—a woman my husband is holding on to, who he can't seem to let go of.

But my eyes are drawn to something else on the title page. At the bottom, handwritten hastily with pencil, are the words: *Remember Maggie.*

A shiver clanks and rips down my spine, splitting me in half.

THEO

I find my wife on the torn, plum-colored chair in the living room, knees drawn up, a book in her lap. A cool, easterly breeze slips through the open windows, the sun only just risen, but Calla looks like she hasn't slept—eyes bloodshot and saggy. "What are you reading?" I ask cautiously.

She closes the book and holds it up for me to see, her mouth flat. The pages of the book are warped, rigid, like it had been dropped into the pond then left to dry. Even the cover is misshapen, curved near the top, and against the matte-black surface, I can just make out silvery gray letters: *Eloise and the Foxtail, Book One.*

And there's something else, something along the corners—it's even scattered across my wife's lap, collected in the seams of the chair, and on the floor at her feet: dirt.

"Where did you get it?"

"The garden," she answers, her own gaze unable to pull away from the book.

"You found it in the garden?"

"Beneath the wild roses. It was in the soil, planted there." Calla's words sound foreign, not really hers, a daydream imagined while she slept. Because books aren't found in gardens.

"Was it on the shelf?" I ask, certain she's confused, and I flick my gaze to the shelves that line either side of the fireplace: books about wild-harvesting and water collection and wind turbines (books that the founders thought they would need when they came to Pastoral), books about the history of the west, poetry volumes of Emily Dickinson and

Walt Whitman, a massive hardback copy of *East of Eden* and several books from Jack Kerouac, Fredrick Douglass, Toni Morrison, and Joan Didion. But there are newer titles too, mystery novels and romance and a few children's books meant to distract the mind during the long cold winters. The farmhouse has always served as a community library, books borrowed and returned. Some lost along the way. Some left out in the rain or dropped too near a bonfire. Slowly, we lose books. And there are never any new ones to replace them. But on the shelves, I see no empty rectangle, no gap where the book could have been retrieved.

"No," she says, her voice edged in irritation. "I found it where I found the silver book."

I want to touch her, feel the temperature of her forehead to see if she might be running a fever, because something isn't right. "Calla," I begin softly. "What are you talking about?"

She stands up quickly, with a jerk of her knees pushing her upright, and she presses the book to her chest—a thing she doesn't want to part with. Her beloved book, covered in dirt—like it really did come from the garden. Now, with her free hand, she reaches into the pocket of her stained jean shorts and draws something out. It's small, balanced in the palm of her hand.

I reach forward to see it more clearly, but she snaps her fingers closed—her eyes resting coolly on me, a warning for me not to touch it. She opens her fingers again, slowly, and this time I peer forward, observing it, the small silver sides, the clasp broken at the top. This too, has a bit of dirt still caught in the creases, but most of it has been smoothed away, either by Calla's fingers or because it's been living inside her pocket. And I can even make out a number, clear and distinct, etched into the center of the book: *three*.

My lungs suck in a breath, like a record stalling mid-song, and the morning sunlight through the windows seems suddenly too bright, a single glaring eye, watching me. Observant. "It's a charm," I say aloud, nearly choking on the words.

"A what?" Calla closes her fingers back around it and slides it into her pocket, out of sight.

"It was on a necklace once, and there were others like it. Five of them."

Her mouth seems to be working on a question, turning it over, making pulp of it. "How do you know that?"

In my back pocket, I find the notebook and pull it out. But just like Calla, I don't want her to touch it, to take it from me. We each have things we covet—our secret, private treasures.

Inside the notebook is the photograph of Maggie St. James. I've pressed it between the pages to keep it safe, to keep it from bending, and I don't want my wife to know I still have it—that I still look at it every night, searching the woman's face for some clue I'm waiting for her to reveal; some truth in the lines along her eye, the slope of her hair just above her shoulders that will tell me what happened to her. Where she is now.

Just like Travis Wren, I'm trying to find her.

"What is it?" Calla asks, nodding to the notebook, but not taking a step closer to me, like she already understands the agreement between us: We each keep our own things. We don't share.

"I found it in the sunroom," I say.

She swallows, eyes no longer blinking, waiting for me to continue.

"It belonged to Travis Wren, the man whose truck I found." I look down at the notebook, an artifact from another time. "He came to Pastoral looking for a woman, for Maggie St. James. It's why he had the photograph of her in his truck. She was missing, and he believed she was in Pastoral. He found her here."

My wife lowers her gaze to the thick, black book in her hand. A moment passes, silence vibrating through the old farmhouse, then she flips open the front cover to a page with the title printed again in black ink on white paper. Calla swivels the book around so I can read it clearly. So there will be no question of the author's name:

Maggie St. James.

And below the printed name, are handwritten words in looping, over-size letters. *Remember Maggie.*

Maggie St. James wrote the book my wife now holds. Travis never mentioned the title of Maggie's books inside his journal. But now, Calla has found one of them in the garden. Buried there—kept hidden. *Why?*

And who wrote those words at the bottom? Who wanted to make sure Maggie wasn't forgotten?

Calla's hands begin to tremble, her eyes shiver. Maybe it's the lack of sleep or the colliding together of too many things, parallels aligning themselves in this singular moment, but the book slips from her hands—like the weight is too much—and as it tumbles to the floor, the pages fan open briefly and I glimpse the eerie, dark illustrations inside. Broad charcoal lines that are smeared and ashen, a rush of images that send a cold, icy prick down to my tailbone.

I kneel down to retrieve the book and so does Calla. But we both stop, our faces only a few inches apart, the book on the floor between us, pages closed. My wife stares at me, a hint of terror in her eyes, like she's waiting to see if I will make a move for it.

"Maggie was wearing a necklace when she went missing," I say. "There were five charms on it, five silver books. But book three was broken off, and Travis Wren brought it with him when he came to Pastoral."

Calla settles back onto the floor, leaving the *Foxtail* book where it sits. "He buried the book in the garden?" she asks.

I shake my head. "I don't know."

"If he brought it here," she says, reaching back into her pocket to retrieve the silver charm, the metal glinting in her palm. "Then he must have buried it. He probably buried both books." She nods to the larger book on the floor between us. Her voice sounds clearer now, more lucid, like she's shaken off the lack of sleep. "And maybe he wrote 'Remember Maggie' on the inside."

"No," I say. "He didn't."

"How do you know?"

"His handwriting in the journal is sharp and slanted. It's nothing like the note in the book. Someone else wrote 'Remember Maggie.'"

"Who?"

Again, I shake my head—I don't have an answer. I peer down at the book, still resting on the floor, a harmless thing, merely paper and ink and glue. And yet, it frightens me: the thick quantity of pages; the dark, lusterless cover that contains only the title of the book; the place where Calla found it—buried, concealed away in the garden, where only my wife would find it.

"You read it?" I ask.

Calla's mouth curves, one side dipped down. "Some of it."

"What's it about?"

"It's just a children's book," she answers, simple enough, but I can hear the shiver in her voice. Something inside the book frightens her, too.

I want to touch it suddenly, draw the book to me and turn through the pages, but I resist. I know she doesn't want me too. "The images inside seem dark, for a kid's book."

Calla nods, eyes still focused on the black cover. "I don't like it."

A bird thumps against one of the kitchen windows, wings flapping manically—confused by the reflection of blue sky in the glass—and the window rattles in its casing. But my wife doesn't turn toward the sound.

"Is there an image of Maggie?" I ask, "an author image, in the back of the book?" If there is a clear photo of Maggie St. James, better than the one I found in the truck, we might finally see who she is, recognize her in the community.

But Calla shakes her head. "The dust jacket is gone. The author photo was probably on the back flap."

My heart sinks.

"You think she was here?" Calla asks now, eyes anchoring themselves to mine. "You think that man, Travis, found her here?"

A knocking begins against my ribs, and it feels as if we're speaking to each other with stones in our throats. "Yes. I think she was here; I think he found her. And then something happened . . . to both of them."

"Maybe they left," Calla surmises. "Maybe he found her and then they went back down the road through the trees. Maybe they . . ."

She was going to say, *Maybe they got sick and died out there in the forest.*

"Maybe," I answer. And maybe they did. Their bodies curled together, illness leeching through their pores, turning everything black: fingernails and corneas and lips. While panic seized their minds. But if they were here and then fled, why did we never see them, never know they were here? And why have these clues been left behind?

"Or maybe something else happened to them," my wife dares to say, the very thing I've been worrying over since the night I found the truck.

Maybe Maggie and Travis never left Pastoral.

Calla scoops up the book into her arms and stands, looking unsteady on her feet. Off-balance. "I'm sorry I didn't believe you before," she says now.

I touch her hand and she doesn't flinch away.

"They were here—" Her eyes are watering at the corners, little dewy drops. "They were in our house and—" Again her voice breaks then reforms. "We have to find them."

BEE

I sleep outside, among earthworms that make shallow tunnels through the loam beneath me, and under a swarm of dying stars so vast and abstract that sometimes I feel an ache in my solar plexus when I peer at them for too long.

Blades of grass press against the nape of my neck, braiding into my hair, knots that twist and bind. I bury my fingers down into the dirt and press myself flat against the earth. I want to remain here, in the dark, and let the ground absorb the life growing inside me.

I want to disappear.

But instead, I lie awake and listen for the cracking of trees, disease spilling out, infecting the air. The hours pass and the scent of smoke fills my nostrils, remnants of the smoldering sage.

We are insipid, ignorant, foolish in our attempts to protect the community.

I rise up from the ground and my legs carry me through the meadow to the creek, to the edge of the boundary. With bare feet, I cross the creek at a place where the banks widen and the cold mountain water is shallow, but it still numbs my toes, and I move quickly, stumbling over the smooth stones I can't see. At the other side, I pause on the muddy bank, not wanting to make a sound.

A foot ahead of me are the boundary trees.

I think of Theo, who crossed down the road and returned unharmed, without sickness inside him.

I step forward, reaching out a hand for the nearest tree. I don't know the boundary as well as other parts of Pastoral. I rarely come this close to the edge—I do not know these trees, their spacing, their broadness, the sound of their leaves against the midnight air.

My fingertips find a smooth trunk, soft like the surface of young skin. It's an aspen tree, narrow around but tall, its tiny leaves chattering high above me.

I move to the right, touching the next tree, and then the next, running my hand high over my head and then down again, feeling the bark. I'm searching for something.

Something.

On the fifth tree, I find it.

A laceration in the wood.

The soft bark has been peeled away, cleaved down its center. I hurry to the next tree in the line, and each has been split open, flesh bared to the night air, sap bleeding to the surface. It's sticky and sweet on my fingertips, collecting beneath my nails—as if the trees were crying, bemoaning their wounds.

This is the sickness. *This* is what we fear.

I drop my hand from the tree and take a step back.

My lungs are suddenly too tight, and my feet stumble back into the creek, slipping over the stones beneath the water, scraping my ankle bone across a rock and feeling the warmth of blood rising to the surface. I scramble up the far bank, away from the border, away from the rot. My hands fan out ahead of me, searching for something familiar. I find a tree: a broad elm, branches sagging low near the edge of the meadow. I slump down against the trunk, my motions stiff, shivering from the cold of the creek, and draw my knees up close.

Blood drips down my ankle bone, across my bare foot, pooling against the ground, smelling metallic. But I don't touch the wound, I don't try to stop the bleeding, I let it spill out of me. And I wonder if maybe I'll bleed out right here, turn pale and anemic beside the creek, until I go limp. A part of me wishes for it. A soft letting go.

I hold my breath and listen to the trees swaying and creaking beyond the border, sick.

A thought enters my mind: I could pass into the forest, over the boundary, and disappear. Some aching part of me craves it, to let the darkness take me. I press my fingertips together, the sap sticky and wax-like on my flesh, and I wonder if perhaps it's already too late. Perhaps I have it now. *Rot, rot, you'll soon die of the pox.*

A memory wants to break against my eyelids, so close I can almost see it, but then it's gone.

Hastily, panicked—my bravado gone—I wipe my hands against the grass and dirt, trying to clean away the tree sap. My fingers find my belly, palm flat against my cotton dress, and another sensation ripples over me: I must protect it. The life inside me. So small, only a heartbeat thrumming warmly in my gut.

And just as quickly, I think of Colette and her baby: how desperate she must feel, how impossibly, painfully helpless.

A line of tears streams down my temples to the grass.

I close my eyes, and a warm, drowsy feeling sweeps over me like bath-water. I dream of a lake made of salty, bloodred tears. I dream the world is made of watercolors, sad and dripping, melting in the summer heat.

In my dream, my eyes can still see, and when I look upon Levi standing in the meadow beside the pond, he is fanged and wild-eyed, with lies spitting from the tip of his tongue.

In my dream, he is the thing I fear.

FOXES AND MUSEUMS

Excerpt from Book One in the Eloise and the Foxtail series

There was no light in the underground.

Only gloom and twilight from the shaft of moon that shone down through the well. But Eloise had a book of matches she'd swiped from her father's desk in his study, and when she struck the match, it sizzled against her fingertips and the flame cast eerie shapes up the walls.

The eyes that had been watching her all blinked in unison, then sunk into the dark, disappearing. Whatever they were, they were not gone, only hiding just out of sight.

The fox bounded away, down the rows of museum shelves, where some unknown curator had been collecting artifacts to be preserved. She chased the fox, because she knew this museum held more than old, dust-covered relics. It concealed a book. A book that would know her fate.

And she would find it.

CALLA

The books I found in the garden, the journal Theo found stashed beneath the bed, were left on purpose—a way to ensure two people weren't forgotten.

The sun dips to the west, while I stand on the porch watching Theo walk up the road for his shift at the guard hut, an uneasy feeling stirring in my stomach, like a scream that keeps growing louder. I wish he'd stay with me, but Parker will be waiting for him, and I know we need to pretend that nothing has changed—that we each haven't found things left in our house like breadcrumbs in a gothic fairy tale.

Once he's gone from view, I force my legs to carry me through the house and out the back door. I pull down laundry from the line that stretches between two elms, the fabric snapping in the wind. The night is warm, overheated, or maybe it's only my thoughts that boil and cook inside me.

When I'm finished, I leave the basket in the grass and walk up past the pond, breathing, *breathing*. Gulping down the night sky, trying to calm my mind. I reach the trees and think of the *Foxtail* book, the chapters I've read out of order—the story unweaving itself strangely, without context: a girl chasing a fox, a girl who finds an underground museum. The book frightens me, the smudged illustrations, the dark, awful forest a place where the girl should not go.

Clouds begin to gather in the sky, blurring the stars, and I feel like Eloise from the story—searching for something, some underground place that might make sense of this ache in my rib cage. I move up the path along the creek, burnt sage still suspended from the boundary trees, hanging from string, waiting for a strong wind or curious birds to tug them down.

But something else catches my eye just off the path, a few feet from the gurgling creek.

Slumped against an elm tree, is a girl.

My sister.

Blood pooling around her legs.

I run to her and drop to my knees, searching for a wound. But when I touch her ankle—smeared in dried blood—she wakes with a start and yanks her legs back, swatting her hands in my direction. Her eyes flash upward, searching for the thing that has touched her.

"It's just me," I soothe.

Her mouth falls open, but no words free themselves from the tangle of her tongue. I wrap my arm around her waist and help her to stand, but once she's upright, she shrugs away from my arms, and begins limping down the meadow, past the pond, toward home.

"Bee?" I call, walking after her. But she doesn't look back at me, doesn't answer.

We reach the porch, and I try again. "Bee, what happened to you?"

She turns around this time, touching the railing with her trembling hand. "The trees are still splitting open," she says, her voice hoarse, as if she's been crying or breathing too-cold air all night long. "We burned the sage, but the border trees are still sick." She swallows, wincing as she shifts her weight away from the ankle that's begun to bleed again. "I felt them."

I take a step back from her, my eyes flinching to her hands, smeared with dirt. "You touched the trees?"

Her eyes flutter a moment, the back of her jaw clamping down. This is why she didn't want me to touch her, to help her back to the house, she knows she might be infected.

"You went past the border?" I try. But a web of knowing braids itself tightly together inside me, like spiders scrambling down my joints. "Did you touch the opening in the trees, the sap?" I ask, even though I know, just by crossing over the boundary, she's probably been exposed.

Bee stares at me, but her gaze is slightly off, looking just past my shoulder, and I move slightly to the left into alignment with her eyes. More for myself than for her. Her nostrils swell. "Yes," she admits, swift and certain.

A half-beat of silence hangs in the air between us, between the wind hissing through the lemon trees, and goose bumps rise on my forearms while a furnace boils inside me. I have a choice: I could run up the trail to Pastoral, I could tell the others that my sister has placed her hands along the bark of a sick tree. Or I could not.

I stare at her, looking for signs of the illness, for blood to blossom like wildflowers around the whites of her eyes. "You're sure?" I ask. She might have thought she crossed over the boundary but been confused about her place within Pastoral. Maybe she only thinks she touched a pox-infected tree, but really it was just one of the old elms near the pond, the bark always rough and cracked. Easily mistaken, especially when your eyes only see darkness.

But she doesn't answer, she turns away from me and climbs the steps, her feet dragging. She touches the screen door, about to step inside, but then her other hand strays across her stomach for a half-second. As if she is guarding something growing inside her. As if she is . . .

Then she opens the door and steps into the house.

I wait a moment, terrified, uncertain, before I follow her inside. The kitchen is warm, suffused with the sound of wind against the eaves and possibly the threat of rain.

Bee reaches the stairs, moving slowly.

"Has something else happened?" I ask. She stops at the bottom step, and in her eyes is a coldness—a biting back of all the things she won't say. An anchor of regret drops into my gut: If my sister and I were closer, if she trusted me, she would tell me what was wrong. She would sink onto the couch and tell me why she's stayed away and hasn't slept in her bed. But instead, she stands as rigid as an oak, hands braced against the stair railing. "I need to know that you're okay," I say, my eyes flicking to her stomach.

A hard line forms from her temples to her chin. "I will be," she answers, and she turns, making bloody footprints up the stairs—a trail passed from the back door up to her bedroom.

She shuffles straight into her room, without stopping at the bathroom to clean the blood from her skin, and limps to her bed. I hear the slump and compression of metal springs as she sinks onto her mattress.

She might be pregnant; she might be carrying Levi's child inside her.

But something in the way she spoke, the way the words cut through the air, I can't help but think there is a plan swimming around in her head—an idea she won't share. My younger sister is plotting something.

I reach into my pocket and pull out the small silver book with the number *three* stamped into the metal. I squeeze my fingers around it, like I could press the truth from it, force it to give up its secrets. Just a drop maybe, a tiny spore of truth. But it reveals nothing.

Like my sister, I might be infected, from the night Theo pulled me through the rain.

We all might have it: Theo, Bee, and me. Death like a ticking clock inside us.

I walk to the front window, where the sky is turning dark with rain, but there's still time—if I leave now, I can make it before the first drops begin to fall.

I pull open the front door and leave the house.

———

The road is dark.

Humidity hangs in the air.

Remember Maggie. The words repeat in my mind, stuck there, glue against the hard walls of my skull. *Remember remember remember.* But who wanted to remember her? Who wrote those words in the *Foxtail* book? Who didn't want her to be forgotten?

Ahead, I can just make out the gate through the darkening sky. I rarely come to the southern edge of Pastoral, where the gate blocks the road, where my husband sits at his post every night, counting the hours, the silence like a long, drawn-out hum. When I approach the guard hut, Theo sees me through the window and stands up quickly, meeting me in the doorway.

"What's wrong?" he asks, pulling me inside, his eyes flashing to the sky where the stars have been smeared out by the clouds.

"Bee went over the border."

"What?"

"She went across the stream, and she touched the bark of an infected tree. I found her bleeding, covered in dirt, and her hands had sap on them. She touched them, Theo."

I don't even feel the tears against my cheeks, but Theo wipes his fingers below my eyes, gathering away the wetness.

"Where is she now?" he asks.

"At home, in her room."

"Did you touch her?"

I shake my head then stop. "I—" I remember finding her, slumped beside the path; her legs were wet from the creek and her shin was bleeding. I reached out for her, but did I touch her? Yes. I helped her to stand up and then she pushed me away—I had thought it was because she wanted to prove she could walk on her own, but she knew what she had done, that she might be sick, and she wanted me as far away from her as possible. "Yeah, I touched her."

Theo pulls me closer, unafraid.

"Should we tell Levi?" I ask.

Theo's eyes cut away from me to the window, and his expression drops, hard lines tugging at his brow. "Someone's out there," he says.

He releases his hold on me and for a moment I sway, unbalanced without him bracing me upright, then he steps through the doorway and out into the night. I follow—the sky swollen with rain, only minutes now until the downpour will begin.

Theo steps around the closed gate, moving carefully up the road, then stops several paces back from the boundary—marked by a sagging hemlock tree on one side and the fence on the other, where the road rises up in the distance then veers away into the forest. A place we can see but we do not cross.

I open my mouth to ask him what he sees, what he hears. But then I hear it for myself.

Voices.

Someone is out on the road, beyond the boundary. I move closer to my husband, both of us squinting into the dark.

There are two people, two shadows on the road, and one of them is limping.

But they aren't moving toward us, toward the gate. They're moving away.

They're trying to flee Pastoral.

THEO

Two people are shuffling through the dark along the edge of the road, where the tall cattail reeds creep up from the ditch.

I inch closer, trying to make them out, but my wife touches my arm—a firm, abrupt grip, stopping me. My feet have reached the very edge of the boundary and she doesn't want me to go any farther. She shakes her head at me. *Don't go past the border*, she says with her soft blue eyes. Even though I've done it many times before.

One of the men is dragging his left foot, a grating sound with each step as he pulls it behind him. And the other man has an arm wrapped around the injured one, helping him along.

These aren't outsiders looking for a way into Pastoral.

These are men from our community, looking for a way out.

"Hey!" I call into the dark.

The two men stop—a quick shuddering halt—and both their heads swivel around, looking back up the road at Calla and me. They had probably thought they were far enough past the perimeter that they wouldn't be seen—they must have crept through the trees on the far side of the boundary, the storm clouds blotting out the bright moonlight, then looped back to the road so they could follow it out of the mountains.

Maybe if I hadn't heard them talking, whispering, I wouldn't have noticed them. But now they stand like two cornstalks, afraid to move.

"Theo?" One of them calls back, voice deep, and I recognize it.

It's Ash—Colette's husband, and the father of the baby who clings to life in the birthing hut.

"Where you headed?" I ask, as if I didn't already know. As if they weren't dangerously far beyond the safety of our borders—although not nearly as far as I've walked. Not by a mile.

The leaves on the trees along the road seem to shiver in reply, bending this way and that in a sudden wind that dies just as quickly.

"We're going to get help for my wife," Ash answers. "For my child."

At the gathering, Ash had spoken up, suggested that perhaps the road was safe and that someone might be able to make it to town. Levi had denied this request, but it seems Ash has no intention of sitting around and waiting for his child to drift away. He plans to do something about it.

"Who's with you?" I ask.

I feel Calla tense her shoulders beside me—she doesn't like this. Doesn't like staring down the road at two people from our community who have broken the one unbreakable rule, the one I myself broke only days earlier. Her eyes dart to the trees, as if she could see the illness moving among the pines and settling like yellow, sticky pollen on the men's skin.

"Turk is with me," Ash answers back. "But he's hurt. Fell over a log up in the trees. Twisted his ankle pretty good, could be broken."

"You won't make it down the road with a broken ankle," I call back to the two men.

They are quiet, faces tilted to one another, speaking in low tones I can't make out. "We can't turn back now," Ash answers finally. "Everyone will think we're sick."

Ash is a large man, broad shouldered and tall—he is the foreman for all construction projects within the community—but even at his size, he can't drag another man through the woods in search of the nearest town. I'm not certain of the distance they'll need to travel, but anything past the abandoned truck will be too far with an injured man. They'll never make it.

"The others will think you're sick even if you come back with medicine or a doctor," I argue. "And they'd be right to think it."

Turk adjusts his balance against Ash, trying to shift his feet but wincing at the movement. "But at least we'll have brought back help for Colette," Turk says, speaking for the first time.

I shake my head. "There might be nothing out there," I say, remembering what Levi told me: that the world beyond our small forest might only be a husk of what it once was. No doctors, no medicine, no help to be found. The illness might have spread until it decimated everything—we might be all that's left. "And even if there is," I say. "You might die before you reach anything."

Calla touches my hand and I think she's going to say that we need to go tell Levi that two men are trying to leave, or that she thinks they might already have the rot inside them. But instead she whispers, "We have to help them."

My gaze cuts down at her, surprised.

"Colette's baby will die if we don't," she adds.

My wife has always feared the woods, her eyes turning quick and white whenever she's too near the tall slanted boundary trees. But something has changed in her—maybe it's the discovery of the books in the garden, the disappearance of Travis and Maggie, or maybe it's that Bee too has gone over the boundary—and now she wants to help Ash and Turk.

I look back to the men, their faces hard to distinguish in the soft light. "Bring Turk back to the border and we'll help him." I swallow, looking to my wife then back to the men. "You can keep going," I say to Ash. "But you'll never make it with Turk and that injury."

My wife draws in her bottom lip, nervous, anxious. She knows it's the right thing to do, but she also knows we're putting ourselves at risk.

The two men speak again in a hush, then I see Turk nod up at Ash. In slow, labored movements, they begin walking back toward us. Their faces come into view the closer they get, and I see dirt and a few drops of blood mar the right side of Turk's face, likely from when he fell. He looks worse off than I was expecting.

They're only a yard away when they lurch to a stop.

Turk almost buckles forward, but Ash keeps him from dropping to his knees. Both their gazes are lifted, looking beyond Calla and me, to something behind us—my heart seizes, unsure what has stopped them dead.

I swivel around, and three men approach from up the road, from the direction of Pastoral.

Levi and Parker appear through the dark first, followed by Henry—one of the original founders, a quiet, soft-spoken man who I've always liked, always admired, and who I asked to forge the ring I used to propose to Calla.

"Evening," Levi says, nodding at me and then Calla. A calm, unrushed gesture.

Parker sidles up beside me, elbowing me in the arm. "Saw them sneaking into the woods past the boundary as I was getting home." He winks at me, self-satisfied with his diligent detective work. "Went and told Levi."

"Gentlemen," Levi says, looking across the perimeter at the two men. His tone is not angry or chiding—it's easy, casual, like Ash and Turk were simply out for a stroll, and the group of us all happened to meet at the same point on the road. A happy accident. Levi rubs a hand across the back of his neck, like he is deciding his next few words. "I understand your desperation. I know this has been hard on all of us." His eyebrows tilt inward, pained by the events of the last few days. "I wish there were something more we could do, but is risking your own lives, risking all of ours, worth it?"

Levi stands dangerously close to the border, the toes of his boots just barely crossing the shadow cast down by the hemlock tree, close enough he could reach out and grab Ash by the collar and drag him across.

"My child will die if we do nothing," Ash says with such grit in his throat it sounds like a growl.

"We all might die if you venture into those woods and bring the pox back with you."

"This shouldn't be who we are," Ash counters, "allowing a child to die because we're afraid, because of our cowardice."

Levi blows out a tired breath—he looks more exhausted than usual, eyelids sloped downward, mouth punctuated by tiny lines. "It's not cowardice," he replies gently, and he takes a reflexive step across the boundary then catches himself, his gaze flicking to his feet. But he doesn't shuffle back across the line made by the oak tree's shadow. He stays only a few feet from Ash and Turk, as if to make a point, to prove that he's not afraid—he will trek into the dark to bring them back if he has to, he will risk catching the pox, just so they will see how far he's willing to go. "It's sacrifice. It's devotion—devotion for this place where we've carved out a life. Devotion to one another. I've devoted myself to you," Levi says, nodding at Ash, looking him squarely in the eyes. "I've devoted myself to every one of you." He keeps his eyes planted on Ash. "And part of this devotion is also forgiveness. You have risked yourselves by trying to leave, and I understand why you've done it, I do." His tone has dropped now, and it wavers slightly, like there is emotion wanting to break at the back of his throat.

Calla reaches out and takes hold of my hand, a tremble in her skin—she's frightened—and I squeeze it back. Touching her like this causes all the space that has lived between us these last few days to sink away, and I feel regret for the thoughts I've had: of leaving, of escaping just like Ash and Turk, going down the road and out into the world—the ease with which I considered leaving her behind.

"Come back across the border," Levi urges, reaching out a hand to the two men. "Before it's too late."

Turk looks up at Ash, waiting for him to speak.

"We all know Turk won't make it more than a mile with that injury," Levi adds. "You've only been in the woods a short time; you might not yet be infected. We've burned the sage into the trees, we've pushed it farther back. But if you go down the road, you'll surely be exposed."

I think of all the nights I've slipped down the road, a few paces farther each night—I've breathed in the air beyond our borders, and not gotten sick. I think of Bee, who has gone over the boundary and touched a sick, rotted tree. And my wife, soaked by the rain. They might not be as lucky as I am, they might not be immune.

And now we face two men who also might be sick. We might be bringing illness into the community if we let them back across. This might be a mistake.

But Levi nods at the two men. "Come back to this side," he coaxes. "We'll look at Turk's ankle. You don't want to die out there, in the cold, in the trees. You don't want to die like that. Rotting from the inside out."

Without a word, Turk releases his hold on Ash and staggers toward Levi, passing over the boundary. Calla tries to pull her hand away from mine, like she wants to reach out for Turk, to help him, but I tighten my hold on her and refuse to let her go.

Ash raises his gaze, unwilling to look Levi in the eyes, then he too passes back over the border into the safety of Pastoral.

I feel a shallow breath escape my chest. Ash wraps an arm back around Turk and they start up the road to Pastoral, Henry following behind. Parker stands fidgety beside me, his hand on his holster, as if he might reach for the gun. He's waiting for the men to turn and bolt for the trees— he wants an excuse to fire his weapon, to finally use it for something other than shooting old cans behind the crop fields.

"We need to get Turk to Faye's house so she can take a look at his leg," I say.

"We're not taking him to Faye's," Levi answers coolly.

Calla squeezes my hand tighter.

"Why not?" I ask, keeping my voice low.

Levi glances down the road, into the dark where the men were trying to escape. "They'll stay in Henry's barn," he answers, eyes unreadable.

"Why?"

"Just to be sure." He gives me a quick look like I should understand his intent: I should know why we need to do this. "We must be certain our boys aren't sick."

In silence, our small group heads up the road, and when we reach the parking area, filled with dead, abandoned cars, we turn onto the path that winds through the trees to Henry's place. His dogs begin barking when we stop in front of the old barn, yapping from the back of the house, but Henry's wife, Lily Mae, calls out to them and they fall quiet.

Henry pushes open one of the massive barn doors, where inside, half a dozen goats are bedded down for the night. Several lift their heads but none stand up—they must sense that this midnight intrusion has nothing to do with them, there will be no fresh hay or grain tossed their way. Just to the left of the door is a small, metal wagon, a handmade doll propped up inside wearing a tiny blue dress. One of the community children likely stowed it away in the barn for the night.

Henry unfolds a ladder from the ceiling and it drops to the floor with a soft thud, a cloud of dust coming away with it. Henry coughs.

"It's only until morning," Levi assures, giving the two men a trusting nod. As if they have his word.

Ash helps Turk up the ladder, but he still winces and groans with each heave of his leg up into the loft. Once they're settled, Henry pushes the ladder up into the ceiling and secures it shut with a lock.

"Do we really need to lock them in?" Calla asks.

"Can't be too careful," Henry answers, but his tone sounds far away, and he slides the barn door closed, slapping his hands against his legs to shake off the dust.

"They weren't in the woods for long," Levi adds. "But long enough. We need to be sure."

I realize now that everything Levi told them at the border was only to coax them back across, to convince them to come with us. And they did, willingly, as if they didn't have a choice. But Levi has no intention of letting them back into Pastoral so easily—he needs to be certain they aren't sick, that they won't infect the others. Or us.

"What will you do with them?" I ask.

Levi brushes a hand through his hair, smoothing down the sides. "We have to see if they're infected."

"We'll know in a few days," Calla says, flashing me a quick look. "We'll see it in their eyes first."

"It might be too late by then," Levi answers.

Calla frowns, like she's unsure what he means. But I know what Levi plans to do, what he's going to say.

"If they have the pox, we have to treat it quickly," Levi answers. "We have to rid it from their bodies."

"How?" Calla asks, but the way her mouth pinches down, she's starting to understand.

It's been years since anyone was treated for the pox, treated in the *old way*. Most in Pastoral believe the ritual is cruel, a barbaric method for leeching illness from the flesh. But the first settlers who built this small town thought it was the only sure way to cure the sick for good.

"We will bury them," Levi says matter-of-factly.

CALLA

The rain finally breaks open from the clouds and descends over the house, beating against the roof.

"We have to get them out of that barn." My head thumps wildly, and in my hand I hold the small silver book I found in the garden, crushing it in my fist. It soothes me somehow. A thing that now feels like mine.

Theo closes the front door behind him. "Calla," he begins, walking past me into the kitchen. "They went over the border. They might be sick."

"So did you. And Bee." My voice is too high; a thin, awful pitch. "She might have the pox, but I wouldn't put her in the ground to find out. I wouldn't do it to you, either."

My husband stares past me at the wall, at nothing. "Even if we got them out of the barn, Turk wouldn't be able to make it down the road."

"Then we'll hide them."

"Where?"

"In our cellar."

I think of Bee, the way she's touched her stomach in recent days, her skin flushed and swollen. She might be pregnant. And if she is, if her child needed medicine, I would hope someone would brave the dark line of trees to bring back help. I would want someone to risk their lives for her, like Ash and Turk tried to do for Colette. But it's not just this. It's the *Foxtail* book, the white-cotton pages dusted with soil, the story of a girl who is unafraid, who marches into the woods beyond her house in search of a place that most would fear.

I have stood at the edge of the forest and felt my skin tingle and my ears thrum with the foreboding itch of what lies inside the shadowed trees. But the book has spurred something awake in me, and now I mistrust my own fear. Perhaps it has betrayed me, made me coil into myself when I should have stared down the road like my husband and wondered what lies at the end. I want to do what's right, not what my fear has made me feel.

The living room feels suddenly cold, a musty dark in that way it does during a rainstorm—the walls fully sated with moisture. "If Levi found out you went over the boundary, he'd lock you up too," I say, tears catching in my eyes.

Theo crosses the room, swift and sure, and draws me into his arms. I press my face against his shoulder, eyes pinched closed. "You know we can't hide Ash and Turk here," he says at last, his breath against my hair. "I want to help them, but there's nothing we can do."

My temples begin to pulse, the feeling I get when I haven't had enough sleep. I think of Travis Wren, a stranger in our house, tiptoeing into the sunroom while we slept. Our very own ghost.

"Everything feels so wrong," I say weakly, pressing my palms to my eyes. Two people came to Pastoral and vanished, now two people have tried to leave and been locked up. My heart roars in my chest, my mind a riot of too many disproportionate thoughts, each crowding out the others, making it impossible to think clearly.

THEO

My wife is upstairs, and I know I should return to the guard hut for the remainder of my shift, but my legs carry me down the back hall and I push open the old, crooked door into the sunroom.

I stand surveying it, looking for something out of place. A strange hum vibrates at the back of my throat, the murmur of a song rising up as if from some memory—a nursery rhyme maybe, something whispered to children before sleep—but when I step down into the sunroom, the memory fades.

I slide my hand along the bed frame, the mattress, looking for something I might have missed. But there is nothing else tucked under the mattress. I pull away the curtains and let in the watery, rain-soaked moonlight. I feel along the window frames for a crack, a place where something might be stashed away. I check the drawer of the small bedside table, but it's empty except for a small bundle of twigs gathered in the corner—signs of a mouse. I glance around the room but there is no other furniture, no place to hide something you might want to be found later, once you had gone missing.

A tiny pulse throbs above my left ear. An unknown nagging. My gaze lifts—to the headboard, the wallpaper—and I notice a wrinkle in the smudged daffodil print, the paper coming away from the wall. Likely water and sun damage from too many years of neglect. I slide my hand along the puckered folds, the glue that once held the paper flat has begun to buckle and melt. My fingers find a seam and I follow it down where it meets with the headboard, and to a strange bulge, a place where the wallpaper is thicker than it should be. I feel into the seam, carefully—afraid I might find a displeased spider or rodent—but instead my fingers discover a folded scrap of paper.

Gently, I pull it free, then sink onto the edge of the bed. The paper is crinkled from the dampness of the wall, but I manage to open it, flattening the creases in my palm.

It's one of Travis's notebook pages.

Torn free from the book then placed in the wall above the headboard. My eyes vibrate, struggling to settle on the words.

> *I can hear them upstairs, their footsteps loosen the dust from the ceiling, sending it down to the bed where I'm trying to sleep. There are ghosts in this house too, each room crowded with their afterimages—all the lives lived in this farmhouse. My head throbs with them.*
>
> *I didn't think it would be like this—all these people living way out here in the woods. It's like they're trapped in time, cut off from the outside, disconnected. I need to get out of here, and I'm regretting not calling Ben before I lost service. It hasn't snowed in a couple days, maybe I'll be able to get my truck unstuck. I have to try.*
>
> *Also: I've been having bad dreams the last four nights, and sometimes I think I hear things in the woods, over their border—like the trees really are breaking apart.*
>
> *I've found Maggie, I just need to convince her to leave with me.*

Travis *was* in this room.

He was here. He heard us at night, moving around the house. And he knew about the rot in the trees—how? Someone told him, someone knew he was here. Someone must remember him.

But why did he tear out this page, why did he hide it separately? Unless he knew something was going to happen to him.

Unless he was worried they'd be found by the wrong person.

CALLA

I don't bother knocking, I turn the knob and enter Bee's room silently, closing the door behind me. My sister is curled on her side, facing the window, a sheet pulled up to her throat.

Remnants of a childhood are preserved inside this room: on the dresser sit two handmade dolls slumped against a small mirror, one is in the shape of a rabbit wearing a sunflower yellow pinafore, the other is a human girl with cat ears wearing a lavender-stained cotton dress and a ribbon made from twine tied in her strawberry-red hair. Bee grew up in this room, humming songs to herself, eyes gazing across the meadow while she counted the different shades of tulips—back when she could still see. Before it was all taken away.

I tiptoe across the worn wood floor and sit on the edge of her bed. Maybe I shouldn't be this close—my sister might have the pox roiling inside her, seeping from her pores, carried on her breath with each exhale. But I've already touched the wound on her shin, already breathed the same air.

But worse than that: I've felt the summer rain against my own skin, felt it soaking into my flesh. The sickness is already in our house.

Bee's hand stirs on her pillow. She's awake. Her gray-blue eyes flutter open, fixed on the far wall she can't actually see. "I heard you and Theo talking downstairs," she says. But she doesn't roll over to face me; she keeps looking away.

"Ash and Turk went over the border."

"Levi plans to do the ritual?" she asks.

"Yes." I touch the hem of a pillowcase where it's been restitched several times. Blue thread overtop white. "You could talk to Levi," I say. "You could convince him not to do it."

Her eyes shiver closed a moment, her breathing changes. "I can't convince him of anything anymore."

"I know something happened between you two," I say. "But you're the only one he listens to."

"No, not anymore." She pushes herself up, the sheet falling away from her shoulders, and I can see that her feet are still caked in dirt, the blood now dried against her leg. Her bed linens will need to be scrubbed several times to get them clean. "And if they're sick, the ritual might heal them."

"Or it might not," I say.

"In which case, it's too late anyway." My sister looks at me with a vacantness I've never seen in her before, tears staining her cheekbones. Instinctively, my eyes settle on her stomach, but there is still no definition beneath the thin cotton of her dress. "We can't save them," Bee says, reaching out and taking my hand. Her skin is soft and uncalloused. Fingernails closely trimmed.

"What about you?" I say. "What if we need to save you?"

She smiles, a tiny curve at the corner of her mouth. "I'll save myself."

I lie down beside her, forming myself into a shell, our knees touching. If my sister is sick, if the rot is working its way through her, then I am sick too. Made of the same flesh. Born of the same blood. We haven't always been close, we haven't always understood one another, but if she dies, perhaps I want to die as well. Perhaps there is no life that makes sense without her: my little sister who has always reminded me of the night sky, endless and beautiful and chaotic. My sister the universe. My sister the anomaly. My sister who is blind, yet now, looking at her, her pupils seem to focus, to dilate, as if some part of her can see the form I make in the bed beside her.

"What if I am not who I thought I was?" she says after a long, sleepy silence, listening to the rain stream down the windows, pouring over the roof as if it's looking for a way in, a way to infect those who hide inside.

"What do you mean?"

Her eyes flutter closed again. Her mouth goes slack. "I'm just tired," she says softly, her fingers burrowing beneath the blankets, drawing them up to her chest. "Will you put on a record?"

I slide from the bed and pull a record from the top of the stack, slip-ping it free from its sleeve, then place it on the player, turning the small hand-crank until the record begins to spin. I keep the volume low then climb back into bed.

Bee falls asleep, and I brush her hair away from her cheekbone. *My little sister the universe.* I feel her forehead for fever, for any sign of the pox, but she is cool to the touch.

We sleep side by side, just like when we were little, listening to the scratch of slow, sad songs. We are two tiny figures in a big-girl bed, and her breathing comforts me, the low, sputtering exhale. Her eyelids flutter for a time before they fall still, and I'm afraid of tomorrow, afraid for Ash and Turk.

What we've built here suddenly terrifies me.

THEO

The gathering begins just after sunrise.

Two holes have already been dug beneath the Mabon tree at the center of the circle. They aren't trenches, long and wide to fit a coffin. Instead, they are only three feet wide and about five feet deep. They are actual holes. As if we mean to plant a tree in them.

But instead, we will drop two men inside.

From my pocket, I retrieve the folded notebook page I found behind the wallpaper, and hand it to my wife seated beside me. She arrived late to the gathering, appearing cautiously from the path, her arms folded, before she spotted me and came to sit on the bench to my left. I thought she might not come at all, but stay in Bee's room, sisters comforted by the presence of the other. But now she sits with her shoulders tensed, come to see what will happened to Ash and Turk.

"What is it?" she asks, holding the folded paper, but I only give her a tight nod.

She senses its furtive nature, and her eyes glance around the group to be sure no one is close enough to see before she unfolds the creased edges. She reads the words quickly, keeping her head bent low, then refolds it again, clamping her palm around the little square. "Where did you find it?"

"Tucked in the wallpaper, above the bed in the sunroom."

"Were there others?"

"No. The notebook is missing more pages, but they weren't in the wall with this one."

She hands the folded square back to me. "We need to find the rest," she says, swift but quiet. "They must be somewhere in the house."

A sudden and abrupt hush settles over the group, and those who had been standing, milling about, make their way to benches, crowding in around us. I turn to see Levi striding up the center row toward the stage, his eyes cast to his feet.

"Something has happened," he begins once he reaches the stage, his gaze directed at the front row where Turk's wife, Marisol, is seated, as if he is speaking only to her. But Marisol's back is rigid, dark thick hair braided loosely over one shoulder, and I wonder if she knows Turk tried to leave, if he told her before he stole away into the dark? Or maybe he did it in secret so she wouldn't worry.

Several members shift in their chairs, an uneasy unified motion. This is our second emergency gathering in only a few days, and they can feel that something is off—something's wrong.

Levi clears his throat, eyes lifting to the whole of the community now—addressing us all. "Two of our members have slipped outside our borders into the place they shouldn't cross."

The stirring of the group stops.

"We need to be certain they haven't brought the pox back with them." Levi's tone is grave, and his eyes sweep to his left where Ash and Turk stand just below the small stage, their hands bound in front of them with rope. Parker stands behind them, his own hands planted on his hips. It occurs to me that Parker isn't at the gate for his shift. Perhaps Levi thought the gathering was important enough that we should all be in attendance— we all need to witness what's about to happen.

"We will perform the ritual, just like the early settlers did. The old ways have often proved the most effective, and if these men do have the rot inside them, this is their best chance of being cured. *Our* best chance of knowing if the pox is already within our walls."

Levi nods solemnly, and Parker leads the two men to the Mabon tree— the broad oak that was planted when the first settlers built this place, long before Cooper and the members of Pastoral arrived.

Turk is still limping, and I doubt anyone has tended to his ankle—it's not worth the risk of treating his wound, spreading the pox, if he's going to die anyway. I glance at Calla seated beside me, hands folded in her lap, and I know what she keeps cupped between her palms—the silver charm she found in the garden. She has it with her always now, even when she sleeps, just like I keep the photograph of Maggie St. James.

Parker is careful not to touch the two men, but he urges them forward to the Mabon tree, until they're each standing over a hole. Someone in the group makes a strange, sputtering wheeze, like they're holding back tears, then Parker prods the two men forward with the barrel of his gun. Obediently, without a word—as if they've resigned themselves to what will happen next—they climb down into their holes, their feet standing at the bottom, only their heads sticking up above the ground. "Lift your hands," Parker instructs, and both men do as he says. I wonder what Levi has told them—this morning before the gathering—if he implored them that this is the only way they might be saved. And now they raise their bound arms above their heads without protest.

If the pox is inside them, this old way might actually rid it from their flesh—the mineral-rich soil said to leech the illness from the bones, draw it clean out, like a sponge to water.

Parker loops one end of a rope around their wrists and the other up around the lowest limb of the Mabon tree. This will ensure they can't dig themselves free from the ground.

Now Parker and one of the other younger boys, Orion, begin filling in the holes around Ash and Turk, packing it in good so the men won't be able to move or shift or wriggle loose.

"I know these next few days will be difficult for many of you, but I ask that you don't try to free these two men," Levi says over the sound of dirt being slumped into the holes. "The early settlers knew this was the only way to draw the pox from the skin. If Ash and Turk are infected, the ground will rid it from their bodies—this is our only hope of saving them."

Turk's eyes are pinched closed and from the front of the gathering circle, I can hear the whimpering of Turk's wife. Someone helps her to stand, and she's led away before the dirt has reached her husband's chest. I think of Colette, Ash's wife, and I wonder if she knows what he's done. If she's been told. These last few days, she has stayed inside the birthing hut where she and her child can be cared for, but does she know the unrest her recent delivery has caused? That her husband is being buried beneath the Mabon tree in the ritual of the old way?

"We will let three days and nights pass, and then we will pull them from the earth to see if they are infected." Levi clears his throat and looks away from the men. He seems a little unsteady on his feet, like maybe he's been drinking again. "We must protect our community; we must have devotion for one another, for this land." His eyes blink rhythmically, his breathing heavy as he continues. "We must be certain that Ash and Turk have returned without illness inside them—a disease that will infiltrate our walls and destroy us." The group is silent, watching as the last of the dirt is shoveled into the ground around Ash and Turk's chests. "We cannot allow darkness into our community."

Levi sways and I think he's going to tumble off the front of the stage into the dirt. He's definitely drunk.

I stand up, feeling the sudden instinct to go help him, but Calla reaches for me, taking hold of my hand. I sit back down. Levi staggers to the side of the stage without saying another word and clomps down the steps. We watch as he stumbles across the uneven grass, then wanders down the center of Pastoral, away from the circle. When my eyes swing back to the Mabon tree, Parker and Orion have finished filling in the holes.

Both Ash and Turk have been buried up to their necks, arms strung above them. Turk's eyes are still closed but Ash's are open. He finds me among the group, his pupils like needles, staring me down. I could help them if I wanted to: I could walk to the Mabon tree and push Parker aside; I could cut down their ropes and pull them from the ground. I could announce to the community that this is inhumane, that Levi has taken it too far.

Because it could just as easily be me in the ground—I have crossed our boundary hundreds of times and gone unnoticed, unpunished. It could be Bee buried in the ground too, it could be any of us.

But I don't do this, because I'm afraid what will happen if I do. So I stare at Ash like a coward.

And when I turn to look at my wife, she's stood up and is walking away from the gathering, back toward home.

CALLA

My thumb catches on a thorn and it tears the flesh back, blood dripping into the soil beneath the rosebush. I've dug away a good two feet of earth, well beneath the roots of the plant. And now I'm digging a wide arc away from the roses, out into the path that winds back into the garden. The night sky is clear and sharp overhead, a carpet of black with little holes punched at random where the starlight peeks through.

I can't help Ash and Turk—they're already in the ground. But I need to find Travis Wren and Maggie St. James; I need to know what happened to them—I need to set something right.

I claw at the soil, the desperation inside me like a wild roaring panic in my ears, in my chest. I unearthed two books in the garden, maybe there are more—hidden clues left by Travis Wren, things he wanted us to find. I draw back another pocket of earth, pushing it aside. The chickens scurry close, pecking at the fresh ground where they pluck fat earthworms from the soil before scuttling away. My fingers feel down into the hole, hoping for something manmade, but there is only more dirt. Small rocks. Old roots from long dead plants that grew here many seasons ago.

The garden offers me up nothing else.

I slump onto my side, knees bent, and although for a moment I feel like I might cry, only heat pushes against my eyes, no wetness. *Is this what my husband felt each night when he left his post at the gate and walked down the road? Is this the desperation that wore at his thoughts, urging him farther and farther away?* Was it this same need? Intangible. Nameless.

That vague longing for something.

Back inside the house, I wash my hands in the sink, picking out the dirt from under my nails. But I feel worse than I did before I started digging up the garden—the throb at the back of my throat is heavier. I leave the kitchen and walk down the back hall, turn the metal knob on the old door, and push into the sunroom. It smells of decaying wood and damp, moldy earth. I'm certain moths and beetles and other critters have made their home in this abandoned part of the house, but in the dim light, at least I can't see them. I know Theo has searched the room, but I slide my palms beneath the mattress; I check every broken seam in the wallpaper; I open each bedside drawer and shake out the curtains, hoping to find more missing pages from the notebook. But the room is bare.

I turn in a circle, my head pounding now. If Travis Wren was secretly sleeping in this room, where would he hide something? What are his options?

Maybe I'm stupid to think it would be this easy. That the page would reveal itself to me. I leave the room and step back into the hall, and then, beneath me, the floor makes a small creak. Inside the sunroom, the floor was hastily laid down atop the earth, without a foundation, without a crawl space beneath. But here, in the hall, the floor was laid properly, atop slatted joists. I sink to my knees and press my palm against the floor. Several boards give a little beneath my weight, but it takes some testing before I find one that is loose enough to be pried upward. I wiggle my fingers along its side and pop the board free. And there, sitting down in the dark hole, within reach, is a glass jar—the kind I use for canning in the fall.

At first I think it's empty, just an abandoned jar that somehow found its way beneath the floor. Peculiar, but not a clue of any kind.

Yet, when I hold it up to eye level, I see that there's something inside.

Quickly, I unscrew the lid, and pull out the thing: a piece of paper.

A notebook page, just like the others.

I found it.

They had a gathering tonight, I watched from the edge of the trees. They think they're safe here, inside the boundary, but I don't trust any of it.

My talent is fading—I touch things and only get a diluted flicker of an afterimage. It feels like I'm a damn windup doll whose batteries are low. I

*haven't been keeping track of the days as well either. At first I was mark-
ing them in the journal every morning, but now I can't be certain how
long I've been here. Nine days? Twelve? They're starting to bleed together.*

Something's wrong, and I need to find a way out of here.

*Maybe the woman at the gas station will call the police, let them
know I never turned up again after that night. But I doubt it. She had an
aversion to cops and no reason to think anything happened to me.*

*I need to leave. But Maggie refuses to come with me, refuses to accept
that she can't stay here. I don't want to do it—but I might have to go
without her.*

I stand in the hall, rereading the note over and over until the words
lose their meaning. The front door clicks shut—Theo is home—and I
hurry down to the kitchen, abruptly handing him the page.

"Where was it?" he asks once his eyes have finished scanning the words.

"Under the floor, in the back hall."

He reads the page again, several more times, before folding it back
together.

"They were leaving us clues," I say. "Messages they wanted us to find."
Our house has been keeping secrets, and now they are being stirred loose,
like dead leaves caught in the corners, blown free by an open door.

"But none of it tells us what happened to them." Theo's eyebrows
buckle together. "Maybe Travis did leave without her, like the note says.
Maybe he left her here."

"Then where is she?"

Theo presses the folded page tight in his palm, like he could squeeze
out more words, more meaning from it. "There were three missing pages
in the notebook. We've found two, so there's one more." His eyes flick past
me. "We have to search the rest of the house."

We spend all night prying up floorboards, running our fingertips
along the creases and puckered edges of wallpaper, we lift old dusty paint-
ings from the walls, and pull all the books from the shelf in the living
room, fanning through them for some hidden, secret page tucked inside.
But we find nothing. If Travis hid the last page inside the farmhouse, he
hid it well enough we can't locate it.

As the morning sun begins edging above the trees, we climb into bed for at least an hour's rest. Our bodies exhausted, our minds rattling with all the mismatched pieces we can't make fit. And I have the feeling, if we could uncover this last page, just one more hint, it all might suddenly make sense.

———

One night has passed since Ash and Turk were buried up to their necks beneath the Mabon tree. And when I enter Pastoral, carrying a mason jar filled with water and fresh slices of ginger, the mood is somber, the early afternoon sun a bright, unwelcome eye. I pass Marla, who works in the community kitchen with Roona, but she doesn't meet my gaze. No one will. Their heads are lowered, moving through the community, tending to their daily work but refusing to acknowledge one another. Maybe it's shame: knowing that we have all agreed to do nothing, to let Ash and Turk be buried for three long, cruel days. We are each just as guilty as the next, as guilty as Levi, for this thing we are allowing to continue.

I walk to the gathering circle, where Henry leans against the Mabon tree, carving something in his hand with a knife. A piece of wood. A figure in the shape of a deer, a giraffe maybe—something he will give to one of the children.

He nods at me when I'm close enough, lifting his eyes to watch my movements. Ash and Turk look worse than yesterday, their hands are a deep blue and they hang slack in their binds. Both men's eyes are closed, heads slumped to one side, barely touching the earth.

"Are they still alive?" I ask quietly.

"Yeah," Henry answers, his tone grave. He's been posted to keep watch over the men, to keep them from freeing themselves (which seems unlikely), but also to keep anyone else from trying to help them.

I kneel down beside the two men, holding the jar of ginger water.

"Don't get too close," Henry warns. "You don't want to catch it."

Turk's eyelids flutter, a strange jerking motion, like he's having a nightmare, and then they finally shiver open. "Turk," I say softly. "Drink this." His eyes are clouded, distant—he might be looking at me, or through me.

"Not sure you should be giving them anything," Henry says, stiffening up from his spot against the tree.

"They need water," I say. "Or they won't survive the three days."

Henry's eyes flash away, to the center of Pastoral. But there is no one nearby. No one dares to come close to the gathering circle now—they can't bear to see Ash and Turk like this, to know what we have done to them, so they stay away. Henry sweeps his gaze back to me and nods.

Turk doesn't speak, but his mouth parts just a little, and I bring the jar to his lips. He drinks, half of it spilling down his chin, until he finally shakes his head—refusing any more.

"What is it?" Ash asks, his voice hardly more than a scratch, and I see that he's awake now too, watching me.

"Ginger water. It'll warm you." I inch closer to Ash and help him to drink. He finishes the rest of the jar, gulping deeply—his eyes are clearer than Turk's, more lucid, but he still looks like he's in pain.

"Can you feel your arms?" I ask, eyes flicking up to where they are tied above his head.

"Not since last night. They hurt for a while, but not anymore."

I fight the urge to wince, to show him the pity I feel. Even if they survive, if the ground really does leech away the pox, they might lose their hands, their arms. They might be worthless after this. Without circulation, I'm not sure a limb can still work, can survive after this long.

"I wish there was something else I could do," I whisper.

"My child will die without a doctor," he says, swallowing hard. "You could help her."

I shake my head at him. "I can't."

"Please." He coughs and the motion seems to cause him pain, the weight of too much soil bearing down on his chest.

Henry moves closer. "That's enough," he says down to me. "You should go before someone sees you."

"Just a minute, Henry," I answer. I look back at Ash but his gaze has wavered, he's looking at nothing, at a spot on the ground.

"Calla, please. I'm not supposed to let anyone get this close. You're putting yourself at risk."

I shake my head but Henry touches my shoulder, and there is fear in his eyes—fear for me. But he doesn't know I've already been exposed in more ways than I care to think about.

Still, I nod and push myself up.

"Let's just hope it works," Henry says, glancing quickly at the two men.

"Yes," I answer, breathless.

I can't leave the gathering circle fast enough, or Pastoral. I can't look at the strain on everyone's faces, the regret writhing beneath their pinched mouths. We have done this to them—to Ash and Turk.

We are all to blame.

BEE

I am quarantined, caged within the box of my bedroom. Three days pass, and now Calla is standing in the open doorway, arms crossed.

"You need to stay here," she says.

I sit at the edge of my bed, feeling the flutter of my heart in my chest, but also listening for the other small heartbeat tapping like rain from the inside out. "I want to go to the ritual," I tell her.

"No."

"I'm not sick, Calla." I stand up and touch the metal bed frame, my ankle throbbing only a little, the cut mostly healed. "It's been several days. I feel fine."

Calla unfolds her arms, her body weight shifting in the doorway, making the floorboards creak and settle. "We need to wait another day or two, make sure you don't show any symptoms."

I'm already certain I don't have the pox—I can hear the clear, steady rhythm of my lungs, air spilling in and out without a rasp. But my sister crosses the room and takes my chin in her hand, directing my face upward so she can inspect my eyes for drops of blood spreading along the white edges. She then lifts each of my forearms to check the veins, for the blue to turn an inky black. Satisfied, she drops my arms back to my sides.

If I have the rot, then so does she. She's touched my skin and slept in my bed and done nothing to protect herself.

"We'll be back right after," she says, and I can hear her straightening up, the bending of joints, her gaze shifting so that she's looking to the window.

Air escapes my throat. "Fine."

I hear Calla and Theo leave the house through the back door.

But I don't sit and wait for them to return, I slink down the hall, the wound on my ankle where I tore it open against a rock still stings when I move, but not enough to stop me from venturing outside and up the path to Pastoral.

Tonight is the end of the ritual.

Tonight, Ash and Turk will be pulled from the ground and we will know if they have the pox inside them. If they've been cured or not. If they will be allowed to live . . . or not.

When I reach the gathering circle, I stay back in the trees, out of sight. The sun is nearly set and I can feel its serrated edges of light breaking across my skin, warming the parts of me that Levi will never touch again.

Levi.

I haven't seen him since I told him about the baby, since he said that he doesn't love me enough to stay with me and raise our child. Since he broke me open. And still, he is a dichotomy of pain and devotion inside my ribs, my heart beating against these two emotions: the weak-kneed desire he stirs loose inside me and the grating anger at the back of my teeth.

I want to hurt him, *and* I want to sneak up to his front porch and beg him to love me still.

I hate it. I hate the way he makes me feel.

A hush sinks over the group gathered at the circle around the Mabon tree. I can't see the two men buried in the earth, but I can hear their low, labored breaths, their struggle to draw in air. Their heartbeats have slowed, the cold of the earth pulling the life out of them.

I strain, trying to hear any hint of the illness, to know if it's truly inside them, but every breath sounds raw and serrated, and I can't be sure. Infected or not, they sound like they're dying.

Levi emerges, walking to the Mabon tree.

The others shift on their wooden seats: bare feet against the dirt, toes wriggling; fabric scraping together as arms are crossed; throats cleared. While my own body fidgets, my mind bulges with a thousand things I want to scream through the trees at Levi. But I stay quiet.

"It's been many years since anyone has left our borders," Levi begins. *He doesn't know how wrong he is.* "And many years since we've had to perform the ritual."

I hate how it feels, listening to the oration of his words, the swooping cadence of each vowel. It makes me feel weak, my eyes heavy in a way that's hard to explain, like I could slip back into the gravity of his arms and believe anything he said. I could fall in love all over again.

This is what he does to me: this man whose baby grows inside me, fingers and toes, a tiny warbling heart. This man who loves someone else.

I press my palms to my ears, muting his voice, and blocking out the rush of wind through the trees. I remind myself of what he's done to me, and the familiar hurt rises again, the hate finding structure and meaning inside my chest. This is what I want to feel—not the other thing. I want to loathe him with a deep, wretched pain that cannot ever be undone.

I release my hands and the rustle of the trees fills my ears again.

"Now," Levi continues, "we will see if these men have been cured. Or if the pox has already rooted itself inside them."

A dull silence falls over the others, a collective breath held stiffly in dry throats. And then another sound, the heaving of two men being pulled up from their graves. Of dirt sloughing away. Of ropes grating against limbs. Of Ash and Turk moaning against the effort.

Someone, Parker I'd guess, and maybe Henry, are tugging against the ropes, which have likely been looped over the branches to help hoist Ash and Turk from the ground. They are being pulled upward by the same ropes that bind their arms overhead—a method to avoid touching the men at all. To avoid contact if they are still infected.

I feel myself leaning closer, away from the tree line, straining to hear. To understand what's happening.

Someone is crying among the group, a woman: Marisol, I think, Turk's wife. Perhaps she shouldn't be here, shouldn't witness this—someone should take her away, but the weeping continues and no one stops her.

The limbs of the Mabon tree creak strangely, the ropes bearing too much weight, and my body cringes against the sound. The men are hanging now, suspended, arms overhead. I wish I could see them, look into their eyes and know if there is darkness in them.

"Their blood will reveal the truth," Levi says. Even at this distance, I can hear his heart rate rise, a club against his ribs—the tension building inside him for what he must do next. He moves beside the two men and I know he holds something in his hand. A blade. A knife. A way to cut through skin.

One of the men groans—Turk—and he sounds like an animal, gritting through an awful kind of pain.

His wife lets out a shrieking cry.

I can't see where Levi has pressed the blade into Turk, but I imagine it's punctured his forearm or maybe his hand, a place where the flesh is thin and pale, easily cut. Levi takes a step back, the only footsteps against the earth, and there are gasps from the group, heads shaking, hands worrying together. A chill coils down the length of my spine, landing in my toes.

If blood, ripe red, poured from the wound, there would be no gasps of shock from the others. Instead, they are seeing something unnatural. Something that isn't right.

I swallow, trying to slow my breathing, my heartbeat, so that my ears can pick out each sound.

Levi walks to Ash, suspended several steps from Turk, and he performs the same test—pushing the blade into Ash's skin. But Ash does not moan in pain, he doesn't make a sound, although I hear his heartbeat quicken in his chest.

The response from the group is the same. Several women begin to cry in earnest, and someone mutters, "no, no," like they can't believe the sight before them. People begin writhing in their seats, disgusted or frightened.

I cannot see the wounds in Ash and Turk's flesh, but I can imagine what's pouring from their veins: mud, thick and black, infected.

"We had hoped the ground would draw out the illness," Levi says, his voice carrying out over the crowd, to the trees where I stand. "But their blood pours from the flesh black as death. The pox has taken hold inside them."

More crying erupts from the group, along with a muttering unease, a restlessness that reminds me of the goats in Henry's barn when they startle and begin stamping the ground, wanting to run.

"This is what we fear," Levi declares. "This is the illness we work so hard to keep outside our valley."

"No!" Marisol cries out suddenly. I can almost hear the tears dropping from her cheeks and falling to the earth, salt returning to salt. Someone near her coos softly in her ear—a worthless effort. Because it's obvious how this will go, the *end* this gathering will arrive at.

My heart climbs up my throat and I feel like I suddenly can't breathe, too many sobs are clotting the air—the group whimpering and shifting in their seats, the noise like static, like a growing roar.

"It's not true," a voice—low and unnatural—speaks for the first time. "We're not sick."

It's Ash who's spoken, and the group falls still again.

"We only tried to help my child," he pleads, "because you all refused to do anything. You'd rather stay safe within your homes than see what's out there, beyond our walls."

No one answers and I'm surprised Levi allows Ash to continue to speak. Maybe he knows it's too late—the men's fate is already decided. The truth of their wounds cannot be denied.

"Ash and Turk have brought the pox back with them," Levi says decisively, a calmness hung on each word. "*This* is why we do not cross the border. This is why we cannot pass down the road and bring back doctors or medicine. These two men are already dead, their bodies devoured by the rot. Two lives have now been given trying to save a child. Two lives lost needlessly." He swallows, a word catching there, as if he's lost his train of thought briefly. "We cannot allow the pox to infect anyone else, we cannot allow this disease to destroy what we've built."

This declaration is met with a sudden cry from Marisol. "Please," she shrieks. "He didn't do anything wrong." She's weeping and I hear her footsteps scramble forward, reaching out for her husband. But someone stops her, hands braced against her shoulder, and she's led away; her wails heard across the community until she is ushered inside somewhere and a door shut, muffling her desperate cries.

I press a hand against a nearby pine, my bones buzzing, my ears filled with too much noise. I wish I could *see* what's happening, yet I can feel the terror in the heartbeats of everyone gathered around the Mabon tree. It's already too late for Ash and Turk: the rot will kill them eventually, painfully. But in their slow deaths, they might infect others. So instead, their deaths will be swift and absolute.

It's a mercy, to end their lives. But I also know, in some small way, it's a punishment for what they've done. Levi will prove his point—and he will ensure our enduring fear of the woods.

I close my eyelids and back away from the gathering circle, gasping for air, needing the silence the trees will bring, my pulse beating at my throat.

I don't need to listen to what comes next.

CALLA

Ropes are tied around the men's necks. A careful, precise act, to avoid contact with their skin.

I saw my sister standing in the trees as the men were pulled from the ground, listening, even though I told her not to come. But now she has vanished from the dark edge of the forest.

She doesn't want to hear the snap of the men's necks, bones separating in places they shouldn't. Many others have left too, retreated into their homes, curtains drawn, pillows pulled over ears to muffle any sound. There will be no work done today, no crops tended to, no loaves of bread baked in the community ovens. The children have been led away as well— but not into the meadow to practice cartwheels and summersaults and braiding dandelion crowns under the morning sun. They have been led to their rooms, to consider the punishment they too could face if they ever tiptoed past our borders. Today's execution is a reminder to us all: *Stay within our walls and you will be safe. Leave and you will know death, one way or another.*

I expect Levi to say something else, some final decree: precise, faultless words to assure his followers that this is the right thing. That we have no other choice. But when his mouth dips open, it only hangs there, the silence of air leaving his lungs is all that escapes. For the first time, Levi can't find the right words.

He must sense the burden of so many eyes on him, expectant, so he quickly snaps his jaw shut and nods to Henry, standing on the other side of the noosed men. And in one swift blow, Henry and Parker knock the wood logs out from under the two men with a kick of their boots. The logs roll away toward the Mabon tree and my eyes flutter, taking a moment to rise, to focus on the feet hanging suspended in the air, shaking violently—legs convulsing where they attach to trembling torsos. Both Ash's and Turk's chests seem oddly expanded, like their lungs have swollen, seeking air. But there is no air to breath, because in the last twitch of their fingertips, it's obvious their necks have been broken. The shaking is only residual, a spasm of muscles. Turk stops trembling first, but it's another moment more before Ash falls still—before they both hang slack against their ropes.

Death has settled firmly into their joints, blood ceasing to pump down veins, but instead pooling in valleys and the hollow places of the body, a black, awful kind of blood—the same inky darkness that spilled from their arms when Levi cut into them—an undeniable symptom of the pox. The ground did not heal them as it was meant to. They would die one way or another, and perhaps this way, with ropes tightened around their necks, was a kindness. To die swiftly. Without the agony of a slow, writhing death.

In the echo of my mind, I hear several women crying.

In the periphery of my vision, I see the remaining witnesses rising to their feet and hurrying away from the stage.

I can even hear my husband, speaking to me, touching my hand. But my eyes are fixed on the two men swaying in the morning breeze. I know how this should feel, I know the wretched pain that should twist my gut, but I suspect that will come later. Right now, I feel only the strangeness of what's been done: how swiftly life can be squeezed and snapped from a person. How easily Levi could demand these two men's death, and minutes later, it's done.

But Levi did not kill these men.

We all did.

THEO

The mirror above the bathroom sink is cracked in two places—I don't recall it ever *not* being broken—and I lean against the porcelain edge only a few inches from the glass, staring at my own reflection. A candle flickers from the counter, making it hard to see anything clearly, but I widen my eyelids, dark pupils staring back.

If the pox is inside me, I should be able to see it—a blackness spreading around my retinas, the rot working its way through my veins. I should be able to feel it too, the decaying of my bones, turning to muck.

Another reflection catches my gaze and I jerk back from the mirror.

"You're looking for the pox, aren't you?" Calla is standing in the bathroom doorway, arms crossed.

Only an hour earlier, we sat at the gathering and watched as Levi pushed a knife into Ash's and Turk's flesh, and what spilled out was not blood, it was something else: dark and ruddy, almost like oil.

I blinked and blinked, wanting the blood to not be what it was. But it was indisputable: Both men were infected. The pox was inside our borders.

Now I wonder, *Is it inside me?*

I turn to face my wife, and she crosses the bathroom, bringing her hands to my cheeks, sliding her fingers up my jawline. She peers close, examining my eyes like she is looking for a stray eyelash or a bit of dirt. Her gaze is soft, innocent, and it makes me think of other times when she has tended to my wounds—a crushed hand when a tree trunk rolled onto my knuckles while chopping firewood, a gash in my shoulder when a length of barbed wire tore through my shirt down to my flesh—careful and precise as she cleaned blood away and bandaged me up.

"I don't see anything," she says now, keeping her hands on my face, as if to prove a point: that she isn't afraid, that she doesn't think the pox is inside me. Or that if it is, she will gladly catch it too—whatever happens to me, happens to her too. Maybe this is love, the things we endure for the other, the willingness to face death, to stare it down, and not be afraid.

Finally, she releases her warm hands and exhales. "We're murdering ourselves," she says.

"They were dead either way." But even as I say it, it feels wrong, a fairy tale told to pacify frightened children.

Calla's eyes shiver, like she's holding in tears, and she walks out into the hall.

I feel unsteady on my feet, the house seesawing around me.

But she spins around before entering our bedroom. "I don't know why you're not sick and neither is Bee. But those two men, they caught it while trying to go for help—it doesn't make sense." Her eyes flicker with something—a strange kind of uncertainty I don't usually see in my wife. Like an oversized thought is pressing against her windpipe, and it's only growing larger. "Why aren't you infected?"

"I don't know."

Her hands twitch at her sides. "Something happened here," she says, and I know she's not talking about Ash and Turk anymore, she's talking about the truck, the notebook, the man who slept in the sunroom at the back of the house and hid pages in our walls and floorboards. "Maybe it's happening still." Her voice falters, tears breaking free and streaming down her cheeks.

I step forward and pull her into my arms. She makes a wordless sound against my shoulder, a sob, and I want to say something to comfort her, but all the words fall flat in my mind. Because maybe she's right—and nothing is what we think it is.

BEE

After the ritual, I don't return to the farmhouse.

I rest in the burrows and hollowed-out earth made by other creatures, where the deer go to rest in gathered herds, nestled beneath an oak. I find soft rounds of soil, or grass tamped down by foxes. Clumps of fur, carcasses of birds. I rest and I wake and I dream of odd fitful things, of voices always beckoning me forth, deeper into the trees.

I have crossed the boundary.

I've done it many times now, careless footsteps, rattling heartbeat.

I have slipped into the trees and felt the fear always at my neck—nipping just softly like a warning, never sinking its teeth all the way in. It craves me, wants to bury me out here in this forest, but I am quick and alert, and I scurry through the underbrush, startling the quail from their roosts under thorny bushes. I am a creature too, more fearful than most things.

I lean against the old, sturdy oaks, listening for the hum, for the crack and splinter of limbs. I dare the pox to sink into me—I dare death to come close.

Two nights now I've been in the woods, past the border, drinking from the stream, pressing my palms to the ground to feel its warmth. Two nights of seeking something that doesn't want to be found.

I creep close to the birthing hut, pressing my back against the wall, listening. Colette and the baby are sleeping—I can hear their soft exhales. I wonder if she's been told about her husband: how he tried to leave and bring back help for their child, but instead brought back the pox. I wonder if she wept until the grief was too much, until she drifted off to sleep, knowing she had lost her husband. And will likely lose her baby, too.

Netta is with her most nights, tending to the infant who still has no name, then dozing in a chair near the front door of the hut. They are counting the days now, the hours, every half-second, knowing there might not be many more left.

I step back into the trees, following the sounds of breaking limbs and a hissing disease. I search for the pox, running my palms up the trunks of sick trees, feeling for sap, for illness. But the pox merely teases me. I need to know that those men died for a reason—because they were sick in a way that couldn't be cured—I need to feel what they felt.

It also occurs to me, I might be going mad.

CALLA

Bee only comes to the house to steal toast from the kitchen or water from the well, but mostly she stays away. I don't know what she's staying away from: me, maybe? Or she's looking for something out there in the dark.

Henry came to the house yesterday, walking around to the garden where I was pretending to collect eggs, but really I had the *Foxtail* book open in my lap—reading through the pages, a cold tickling down my spine, searching for some clue about what happened to Maggie, some hidden message in the story she wrote. When I heard Henry approach, I snapped the book closed then tucked it into the basket beside me that held half a dozen eggs. Henry stood for a moment, a cold expression drawn along his eyebrows, and I thought something was wrong—I thought maybe he came looking for Bee or Theo, that somehow Levi had discovered that they went over the boundary.

But instead, Henry said, "Tomorrow there will be a celebration."

"For what?" I asked, placing two nearby eggs into the basket then standing up. I could think of no reason for the community to celebrate—surely any birthday could be delayed because of recent events. The community needs time to heal, to forget.

"A wedding," Henry answered. He pushed his knuckled hands into the pockets of his loose, acorn-brown cardigan, then bent his shoulders forward as if he were cold.

"Whose?"

"Levi's."

I frowned and instinctively looked up to Bee's bedroom window, even though I knew she wasn't inside.

"He'll be marrying Alice Weaver," Henry explained, sensing my confusion.

I brushed my hands along my apron and wondered if Bee knew, if this was why she's stayed away.

"Okay," I replied.

"The ceremony will start after dark." I could see that Henry was just as unnerved by this. Perhaps not because Levi would be marrying Alice instead of Bee, but because he felt it was too soon. We only just buried two of our own in the cemetery, and now we would celebrate the union of two others. But maybe this is what Levi intends—to give us a way to move on. "Perhaps the normalcy of it will be good," Henry added.

I nodded, and we stood silently like that, both of us weighing the strangeness of the last few days, before he turned and left.

Tonight, once the sun has been pulled down by the trees, Theo and I walk to Pastoral. We move with the same dulled quiet that has rested over us in recent days, the nagging sense of waiting that has no words—like we both know something terrible is coming, the hours a dangerous ticking clock.

We're nearly to Pastoral, the moon full overhead, when Theo asks, "Is there a nursery rhyme in the book?"

"What?"

"In the *Foxtail* book, is there a nursery rhyme, or a lullaby?" It feels like something he's been thinking about for some time, a thought that's been worrying at his bones, and the question has finally bubbled to the surface.

"Maybe. I haven't finished it yet." At times I read the book at a panicked rate, like I need to get to the end before I can take another breath. Other times, the words inside its pages make me feel like I'm slipping out of my own skin, into a fictional world where I don't belong. I don't like the way it slithers into my thoughts even when I'm not reading it, and sometimes I wonder if maybe I shouldn't know how such tales end—I shouldn't know what happens to a girl who vanishes into the woods.

Tonight before we left the house, I tucked the book into the back of the closet behind a stack of old dresses that need mending, near a spider's web long abandoned—where Theo won't find it.

"There's a lullaby I keep hearing," he says. "I think it's a memory."

"A memory of what?"

He shakes his head and glances at me sidelong, like he's afraid to say. "I'm not sure."

In truth, I know what my husband is asking: He wants to know about *the* lullaby. The one mentioned in chapter seventeen of the *Foxtail* book, the lullaby that coaxes the fox from the forest. The one that turns Eloise into the villain.

I lied when I pretended not to know.

FOXES AND MUSEUMS

Excerpt from Book One in the Eloise and the Foxtail series

The lullaby was written in an old book Eloise found buried beneath the roots of a snowbriar tree, near the far back of the underground museum. Her palms were caked with mud by the time she pulled the book free and slumped back on her heels, holding the book to her tiny chest.

Worms wriggled beneath her feet; bats swung from the ceiling of the museum. But she paid no mind to the dark, crawly things that watched her. She only cared about the book.

She placed it on her lap, legs crossed beneath her, knees muddied, and flipped open the front cover. But the first page was empty. So was the second. She fanned through the pages and found them all blank— only smooth white paper stared back.

Tears welled at the rims of her eyes as she flitted through the pages, desperate, heartbroken. But then, at the very end—at the last page within the book—she found writing. The ink was bold and sharp, still wet, as if it had been pressed to the page only moments ago. But the words were not a magic spell or a curse, as she had hoped.

It was a lullaby. A song sung to babies to help them sleep.

At first, Eloise was angry, and she thought of closing the book, dropping it back into the earth and covering it with soil. But she felt a tickle at the back of her throat; her vocal cords beginning to hum the words aloud. And soon she was singing the lullaby with her head craned back, as if she were commanding the stars far above the dark chamber of the museum. She sang the words bright and clear, *Let the night woods bury you alive; let the dark swallow you whole. You are not a girl tonight; you are a beast stripped of your soul.*

When she climbed back up through the old, crumbling well, the book held carefully in her arms, she stood once again aboveground and watched as dawn inched through the alabaster trees. Night becoming day.

But she was not the same.

Eloise was no longer the heroine of this story—she was something else. She was the dark between tree branches, she was the vile thing that is hidden in corners and low places.

She was the shadow.

The monster.

Called by a name that would not be spoken, unless you desired to summon her close. To look death in the face. To be changed into something that was not yourself.

THEO

Candles have been lit along every surface, illumining the center of Pastoral in a soft, phosphorescent glow. It's a strange sight, the community lit up for a celebration—a wedding—when only days ago we hung two men from the Mabon tree.

The ceremony is a simple exchange of vows: Hand-forged rings are pushed onto fingers and when Levi and Alice kiss, there is a soft applause.

We are numb, weary, and we move through the motions by necessity.

After the ceremony, the group gathers around a long table placed in the tall grass near the crops, framing an open space between the trees. Candles line the table between heaping bowls of summer squash and ripe tomatoes and seasoned snap peas. It's a feast, a celebration of abundance within the community. Bodi is playing his guitar beneath the swaying lights while Cyrus sings—an old tune from the outside world, about war and changing times. Some sit in the grass with plates of food, others dance slowly, moving with the music.

On a night like this, the mood of the group should be jovial, even raucous—at our wedding, most in the community stayed up late singing wildly to the stars, laughing from deep within their chests, then fell asleep among the crops or curled up on benches inside the gathering circle. We all woke in the morning with the sun burning our faces and wine swimming in our bellies. Calla and I wandered home, still a little drunk, stupidly happy, then slept for the remainder of the day—as husband and wife.

But tonight, a thick, unnamable pallor sticks in the air, to the roofs of our mouths.

Calla and I stand beneath one of the swaying elms. "This feels wrong," she mutters to me, rubbing her hands up her arms, looking uncomfortable. Neither of us want to be here.

Henry and his wife, Lily Mae, approach from the feast table carrying mugs of apple wine.

"Nice ceremony," Henry comments, coming to stand beside me, looking out at the somber festivities.

I nod, my voice too tight to speak.

"Haven't seen Marisol though," he adds.

Turk's wife was an obvious absence at the wedding. Surely her grief is still too wide and painful to face anyone yet. Perhaps Levi even asked her to remain in her home, because seeing her would be too stark of a reminder for the rest of us. *Just until enough time has passed*, I imagine him saying.

Levi appears from the eastern edge of Pastoral, his new bride, Alice Weaver, on his arm. They move to the center of the group, and Alice's hair, a deep copper color, shimmers in the candlelight. She's a plain-featured woman, with an abrupt nose and a small row of teeth, but she's also known to laugh easily—a bright, quick sound.

I wonder if this is why Levi has chosen to marry her instead of Bee: Alice will serve as a docile, soft-spoken wife, a wife who won't upset the order of things. While it isn't talked about openly, many in the community knew of Bee and Levi's furtive relationship, and I had hoped he wouldn't break her heart—that he would take care of her. But he seems to be unraveling in recent days.

The low chatter of voices around us falls quiet and the music draws to an end, everyone turning their attention to our leader.

The first words from Levi's mouth slip out in a jumbled, unintelligible slur, and he has to clear his throat before he starts again. "We made a promise—" His voice breaks off, and Alice grins uncomfortably at his side, her posture stiff. She is the only thing keeping him upright. "To honor this . . . land. And it would . . . provide for us. It would—" He waves a hand, gesturing to the terrain around us, the trees, the crops to the north of us. "It would give us this food to nourish us, make us strong. Make us . . ." He sucks in a deep breath, like he's forcing his lungs to breathe, and it's clear he's lost his train of thought. "A toast to our community. Our commitment to one another."

He says nothing of his marriage, of the reason why we have all gathered, he doesn't even utter his wife's name once. Yet Alice's face maintains its perfectly upturned grin.

Glasses of fermented apple wine are raised in the air and clinked together, and Levi sinks into a chair near a stand of trees, his gaze blurred over as the music resumes along with the chatter. Alice tries to offer him something to eat, but he brushes her away, and she slips off to the Mabon tree where a group of women have gathered for the ribbon binding ceremony.

There is nothing lighthearted about Levi's mood tonight—he's drinking to forget, not to celebrate.

"Had a little too much of Agnes's wine," Henry comments under his breath, nodding at Levi.

"Easy to do, on your wedding day," I answer, as if I needed to defend him, certain this abrupt marriage was intended to distract himself, and maybe the rest of us too.

"Any word of Colette's baby?" Henry asks, looking to Calla. He assumes we might receive daily reports on the infant's health from Bee. But we haven't seen Bee in days.

Calla shakes her head and sinks back, looking away from Henry and Lily Mae. She doesn't want to talk about Bee—her sister who has become a ghost.

I take another sip of the wine in my hand. It's dull, barely alcoholic, but there is enough warmth to coat my insides and make me feel loosened along my edges.

"Haven't seen that sister of yours around much," Lily Mae says, swallowing a slow drink of her wine. "Used to see her sneaking out of Levi's house nearly every morning. But not lately. Then Levi up and marries Alice Weaver. A little odd, I'd say."

My gaze swivels to Calla, and I can feel the heat from her skin, the fury boiling up inside her.

"It's none of my business what my sister does," Calla answers, flashing Lily Mae a hard look.

"Everything that happens in Pastoral is the business of us all," Lily Mae replies with a little upturn of her chin.

I know my wife should just let it go; it's not worth the argument. But she swivels beside me so she's at a better angle to meet Lily Mae's eyes dead-on.

But Henry pats a hand against his knee before Calla can speak, before she can spit some insult back at Lily Mae. "Isn't that the price for living this way," he says with a grin, attempting to lighten the thin band of tension stretching from his wife to mine. "No way to avoid knowing your neighbors' comings and goings. For better or worse, I suppose." He raises his glass of wine in the air as if the four of us might toast to this, but no one else lifts their glass to his. So he takes a drink alone, closing his eyes and savoring the sharp twinge as it slides down his throat.

Calla looks away and the music begins again, an upbeat melody, and more members gather in the candlelight, swaying with the thrum of wine now pumping through their veins. They want to forget what's happened, they want to drink and dull the pain inside them. And I don't blame them for it—I'd like to forget too. But I also know forgetting won't undo what's already been done.

I need something else: reparation maybe. I need to peel away the lies and reveal the beating heart of what's really happened here—to Ash and Turk, to Maggie and Travis. Bloody and awful as it might be.

Calla leaves my side suddenly, crossing through the candlelight to get another mug of wine. Or maybe just to escape Lily Mae.

Henry makes a joke about Agnes not fermenting his apple wine long enough because he gets impatient, but I'm hardly listening. My gaze follows Levi as he stands from his chair and wanders to the edge of the trees, just back in the shadows.

Henry says something else, asks a question about our canned fruit storage, but I offer him a quick smile and my apologies. There's something else I need to do.

I weave through the group, into the shadow of the trees, moving toward Levi.

BEE

My head feels clear. Crisp, like a cold December morning.

I hadn't noticed it before, but a gray, whirling cloud had settled inside my skull. *How long had it been there? Years?* And now it's begun to lift, evaporating from behind my eyes.

It's been days since I've seen Levi, and maybe the time away has cleared my thoughts. Not just in the way that love blinds, but in a real, tactile way. As if I had been tangled in reeds before, legs trapped in mud, hands clawing for a surface that wasn't there. And now my body has begun to shed its old skin, slithering free of the binds he held around my wrists—tendrils of him braided into every strand of my being.

But now he's gone.

Nights spent outside, sleeping under the stars, have peeled away something inside me. And sometimes when I wake—the sky still dark—I swear I can see up through the trees, tiny dots of light coming into focus. A fabric of stars winking back at me.

It feels as if I'm waking up, the blackness dissolving.

And something else is forming in its place.

THEO

Levi is swaying when I reach him, eyes glassed over, yet there is an edginess to the way his shoulders tilt heavily to one side, his mouth drawn too tight against his teeth.

"I did it for them," he says when I reach him, as if I've walked up and interrupted him midsentence, even though he's standing alone.

"Did what?"

His upper lip snarls, watching those who are swaying beneath the rows of lights. "They don't know what's out there, but I do—" His voice breaks off and he hiccups, tipping slightly onto his left foot before righting himself.

I feel sorry for him, seeing him like this—he's not the man he was a week ago—before Colette had her baby and Ash and Turk snuck over the border. Some part of him has rattled loose.

His chin tips back and he peers up through the trees, like he's trying to see the stars. But I suspect everything is a blur to him right now. The world blotted out. "They're all sheep," he mutters, his half-closed eyes snapping back to me. "But not you." He takes another drink. "You're smarter than them." I think he's going to say that I'm the only one he trusts, the only one he can confide in, but his mouth pinches closed and he breathes, steadying himself. Or he's thinking some other thought he refuses to share.

I pull out the photograph from my pocket, keeping it curled slightly against the shape of my palm, and I hold it out for him to see.

His chin lowers, eyes flickering across the image. "What is it?" he asks, like he can't tell what he's looking at. He sways forward, spilling some of his wine onto the grass, then blinks down at the photo but doesn't touch it, doesn't try to take it from me. For a tiny half-second, I think I see something in his eyes, maybe it's recognition, a twitch of his eyelashes, a puckering of his mouth. Or maybe it's just the booze causing odd little convulsions in his face muscles.

"Where did you get it?" His voice is flat and measured, giving nothing away.

I draw the photo back so only I can see it. "I found it."

"Where?" This question comes as a punctuation in the air.

Beyond the border, I think. Down the road until I could no longer see Pastoral behind me. Much farther than Ash or Turk trekked. Deep, deep into the woods.

But Levi looks at me like he already knows, or he suspects. And we stare at one another, looking for the lies, looking for the cracks in the other person.

"Do you know who she is?" I ask.

Levi's right eye squints nearly closed and he shifts his jaw back into place. "Should I?"

"Her name is Maggie St. James."

He blows out a breath, almost as if he's relieved. Or again, it might just be the alcohol making his gestures seem like they have meaning when they don't.

"There's no one in Pastoral with that name," he answers, turning his attention away from me. "You know that."

Across the way, at the Mabon tree, Alice and a small group of women have finished tying lengths of dyed fabric to the lowest limbs of the tree, and now they stand in a circle around the trunk, each holding the end of a fabric strip, singing softly as they begin to weave in and out through one another, wrapping the trunk of the Mabon tree in a crosshatch pattern. It's a way to bind the marriage of Alice and Levi, to brand it into the tree. The same tree where only days ago, two men's necks were snapped.

"Maybe she passed through here years ago," I say.

"We haven't had anyone new come to Pastoral in over ten years," Levi reminds me. Not since Cooper died and the forest became unsafe.

I nod, looking down at the photograph in my hand, at the half-image of a woman who is screaming at me with her visible eye. Begging me for something—*to find her*. "But what if this woman did come here," I press. "Maybe she snuck in and then something happened to her."

"Like what?"

"I don't know." I turn the photo over and read her name handwritten in black ink on the back. "I think a man came looking for her, too. A man named Travis Wren."

Levi juts out his lower jaw then slides it back. "Why do you think that?"

"I found a notebook in our house, in the sunroom. It was written by a man named Travis Wren." I hadn't planned on telling Levi about the notebook, it felt like something I needed to keep secret, but now I find myself wanting to convince him, make him understand that two people are missing. And it's better—less risky—to tell him about the notebook than about the truck I found down the road. Than to admit that I went over the perimeter.

"And you think that man was in your house?"

"I do," I answer.

"And this Maggie St. James also?"

"Maybe."

He brings the mug to his lips, but it's empty. He shakes his head. "If those people were here in Pastoral, if they were in your house, we would know." He looks up at me, unblinking, mouth pulled into a strange curve. And there, in the subtle twitch of his eyes, I can see that he's trying to maintain control—of his temper, of me.

At the Mabon tree, the women are just finishing binding the tree with fabric, and their singing slows to a stop. They fold their arms around Alice now, protecting her—a show that they will always be with her, even as she enters this new marriage and her role as a wife. Then the women break apart, smiling, laughing at some private shared joke.

"Travis could have snuck into the house at night, slept in the sunroom, and we wouldn't have known."

"And the woman?"

I shake my head, turning the photograph away. "I don't know—I'm not sure where she was. But I think they were both here, in Pastoral, and we need to find them, we can't just—" My words break off. I sound manic, out of breath.

"You need to let it go," he says gently, like a parent consoling a child who's had a bad dream. *Just go back to sleep and everything will be fine by morning.* He clears his throat, then adds, "My eyes are sore from crying, my lungs are sore from coughing, my knees are sore from kneeling, and my heart is sore from believing. If you are sore and tired, then come into these woods and sleep."

It's a quote from Cooper, our founder, and I suspect Levi speaks it now as a reminder. He thinks I've forgotten why we're here, or maybe he thinks I've forgotten who he is: our leader. I've pushed him too far, and I can see the strain now cut into his forehead.

He sets his empty mug in the grass at his feet, swaying as he rights himself. "It's late," he says finally, patting a hand on my shoulder, and nodding.

He takes a few steps forward, then staggers away along the edge of the trees so he won't be seen and disappears into the dark.

I watch the place where he vanished, a thread of knowing weaving itself tighter and tighter until it feels like my mind will snap. It wasn't what he said exactly, it's the way his eyes cut slantwise over to me, the thick rasp of his breathing. He might be drunk, but it's more than that.

Levi is lying.

I stand on the porch of Levi's home, concealed in shadows, my shoulder pressed against the log exterior.

Peering through the front window, I watch Levi walk to the cabinet and drag out another bottle of whiskey. The dark, tawny liquid splashes onto the wood table as he fills a glass, holding it to his mouth, before knocking the whole thing back in one gulp. He sets the glass on the cabinet but doesn't refill it.

The fireplace is lit in the living room, candles glowing throughout the house—one of the community members must have lit them earlier in the night so our leader and his bride could return home and not be forced to fumble around in the dark.

He walks to the fireplace and tosses something onto the flames. It looks like a small piece of wood, kindling maybe. And then, through the muffled barrier of the windows, I hear a sound, like a back door shutting. Levi turns his head, listening. For a moment there is only silence, and then footsteps.

"Levi?" a voice calls into the house.

I recognize the sharp upswing of her voice. It's not Alice Weaver, come to look for her new husband.

It's Bee.

Levi walks to the back of the house, where the kitchen faces the forest beyond. Bee's voice is low and I can't make out their words, but soon they appear again in the dim light of the living room, Bee's hand in Levi's, and he leads her up the stairs.

When they're out of sight, I enter the house quietly and leave the door ajar behind me, to allow for a swift exit. At first, I don't know what I'm doing, why I'm here—or what I'm hoping to find. Maybe some proof that Levi knows more than he'll admit. So I walk into his office, keeping my footsteps light.

The interior of his office is filled with dark wood furniture, and the heavy cotton curtains are drawn closed. I've never spent much time in here—I've never had reason to—but now, I eye Levi's mammoth desk: a thing that was here long before Pastoral was founded, the kind of solid antique desk that will last another hundred years, with thick wood legs and a smooth, lacquered top.

I move around it, where the wood chair sits pushed forward, and I begin opening drawers, peering into the cavern of each one. I find another bottle of whiskey, a few books on native plants, a box of keys—car keys that once powered the abandoned vehicles now decaying in the parking lot to the south. Nothing relevant. Nothing to explain any of the questions clanking around inside me. In fact, I'm not even sure what the right questions are, what I should be looking for.

I leave the office and step back into the living room.

The fireplace burns low, candles lit along the mantel, and I think of Alice Weaver—still out celebrating her recent marriage to Levi, while her husband is in his house, upstairs with another woman. And I realize suddenly that I don't want to be here.

It's time to leave before I get caught.

But as I move to the open door, my eyes jerk twice over something in the fireplace. A thing I dismiss at first, then glance at again.

Something rests among the burning logs—square, manmade.

I move away from the open door and kneel down beside the fire, my left temple throbbing with strange little pulses. I use one of the heavy iron pokers to dislodge the thing from the fiery logs and watch as it rolls out onto the floor.

It's a wood box.

Its edges are still burning so I push it back into the ash of the fireplace, putting out the flame. I blow the soot away, waiting a moment for it to cool before I lift it up. It's small, about the size of my palm, and it's still warm, but not enough to burn my hand. This is what Levi tossed into the fire when I watched him from the porch. I had thought it was only a scrap of wood—I couldn't see it clearly through the window.

Now, I have spared it from the flames. The hinges have melted some but I manage to pry open the lid, ash falling away from the cracks.

Inside is a heap of metal.

Shiny, silver.

My eyes vibrate for a moment, certain I'm not seeing it right.

I pull out the thing inside, holding it in my palm: a necklace. And hanging from the long silver chain are four charms: four tiny books with numbers stamped onto their covers.

Levi had tossed the box onto the fire, he had tried to burn it—maybe he thought the necklace would melt inside the wood box—be reduced to a puddle of shivering metal.

But it didn't burn.

And there is something else in the box. Folded and pressed into the bottom. I pry it free: a piece of paper, a note, unburnt. My hands begin to shake as I unfold it quickly, my eyes darting over the words. I already know what it is. What I've found.

It's the third page from Travis Wren's notebook.

The last missing note.

BEE

It's a mistake coming here.

I open the back door, the divot in the wood floor familiar as I step into Levi's kitchen. It smells of candle wax, and a fire is burning from the fireplace at the other end of the house, the snapping of embers like little bursts in my ears.

Levi is alone in the house—Alice Weaver isn't with him, I heard her clear buoyant laugh back at the party as the others swirled around her, running their envious fingers down the fabric of her dress, a gown that's been worn by many women in the community on their wedding days. A dress that I've been told is no longer a pure white, but the color of hen eggs, speckled along the hemline from the stains that refuse to be washed out.

Alice Weaver absorbed their praise and admiration, she breathed it into her lungs as if it was always meant for her. But it should have been mine.

I slither like a cold, autumn shadow into Levi's house, my words waiting at the back of my throat, the things I will say to him, the venom burning a hole in my trachea.

But when the door clicks closed behind me, I hear footsteps across the hardwood floor, the heavy breathing of Levi after he's drank too much.

I say his name into the dark. "Levi?"

He is suddenly in front of me, alcohol on his breath, a hand grabbing my arm, fingernails pinching my skin. He is sloppy, heavy limbed, rougher than he would normally be.

"Come with me," he slurs against my ear.

I feel my body go limp, a strange acquiescence cascading through me, as though my skin is unable to resist his touch—all the while my mind screams against it, against him. But I allow him to lead me up the stairs. And from some distant echo in my ears, I hear someone else: someone on the front porch, leaning close to the exterior walls of the house.

I was wrong when I thought Levi was alone: Someone is watching him through the window.

But then we are at the top of the stairs, and I don't resist. I feel only a tingling in my toes, the tips of my ears, a storm of thoughts crashing against my skull—yet they seem unable to form into anything that might resemble words. I am mute.

A girl who has forgotten why she's come.

We are in his bedroom before he finally releases my arm, and I sink onto the foot of his bed. The room smells like cinnamon, cardamom—like Alice, this room where she has slept. And yet, the fury I had felt walking to Levi's house, my cheeks burning hot, has now left me. I find myself suddenly unable to say all the things I had planned to—unable to resist any words he might whisper against my ear.

How easily the ache in my heart-center returns, the *want* that can only be sated with his hands against my cold, cold flesh. I am weak. This man makes me pliable and meek in ways I don't understand.

Levi walks to the dresser and opens the top drawer where his laundry has been neatly cleaned and sorted and folded by several woman in the community. Levi is always tended to, the necessities of his daily life organized around him. I wonder if this will change once Alice Weaver takes up residence inside his home? Will her hands toil over the fabric that lies against his skin, will she mend the clothes that need stitching, will she hang his sheets to dry on the line outside? Will she fold herself into his life seamlessly, ridding me from it completely?

"I'm sorry about everything," Levi says, reaching into the drawer and pulling out the flask he keeps hidden there. He unscrews the top, the sound of metal, and takes a drink—his throat swallowing stiffly.

I don't answer him, instead my ears absorb the sound of his heart beating heavily in his chest, the rapid thud, the booze swimming through him and making his skin radiate heat. He walks to me, careful and slow, and my own heart claws against my ribs—betraying me, wanting to reach out and touch the surface of his flesh, to stand up and kiss him. But I don't allow myself to do this stupid thing.

He has married another woman tonight. He is bound to her now, not me.

"I know that I hurt you," he says, words smashed together, and I realize he has brought me upstairs to avoid anyone seeing us together, glimpsing us through a window, alone on his wedding night—when he should be with his wife. He sits on the bed beside me. *So close.* "I know I've made everything worse." His hand lifts and I think he touches a strand of my hair but I can't be sure. He lets out a hollow breath of air, like someone has punched him in the stomach, and he turns away, his voice directed at the doorway. "You make this hard for me." I want to remember the feel of his lips on mine, I want to forget everything he said to me before, I want to forget that later tonight, when the party has ended, Alice Weaver will sleep in this bed beside him. In the same place where I have dreamed and dozed and felt the sunrise.

He makes a weak, shuddering sound, like tears might have broken over his eyelids. But then he says, "I have obligations here, in Pastoral." He takes another drink from the flask, as if fortifying himself, stuffing down whatever he's afraid to feel. "Alice understands that, she understands what it means to be my wife."

The words fall like a hammer against my kneecaps, shattering bone.

And I don't? I want to scream. I know Levi better than anyone, better than he knows himself. *Better than docile, perfect Alice Weaver.* But the anger feels buried in my marrow, tamped down by a calm buzzing in my eardrums.

"You have always been fearless, wilder than the other girls, especially when we were younger," he continues. He smells like sweat and the sharpness of whiskey. He smells like summer grass, green and sweet under a hot sun—he smells familiar—but his words bite at me as if he were a stranger. "It's what I've always loved about you. But it's also why you're dangerous. You put everything at risk."

"Why?" I ask, my voice a distant thing, stuffed into the spaces between my ribs.

"Because I think someday you'll leave me. You'll try to leave Pastoral."

I shake my head, but the motion is dizzying, eyes blinking, fluttering up and down, and I think I see candlelight across the room—a flickering that can't be anything else. But when I squint, it's replaced by darkness.

Levi stands up and the absence of his body next to mine makes me shiver. "Those men leaving, trying to escape, it feels like it's only the beginning. Soon others will try too."

"They weren't trying to escape," I explain. "They were going to get help."

"There is a thin line between escape and sacrifice." I'm not sure of his meaning, but I hear his footsteps move to the window, and I imagine him staring out at a starlit forest, the moon suspended low in the sky. He's so far away, I couldn't touch him even if I wanted to. "I can feel a change in them, all of them," he says, carefully tracing the words he wants to say before he lets them leave his lips. "They don't trust me anymore. They think of the outside world, of what they *don't* have instead of what they do."

I run my fingers along the quilt beneath me, feeling the familiar stitching, the pattern sewn together in little triangles. There are no holes, no torn edges in it—unlike most things in Pastoral. It has been mended and well-kept. "They still trust you," I say, my own mind slipping back into old patterns. Always comforting, always reassuring. Even now, I can't help but buoy him up. It's what I've always done—I am the guidepost for a man who sways so easily off course. "They just need to know that you trust them in return, that you make decisions for them, not for yourself."

"Everything I do is for them," he snaps, his body twisting around, his voice now directed back at me and not at the window. "Those men would have undermined everything if they'd made it any farther down that road. If they'd gone into town."

"Why?"

He crosses back to the bed. "We don't know what's out there," he answers, mostly to himself. "We don't know what's left."

"What are you talking about?"

He breathes and takes another drink from his flask. The room smells of alcohol, it saturates the walls, the linens, Levi's skin. As if the house itself has been soaked in whiskey.

"They were traitors," he answers at last, with a quick finality.

"They weren't traitors," I argue. "They only wanted to save Ash's child."

His breathing grows deep, a heady weight to each inhale and exhale. "It doesn't matter why they did it, only that they did. They had to be punished."

"They were hung because they were sick. Not because they were traitors," I correct.

He makes a strange sound from the back of his throat. "They see what they want to see." He sinks back onto the bed beside me, his body too heavy to hold up.

"Who does?" I ask, unsure what he means. "Ash and Turk?"

He shakes his head, I can hear the subtle shift in the air. "No, Bee." He sounds tired, like he's fighting the sleep tugging at his brain.

"Tell me what you mean," I press.

He sways closer to me. "The others," he says. And when I frown at him, still unsure what he's saying, he adds, "You ask too many questions. Too many things you shouldn't worry about."

I open my mouth but then his hand is at my throat. Not hard, not violently pressing, but smoothing across my skin up to my ear. He tugs at the ends of my hair, like he used to do when we were kids, when he would sneak up behind me and pull my hair, a reminder that he was there. Always close. My companion, my best friend, and sometimes my shadow.

"I loved you," he says now, and it sounds as if tears are pushing against his eyelids again. As though I was the one to hurt him, I was the one who has married someone else. "You were always better than me. Smarter even—I always knew it." He exhales deeply. "Even when we were kids. It's why I had to—" His voice breaks off.

I pull away from him, and start to stand, but he reaches out quickly and grabs my wrist. "Bee," he says, drawing me back down, back beside him. "After tonight, I will belong to Alice."

"You already belong to her." *You're already married*, I want to scream.

He sighs. "But it's always been us. . . you and me. Even when we were younger. I always thought I'd marry you, that there would be nothing that ever pushed us apart."

"But you've chosen her," I say. "*You* pushed us apart."

"No," he answers. "I didn't push us apart—this place did, this community."

I shake my head, feeling my own tears swelling against my eyes. I don't want to hear him say this, any of it. It only makes it worse—the pain he's cut into me, the betrayal of marrying someone else. He has hurt me more deeply than anyone ever could. And I hate him, hate him, *hate him*. "I'm not yours anymore," I manage.

He brushes his thumb across my cheek, catching the wetness. "That's not true," he says, his voice breaking a little, his own hurt rising to the surface. "I'm still yours."

"No," I say, and again I stand. But he follows me to the door, grabbing my hand. And when I turn back to him, to shout for him to let me go, to shout that I hate him: that I will never forgive him for this thing he's done, for loving me but still marrying someone else, for denying our child—the tiny ember of light inside me—but instead, his hands find my arm, my face, and he pulls me to him.

I don't want him to touch me like this—I don't want the heat of him so close, reminding me of too many nights when we folded ourselves together beneath the sheets. I don't want any of it. And yet, his lips are against my ear, muttering things I won't recall by morning. His hands are in my hair, his words in my chest, and I feel myself sinking, slipping, and then my mouth is on his. This man I hate, this man I could press the life out of if my hands found his throat.

But instead, he whispers my name again, over and over, and his hand has found the hem of my dress. I hate him, and I press my lips against his mouth. I hate him, and I dissolve against his touch, the familiar pulse of his breathing, his heartbeat in my ears.

I hate him.

I hate him.

My back presses against the closed door and I pull him to me.

I hate him.

His lips are on my throat, my hands along his spine. Digging. Making trenches. Hating.

I forget that he doesn't want me.

I forget that he is married, bound to another.

I forget—for the tiniest of seconds—that I hate him with everything I am. *Hate hate hate.*

And I let the hate become something else: a burning. A need, that is deep and silent and worries not about tomorrow or how this will feel in the morning.

I let myself love him one last time, against his bedroom door, against the soft cotton of his summer-white sheets. And for a moment, I think I can see the ceiling, the tiny blue floral pattern of the wallpaper. I think I see the window, looking out at the tall pines.

I think I see Levi's face: the lines around his too-green eyes, the perfect structure of his nose and jaw, the form of his lips as they trace along my collarbone.

For the briefest moment, I can see again.

And it terrifies me.

CALLA

A lie is a lie is a lie.

It tastes the same when it leaves your throat, regardless of intent.

Living in Pastoral, you look for ways to keep some part of you hidden, some singularity from the group. But the lie I told my husband is different—I lied because I'm afraid, because the things scrabbling back and forth inside my mind frighten me. They make no sense, not in the way they should.

I told Theo I've never read the nursery rhyme inside the *Foxtail* book . . . but I have.

I've been reciting it every day, a melody that swings in and out of focus when I'm trying to sleep, trying to breathe. I've read it so many times, traced the letters with my fingertip, that now it feels as if it's branded into my skin. It frightens me, the sureness of the words. So I keep them a secret, for now. I don't tell Theo.

But my husband has lied too.

And so has Bee; there is a lie growing inside her—a tiny thing, but soon it'll be too large to ignore.

I stand in our bedroom, holding the Foxtail book I pulled from the back of the closet, my fingers worrying over the edges of the cover, as if I could peel it apart, turn the book to scraps—shreds of paper falling to the floor. I watch through the window for my husband to return from Pastoral. He went to speak with Levi after the ceremony, and I walked home alone. But the longer he takes, the more certain I am that something's happened.

When he finally appears in the far field, he's moving quickly, head down.

I tuck the Foxtail book beneath my pillow and listen as Theo enters the house, then climbs the stairs two at a time, appearing in our bedroom doorway. "Is Bee back yet?" he asks quickly.

I shake my head.

"She was at Levi's when I left."

"Why was she there?"

He crosses the room and extends his hand out to me, ignoring the question. "I found this."

I can't tell what it is in the dark of the bedroom, but when he holds it up to the window, a silver chain unravels from his fingertips, shivering like water in moonlight. He places the chain in my palm, letting me hold it, letting me observe it closer. Letting me *have* it. As if it's mine to keep. This isn't like the notebook—which he's never let me touch.

At the end of the chain are several charms. Tiny little books.

"There are four of them," he says.

I touch each one with my fingertip, finding the numbers etched into the silver covers: *one, two . . . four, five.* The number *three* is missing.

My lungs blow out a quick breath, and I reach into my pocket, pulling out the tiny charm I found in the garden buried beneath the rosebush, and I place it beside the others. The clasp is broken, but I'm able to bend the soft metal and clamp the ring around the chain, placing it back with the others where it belongs. "Where did you find it?" I ask.

His expression is tight, and I can't tell if he's looking at me, or at the necklace in my hand. "In Levi's house."

"Where in his house?" I press.

"The fireplace. He was trying to burn it."

I squeeze the chain in my palm. "Why would he do that?"

My husband's eyes flick to the window like he's heard something, but then his gaze falls back on me. "I don't know. But Maggie St. James was here and Levi lied about it. They were both here—Travis and Maggie—and he knew."

"Levi knew about Travis?"

Theo slides his hand into his pants pocket and pulls something out. A piece of paper. "I found this with the necklace. He was trying to burn them both."

I take it from him.

Things have changed.

Levi asked me to stay in Pastoral, he thinks my ability to see the past in the things I touch will help the community.

But I refused his offer. I told him I would leave as soon as the snow thaws.

He said it wasn't safe beyond the border, that I couldn't leave. He tried to stop me . . . and I pushed him. We struggled, breaking one of the old windows—a piece of the glass cut my scalp above my ear.

Maggie stitched me up, but a desperation is building inside me. I have to get out of these woods. I need to hide my notebook and these pages—evidence that I was here. Maybe Ben will come looking for me, or the St. Jameses. But I doubt it. They likely think I've abandoned the case. I haven't been reliable enough for anyone to worry if I don't return.

And there's something else. Things are more complicated with Maggie now. I can't just leave her behind . . . I care about her in a way I never should have allowed myself to.

We will leave together, or not at all.

Theo walks to the window and peers out at the evening light.

"Levi knew they were here?" I ask, breathless.

Theo nods. "He knows a lot more than he's saying."

A headache forms quick and blunt behind my eyes, and I walk to my husband at the window, staring out at the meadow, each of us looking for answers in the tall summer grass made pale and sorrowful by the drowsy moonlight.

"Was he talking about the window in the sunroom?" I ask. "It was broken by a tree branch during that storm two winters ago, not by a fight."

Theo's face has gone cold, muted, like he's not sure of anything anymore. "We thought it was a storm when we found the broken window the next morning, but maybe we were wrong."

"And we just slept through it? Two men fighting, breaking a window?"

"Maybe we didn't hear it over the storm."

I shake my head, but keep my eyes out at the distance, beyond the meadow grass, to the line of border trees. "It doesn't make sense. If two outsiders came to Pastoral, why would Levi try to hide it? Why keep it a secret? Even if they were sick, he would perform the ritual like he did with Ash and Turk." It feels as if we're tiptoeing toward the truth, but not moving fast enough, and it's quickly slipping away.

"I don't know," Theo answers. "But Levi's been lying about all of it."

"We need to confront him—ask him about Travis, about the broken window, ask if he was here in our house that night."

Theo scrapes a hand across the nape of his neck. "No," he says flatly. "Levi tried to destroy the necklace and the page; he doesn't want us to know Maggie and Travis were here. He's trying to hide whatever happened to them." For the briefest moment, my husband looks scared, frightened in a way I've never seen in him before. "Maybe none of this is what we think it is."

"Then what is it?" I ask, knowing my husband doesn't have the answer. But wanting him to tell me something all the same, anything that will slow the desperate rattle of my heart.

Perhaps just like Eloise and the fox, we have feared the wrong thing—when we should have feared what's right here, within our own borders, within our own walls. The beast is already inside the castle, tearing people apart, yet we stare into the woods waiting for it to appear.

Something bad happened here.

Something that screams inside me, begging me to *see*.

FOXES AND MUSEUMS

Excerpt from Book One in the Eloise and the Foxtail series

Power felt good to Eloise.

It surged through her veins like electricity down a tree trunk during a lightning storm. She took to it quickly, as if she was meant for darkness, for the vile thoughts that now rattled through her.

The fox who she had followed into the woods now feared her—*it knew what she was*. What she had become. Yet, it had no choice but to obey her words, to trail her through the trees, to hunt for rabbits when she was hungry, to sleep beside her and keep her warm when she was cold and tired. For Eloise would never return to her strawberry-pink room in her house at the edge of the forest.

Eloise would become a missing child, believed to have vanished straight from her bed while she slept one cool, autumn night—taken or wandered off, her parents would never know for sure. Flyers posted to streetlamps and search dogs sent into the forest would never recover the missing girl.

Eloise belonged to the woods now.

She was a shadow. She was the cruel, howling thing that could be heard during a full moon. She was the monster who crept into other children's dreams.

But this is how monsters are made: from innocent things.

BEE

The scent of rot is everywhere. In my nostrils, behind my ears.

I wake, knees to chin, my face pressed into the cold dirt, my dress torn at the hemline—threads snagged on a rock a few feet away. But I don't know how I got here.

I was in Levi's bed, his hands were in my hair, fingers tracing long, lazy lines along my sun-freckled flesh. But now I'm lying against the hard ground . . . a knife in my left hand.

The smooth wood handle is held tightly beneath my gripped fingers, and when I open my palm, the muscles of my hand ache, cramping down the center to my thumb. I let the knife fall to the dirt and I push myself up, ears ringing, the sounds around me swimming in and out of focus.

I can hear the creek some distance away, and the cold wind blowing through the trees at my back.

And I know: I'm beyond the boundary.

I don't remember leaving Levi's house, slinking down the hall away from his bedroom before his wife returned. I don't remember wandering into the trees, carrying a knife. *Why do I have a knife?*

My mind feels frayed, little webs of pain peeling away from my bones, memories I can't seem to pluck from the dark. I push myself up, sitting with legs tucked beneath me, and brush away the dead leaves sticking to my skin. I must have stumbled through the woods, the hem of my skirt catching on thorns and jagged rocks until I collapsed in the dirt and fell into a strange sort of sleep.

I touch my cheeks and the hollows of my eyes, feeling separate from my own skin—like I'm clawing my way back from my dreams.

This isn't the first time I've slept outside the valley, past the border of Pastoral, but it's the first time I have no memory of how I got here. These last few nights, I have stepped over the creek and into the sacred trees—I have allowed myself to be judged, appraised—I have touched the wounded elms and welcomed illness into my flesh, but it never came.

Something skitters away to my right, but it's only a night creature—voles and bats and ground mice who seek out the scraps left behind by the more discerning daylight animals. I reach my hand across the ground and find the knife, the edge still sharp, but caked in mud. I grip it tightly and push myself to standing, holding the blade at my side.

Why do I have a knife? Why do I have a knife?

I press a palm to my left eye, to stop the humming. Did I hurt someone with this knife? *Levi?*

But there is no scent of blood on the blade—that awful metallic smell that burns the nose. The knife smells only of mud and earth and wood. The bitter sweetness of fresh sap. When I woke, I was gripping it tightly, as if I had wielded it for protection. For some unknown purpose.

My legs tremor, and I reach out for a tree to steady myself. My palm meets with the rough, scabbed bark of an evergreen, the scent of its needles fragrant and rich in the midnight air. And then my fingers feel it: the sap spilling down the trunk, the wet, honey-like texture. Sticky like glue. My hand follows the trail of sap, until my fingers fall inward, into the soft white center of the tree—where it's broken open. I can smell it, the woolly fragrance of freshly split wood, that soft green scent.

The tree is sick. Bark peeled back, trying to rid itself of the pox.

My fingers slide along the edge of the wound, feeling its shape, the sharp serrated curve about three feet long, top to bottom. It's only recently split open—the wood still fresh and tender inside.

The whole forest is infected.

I turn away from the sick tree and move swiftly through the dark woods, over the creek, and back into the safety of Pastoral. Fear boils in my gut, fear for something I can't quite explain—not just the pox, but another thing. Yet, the knife in my hand comforts me, the balanced weight of it, and I pick my way back to the path. Back to the farmhouse.

The buzzing in my ears—behind my eyes—growing louder.

THEO

My wife has fallen asleep, her hand still clutching the necklace I found in Levi's fireplace. But I sit awake at the edge of our bed, my mind ratcheting clumsily over thoughts that keep doubling back on themselves. A machine that repeats the same motion, stuck in a maddening loop.

How did Levi get Maggie's necklace? And Travis's last notebook page? Why was he trying to burn them, melt them down to nothing?

When I showed him the photo of Maggie, why did he lie? Why did he say he didn't know her?

What did he do?

Calla exhales softly, her breath stirring a strand of her dark hair. And then I see it: something beneath her head, beneath the pillow—the sharp corner obvious against the soft edges of the white linen sheets. Quietly, gently, I pull the thing loose from beneath her pillow.

Calla stirs once, her foot kicking at the blankets, sending the green patchwork quilt to the floor. But she doesn't wake.

It's the book: the *Foxtail* book written by Maggie St. James. My wife has kept it hidden from me, as if she feared what I might read inside. This book belongs to her, while the notebook I found in the sunroom belongs to me. We each have our own secrets that we covet and keep close, so the other won't see—but what do we fear they might reveal? What unknown words live inside?

I stand up from the bed, the *Foxtail* book in my hand.

It's heavy, a book you don't simply open and read before sleep—a chapter here or there. You must commit to it. A book like this demands something of its reader.

And holding it now, I wonder what Calla discovered inside.

I move toward the open door, nervous that Calla might wake and catch me with her precious book, when something passes by out in the hall. At first, I think it might be Bee—sneaking through the house, tiptoeing into her room to change her clothes, to get something to eat, before retreating back out into the woods where she's been spending her nights. But when I walk to the doorway and step into the hall, I see the flash of hair—of a woman I don't know—hurrying down the stairs.

It's not Bee.

But the woman isn't entirely unfamiliar either.

I don't call out to her, instead I move quietly down the stairs and through the house after her, the *Foxtail* book tucked under my arm. She opens the screen door and ducks outside, dashing up through the meadow beneath a clear, night sky. I stop on the back porch and watch her, her blond hair sliding across her shoulder blades, her gait long and deliberate, pale arms moving with the ease of a deer knowing its path through the tall grass. She's humming a tune, words slipping gently from her lips.

I blink and refocus, I hold the book tight against my side—she isn't a ghost, a specter set loose from the old farmhouse. This is something else: an *afterimage. A word that drips through my mind, unmistakable.*

This is a moment from the past.

The soft-blond hue of her hair reflects the moonlight, but it's not quite how it was in the photograph. Her hair has grown out several inches, and at the roots, I can see the dark brown shade of her natural color.

Maggie St. James.

Maggie.

She reaches the pond, the lemon trees shivering as she approaches, and a man is waiting for her. She isn't alone. He pulls her to him and they kiss, embracing beneath the half-domed moonlight, before they begin shedding their thin summer clothes and wade out into the pond, arms tangled around one another.

Travis Wren came to Pastoral and he found Maggie St. James.

He found her, and he also fell in love.

My hands shake at my sides and I drop the book onto the porch at my feet. My eyes blur over and I bend to retrieve the book, my head pounding suddenly, a feeling like I might be sick. When I stand back up, the visage of Maggie and Travis in the pond, are gone. Not even a ripple remains across the surface of the water.

My left temple begins to ache just above my ear—an old, distant pain. The memory of it just out of reach—like so many things.

I struggle to take a breath. *Something happened here.* Maggie and Travis lived within the walls of this old house. Not ghosts. Not phantoms passing through the hall.

Maggie and Travis are still alive.

Maggie and Travis never left.

CALLA

The house is hauntingly quiet.

My husband is gone from the bed and the *Foxtail* book is gone from beneath my pillow.

It's late—middle of the night late—saturated with the kind of stillness that comes when even the midnight creatures stop their scurrying beneath floorboards and night owls have eaten their share of field mice and have returned to their roosts to await the dawn.

I walk to the mirror over the dresser. In my hand is the necklace, all five charms suspended from the end. I know I shouldn't, but I unclasp the hook and place the delicate chain around my neck, securing it there. My reflection in the mirror feels instantly like someone else: dead eyes staring back, a woman who isn't in the right skin. My fingers trail across the chain, observing the way it lays over my collarbone, a comfortable weight.

I am wearing a necklace that belonged to a woman who has vanished.

I leave the room and my feet carry me down the stairs—feeling as if the necklace is mine now, right where it belongs.

Nothing stirs in the house—not even the walls creak, the timbers holding their breath—but I move down the back hall to the sunroom, feeling the same curiosity that buzzed through me the last time I entered the room. But this time, I find the door ajar, and my husband sitting at the end of the bare mattress.

He's holding the *Foxtail* book, and his eyes lift.

"Calla?" he says, like he is trying to shake away a bad dream, like he wants to be sure of my name. Of who I am.

"Yes," I say, flat and strange.

THEO

"Why are you in here?" Calla asks, touching the doorframe, the entryway into a room she's rarely stepped foot into.

I stare at her long dark hair, ribbons of auburn that sometimes reflect hues of cinnamon in the midday sun. She has always been a puzzle to me, pieces scattered that don't quite fit. I didn't understand it until now.

The pieces were never hers to begin with—they belonged to someone else.

When I don't answer her, she drops her hand from the door. "You shouldn't have taken that," she says, nodding to the *Foxtail* book in my hands. *Her book.*

Hers.

How do I explain what I now understand—what I remember—to this woman I also love, who I don't want to hurt?

Calla walks across the room and plucks the book from my hand. She holds it to her chest, as if it contains all her secrets—and maybe it does. Her gaze passes over me, surveying me, disappointment rimming her blue, sapphire eyes.

What does she remember?

But she swivels around and crosses to the door, disappearing out into the hall.

My mind is a storm—flickers of light and then great swathes of dark. It takes me a moment to react, to go after her, and when I find her again she's in the kitchen, the book sitting harmlessly on the kitchen counter. She stands at the sink, the faucet turned on, water rushing through her hands, then she rubs her palms over the back of her neck to cool her skin.

The house is warm, but it's always this way in summer—left to the mercy of the seasons—and we can only hope for a breeze to pass through the open windows to sedate our overheated flesh. I watch Calla and wonder: How many times has she stood at the sink, hands working the bar of lavender soap, rinsing dishes and sturdy glasses, eyes cast out the window to the meadow, longing for something she's never spoken aloud, not even to herself? Perhaps not as many times as she thinks. As many as I once thought.

I fight the words in my throat, the ache expanding in my chest, becoming a fist-tight pain.

She needs to know the truth: a truth that will capsize everything she thought she knew, turn it wrong side out.

The man I am, standing in our kitchen, is not real. And neither is she.

"Calla?" I say, but she won't look at me. She pivots to a drawer and retrieves two spoons. "What are you doing?"

"We're awake now, might as well make breakfast." She stands on tiptoes and pulls down the jar of dry oats from the upper cupboard. She begins to hum a tune—softly at first under her breath—while she pours the oats into a bowl. It's a melody I now recognize, the lullaby I heard Maggie humming last night when she left the house and went to the pond. It's the one Calla said she didn't know when I asked her about it on our walk to the gathering. She lied.

"You do know the lullaby," I say to her.

She stops humming but keeps her eyes on the two bowls on the counter in front of her. "It's just something I remember from when I was a kid."

I move closer to her. "That's not true," I say. She still won't look at me, but her hands fall flat against the kitchen counter, pale white palms pressed into the wood, like she's bracing herself. "It's not from your childhood," I tell her.

Her eyes are slow, shifting one millimeter at a time as they inch higher to click on mine. "What?" she asks. The word sounds mechanical, squeezed out through clenched teeth.

And then I see it. "You're wearing the necklace?" I ask. It lays flat against her chest, the tiny books pressed together. Her hand reaches up to grasp it, but her mouth is still, no words falling out.

Slowly, I pick up the *Foxtail* book from the counter and Calla's eyes watch me, shivering. I think she might cross the space between us and yank the book from my hands again, but she only stares—a marionette doll whose arms and legs have gone slack, but her glass eyes still blink in slow, eerily lidded motions.

"Here," I say, flipping through the pages of the book. I'm searching for the nursery rhyme, and it takes me longer to find than I think it will—I haven't looked at the book in years, *another lifetime ago*—and it takes a while for my memory to locate it. But when I do, I slap my palm to the page and walk to my wife's side, turning the book for her to see. "You've been humming that lullaby because you wrote it."

She peers forward at the page, her eyes no longer clicking open and closed—they have begun to water—and I don't know if she's crying or if she's focused so closely on the book that she's started to peer into the past.

I flip back through the pages again, all the way to the front, where the name of Maggie St. James, the author, is stamped onto the title page. "You know the lullaby," I say again. "Because you wrote this book, Calla."

She breathes, swallows, but her eyes refuse to blink.

I drop the book onto the counter and pull out the damaged photo of Maggie St. James from my back pocket. Even now, as I stare down at it, I'm having a hard time rectifying it: the distorted photo of the half-visible woman staring up toward the camera, with the woman standing before me in the kitchen. My mind still doesn't want to believe, to push the two images together.

Calla runs her fingers over the photograph, moving slowly, as though she could feel the features of the woman's face, and when her eyes lift, there is fear pooling in them. Her lips begin to tremor.

I'm about to reach forward and pull my *wife* to me, when her mouth dips open. "I know," she says, eyes skipping back and forth between mine. "I remember it. I—I remembered the story of Eloise before I even read the book. I remembered every word of it."

I don't nod; I don't move. I just stare at her, wanting to touch her, absorb each word into my skin so it won't be true—take away the past that's been buried inside each of us, scrub it away and make us forget. But I can't; I don't know how. The truth has found us, and now it stabs at the backs of our necks, refusing to be ignored.

"I'm not your wife," she says, and the wetness at her eyelids spills down her cheeks. "Not really." I can see it in her face—the memories clotting together, breaking across her skin, cutting her open. It hurts her to say it aloud. "I'm scared," she says, tears falling in trails down her cheeks, suspended on her chin, and finally I pull her to me, bracing a hand against her tiny skull, fingers woven through her dark hair. *Dark hair that used to be dyed a stark shade of blond.*

She lifts her head, her heartbeat thundering wildly against my chest, and she winces before she speaks, like she's afraid to hear herself say the words aloud.

"I'm Maggie St. James."

CALLA

I twirl my fingers around the tiny books hanging from the necklace, counting them out of habit. *Habit: a thing I've done before.*

A thing Maggie St. James used to do, back before I came into these woods, before I forgot.

My fingers fall away from the necklace, and I hold a hand over my eyes, the morning sun creeping up over the evergreens, a semidarkness that reminds me of long winters when the sun never fully breaks through the clouds, and the sky remains stuck in a strange gray permanence.

"Maybe it's the pox," I say, glancing to Theo—my husband—a man who once had another name: *Travis Wren*. But something happened to us— our minds stripped clean and replaced with something else, memories that weren't quite ours. We're standing on the back porch, two drowsy outlines beneath the pale sky. I needed to free myself from the walls of the farmhouse, I needed cool air against my skin and the quiet rustle of early dawn in my ears. "Maybe it makes us forget," I say. "Maybe we're sick; maybe we've been sick this whole time. Years."

Theo has been going down the road, beyond our valley, and isn't it possible he brought the pox back with him? The *rot* seeping into our brains, turning it to muck, making us forget.

"I don't think we're sick, not after so long. We'd be dead by now." Theo's jaw slides back and forth, working over something, a slippery thought he can't quite keep hold of.

"I think I buried the book in the garden," I admit. "And the charm." Again, I want to touch the necklace, coil my fingers around it, be soothed by the shape and structure of it. But I resist. It feels unnatural, the parallels of who I used to be and who I am now, the boundary lines too vague to sort through.

Theo shakes his head, eyes wavering against the approaching sun. "Why?" he asks. "Why would you bury them?"

"I was afraid, I think." I scratch a finger along the inside of my wrist, anything to occupy my hands, to keep them from touching the necklace. "I hid them so no one else but me would find them."

Remember Maggie, the inscription said. My mind skips back, like a stone across the pond, memories that feel mirrored, prism-like, and not quite solid. *I* wrote the note inside the *Foxtail* book—but it wasn't a message meant for someone else, to remind them that Maggie had been here, the message was meant for me. I buried the book in the garden because I knew only I would find it. It was just deep enough, just shallow enough, that eventually, while pulling up a clot of weeds, I would easily unearth it.

I wanted the book and the charm to be found—by me. *Remember Maggie*, I wrote. I was telling myself not to forget: who I was, who I had been.

"Why did this happen to us?" I turn to face my husband, and his chin is tilted to the sky—the horizon becoming a murky dark hue, a purple bruise not yet bloomed. And in his eyes, I see the same uncertainty I feel in my own chest.

Memories of two different pasts: A childhood spent in Pastoral coils together with memories outside of this place. If I close my eyes and pinch them tight enough, I can feel the foamy sea around my ankles, my shins, and the brine of the salt air in my throat. I can taste the ocean, a thing I shouldn't know, a memory I shouldn't have.

A tree of anxiety grows inside me, stabbing me with its limbs. "You're Travis Wren," I say plainly, to hear myself say it aloud, the name knotting together in my stomach.

"Yes," he answers, flat and cool.

"How much do you remember from before?"

"A little now."

"You came to Pastoral to find me?" I ask.

He nods.

"Why?"

His face goes tight, trying to pluck a moment from his past—but the memories collide and break apart as soon we try to focus on them, just out of reach, like an insect that keeps skittering away.

"You were missing for five years," he says, shaking his head, like he's unsure of his own words.

Five years. Five years gone. I try to insert that number into my mind, a piece that should slide into place, clicking perfectly, but it only wobbles around in my skull, never settling, never finding its place among the other memories that don't fit.

"Your parents hired me," he adds.

"My parents?" I try to draw them forward in my mind, but there's nothing there.

"I met them, in their home. Your childhood home."

I turn now, my body facing his. "Where was it?"

The sunrise shivers through the trees; a bird begins to chirp. Theo frowns. "I'm not sure. I'm sorry, I wish I could remember."

I nod, understanding, and try to think of a home beyond Pastoral, a bedroom where I grew up. A place different from this. I see a doll with perfect glass eyes placed beside a blue ballerina jewelry box that used to play a tune when you opened the lid, but had long ago sputtered and died. And then the flash is ripped away just as quickly, gone.

I scan my husband's eyes, the cool river of them. "Why you?" I ask. "Why did they hire you? Were you a detective?"

A strange tension pulls along his forehead, and for a half-second I barely recognize him—he becomes the man he used to be. He is Travis Wren. "No," he answers. "But I could find missing people."

"How?"

The sky above us brightens, the sun inching above the trees, yet a mantle of rain clouds is already crowding out the blue, sinking down from the north. "I don't know. I saw people . . . could see what happened to them."

"What do you mean?"

"I'm not sure. Maybe that's not right." Even when he tries to draw the moment forward, it sputters away. "But I had your charm with me," he says. "Number three. You dropped it beside the road."

"What road?" I know I'm pushing him, forcing him to strain into the backwoods of his mind, but some part of me is afraid this won't last, this glimpse of the truth, of memories we shouldn't have. If we do have the pox—if we're sick and the illness has stolen parts of our mind—this moment of clarity might not last. By midday, it might vanish all over again: I will be Calla and he will be Theo, and the necklace and the *Foxtail* book will only be clues to a mystery we'll never unravel.

"A main road, a paved road. There was an old, collapsed barn there too. And a boy broke his arm jumping off the roof of a house, but it burned down a long time ago."

"How do you know that?" I ask, squinting at him. "About the boy breaking his arm?"

He looks at me but doesn't answer, because he doesn't know—he doesn't understand his own memories. And it makes me question if what he recalls is real, if we can even trust our own thoughts.

"I didn't mean to get lost," I say finally, fighting the tears that begin to press at my eyelids. I remember walking through the trees, sleeping in a bed in a farmhouse that wasn't mine, but all too quickly felt familiar.

Why did I come here? Why did I leave my life and go in search of Pastoral? This is a black spot in my mind I still can't pinpoint.

Theo looks south, in the direction of the gate and the guard hut. "We both forgot who we were." His voice sounds clear now, like this is a truth he's sure of: We both used to be someone else. But we left clues for ourselves—buried in the garden, tucked beneath the mattress in the sunroom—whatever we had left, whatever would help us remember.

I can feel the hard dirt under my hands when I dug a hole beneath the wild rosebush long ago, my eyes glancing to the meadow, panic in my throat. I placed the *Foxtail* book in first, touching the pages gently with my fingertips, worried the insects might begin to eat at the corners, or that the rain would soak into the soil and ruin the paper. But I didn't want to bury it too deeply and risk never finding it again. I set the tiny charm on top, near the surface, like a gravestone: a hint that more things were buried beneath.

After tamping down the soil, I closed my eyes and whispered my name, my real name: *Maggie St. James.* I said it three more times, imprinting it onto the curved lobes of my skull, my bones—I knew I was starting to forget. I went inside and stood in the bathroom, water running in the sink, scraping my fingertips through my wet hair. It was still blonde then, but it was beginning to grow out, just past my shoulders, and I was fighting to remember something—searching my mind for the way back through the woods. I was struggling to keep hold of who I used to be. I muttered aloud, *Don't forget.*

It's one of the last things I recall from before.

Before the wall of black swept over my mind like a storm, and replaced my old memories with new ones. Memories of a childhood in Pastoral, of cool autumns wading in the stream, of Bee beside me as a little girl, laughing as she chucked stones from the creek up onto the soft, sandy bank. She was searching for skipping rocks, smooth flat stones that we could take to the pond and see who could skip them the farthest. But now, when I search for this moment in time, I only recall Bee telling me this story, of something she used to do—alone. I was never there beside her at the creek shore, I only imagined it: a childhood spent with Bee. And now, I can't find any true memories of Pastoral when I was young. It was a childhood that never really existed.

My mind distorted truth with fiction, it created a messy, disjointed fairy tale that is hard to unravel.

"Do you think there are others?" I ask. "Do you think everyone in Pastoral has forgotten who they used to be?"

Theo is quiet for some time, then says, "No, not everyone."

"How can you be sure?"

"I'm not. It's just a feeling."

I let myself touch the necklace at last, be soothed by the metal edges of each of the five books. I never intended to lose myself in Pastoral, I never intended to stay. "Then why us?" I ask.

Theo touches my hand, weaving his fingertips through mine. Still, he doesn't answer.

"Say something," I plead. "What do you think this is?"

His hand fidgets in mine, loosening his grip then tightening again. "I think we've been believing a lie for too long." He pulls me into his arms, and I press my cheek into his shoulder, tears streaming down my chin, soaking into his cotton shirt. The sun lifts fully above the tree line, and I want to believe that he is really my husband, that we grew up in these woods. I want to believe that I really love him—that it's not merely a trick of my mistaken, amnesic heart.

But he won't tell me what he's thinking, and maybe I don't want to hear: I want to pretend a little longer that everything is just as it always was. Plain and featureless and good.

My husband is my husband.

My life is my own.

But the longer we stand here, a new working of fear wedges itself between us. And I know: He's becoming someone else. He is not Theo at all; he's Travis Wren. A man who came looking for me, who suffered the same fate as I did.

And now, with the thud of his heartbeat against my ear, I know he's thinking the same thing: We can't stay here.

This life is a lie.

FOXES AND MUSEUMS

Excerpt from Book One in the Eloise and the Foxtail series

Eloise spent an uncounted number of days and nights within the woods.

Weeks passed and then years.

The trees wove themselves into her heart, and soon she became just as hard and rough as bark.

It wasn't long before she began to forget her old life, her home at the edge of the woods, the soft feel of her paisley-printed sheets. Her mother's kiss against her cheek before bed.

She was a forest thing now. And even her name faded in her mind, became a smudge she barely recalled.

But when you become familiar with the dark, with slithering, rotting things, you forget the feeling of sunlight. You forget what you should miss.

And then there's no going back.

CALLA

Bee returns.

I'm standing on the back porch—trying to set right the patch-work of thoughts coming unstitched inside my head, trying to figure out how to leave Pastoral, but the ringing in my ears is too loud, my skin too tight against my bones—when I see her moving down the meadow. Her hair is unbraided, spilling over her shoulders, across her face, and she reminds me of a song, turning round and round on her record player.

When she gets closer, I can tell something's wrong; a cold, awful knot of hate and fury turning her features in on themselves.

I say her name. "Bee?" And just the word against my lips sends a sharp, uncertain pain down into my gut. *My sister is not my sister at all.* She stops at the bottom of the porch steps, mute, and she's hiding something in her hand. "What happened?" I ask.

The rims of her eyes are bloodshot; her nostrils swell like she might be sick—a wave of discomfort blazing across her face. She shakes her head, mouth unmoving, and I see that her bare feet are thick with mud, and when her head lifts, it's as if she can see me—her pupils expanding.

I swear she's looking right at me.

"It was me," she says, finally turning her hand and revealing a knife clutched tightly in her palm, the blade dulled, smudged with dirt.

"What was you?"

"I carved the border trees."

I shake my head at her. "What are you talking about?"

"I woke up in the woods . . . and I had this knife. I don't know where it came from, but I—" Her voice warbles, a bird losing its pitch. "I don't remember doing it. But I can feel the memory in my hands, cutting into the wood."

"I don't understand." My own voice cracks. "The trees are sick; it's the illness that splits them open."

"No," Bee says, lowering her arm to her side but still clutching the knife, fingers trembling. "It's me. It's always been me."

"You're tired," I tell her, because there is fear in her eyes, and I try reaching out for her, but she senses the movement and flinches back, stepping away from me, farther from the porch.

"I'm not tired," she snaps, her voice a thin wire pulled taut, vowels that want to break against the tongue. "I've been asleep for years." She presses a palm to her right eye and winces. "Something's wrong with me. My head feels muddy."

I take another step closer to her, and I wonder . . . just like Theo and me, have her memories been smudged out? A kaleidoscope of images crushed together, now splintering like old wood.

"There's nothing wrong with you," I tell her, watching as tears pool against her eyelids. "Give me the knife, Bee." My own head throbs, too, many parallels crushing together at once: *Bee is not my sister. None of this is what it should be.*

Her chin tilts to one side, like she's considering the request, but then she says, "I can't. I need it."

"Please." I move softly toward her, trying not to make a sound. "You're right, our memories aren't what we thought they were."

There is a vagueness in her eyes, a grinding of her jaw. "I can't stay here," she mutters, turning her head toward the meadow and the forest beyond, as if it were awaiting her return, silently calling her back. She takes another step away from me, into the grass.

"I know," I say, mirroring her movements. I could tell her the truth: that I am not her sister, and she is not mine. But the wildness in her gaze makes me think I shouldn't, not like this. Instead, I reach forward quickly and grab for her arm, trying to snatch the knife away from her.

But she shrieks, jerking away from my touch, and when she tries to spin around, twisting out from beneath my grip, the knife in her hand swings forward and the blade slides delicately across my forearm. Warm blood beads instantly to the surface.

I release her arm and press my other hand to the wound—the cut is deep, a swift peeling open of flesh, like butter, easily separated—and the bright red soaks between my fingers, dripping onto the dirt at my feet.

Bee staggers backward, her mouth agape. She must know what she's done because she touches the end of the blade then presses her fingers together, feeling the sticky blood.

The shock tears across her face. Eyes wide.

"It's okay," I mutter to her. "You didn't mean to."

She shakes her head, repetitive and quick, staring through the darkness of her unseeing eyes—her pupils resuming their blankness, their voided focus. This single violent act has unmoored her.

"Bee," I say, reaching out for her with my good arm, and this time she doesn't flinch away; her body has gone slack. But she keeps the knife held tightly at her side, refusing to give it up. "I have to tell you something," I say. "I have to tell you the truth."

THEO

We had thought a man was living in the decaying sunroom, a stranger sneaking in and out of the house at night, unseen.

But that stranger was me.

And I wasn't there in secret.

Broken bursts of memory surface inside me: driving into these mountains, sleeping in the drafty sunroom while snow blew down from the sky. But when I discovered that Calla was Maggie St. James, I knew we had to leave. A storm thrashed against the walls of the farmhouse, and Levi was there, in the sunroom, telling me I couldn't go. I remember the air leaving my lungs as we fought, the single-pane window shattering, and the glass slicing open the flesh above my left ear. I can still see the shock in Levi's eyes—he hadn't intended for it to go that far.

I touch it now, feeling the tender spot just above my ear that has nagged at me, ached late at night, but I couldn't seem to recall the injury that caused it.

That same night, Calla stitched my skin back together at the kitchen table. Something had changed between us in the month I had spent in the sunroom, in the farmhouse—I was falling in love with her. I kissed her for the first time that night, and the following morning when I woke in her bed—the sun streaking through the curtains—I told her we had to leave once the snow thawed. And she agreed.

I must have known something was going to happen—maybe I felt my memories slipping away—so I hid the notebook pages inside the house, the last reminder of who I used to be before a kind of madness took hold. But the last page—the third one—I kept in my pocket for several days, unsure where to place it so it wouldn't be found, except by me.

It's one of the last memories I have of *before*.

Now the man I used to be begins coming back into focus like a tide rising and falling against the shore of my mind. I stand in the kitchen, holding the photo of Maggie, trying to see my wife in the distorted image, in the soft blue eye staring up at me, when the screen door bangs open.

Calla pushes inside, her face pale, one hand pressed to her forearm. "She didn't mean to," she says, blood dripping steadily to the floor. Behind her, moving like a frightened animal, is Bee, a knife held at her side.

I make Calla sit at the dining table, and I peel back her hand, revealing a deep cut, while Bee crosses to the stairs and her footsteps can be heard climbing up to the second floor, and then the sound of the bathroom door shutting.

"It was an accident," Calla says, pinching her eyes closed.

The knife has gone through several layers of flesh, and I grab one of the kitchen towels, pressing it to the wound. "I'll go get Faye," I say. "You'll need stitches."

But Calla shakes her head. "No."

And I understand: She wants this to stay between us. If Faye knows, then so will others within the community, and they will want to know what happened, why Bee cut her own *sister*. There will be questions and whispers, and right now, we can't have either.

So I blot away the blood, then using strips of fabric, I begin to wrap Calla's wound. "Why does she have a knife?" I ask, keeping my voice low so Bee won't hear.

Calla glances down at her forearm, where I tie the fabric tight at the ends. She cringes then looks away. "She says she's been carving the trees—that she's always done it. She says it's not the pox splitting them open, it's her."

My eyes flash to the back door, the forest beyond. "Why would she do that?"

"I don't know. It doesn't make sense."

I think of the sickness waiting inside the trees at our border, until they finally peel open and breathe one last sigh—the pox turning the forest air stale with infection. But why would Bee carve the trees? What reason would she have?

My mind strays back to Levi, of the necklace and the notebook page he was trying to burn inside his fireplace. He wanted to make it vanish—just like Maggie. He was trying to make it all go away.

But guiltless people don't burn things.

"Maybe we don't belong here," Calla says, clearing her throat. "We have whole lives we left behind out there."

I try to remember the things waiting for me on the outside. But I only see the truck and an endless road. Surely there is more: family and friends I just can't quite recall.

"I think we have to leave Pastoral," she says finally. "Before we forget again."

Doubt crisscrosses my thoughts, but I nod at her, because I know she's right: These aren't our lives. The real us is waiting somewhere beyond these forest walls, our memories and our past waiting for us.

"Okay," I say.

BEE

I sink into the bathtub, and my skin pricks from the lukewarm water like little beestings.

I need to wash myself clean: The creases of my skin are caked with soil and prairie grass and tiny wildflowers pressed flat; they form a new landscape of my body. A restlessness is building inside me, a bewildering need I wish I could scrub away, but pain like this doesn't wash off. I need something stronger. I need nails and wire. I need a knife—like the one resting on the bathroom counter beside the sink.

I hold my breath and sink below the waterline, remembering the feel of the cold creek when I bathed in its shallows, leaves floating past me, tickling my shoulders and elbows like delicate fingers. I bring my eyes, my mouth, my chin, back above the waterline, listening to the clicking and snapping of locusts through the open bathroom window, sawing between my thoughts, dividing me into sections.

Perhaps I am two people, one waking and one sleepwalking.

Perhaps I am capable of monstrous things.

I've been carving marks into the border trees—*for how long? Years?* But why do I do it?

I think of the cells growing inside me, duplicating themselves, amassing into something larger. A body formed of my body. A baby who wants to be born, stubborn, resilient—like her father—a baby who doesn't know what I really am.

I touch my bare stomach, the flesh marred by goose bumps, when a soft tap comes at the bathroom door, and then Calla's voice on the other side, "Bee, can I come in?"

I draw my knees to my chest, hair dripping, neck pressed to the back of the tub. "Okay," I answer.

I hear the creak of the door opening, and then my sister's careful steps as she slips just inside the room and closes the door behind her.

"I'm sorry I cut you," I say. My voice sounds broken, nervous, like I haven't used it in some time.

"It was an accident." She clears her throat, and I imagine her gazing out through the narrow window, the soft white curtain churning gently in the wind. Or maybe she's looking at the knife, resting beside the sink. There is a long pause, and I wonder if she's forgotten what she wanted to say. I hear her hands press together. "I'm not who you think I am," she says at last, and the words are not what I expected to leave her lips. "Theo and I, neither of us, are who you think we are."

I lift my head from the edge of the tub and sit up straighter.

"Theo came to Pastoral two winters ago; it was his truck he found down the road, and I—" Her voice breaks off, and suddenly I don't want her to continue; I don't want to hear what she's going to say next. I have the feeling it's going to break me open, sever me into more halves. "I used to live on the outside," she says, each word a tiptoe, a creeping dance around the truth of what she's getting at. "My name was Maggie St. James. I was a writer, but then I came here. It was many years ago, five . . . no, seven years now, I can't really remember, but I know—" The bathwater has gone cold, and I don't want to be in this room, I don't want to hear the rest. "Bee, I'm not . . ."

I know what she's going to say, because somewhere in the faltering cracks of my mind, I think I've always known. I feel it in the cold water pressed against my skin, the bitter sharp line of truth and lies has been threatening to split me apart for too long—a calloused wound I've been rubbing over and over again, trying to peel it open, to see what's beneath, but also afraid it would hurt too badly. A knowing that something isn't right in this house, that at times, Calla and Theo have felt like strangers. And yet, also two people I couldn't possibly live without.

Calla is not my sister.

And I'm not hers.

But I don't want to hear her say it, because I remember summers with her when we were kids, I remember when our parents died and she ran out to the pond and I sat alone in the house, crying silently by myself.

Or maybe I cried alone, because she wasn't out at the pond, because she wasn't there at all. Because they weren't her parents and I had no sister and I was always alone. I press the heels of my palms to my eyes—my mind a mess of too much noise.

Before she can say the words aloud, I ask, "Why do we remember things that didn't happen?"

Her breathing is low, strange. "I don't know, but I do know Levi has lied to us, and we can't stay here. Not anymore."

I turn my head away, toward the window, listening for the birdsong, for the insects tapping against the glass, needing a reminder of why this place is my home. But my heartbeat is too loud in my ears, the blood roaring now, as if it's looking for a way out. "I'm pregnant," I say.

Calla is quiet, and then she says, "I know."

And I know my sister is right: *We can't stay here.* Levi has broken me, and I won't raise our child and watch him look at her with bland indifference, as though she means nothing to him. I won't watch him raise a family and feel the blotting out of my soul as he slowly forgets about me. I think of Colette, how Ash went over the boundary to save their child. He loved her enough to risk his life, while Levi doesn't even love me enough to raise the baby growing inside me.

The idea that's been taking shape in the far back of my mind, finally rises to the surface. "I won't leave without Colette and her baby," I say. She deserves more than this place, more than what's happened to her. She's already lost her husband; I won't let her stay and watch her child die too.

Calla fidgets with something, a small metal sound *tink tinking*, as if she's wearing a bracelet or a necklace I can't see. "We'll leave tonight," she answers.

CALLA

What does a person pack when they're leaving their home and likely not coming back?

I stand at the back door, the small cotton sack filled with a loaf of bread, a jar of sweet blackberry preserves, two candles in case it gets dark (I have no idea how long the trip out of these woods will take), and my best sweater—no holes at the collar or hemline. But somehow, they feel like the wrong things.

Nerves wind their way up my tailbone, and I touch the necklace around my neck. It belonged to me once: the old me, the watercolor me, forgotten, dripped from canvas onto the floor and faded into the cracks. Only a smear of gray colors now. I recall opening a black box with gold ribbon, and inside lay the necklace with a single charm hanging from the end. I held the chain up to the afternoon light, through a window that overlooked a city and a bayfront in the distance. I wrote five books in the Foxtail series, and I received five silver charms, each sent to me from my editor—a women whose name I can't recall—once the books were published.

"You ready?" Theo asks, his voice breaching my mind, pulling me back. He stands at the front door, holding it open for me.

Bee has already left the house, gone to get Colette and the baby, while Theo and I will go to Levi's and retrieve the keys to his truck—which he believes are in a drawer in Levi's office—then we will all meet on the road near the gate, where we will flee together.

I nod at Theo, releasing the necklace—the cut on my forearm throbbing—and when he closes the door behind us, I look back over my shoulder. The life we built in this house felt real, a lifetime's worth, but it was never ours to begin with.

"You okay?" Theo asks.

"We might never come back here," I say, choking on the words.

He touches my hand, tightens his fingers through mine, and we walk away from the house. But I don't look back again, for fear I'll change my mind.

PART FOUR

THE ROAD

BEE

The knife is tucked into the waistline of my skirt.

I didn't mean to hurt Calla, but now I know the feeling of flesh peeling open beneath the weight of the blade. And it wasn't so bad. I could do it again—if I needed to.

I make my way up the path to the birthing hut, my skin still damp, but my body buzzing. I don't fully understand why my sister is not my sister, why my memories feel clotted with moss and dust, but there is also a clearing away, a sharpness to my thoughts that I haven't known in years. Like the broken memories are being swept out by a sudden autumn wind, and I'm finally beginning to separate the fairy tales from the truth.

When I reach the birthing hut, I can hear the voices inside: Faye and Colette, even the soft whimpering of the baby who has yet to be given a name—Colette too afraid to name her, knowing she might not last long enough to bear it properly.

I stand outside the closed door of the small domed building, not knowing what I'll say when I enter. I need to convince Colette to come with me—make her understand. I touch the knob, about to push the door inward, when it swings wide and Faye steps out—I can smell her lemony scent.

"Bee," she says, startled. "Where've you been?"

Sleeping in the trees, past the perimeter where I shouldn't go.

"Are you okay?" she asks.

I rub my palms together, trying to focus on Faye, hoping I might be able to see some outline of her standing before me. But everything is dark. "I need to speak to Colette."

She is quiet a moment, then I sense the subtle shift of her chin as she nods. She pushes the door wide behind her, and I step through, walking to Colette's bedside. The baby is in her arms, making the soft gurgling noises that babies do at this young age.

"Bee," Colette says when I touch her arm, her voice thin and wiry, like she hasn't been sleeping. Like her husband's death has left her raw, and now she has to force her lungs to take every inhale, to keep her heart beating and not seize up beneath her ribs. I suspect the baby is the only thing keeping her alive.

"We need to leave," I say quietly, only a whisper in the air. "The baby won't survive here."

But before Colette can speak, I hear Faye behind me, shifting closer from where she had been standing in the doorway. "What are you talking about?" she asks, her breathing slow, measured—the inhales of a woman who has learned to calm her own heartbeat, to remain always in control. "You know we can't leave," Faye adds. "It's too dangerous." They are words we all know by heart, a mantra we live by, but we die by it too—painfully, wretchedly, necks suspended in nooses.

"I can get us safely down the road," I say.

"How?" Colette asks, her voice so brittle it shreds the air.

"I've been in the woods. I know how to pass through without catching the pox."

I hear Faye take a step back away from me.

"I've been beyond the border many times," I say, lifting my hands toward her so she can see that I'm not sick. "And I've never caught it."

"How?" Faye asks.

I will need to lie to convince them, because if I tell them the truth: the notion that is clattering around inside my head—that perhaps the pox is not what we think it is, that if we flee through the trees we won't get sick—they will think I've gone mad. So instead I say, "I carry a bundle of sage. And I can hear the trees splitting open. I know when they are sick; I know how to stay clear of them."

Faye's feet shuffle on the wood floor, uneasy. "The child would never survive the journey, it's too far for her to be outside. It's not possible."

I swivel my eyes, hoping I'm looking directly at her, hoping she can see that we don't have another choice. "We won't be walking," I explain. "We're going to drive."

"How?"

"Theo found a truck down the road, just past the border. It hasn't been there long; it should still run." I leave out the part about who the truck belonged to, how it got here, or that Calla isn't really my sister.

"Bee—" Faye says in a low muttering hush, as if just my words were a betrayal to the community.

"What if we can save the child—" I interrupt before she can tell me all the reasons why this is a bad idea. "What if we can bring back medicine. What if there are things out there that can help us."

"Whatever is out there might also kill you." Her voice is directed away from me, her face straining toward the door, as if she's afraid someone might be outside listening. "You don't even know what's beyond our woods, in the outside. You've never seen it."

I shake my head. "Faye, some part of you must know that something isn't right here. There are lies built into the walls of this place; we just can't see them." My chest grows tight and heavy, and I suddenly want to be free of the birthing hut. "Some part of you must know that we have to try and save the child."

Because what if it were my baby who was sick, but no one was willing to risk leaving the valley to help her? We need to do this—we need to try.

"Okay," a voice says. But it isn't Faye's, it's Colette's, her small hand clamping around my wrist. "When do we leave?"

"Now." I swallow, realizing the seriousness of what we're about to do. "We'll meet Theo and Calla on the road. But I just need to do something first—gather your things and I'll come right back for you."

This isn't part of the plan. Calla and Theo and I never discussed this, but it's something I must do before we leave, one last moment of defiance to prove to him that I don't love him anymore. I want him to know that I'm leaving, and I'm not coming back.

I slip out of the birthing hut, and into the trees.

We are betraying the foundation of everything we've built here by leaving. We are breaking with the principles of everything Levi has taught us. He would have us believe that we will be infected with the pox if we go over the boundary, but if I'm the one who's been carving the wounds into the trees, then maybe they're not sick at all: no illness weeping from their fleshy white centers, no elm pox congealing in the air between the trees, waiting to infect those passing through.

I'm no longer sure if there is danger in the woods at all.

Or only the danger that lives in corrupt men's hearts.

I hurry through the dark. *No turning back.* This is the only way to save Colette, to save the baby.

And myself.

———

The sky is a muted shade of twilight as the sun dips beyond the pines. I can't see it, not exactly, but I can feel its delicate azure quality against my skin.

I stay back in the trees, where I won't be seen. Still, my stomach tightens into itself the closer I get to Levi's house, until I am made of knots and twisted fibers, just like the sage bundles that hang from the trees.

It's early evening. Levi and Alice are surely still somewhere within the community, but I am quiet as I sneak up to the back door and turn the knob, slipping inside.

If Levi catches me, I doubt he'll believe whatever lie I tell—not now, after everything that's happened. There is a part of him that fears me— and always has. He knew I would betray him someday, that he would lose control, and he was right. A fury boils up inside me, embers that smoldered for too long, and now have been set ablaze.

The house is quiet—vacant. I'm sure of it.

Even if he and Alice were asleep—which they wouldn't be at this evening hour—I would hear their breathing through the walls, the weight of them lying in bed, and the pressure through the floorboards. The house would tell me if they were here.

I hurry through the kitchen into the living room. I touch the walls only a few times, to be certain of where I am, but otherwise I move without need for markers. I know this house nearly as well as my own.

Inside the pocket of my skirt, I pull out the dried daffodil.

I plucked it from between the pages of the dictionary in my bedroom before I left the farmhouse. At first, I thought maybe I would take it with me, the one thing of value I didn't want to leave behind, but as I strode up the path toward the birthing hut, I realized it wasn't that at all. I needed to give the flower back. At one time, it meant something to me, the first thing Levi gave me when we were young and clear-eyed with our hands always woven together, our mouths pressed as one.

But now, the delicate white petals only remind me of what Levi has done: broken me. So I will leave the dried daffodil behind, placed in his house, a symbol that I am leaving and never coming back. That I don't love him anymore.

My fingers trail along the edge of the couch, considering where to leave the flower. Maybe I should climb the stairs and place it on his pillow, where Alice would see it when they slid into bed, a tiny perfect daffodil pressed flat, left for them to find. She would ask questions, she would demand to know who left it.

But somewhere in my gut, I know it doesn't matter what Alice thinks, if she leaves him or not. Because *I'm* leaving and not coming back.

I walk to the fireplace and feel the wood mantel, a good place to set it, a fitting place. He might not notice it tonight, it might take him a day or two, but that would give us time to get far away from Pastoral before he realizes the truth.

I'm about to place the daffodil on the mantel, when I hear the back door off the kitchen swing open. *Levi's returned.* And he's not alone, there's another voice—*his wife.* I can smell her clove and sugar-sweet scent.

I freeze, a stone sinking into my gut—but I need to move, get out of here before they see me. I drop to the floor and scramble behind one of the chairs.

Alice whispers something I can't make out, then laughs. *She doesn't know the awful, traitorous things he's done to me. That someday he might do to her.* But hearing them together, causes a new rage to simmer up into my throat. I want to cry, I want to wail from some primal part inside myself. But most of all, I want to hurt him.

Their footsteps carry across the kitchen. More furtive words, vows of devotion, I'm sure. *I hate him.*

I wait for the sound of their feet moving up the stairs and down the hall to his bedroom. For the rush of clothes being peeled away. For the heaviness of their breathing. But none of it comes. Instead, I hear the soft click of the back door again. And then nothing.

Maybe they only slipped inside to steal a kiss away from the eyes of the others, and now they have returned to their evening chores—Alice to prepare the yeast in the community kitchen for tomorrow's loaves, Levi to survey the daily routines of the community. Perhaps they have left.

But I stay crouched, listening, wanting to be sure before I rise and bolt from the house. I draw in a tight breath, holding it in so I can better hear. But my heartbeat is too loud, hammering wildly against my eardrums, making it impossible to pick out distinctive sounds.

And then . . . a hand is on my arm, yanking me upright.

I cry out, the breath leaving my lungs in one shuddering exhale.

"What the hell are you doing in here?" Levi's hands grip my upper arms, squeezing so hard I let out a small cry of pain, dropping the dried daffodil to the floor. He doesn't even see it—doesn't notice. He pulls me away from the chair, away from the flattened little flower. "Why are you in my house?" he barks, his voice so close to my ear it feels hot, sharp against my skin, and I smell the alcohol. He's been drinking again.

"I'm leaving Pastoral," I spit. They are words I shouldn't say, but they feel so good when they leave my lips, the defiance tucked under each one. The betrayal.

His breathing turns shallow and he tightens his hands on me, dragging my face close to his. "You're not going anywhere." This is the anger I've always known was inside him, bottled up, kept hidden. And even if he doesn't want me anymore, he won't allow me to leave Pastoral. To leave *him*. Not because he's worried about me crossing the border into the woods and catching the pox, but because he needs control. Always control—especially over me.

"You thought you could leave and I wouldn't find out," he says, his teeth mashing together. "That I wouldn't come after you?" He laughs, quick and serrated, then yanks me toward the stairs.

Alice is no longer in the house, the sound of the back door shutting moments ago, was her leaving—maybe she really has gone back to finish up her work.

"I always knew you would try to leave," he says, words mumbled, hardly making any sense. "I'm surprised it's taken you this long." He drags me up the stairs, my legs giving out, unable to keep up when I can't see each stair before it comes. I fall to my knees but he doesn't slow; he keeps pulling me up, my shins banging against each step, tearing open the flesh. "You probably thought you'd take Colette and her baby with you too." His hands pinch into my flesh. "You wanted to get help for her from the start; you never trusted my decision."

"Levi," I plead. "Stop."

"I've done everything for you," he says. We've reached the top of the stairs and he yanks me forward. "Since we were kids, I've taken care of you. And now you just want to leave me?" Each word lashes from his mouth, and he doesn't sound like himself.

I hear the quick unlatching of a lock and a door swinging open. I know where I am, in the hall just down from his bedroom. This is the closet— the one he keeps locked for reasons I've never understood. He releases his hold on my arm, and I feel the white-hot pain of circulation rushing back down to my fingertips. Then . . . he shoves me inside the closet. I stumble and reach out to brace myself for whatever is in front of me, but my fore-head slams into a sharp wood corner. Blood seeps into my eyes.

And for the first time, I think: *Maybe he's going to kill me.*

I touch my forehead, feeling the sticky warmth on my fingertips, and it smells like metal.

"I won't let you leave me," Levi says now, his voice softened slightly, as if I should understand. "I won't let you take my baby."

My jaw quivers; the warmth of blood runs down my legs where they scraped open against the stairs, and along my temple, makes me dizzy. "Levi, please," I say, but the door slams shut and the lock slides into place from the outside.

I am in a closet, caged.

His footsteps move away down the hall, followed by the thud of his heavy boots on the stairs.

———

My palms slide along the closet walls, locating the shelves, the line of coats hung from metal hangers, this narrow space where I am now confined.

I find the door, but there's no knob on this side, only a smooth wood surface. I lean my shoulder against it with all my weight, but it doesn't move. Not even an inch.

I hear the bang of the back door and I know Levi has left the house.

My knees burn where he dragged me up the stairs. My head throbs, and I press my hands against the door, willing it to open—but I'm starting to realize, there's no way out of here until Levi unlocks it from the other side.

I sink to the floor, drawing my legs up to my chest—my heart beating too fast, the air sick with the stench of fresh blood. I think of all the times I slept folded in Levi's arms, the times he kissed me on the forehead as the warmth of dawn crept through the curtains of his bedroom window. How I trusted him. How I imagined us walking through the community together as the years wore on, our hair turned white-gray, but our hands always folded together.

But now I see: These were the imaginings of a teenage girl, a girl who fell in love with Levi in a meadow buzzing with fattened honeybees, wildflower fluff drifting lazily through the warm breeze, cool blades of grass poking up between my toes. I fell in love with him easily, and now I have allowed him to break me.

I am a stupid woman. Believing in stupid, impossible things.

I press my palms over my eyes and squeeze, making everything even darker. A black so black it feels like I'm tumbling forward through the floor of the closet. I dig my fingers through my long hair, catching on the knots, pulling them free. My mind feels like a bruise that will never heal.

The blood at my shins and temple has started to set, no longer rushing, but clotting over—becoming scabs. The body heals quickly, an efficient machine, but the heart is worthless at such things. It burns long after the hurt has worn away.

I drop my hands and blink up at the pitch-black closet, but the darkness has melted slightly. Bled into the background. Shadows take shape, as though I am waking from a dream and trying to orient the familiar objects in a room.

The wool jacket hanging above me.

The pair of blue overalls, stained muddy at the knees.

The wood shelf at the back.

These things come into focus as if looking through pond water.

I blink several times, trying to settle my gaze on the pair of overalls above me, but my vision turns grainy whenever I focus on any part of it for too long: the hem of the legs, the two silver buttons on the chest, the metal hanger it's draped from.

And yet, I can *see* overalls.

Not clearly, but they're there.

With aching legs and a throbbing head, I push myself up from the floor and touch the heavy jean fabric, pressing it between my thumb and forefinger, to be sure it's real. Not just a cruel trick of the dark.

I release the leg of the overalls and scan the small, square room.

The more I blink, the more things become clear. As if whatever clouded my eyes is being washed away from my retinas. I reach my hands out to the shelf where I hit my head when Levi pushed me in, I feel the sharp corner, and my forehead throbs with the memory, the impact.

My body is bruised and bloodied and sore, but my eyes are beginning to see, so I push away the pain.

On the shelf are rows of books.

My fingertips slide across the spines, some thin and hardly measurable, others are thick with indented lettering. I haven't read a book since I was a teenager, since before I lost my sight.

I bring my face closer to the books, making out the letters: letters that form words that form titles. My brain is slow to recall the formation of these symbols, how they become sentences that tell an entire story— a narrative. For so long, I've absorbed information through the sounds of the trees and the direction of the wind and the unique exhale from someone's lungs.

Now, my mind is trying to sort through these stamped letters and deduce their meaning.

Their titles:

How to Govern a People by E. S. Warren

A Return to Simple Living and Native Farming by Allison Carmichael

The Art of War by Sun Tzu

Mastery of Magic and Ancient Card Tricks by Bert Ferny

This last title sits stagnant in my mind. It rolls around inside my skull, pinging against memories that have gone dormant but are now waking. I slide the book out and peer at the cover: a deck of cards fanned out on a stone surface, the joker is the only card facing up. A scattering of stars adorns the top third of the cover against a black background. I remember this book, remember seeing it in Levi's lap when we were kids.

I'd lie on my back in the meadow beyond the farmhouse, the sun warming my face, while Levi practiced his card tricks. He'd let me choose a card from the deck then he'd shuffle it back in, a moment later magically plucking my card from the stack, and show it to me with a wide, gaping grin. I'd nod and we'd start again. He was always good at it, and he liked to practice his tricks with me before showing them to anyone else in the community. He wanted to get them just right, and I'd smile watching him concentrate so deeply that the freckles on his nose pulled together.

We were young then, thirteen, fourteen, and we'd weave our hands together under the hazelnut trees—shy and wary, giggling softly—before we'd run up the path to Pastoral to beg Roona for scraps of dough from the sweet lavender bread she was baking.

I slide the book back onto the shelf, not wanting the memory to tear me open any further.

If these are the books he's kept hidden all this time, the things he's kept locked away and safe inside the closet, then maybe he doesn't have any secrets after all. Maybe he's more transparent than I realized. A man who is afraid of losing his power, his control over his people, but nothing more sinister than that.

I rub at my eyes, my vision clouding briefly then re-forming.

My eyes settle on another row of titles, lower on the shelf:

Ways to Outthink the Brain by Helga Boar
The Structure of the Mind after Birth by Reginald Cartersmith

And then my gaze falters, skips to a book I remember like a spark across my synapses: the book Levi started reading once he abandoned simple card tricks and the magic of making dandelions and hair ribbons disappear. The book he would read with furious intensity. He would even recite passages to me, as if he were devouring each word and he wanted me to devour them too. He wanted to see if he could do it, if he could really make someone see, hear, smell things that weren't truly there. If he could make them forget.

I slide the book out and hold it in my hands. It's a heavy book, dense in content and page count. And it's not a kid's book, not for birthday party games. This is a clinical book, a practical application book. It took Levi years to read it all the way through, to understand it.

I let my fingers slide over the letters. I will my unpracticed eyes to focus on the words, and the memories snap through me with sudden, sharp accuracy.

I remember nearly everything.

Everything.

Hypnosis and Practical Applications to Alter the Function of the Brain by Dr. Arthur Trembly.

CALLA

The night sky is teeming with stars, but there is a bite to the air, the possibility of a storm.

We reach the edge of the community and duck into the tree line, not wanting to be seen. Candles throw light against windowpanes and children have been herded into their homes for bed. Pastoral is settling into an evening hush.

We pass the community kitchen and through the windows, I see two figures inside—Alice and Roona—working late as they often do. At least we know Alice won't be home when we get there.

At the east end of the community, we cut across the main path, moving secretly to the front door of Levi's house. It's dark inside, not a single candle lit.

Hopefully Levi has drunk too much, as has been his nightly ritual lately, and is passed out in bed—an immovable human form that wouldn't wake even if we thumped him on the head.

But we can't be certain, so Theo pushes open the front door slowly, listening for any sounds. He looks back at me and holds a palm up, gesturing for me to wait here on the front porch, but I shake my head at him. *I'm not waiting out here alone.* "No," I hiss. "I'm coming too." He drops his hand and nods; it's not worth the argument—we don't have time—so he turns back for the open door and we both slip inside. The house is cold, drafty, and we move into the office off the living room. My shin thumps against a chair and I let out a wheeze, buckling forward. Theo snaps his gaze back at me and I cover a hand over my mouth, listening for someone moving down the stairs, for Levi to wake. But there is no sound. No movement on the second floor.

Either Levi really is passed out or perhaps he's not even home, gone somewhere else within the community.

Theo reaches the broad wood desk and his outline bends low, opening one of the drawers. Books line the shelves on the far wall—I can smell their damp, inky scent—and the curtains over the window are drawn closed. Theo pulls out a tangled heap of keys from the drawer, keys to every vehicle that's ever come to Pastoral, and he places them on the desk then begins sifting through the pile, searching for one key in particular.

"Do you know what it looks like?" I hiss.

He doesn't answer, his hands working methodically through the keys secured on metal rings, others attached to woven fabric, while some have multiple keys tied together. But then Theo lifts one up, bringing it close to examine it. Hanging from one end is a square piece of metal that reads: *Lone Pine Lake*. It's a souvenir, the kind of thing you buy at a gas station or at a small, lakeside store near a campground. A memento.

Memories swirl and collide through me, recalling such places: campgrounds and winding highways and car radios and the smell of tents newly erected after sitting in attics and garages for too long.

"I think this is it," Theo says, holding the key up for me to see. And then he is quiet a moment, staring at it, and I wonder if he's recalling a similar flutter of memories. "This is the key to my truck," he states, as if to solidify it in his own mind.

He pushes the key into the pocket of his jeans, and looks at me, nodding. *It's time to go.*

But that's when I hear it: the banging through the walls.

An echo coming from inside the house. Upstairs.

At first I think it's Levi—he's woken, he's heard us, and he's stumbling for the stairs, bumping into furniture, still half-asleep and fully intoxicated.

But then I hear a voice; someone shouting for help, fists pounding against a door.

I walk carefully into the living room, to the stairwell, straining to hear. And I know the voice: It's Bee.

THEO

Her voice is hoarse against the grain of the wood door. "Let me out!"

Bee is trapped inside the closet, and Calla reaches for the knob, but a lock has bolted the door shut. I reach up to the top of the doorframe, feeling for a key, but find only dust.

"Stand back," I say to Calla.

Her eyes swivel to mine, and she steps away quickly. I ram my shoulder into the door, but it doesn't move—the wood frame is solidly built. I spin around, looking for something I can use to it pry open. But the hallway is mostly empty.

"Calla," Bee pleads from the other side. "Please, open the door."

"We're trying," Calla whispers, as if she needs to be quiet, as if Levi might return and hear us in the house.

I bolt back down the stairs, and in the living room I find an iron poker hanging from a hook beside the fireplace. I grab it, and for a split second, an image flashes across my vision: of Levi holding the metal poker and jamming it into the fireplace to spur on the flames. His face turns, looking back at someone behind him. "You could be valuable here," he says. "Part of our community. It's a better life than what you left behind." And then another face comes into focus, the man standing behind him in the living room: It's me.

I drop the poker to the ground and press a hand against my eyes. The afterimage was from years ago, when I first arrived and Levi tried to convince me to stay. I swallow and take a deep breath, letting the image recede. In my other life, *as Travis Wren*, I would see glimpses of the past in the objects I touched—but that talent has gone dormant, forgotten, along with everything else. But now perhaps it's stirring awake, a creature blinking its eyes open after years of hibernation. First, I saw Maggie moving through the house and out to the pond when I held the *Foxtail* book, and now the metal poker.

Slowly, I bend and pick up the poker from the floor, but when the image of Levi starts sparking across my eyes, I blink and stuff it back down. When I can feel it fading like shadows on a cloudy day, I open my eyes and head for the stairs, taking them two at a time.

I don't tell Calla what I saw—there's no time—instead, I wedge the sharp end of the poker into the space between the door and the frame, and pull. Surprisingly, the wood begins to crack and separate as soon as I apply force, prying the door free. One more good shove and the lock mechanism breaks and the door pops open.

Bee tumbles out as though she'd been leaning against the door, blinking wildly, blood along her cheek and dripping down her shins to her feet. Calla grabs Bee by the arm and holds her steady. "I heard you," Bee says, breathing deeply, eyes too wide—like a terrified animal whose heart is about to burst. "I heard you downstairs. I knew it was you."

"What are you doing here?" Calla asks. "You were supposed to go get Colette and the baby."

Bee draws her arms away from Calla and wipes the hair back from her face, stained red with blood, and stands up straight. "I know," she answers, blinking, blinking. "He lied," she chokes out. "He lied about everything."

"Who?"

"Levi." She looks down the hallway, to the stairs. *Looks* down the hallway—as if she can actually see the hall and the stairwell. Her pupils narrow and contract, skipping from Calla's face to mine. "I don't think there is a disease," she says. "There never was. We could always leave Pastoral."

Calla moves closer to Bee. "But Ash and Turk were sick, their blood was black."

Bee shakes her head. "He made us see what he wanted us to see. He's been lying all this time, hypnotizing us. The pox, the border trees, none of it's real."

Calla flashes me a look, and I know she's thinking the same as I am: Was it Levi who made us forget who we used to be? Erased our old lives and replaced them with something else. Lies woven into more lies.

"We have to go," Calla says, grabbing Bee by the arm and tugging her toward the stairs. "We have to get out of Pastoral."

We scramble down the stairs and flee out through the back door, into the dark—three figures moving among the tall, shadowed pines. Three figures who are starting to remember who we really are. And one who might be able to *see* when yesterday she could not.

CALLA

We have the key to the truck.

Theo is ahead of me, his dark shirt swaying in and out of focus in the dull moonlight, while Bee moves beside me. We make our way around the back of the community, along the garden fence where the pale-yellow stalks of corn are now taller than our heads—reaching toward the scattered night sky. We won't be here for the harvest; we won't peel back the husks and taste the sweetness of corn when the kernels pop on our tongues.

My heart burns at the thought of it, the lost moments we will never have, but we keep going.

My throat burns too—strangely—the night air cutting like glass in my lungs, the taste of smoke on my tongue. Of ash.

Something is burning.

The fire comes into view like a bloodshot sunrise just breaking through the trees, all crimson and violent.

The birthing hut is on fire.

"Holy shit!" Bee screeches, her voice a metallic, half hiss. Her legs kick into a run, and she moves with an odd sureness, as if she can see the uneven ground ahead of her.

At the door into the birthing hut, she stops, a hand reaching forward, but Theo is there and yanks her back before she can touch the handle.

"They're inside," she breathes, flashing a panicked look up at Theo. "They were waiting for me to come back."

The wail of a baby rises above the growl of the fire—a terrifying sound. And above us, sparks wheel up through the trees, embers disappearing into the dark. A loud crack shudders through the air, and I jerk my gaze back to the hut.

Theo rams his shoulder into the door, but it doesn't open. He breathes, chest expanding, then throws his body against the door once more, and this time it breaks free and he tumbles inside.

The wind changes direction, turning the air thick and ashy, and I think: *This fire didn't happen by accident.* Someone set it ablaze. Someone who wanted a problem to go away.

Theo disappears into the birthing hut, and I stop breathing, stop blinking.

The baby has gone quiet.

Gray smoke spills out through the doorway; embers sail among the treetops, greedy for more tinder, anything that will satisfy its hunger, while Bee fidgets a few paces back from the door, hands twitching at her sides.

Too much time passes. Too many minutes.

I look behind me, and think of running back through the trees to Pastoral, yelling for someone to help. Wake the others. My bandaged arm throbs, my panicked heart pumping blood too quickly through my body.

But just as I start to turn toward Pastoral, Faye appears in the doorway, the gray of her hair the same color of her skin, coated in smoke and ash. She coughs then buckles over, dropping to her knees in the grass. Bee is at her side, touching her, telling her to breathe. Colette appears next, but her eyes are wide and watery, like she doesn't know where she is, or how she got here. Like she's lost track of the days.

She stumbles, then spins around, looking back at the door just as Theo emerges from the wall of smoke. He's holding the baby to his chest, and Colette nearly falls trying to get to him, reaching out for the tiny infant wrapped in a blanket. Theo relinquishes the bundle into Colette's arms, and the baby makes a small sound, a whimper—*she's still alive.*

But behind them, the birthing hut continues to burn. "We need to get them out of here," Theo says.

I nod. Chin wobbling up and down, no words coming out—in shock.

Theo turns to Bee, who has placed her hands on the small baby, feeling for the sputter of her heartbeat beneath the rib cage. "We need to go," Theo says to Bee. "Now."

She responds with a quick, assured nod—more lucid than I am. Her eyes sway to me and her mouth tugs into a tight line of concern, like she can see the lost look in my eyes.

And I know now, with her gaze on me, that she can *see*.

Her eyes blink, the gray not so gray, but a deep tragic blue. Perhaps it's always been that color, the same hue as the sky. Maybe I only imagined it was a sad, milky bluish-gray.

She turns away from me, a hand on Colette, and starts leading her toward the path that will take us back to the farmhouse and then out to the road.

But before I can fall into step after them, a voice breaks through the air behind us. "What the hell happened?"

I spin around and see Parker standing in the trees, head craned upward, a hand over his eyes as he follows the pinwheeling trail of smoke and flames up into the night sky.

No one answers him.

Eyelids blink.

We need to get out of here, but not with Parker standing a few feet away, watching us.

"Someone started a fire," Bee answers finally, her tone accusing, staring Parker down, like she thinks he might have done it: set the structure ablaze.

"I see that," Parker replies, his voice thin and soft, still a kid really—and he lowers his hand, looking far too bewildered to have started the fire. He's the only one awake at this hour, and he must have seen the smoke or the flames from his post at the guard hut and come to investigate. Everyone else in Pastoral is sound asleep. "Y'all okay?" he asks, taking a step closer, nodding at Colette with the baby in her arms.

"We're fine," Theo says, giving Parker a blunt nod, as if it's a gesture Parker will take to mean that he needn't concern himself with any of this. *We have it under control. You can go back to your post.*

"Well shit," Parker says, scraping a hand down his neck, like he's trying to sort out how he might extinguish the flames, or explain it to Levi—as if this were his problem now. But then his eyes jerk back to us, the young features of his face hollowing out, eyebrows stuffed together. "Why are you all heading into the trees instead of toward Pastoral?"

Theo steps forward, closer to Parker. "Just figured we'd go back to our place, let everyone rest, and wait for morning when we can see how bad the damage is."

But Parker's expression doesn't soften. Maybe he knows Theo well enough to know when he's lying, or maybe something in his gut tells him this isn't right, that we wouldn't just flee back to the farmhouse without telling someone there was a fire, or trying to put it out to keep it from catching on the surrounding trees and spreading to other structures. Parker knows we're full of shit.

"You're trying to take that baby out of here, aren't ya?" he says. "You're planning to go past the border."

For the briefest moment, his mouth goes slack, like maybe he understands our intentions and won't try to stop us.

"You don't have to tell anyone you saw us," Theo says calmly, cool as winter air. "When you discovered the fire, there was no one here. We had already left." Theo has given him an out, a way to explain away our disappearance. He nods as he says it, meeting Parker's gaze, hoping Parker will see that it's the right thing to do, and help us.

Parker chews on the side of his lip, as if testing out this story, seeing how it sounds in his head—if he thinks the others will believe him. He and Theo have been friends a long time. But in truth, it's only been two years since Theo arrived in Pastoral. A man with a different name.

Without warning, the western wall of the birthing hut collapses inward, and the sound is tremendous—wood splintering, sparks *whooshing* up into the sky like a tornado of angry bees. If the others in Pastoral haven't woken at the sound of the fire, this thunderous crash will surely wake someone.

Parker makes a quick movement, and at first I can't tell what he's doing. His arm jerks to his side and when I'm able to focus again, I see that he's pulled the gun from his holster.

"Whoa, easy." Theo lifts both his hands in the air, palms facing Parker. "What are you doing?"

"I can't let you leave with that baby," Parker says. But his voice isn't sure or strong, it's shaking, trembling along the slope of each vowel. "You'll catch the pox; you'll be infected. I can't have you bringing it back with you, risking everyone else."

Theo shakes his head. "We won't come back."

I see Faye and Colette exchange a look. They hadn't anticipated that we would never come back. That this would be goodbye.

"We just want to help Colette," Theo says. "Let us take her into town for medicine."

"You can't," Parker answers, keeping the gun trained on Theo, his closest target. "It's too dangerous. You won't make it that far, you'll get sick, I can't let you go."

"No one has to know we were here," Theo says, stepping closer to Parker. But Parker keeps the gun trained at Theo's chest, finger itching at the trigger, tapping it lightly. "You can go back to the gate, sit down in your chair, and pretend you never saw the fire."

Parker's feet shift in the dirt, stirring up clouds of dust around him.

"Please, Parker," Theo says. He's only a couple feet from Parker now. He might be able to reach forward and yank the gun from Parker's hand. But he also might get shot, a bullet straight into his stomach. And out here, without a doctor—a surgeon—he likely wouldn't survive.

But then there is movement, a sound from the edge of the trees.

A branch breaks underfoot and Parker whips his head around to see what it is. The wind stirs, sending more ash and sparks up into the already-gritty sky, and I can just make out the outline of someone partly hidden in the dark, standing several feet back in the trees—watching us. I try to make out who it is, but there is too much smoke and too many shadows, and when I blink, for a moment I think there might not be anyone there at all. Only tree limbs pretending to be arms.

I swivel my gaze back to Parker in the same instant that Theo dives toward him, and there is the blunt exhale of air—of one body slamming into another. Both men struggle for the gun, while spasms of firelight erupt behind me, and a half-second later, the gun discharges. Both Theo and Parker hit the ground hard.

A sound leaves my lungs—a shriek, a scream, a struggle for air. I'm certain that Theo's been shot and I try to take a step forward, to run to him, but then I feel the white-hot throb. My chin dips, eyes lowering, and my fingers find the wound, touching the blood already pooling across my shirt—tacky like honey.

"Calla!" someone screams. It's Bee, and the seconds flash forward in strange staccato. She is standing over me now, and I'm on the ground, her palm pressing against the wound.

"I'm okay," I sputter; I gurgle. But it's like she doesn't hear me, her eyes watering, head whipping around to yell for help.

From the corner of my vision, I see Theo stand up from the ground, breathing heavy, dirt and soot smearing the lines of his face. He's wrestled the gun free from Parker and he holds it at his side. Behind him, Parker also scrambles to his feet, but his expression has lost all its hardness. He looks frightened, like a little boy again, staring over at me with regret piercing his eyes. He didn't mean to do it, and I try to lift my arm toward him, to tell him it's okay. But Bee touches my hand with hers, forcing me not to move.

Theo is at my side then, touching my face. "Calla?"

I watch as Parker turns, taking several steps back away from us, and his body seems to be shaking. Or maybe it's my own—a tremble moving up my torso, making my eyes wobble in my skull. Parker vanishes into the trees, and I know he will go wake the others, tell them what's happened, or maybe he will sprint back to his home, slide into bed, and cry against his pillow. Too afraid to admit what he's done.

The burning ache becomes a searing, flesh-torn-open kind of pain, and I blink up at the trees, trying to breathe. "I can stand," I say, attempting to move my hands beneath me. I know we don't have much time; we need to get out of here.

"No," Theo says, his palm held against my ribs, the place where the bullet tore through my flesh. A piece of metal is lodged inside me, and it feels like its wriggling deeper, a beetle through alder wood. *It's not that bad*, I tell myself. It's only flesh and muscle, fractured bones perhaps. It can be stitched back together. But the trees above me begin to swirl and change shape; I worry I might pass out.

Bee stands up and then Faye is bent over me, talking to Theo, but their words are far-off chatter, not meant for me.

And my focus is only on Bee. She steps toward the trees, where Parker vanished—she's looking at something.

Another figure slinks back into the evergreens.

Someone had been watching us, and now they're trying to slip away unseen.

But Bee *sees* him, and she glances back at us. "Just go," she says. "I'll catch up."

"No!" I try to call out, but she doesn't look back. She sprints into the forest, into the dark, where the light from the fire doesn't reach. And she disappears.

"We can't stay here," Theo says, his face only a few inches from mine. There's no time left, others will be here soon; they will have heard the gun-shot, a sound that rips into dreams and wakes even the deepest sleepers.

Faye tears something, a piece of fabric, and ties it around my lower ribs, cinching it tight. The sudden pressure shoots a dagger through my body, and I let out a low moan.

"I can walk," I mutter, but both Theo and Faye ignore my words.

Theo's hands slide beneath my body, drawing me to his chest, and lifts me up into his arms. The motion makes me feel like I might vomit, the swing and jolt of it, but I press my face into his shoulder, my eyes against the fabric of his shirt—I tell myself this is all there is, my eyelashes against the soft, worn cotton of his shirtsleeves, my breathing against his collar-bone. I have no body, no pain, I am only lungs and eyelashes against the sturdy warmth of my husband. Nothing else.

"You have to get as far past the boundary as you can," Faye says, touch-ing my back between my shoulder blades. "I'll try to stall them."

"Thank you," Theo says.

There is a pause, an exchange of looks—a goodbye between Faye and Theo. We might never see her again.

Theo moves into the trees, and the pain finds me, it drives up my rib bones, up my spine, clawing its way into my mind, screaming at me: *I am here! I am a fire burning a hole through your flesh. I am cutting you open, making you bleed.*

I press my face harder to Theo's chest, I bite down, clenching my teeth, my jaw aching.

You can't carry me all the way to the truck, I think.

Or maybe I say it aloud.

"We don't have a choice," Theo answers.

We move down the path, Colette leading the way, clutching the baby to her chest. I try to open my eyes again, to peer back over Theo's shoulder for signs of anyone coming after us, but I can't seem to raise my eyelids now.

We're leaving Pastoral. We're leaving my sister behind.

Yet, I know why she went after him.

Him.

In the river of my mind, I'm starting to remember: *He* might be to blame for everything that's happened. Everything we can't remember. The man that Bee once loved.

And now she's gone to set things right.

BEE

He's a monster.

He set the fire and watched it burn, knowing Faye and Colette and the baby were inside. He knew that if they were dead, no one else would try to leave to go get help for the child. And he watched Parker point his gun at Theo, probably hoping he'd shoot us all to keep us from leaving. We are traitors, after all. A problem to be dealt with.

Better dead than alive to tell all his secrets.

But with my eyes peering through the dark, seeing for the first time in too long, I trail Levi through the trees. His footsteps are an echo across the hard summer ground, his shadow scattering among the tall pines.

Drops begin to fall from the sky, a storm sinking over the valley— but I no longer fear the rain.

Levi ducks around the backside of Pastoral, and the community gardens come into view—rain catching on the neat, tidy rows of cornstalks and vegetables, on bright green leaves, and my eyes stall briefly, marveling at the sight. I had forgotten the shimmery quality of raindrops, and it sends a spark of emotion through me, a feeling like I might cry.

But Levi has stopped at the corner of the garden, only a few yards away, his shadow stretched long and lean in the moonlight, watching me.

Maybe he knew I was following him all along, and now he's led me here, to the garden, away from the eyes of others. Where he can end it.

"You escaped the closet," he says softly, with tenderness in his voice, a sound that now makes me cringe. He moves closer but I don't back away. "You've always been strong-willed."

I feel my jaw tighten, my eyes blink then refocus, afraid my vision will slip away at any moment—only a temporary reprieve from the dark. "You were just going to let them burn?" I ask.

"Sometimes there must be sacrifices to make the community stronger."

"Is that what you planned to do with me—sacrifice me?"

"I hadn't decided yet." The hard ridge of his jaw shifts side to side. "You can *see*," he says, but he doesn't sound surprised. "You're looking directly at me."

"It wore off, whatever you did to me."

"I wondered if it would, if I stopped reminding you that you were blind." My temples pulse, fury seething up inside me. "I knew you would leave me someday, if I didn't make it hard for you. If I didn't make it impossible. You were always so fearless; you would have risked everything when we were younger to leave Pastoral, so I had to stop you, make you believe you were weak." His head tilts to the side, like he's trying to see me more clearly, raindrops cascading over us.

"You made me think I was blind."

His expression sinks a little. "I did it because I loved you," he clarifies.

I wince at his words and I can feel the hardened blood at my temples, along my cheekbone. "That's not love." All those summer days in the meadow, listening to Levi read from his books while I wove blades of grass together at my feet. We were teenagers when he started reciting words to me, asking me to slow my breathing—he was practicing something from one of his books: *hypnosis*, he told me. It felt like a game. A silly thing we laughed about. He would tell me it was snowing, even when the sky was clear and warm and blue. I would shiver and draw my knees close. He'd tell me to sneak from my room in the middle of the night and meet him at the pond. He got better at it, at fooling my mind into doing whatever he said. And that summer, I talked of leaving Pastoral, of running away together, but he wanted to stay, he always had. He knew he would lead our community once Cooper died; it had already been decided. Cooper had raised him as his own son, taught him how to govern, how to lead. Levi would move into Cooper's house and take over his position within the community.

But still, I wanted to get far away from these woods; I wanted to see what was beyond.

One mild summer day, the season shifting into autumn, Levi began practicing a new trick. He placed his fingertips against my closed eyelids—soft and delicate—and told me to imagine a darkness so complete that it spread over my whole body, spilling across my eyes, until all I could see were shadows. Until the sky became a smear of gray, and everything around me bled of its color.

He was taking something from me.

If I had known what was happening, I might have refused, but instead I let myself tumble into the smooth cadence of his voice, the scent of his skin—pine and earth—filling my nostrils.

He whispered about darkness and shadows, until finally, one afternoon, the blackness crept across my vision and didn't recede. Until the landscape was blotted out and he was the last thing I saw.

I forgot that he was to blame. I forgot that his words into my ears started it all.

He took that from me too: my memories. A swift pluck from my mind, *you won't be needing those*, and they were gone.

And now I wonder: How long after that until a new idea entered his mind?

If he could convince me I was blind, he could convince the people of Pastoral of just about anything. A year later, Cooper died and Levi became our leader.

"You lied to me—to everyone," I say.

"I kept you safe."

"From what?" I ask, eyebrows raised, challenging him to tell the truth. No more lies. No more whispers against my neck to make me complaisant, to make me his. "The pox?"

"The real world is dangerous," he answers. "It's broken and diseased. People suffer out there from things you can't even imagine."

"You don't know that," I say. "You've never left Pastoral."

"Cooper told me what it was like out there; he told me I needed to protect the community from the outside. Do whatever it takes."

"He didn't want *this*." I close my eyes briefly then look back at Levi. "Is it real or not?" I demand. "Are the trees sick?"

"I created a story that you would all believe." He breathes, and in his eyes I see the boy I remember from when we were kids. The gentle curve of his mouth, the softness that once lived in his bottle-green eyes that's now gone—the boy I loved so deeply I would have believed anything he said to me. "Cooper told me the story about the early settlers who lived here, about the young girl who disappeared, how they saw her stalking through the woods looking wild and feral, diseased, as if she was sick. As if the trees themselves had infected her with something."

"So you used that story, and you made up a new one?"

"Maybe the settlers were right, and there really was something in the trees." His eyes skip away to the garden, drops of rain exploding against the cornfields, long leafy stalks twitching from the impact. "At first I only told the group that the road was unsafe, that we should close our boundaries and protect ourselves from the outside world. But they didn't want to do it, they still talked of leaving, trading with the outside." His temples twitch, like he's admitting something he's never talked about before, and it's causing little stabs of pain behind his eyes. "I needed them to fear the woods, the road. I needed them to fear for their lives." He swallows, and a strange, long-suffering look tugs at the features of his face—the truth of what he's done sinking into his chest. "Every week at the gathering, I told the same story: about the illness in the trees. And soon they couldn't remember a time when they didn't fear the pox. They believed it so completely. Even you."

"You made me carve marks onto the trees," I say. "You used me."

He nods, no longer hiding what he's done. "I needed a way to make the pox real, to make the others believe without question that it waited outside our borders."

I shake my head. "And you buried Ash and Turk in the ground, you cut them open and made everyone think they were infected."

A coldness washes over his eyes. "The others saw what I told them to see."

"You killed them and you didn't need to."

Levi takes a step closer to me, his forehead pinched flat. "I had to do it," he says. "I had to prove a point. If you leave Pastoral, you will be punished." His eyes press me to the earth. "I did it to protect what we've built here."

I think of the others over the years, the ones who've slipped past the perimeter, their bodies sometimes seen in the woods—but we would never dare cross over the boundary to retrieve them. We believed the pox was to blame for their deaths, but it was Levi, teaching us the rules of the world he's built, teaching us to obey. All this time. He was killing members of our community to protect his lie, to make it true.

But what he's really done is make himself a murderer.

Now, he stands a foot away from me, looking hard-faced and indifferent, but I know his burdens have been unraveling him. An albatross of guilt. The alcohol numbing what he doesn't want to remember.

"You've been killing us," I say coldly—he is the monster we should have feared, not the disease. "You've made us prisoners."

"No," he says. "I've created a place where nothing can harm you."

"Except you."

His eyes dip quickly to the ground then back up, his pupils turned icy-cold, like he's calculating something: the time it will take to reach forward and clamp his hands around me. "I needed a wife who wouldn't abandon me, who wouldn't turn against me," he says now.

I take a step back, bile rising up into my throat.

"You were always the one I wanted," he says. "The one I couldn't live without." This might have been true once, but not anymore. He loved the girl I was when I obeyed, the girl who didn't question him in front of the others, who was blind and malleable and nodded when he asked me to carve marks into the border trees. But now, I cannot be trusted.

Now . . . I am dangerous.

"I gave you everything you wanted. I gave you a sister, I gave you things to lose—reasons to stay."

My mind is wheeling faster now. *A sister.* And when I search the length of my mind, the deepest cavern, I see the thing that burns holes into the soft tissue of my heart: Calla and I never shared a childhood together. She appeared later, much later, coming to live inside the farmhouse—an outsider. But how swiftly I came to believe that we belonged together.

And now she's fleeing Pastoral, a bullet inside her, and I might never see her again.

I should turn away from Levi and run into the trees toward the farm-house, toward the road—I could still catch up to them if I go now. But Levi moves swiftly, stepping forward, and he grabs both my arms, as if he senses my urge to bolt. My muscles stiffen at his touch, recoiling, when days ago I would have softened in his arms, sunk closer. Pressed my skin to his.

But not now.

He pushes me back against the wall of the garden shed—my spine dig-ging into the horizontal logs. The gash along my temple throbs, blood hardened like a shell on my skin. I know I'm outweighed, and he leans into me, breathing into my hair, yet I can't tell if he's going to bend close and kiss me or wrap his hands around my throat and push the life clean out of me.

"I could have killed her when she first arrived—Maggie St. James. I could have killed Travis too. I could have done it and no one would have known." He makes a sound through his throat. "But I couldn't allow the others to see that an outsider had passed through our forest without catching the pox, so I made them forget." He says this as if he is merciful, as if he has done a good thing. A man with a moral compass. "I barely had to push them together—Travis and Maggie. I gave them a few memories, and soon they believed everything. You all did. You wanted to believe the world I created for you." He deepens the pressure against my throat, his eyes widening. "The mind is a weak, pliable thing, so loose and full of holes, easily manipulated. You wanted to believe Calla and Theo had been here all along, since the beginning." He stops and brushes a strand of hair away from my eyes. "Sometimes I wonder how far it could go. What I could make you believe."

I turn my face away from him, disgusted, afraid. "Like tricking me into loving you," I say.

"If I wanted to, maybe."

It wasn't only the hypnosis that made us all believe, it was him. Levi had a way of convincing us, cajoling us with his words—he told stories that we wanted to believe. We were the dumbest of sheep, following a monster toward the carving knife.

I squirm away from his arms, but he presses tighter against me, his mouth only a few inches from mine. "But instead, I'll use you to help the others believe my story. I will tell them that you became sick, infected with the pox, just like Ash and Turk. I will tell them how you tried to leave with Colette and the baby, how you went into the trees. You died quickly, before the ceremony could be performed, so I buried you in the cemetery. A kindness, really. And the others will know without question that they cannot leave; they will know how dangerous it is inside our woods. Your death will make them understand, once and for all."

He slides a hand up my stomach, where our child grows inside me, pausing there, as if he could feel the life against his palm. But then he lifts his hand to my chest, to my throat, his eyes following the movements, savoring each moment, each final breath I take. "You always were my favorite," he says. "I always did love you, even when we were kids." His fingers slip easily around my neck, feeling the pulse beating there, the blood pumping through me. Keeping our child alive.

"No, Levi," I mutter, struggling to find my voice. "You'll kill our baby too."

His eyes harden for a moment, lips puckered together. "I will make you both martyrs," he says. "I will sacrifice your lives to save the others." Some part of him has always feared me, feared that someday I would remember, that my sight would return—that I would tell the others what he's done, who he really is. He was afraid he'd lose control. And now he's taking it back.

Without blinking, he presses his palm against my throat, flesh against flesh, fingers pinching into my vocal cords, and he squeezes.

It only takes a few seconds for my lungs to burn. For my body to start fighting it, convulsing against his weight, struggling for air. For just one more gulp.

"You don't need to feel any pain," he coos softly, using the voice I remember now—the soothing tenor of his words spilling into my ears, becoming truth. The voice he uses to hypnotize, to get what he wants. But I wince away from it: I don't want his words inside me, slick with lies. My fingers claw at his chest, his neck, trying to push him off, but the world has gone dizzy, flecked with little sparks of light.

Fear flames up inside me, burning away the hurt and the pain until there is only terror.

I drop my hands—remembering—and my fingers search for something I know is there, tucked into the waistband of my dress. I find it easily, the hard wood handle, the smooth weight of it, and I pull it free, tightening my grip around the base of the knife. I try to swallow, to summon what strength I have left—while the pressure of Levi's hands deepens against my throat—and I thrust the knife forward.

The blade sinks through fabric, through flesh, down into the soft place of his torso.

Warmth seeps over my hand.

Time slows, stretches outward. Levi's eyes go wide, a quick expansion of his pupils before they narrow to pinpricks.

His hands release from my throat, a sudden giving way of pressure, and he staggers back, his mouth hanging open, fingers twitching in front of him in shock. I cough, sucking in gulps of air, but I don't let myself sink to the ground, I don't let my legs give out. I take a step forward and wrap my hand around the handle of the knife once again, keeping Levi from pulling it out. My eyes settle on the small scar along his chin, the scar I've touched and kissed ever since we were teenagers, and I think: *I will give you another scar. One you won't heal from.* And I press the blade in deeper, watching as he winces away from the motion.

My heart clobbers against my chest bone, beating, *beating*, thudding so hard it hurts. I've always known his weakness: me. And even now, he underestimated how far I'd go, what I'd be willing to do to make things right.

He drops to his knees, a look of bewilderment pooling in his eyes, and he makes a sputtering sound, blood in his throat, suffocating him. I lower myself too, keeping my eyes on his, wanting my face to be the last thing he sees. The last thing he remembers.

I draw the knife out, smelling the metallic scent of blood on my hand, and I open my mouth. "I want you to feel it," I say, each word bitten through clenched teeth. "I want you to know I've taken your life from you. I've taken everything." Blood trickles from his mouth, an awful sight, but I don't look away. "I was always stronger than you." A smile forms on my lips, and Levi's eyes flutter rhythmically, like he wants to speak but can't. No more lies from his lips. No more cajoling words. "You've always been weak." His eyelids convulse, struggling to keep themselves open, and

I thrust the blade in again, harder this time, up to the hilt, but lower in his torso—searching for his kidneys. For the spot that will end his life. And I can see the change in his face; the color leaves him. His skin turns the shade of goat's milk. "Fuck you," I hiss, and I watch as he slumps to his side, arms like two sagging cornstalks, looking sad and awful and dripping in his own blood.

I yank the blade back out and stand up, my body trembling but suddenly warm, on fire.

I've killed him, the man I loved . . . and he deserved it.

Rain cascades down from above, streaming across his face, diluting the blood where it soaks into the wet ground.

A few yards away, the tidy rows of corn smell sweet and a little like dust, the husks peeling away in places, revealing the yellow teeth beneath. I think of the summer harvest, the taste of corn on the cob eaten at sunset while we all gather around a bonfire, telling old stories and laughing at old jokes.

I breathe, shaking from the cold—from what I've just done—and I touch my stomach, feeling the fish-flutter pulse of the baby inside. *My child.*

I have lived a partial life, half in darkness. But now I feel something else: a strange calm, an ease I haven't known since childhood. A feeling I've missed.

The sky turns pewter, watery-gray, and a new certainty settles in my bones: I will raise my daughter within this forest, bright-eyed and wild-hearted. She will march unafraid beyond borders, and into dark feral lands. I will teach her how to swim in the pond beyond the farmhouse, *just as I did*, to harvest lemons and hazelnuts, and to sleep under the stars when the nights are warm and quiet.

And when I touch the bridge of her freckled nose, the shell-shape of her tiny ears, I won't think of *him*. Because she will be all mine.

PART FIVE

THE OUTSIDERS

THEO

I used to find missing people.

Until two winters ago, deep in the mountains of northern California, I became one of the missing.

I open the oil-stained door into the Timber Creek Gas & Grocery, the little bell chiming over the door, and a cold wave of memories crashes over me, as if stepping back into some far-off distant dream. The same gray-skinned woman sits behind the counter under the searing buzz of fluorescent lights, staring lazily out the window, her finger tapping the same brand of cigarettes.

"Do you have a phone?" I ask quickly from the door.

Her wiry eyebrows lift, giving me the same look of annoyance I remember from the last time I was here. "Yeah, but it's not free to use. I'll have to charge you."

"I need you to call an ambulance."

At this, the woman's face draws back, like strings tugging her wrinkled features upward. "I remember you," she remarks, nodding to herself. "You came through here a few years back, looking for that woman." She releases her hand from the pack of cigarettes. "You ever find anything?"

"Yeah," I answer hastily. "Now please, call an ambulance. She's been shot."

The yellow-whites of the woman's eyes flick to my hands, where Calla's blood stains my skin, dripping onto the linoleum floor, and the woman's gaze stalls a moment, unblinking, before she turns and fumbles for her phone.

I don't wait to hear what she says to the police; I hurry back outside to the truck and press my hands against the bullet wound in my wife's stomach, while Colette and the baby sit quietly beside her on the front bench seat, all of us silent, all of us unsure what will happen next.

The rain lets up and the sky turns pale and waxen after the storm.

The police arrive in a noisy swirl of bright lights, and Calla is hoisted into an ambulance and taken away. Colette and her baby are whisked off too. The minutes move fast now, everything a blur of voices and movements—they ask questions about the bullet in Calla's ribs; they ask where we've been; they want to know our names.

"You all just appeared out of the forest?" a young officer with a doughy face asks, as if he too has sidestepped into a not yet fully formed dream, and he's unsure if this is all some prank. "After all this time?"

I tell a story, but not the right one. Not the *real* one. Because there is a strange ache inside me—the need to protect the place that was our home. To keep it secret, even now.

"Are there others out there?" they ask.

My stomach turns. *Others.* Maybe they want to be found, or maybe they want to remain hidden, solitary in the forest that is their home. Maybe it's not my decision to make.

The sun is sinking to the west when they finally take me to a hotel an hour away—when they decide I have nothing more to tell. The hotel has an outdoor pool and continental breakfast and TVs with the volume turned up too high in the lobby. My ears buzz and thump, and I want to go to the hospital to see Calla, but they tell me I won't be able to see her or Colette until the morning. *Might as well rest*, one of the officers says.

Might as well.

Might as well do nothing. Might as well sit inside a strange, stale room with not enough sunlight or air or space to move.

My head hurts, straining to make sense of this place where I once belonged.

I touch the TV remote, the ironing board in the narrow closet, the bar of soap beside the sink, but they threaten to reveal images of the people who have stayed in this room before me, of maids and crying children and one-night stands. My talent is returning to me in bursts, a jarring staccato of glimpses that I don't want.

It's sat dormant for so long that the creeping-back-in of memories that aren't mine feels like a terrifying intrusion. We only just escaped Pastoral, and my mind is still a little cracked, bruised, and unsteady. I'm still not sure who I am.

So I lie awake, alone in a bed that smells like something I've forgotten how to describe: like metal, like bleach that doesn't come from the earth, and I stare at the low ceiling thinking of Calla. Of strangers gathered around her, of needles poking her flesh, and the clicking of machines.

In the morning, there are no officers waiting for me in the lobby—even though they said they'd pick me up first thing and drive me to the hospital. I stand for a while beside the checker-patterned lobby chairs, staring out at the hotel pool. It's still early, and only a single woman is reclined in one of the lounge chairs, reading a book beneath the shade of a large umbrella, the shivering blue rectangle in front of her winking up at the clear sky.

Several feet away, the lobby TVs are making my ears ring with an ad for a bathroom cleaning product, and then a women's sanitary pad, and a storage unit facility that offers the first month free. Clean and organize. Clean and declutter. These slogans feel like insects nibbling at my eardrums.

I start to move toward the sliding lobby doors, needing an escape, when I hear a name bellowing from the TVs: *Colette.*

I pause and crane my head back, listening to the voice warble from the speakers, wishing I could turn the volume down two clicks. It's a local news station, a man with silver hair and a woman with unnatural blue eyes, peering out through the TV screen. ". . . the woman and her baby were taken to the hospital yesterday after having fled a remote part of the forest about an hour south of here. But it wasn't until early this morning when the identity of the unknown woman was discovered. Authorities have determined that she is indeed Ellen Ballister, the young actress who vanished eleven years earlier from her home in Malibu. And since then had been believed to be dead."

I feel the ground beneath me sway just a little. A man walks through the sliding doors into the lobby behind me, glancing up at the TVs. He shakes his head and tilts his gaze to me. "Hell of a story, ain't it? Her husband said she left a note eleven years ago, saying she was going up the coast, needed a weekend away, but she never came home. Somehow ended up in those woods. Has amnesia, they're saying. Can't recall what happened to her." He shakes his head again, but there is a wink in his eyes, like he's thrilled at the spectacle of such a story. "She even had a baby with another man in those woods. You can't write this shit. Fucking crazy."

The man stares at me a moment, waiting for me to respond, to nod in agreement, but I offer up not even a twitch of an eyelash. Somehow *Ellen Ballister* found herself in Pastoral—maybe she went in search of it, like Maggie did, or maybe she found it on accident (which seems unlikely) but either way, just like us, she forgot who she really was. She forgot she was someone else outside those walls.

But now she's returned, with a newborn baby.

I turn away from the TVs and the man, and stride out through the doors. Word has gotten out, and I suspect it won't be long until they come asking questions of Calla and me.

———

A young officer is standing beside his patrol car just outside the lobby doors, hands in his pockets, eyeing the hotel pool like he'd rather be floating faceup, smeared in sunblock, than waiting for me.

"Sir," he says to me, not using the name I gave police yesterday: Theo. Maybe they suspected it was a lie, or at least not entirely truthful, so they're waiting for the rest of the story to reveal itself. For me to fess up.

He opens the passenger door, not forcing me to sit in the back, and we pull out of the hotel parking lot. I'm careful not to touch anything inside the car—I don't want to see the faces of those who've been arrested, handcuffed, and forced into this automobile.

The clouds are low and suffocating overhead, but the day is mild, slightly humid, and smelling of car exhaust. My police escort isn't the talkative type, thankfully, and we sit in silence as we pass a handful of fast-food restaurants, a coffee hut, two hardware stores, and a church. It's a small town, but it feels dense, the buildings crushed closely together, houses divided by fences.

I feel like I'm not in my own skin, watching it all whiz by, but after another mile more, we arrive at the hospital at the top of a sloped hillside.

The young officer with the short haircut and bored eyes gives me a nod when I open the door. "I'll wait for you here."

Calla's hospital room is on the second floor. All bleached-white surfaces and ticking machines. Her eyes lift when I enter the room, and she holds out a hand to me, tears already wetting her eyelids.

"I'm sorry," I tell her, my mouth against hers.

She shakes her head, tears streaming down her cheeks. "Not your fault."

"I should've gotten the gun from him quicker. I should have told you to run."

Again she shakes her head, smiling. "I wouldn't have left you alone anyway. You know how stubborn I am."

I nod and she pulls me down to kiss her again.

"I wanted to come see you last night but they wouldn't let me."

"Doctor says I can probably leave tomorrow. Or the next day." Her mouth falls flat and she looks pale, weak, but she's alive. "The bullet wasn't deep, just between my ribs. I should heal fine."

I squeeze her hand between both my palms. I should have been here when she woke up, should have been here to talk to the doctors; I never should have let her be alone.

"I told them it was a hunting accident," she says. "That no one was at fault."

We've told so many lies since we've found our way out, like we're afraid of the truth—like we're protecting the place we left behind.

"It's cold here," she says at last, and I release her hand to draw the white hospital blanket up to her chin, tucking it close. But she adds, "Not that kind of cold."

I smile for the first time. "I know what you mean."

She traces circles with her finger inside the palm of my hand. "Did you tell them where we came from?"

"No. Only that we were living in the woods, that's all. I didn't tell them about the others."

"Maybe we should."

"It will change everything if we do. And maybe they're better off in that forest than out here."

"Better living a lie?" she asks. "Living in fear with Levi?" She winces and touches her left side where the bullet was dislodged from her torso.

I touch her shoulder, wishing I could take the pain from her, stuff it down inside my own rib cage.

"I don't know." I don't know what happens now, where we go from here. I'm worried about those we left behind, worried what will happen to them if we do nothing. And a small part of me is also worried I won't be able to remember the man I used to be, the man I was *out here*. From the man I became. I'm worried I won't be able to tell the difference between the two.

Calla's expression settles. "How are Colette and the baby?"

"Colette's real name is Ellen. She was an actress before she came to Pastoral. It was on the news in the hotel."

"You're staying in a hotel?" Her eyes smile a little.

"Yeah."

"How is it?"

"It smells like damp laundry."

She laughs then immediately cringes, grabbing for her ribs again. Her eyes begin to droop closed; whatever drugs are in her IV are making her drowsy.

"You should rest," I say.

She swallows and forces her eyelids open again. "Maybe you're wrong," she says, the sleepiness heavy in her voice. "Maybe Colette's real name isn't Ellen. Maybe her real name is the one she had in Pastoral." She smiles gently, touching my hand. "Maybe that's the only one that matters."

"Maybe," I answer. But she's already asleep, snoring softly, her dark hair draped across the pillow.

CALLA

My name is not Calla. I am Maggie St. James.

Seven years ago, I went into the woods and forgot how to get back out.

But now, I wake in my hospital bed, the clean hygienic scent nauseating—I can't think of a worse smell than a sterilized room. I prefer the scent of dirt and pollen, old books and old wood.

Three days I've been here, but they say I can go home now. *Home?* Where is that?

A nurse told me that Colette—*Ellen Ballister*—left the hospital. Her husband and family came to collect her through a sea of reporters and cameramen anxious to get an image of the starlet, returned after all these years with a baby in her arms—a baby fathered by a man who was not the husband she left behind. A baby who, the nurse also tells me, should survive.

She also finally gave the child a name: Clover Clementine Rose.

A Pastoral name—a good name.

Theo comes to pick me up just after noon. I climb into the old truck and roll down the window, resting my head back against the seat and feeling the wind against my face. But the drive is short, and too soon Theo is helping me through the lobby of the hotel to an elevator.

Inside our room, I walk to the window and stare out at an unfamiliar landscape. A world crusted over with concrete and blinking streetlights and car horns.

"Your parents called the hotel," Theo says from behind me. "They know you're here."

I turn back to face him. "How?"

"Police notified them. Found you in the missing persons database, most likely." Theo is standing only a few paces away, like he's ready to reach out and grab me if I start to feel weak. If I collapse beside the window.

On shaking legs, I wobble the few steps to the bed, sinking onto the end with a hand against my ribs. "What will I tell them?"

"The truth," Theo answers.

I shake my head. "I don't even know what that is."

————

I know I should call him Travis. And he should call me Maggie. But we can't seem to shake the names of who we've become. *Our Pastoral names.*

We sit in the lobby of the hotel, my body thrumming with nervous energy. The TVs are droning from the far corner of the long, rectangular room. An older couple is watching the news, their heads inclined back, listening to the voices blare about stock prices and the worst flu on record and a shooting out east somewhere. Death toll unknown. This is the framework of a society we've left behind, the things I was once numb to. But now, each one is a papercut across my skin, little wounds that burn more than they ever did before.

"They're here," Theo says, standing up from his chair and nodding through the glass doors at the parking lot. He runs his hands down his pant legs, like he could wipe away the nerves.

My parents are walking across the pavement, hand in hand. They seem familiar, but in that distant, watery way. And I'm unsure how I'm going to feel once they're only a few feet from me, arms outstretched—these two people who've spent seven years searching for their daughter. For me. I should feel bad for them, for the worry that's carved hard lines into their faces, for the sleepless nights my disappearance has caused. But oddly, I feel nothing. Only a knocking against my ribs.

They move through the sliding glass doors, eyes scanning the lobby, and when they see me, tears break across both their faces. A moment later, I'm in their arms, my mom muttering my name—the wrong name. "Maggie," she says. "Maggie, are you okay?"

But still, I don't know what to feel. What to say. My stitches throb beneath my shirt, the pressure of their embrace too much, and my head is an anvil. I should know these two people, but my mind struggles to place them into the sequence of my life, a slideshow all mixed up and out of order.

I pull away from them and they look to Theo—to *Travis*.

"Thank you," my mom says through the wash of her tears, hardly getting the words out before she pulls Theo into a hug, sobbing against his shoulder. After all this time, he's brought me back to them—he did the job they hired him to do.

The racket in my chest rises up into my throat, and I sink back down into the lobby chair, trying to keep the room from spinning. To keep the nausea at bay.

My parents sit on the small sofa opposite me, hands wringing, staring at me as if they're trying to superimpose their memory of me from seven years ago over the woman who sits before them now.

"Are you alright?" my mother asks, leaning forward, as close to me as she can get—a strange show of affection from a woman who rarely showed any when I was little. A piece of my past I *feel* more than I remember.

I nod but my body feels as if it's convulsing. Theo sits down beside me, and I can feel him wanting to touch me. But he holds his hands stiffly in his lap, afraid for my parents to see, to know what we are.

"The police said you were found near where your car was abandoned," my dad says. "That you'd been up in those woods all these years."

My gaze flinches to my mom, but her expression looks suddenly tight, creases pulled together at her temples.

"I—" I begin, then catch myself, twirling the ring on my finger—my wedding band. I don't know where to start, what to say. How do I explain the last seven years of my life? Tell them that who I am now is not who I once was. I prefer the dampness of soil beneath my toes and the hush of an autumn twilight over cappuccinos and crowds and noisy movie theaters. That I don't think I can ever be that woman again; that I don't know who I'm supposed to be. That seeing them again is both relief and strain inside my rib cage, pressing on the hole where the bullet was pulled free. That I feel like I can't breathe. Like I might vomit right here in this hotel lobby with its screeching TVs and the whoosh of the sliding glass doors as hotel guests come and go, dragging rolling suitcases and yelling children and cell phones that *ding* and *buzz* and *chirp*.

Finally, Theo reaches out and takes my hand, squeezing tightly, anchoring me to him. And I hear the word pulsing against my temples: *husband, husband.* The memory surfaces now: of Levi saying this word to me over and over until it became true. He convinced me of its meaning, made it impossible to think of Theo as anything other than my husband. But he didn't make me love Theo, didn't make my heart twine into knots whenever he touched me—those thoughts are my own. Theo is my husband because my skin cannot bear to be without him, not because Levi made us marry.

I smile at Theo, the familiar touch of his hand calming the roiling in my stomach.

But when I swing my gaze back to my parents, my mom's expression has gone slack, the pink color washed from her cheeks. My dad's posture has hardened in his chair.

I swallow again and this time find my voice. "This is my husband, Theo. You know him as Travis. We've been married for two years." My voice catches, threatens to sink into my stomach, but then re-forms. "Although it feels like much longer—for both of us."

The hiss of the TVs works its way into my ears. A phone rings from behind the lobby desk and a woman answers, speaking low enough that I can't hear.

At last, my mother asks, "What happened to you out there?" Her bottom lip hangs open, hands clasped together so tightly that her knuckles turn as white as her slacks.

"I became someone else."

———

My parents are staying in a room on the third floor of the hotel. An elevator ride above us. They ask us to join them for dinner at an Italian place up the road, Martoni's Eatery, but I tell them we'd prefer to stay in, that the noise of a restaurant would be too much. But in truth, seeing them again, making conversation, pretending that we can resume life as it once was, is more than I can deal with right now.

My head hasn't stopped swirling since we saw them in the lobby, my mother's deft stare, concern and agitation puckering at the corners of her mouth. She was shaken by the sight of Theo's hand in mine; the woman I've become, the secrets I carry. But she carries them too—I can feel the strain of them in her eyes.

Theo and I are back in our room, and I sit at the edge of the bed, my shirt drawn up, while Theo peels away the gauze and white cloth from my wound, revealing stitches and a surgically clean incision. It's a small opening, the place where the bullet tore through the layer of flesh and wedged itself against my lower ribs. If Parker had been any closer to me, if his gun wasn't so old, so rarely fired, perhaps the bullet might have traveled deeper into my torso. Hit organs that could have killed me. I got lucky, I guess.

Theo dabs the incision with peroxide then secures a clean bandage with tape.

"It's healing good," he says.

I touch his hand and he lifts his eyes. "I'm scared," I tell him.

"I know. Me too."

A knock thumps softly against the hotel room door. Theo stands and I lower my shirt, breathing deeply to test the restriction of the gauze. He opens the door and my mother is standing in the hall, shoulders rounded, hands clasped, looking out of place in this hotel. Looking like she's a long way from home.

"Maggie," she says, still standing in the hall. "Can I speak with you?"

She doesn't know my new name, my Pastoral name, and hearing her say *Maggie* grates against my eardrums. A past creeping its way back in.

"I'll leave you alone," Theo says, and before I can object, he strides past my mother and down the hall. I imagine him sitting in the lobby alone, or maybe he'll retreat to his truck, waiting until it's safe to return to our little room. *All we have left.*

Mom steps through the doorway, letting the door close shut behind her. "It's good to see you," she says, and already I see the pain—some foreign regret—gathering in her eyes. "It's been so long."

"I know."

She crosses the room but doesn't try to draw me into another hug. Perhaps she senses that I don't want to be touched right now, that I'm struggling to make sense of my surroundings, of her, of everything.

"I could use a cigarette," she mutters, crossing her arms and smirking to herself. I've never known my mother to smoke, but maybe she started after I went missing. A nervous addiction. I wouldn't blame her.

She lowers her arms again, fidgeting, before meeting my gaze. "I don't know what happened between you and Travis out there. Or how it is that you're married, but—" Her voice sputters away, maybe she's decided not to say whatever she was thinking. She starts again. "The police told us that you're having a hard time remembering things about your life before you left."

I push myself up from the bed, a slow effort, and thankfully she doesn't try to help me, just watches as I walk to the window overlooking the parking lot. A pool sits far below, glittering an unnatural shade of blue under the early evening sun. "The memories are coming back, slowly."

"Do you remember the stories I used to tell you, about the place where I used to live?"

I swivel around to face her, leaning my hip against the window frame. Steadying myself.

"It was a place called Pastoral," she says.

My throat dries up.

"I know that's where you were," she continues. "I know you went back to where you were born."

I touch the edge of the window to keep my knees from buckling beneath me. "I was born in Pastoral?"

Her eyebrows crush together. "I never wanted to tell you the truth. But you were so mad at me that day; you needed to understand—"

"What day?" I press, cutting her off.

"At the ferry." She frowns, as if just now realizing how little I remember. And maybe she's trying to decide if she can backstep her way out of this, avoid telling me anything. But it's too late now.

"What happened at the ferry?"

She rubs her palms against her knees, craving a cigarette worse than ever, I imagine. "It was a week or so before you disappeared. You came to the house for dinner—you don't remember?" She looks at me, but she must see in my eyes that I need her to keep going, I need her to tell me what happened. "You were angry with me. You said—" Her voice breaks off, and for a split second she glances to the door, her exit, her way out of here if she wants to bolt back out into the hall and escape whatever it is she doesn't want to say. But then her eyes sweep back to me. "You said I hadn't been a good mom; you said I loved your brother more than you. But that's not true; it's not." She's fighting the tears now, but it's a helpless effort; they spill down her cheeks in little damp trails. "You said your father was the only one who really cared about you."

I release my hold on the windowsill, *remembering now*. Remembering that day on the wharf, waiting for the ferry. "And you told me that he wasn't even my real father," I say so she won't have to.

Her jaw trembles. "I never planned to tell you, I didn't mean to." She touches her face with her hand, smearing away the tears and mascara, making an ashy smudge at the corners of her eyes.

It was raining hard that day, the sky indistinguishable from the sea, and I remember the anger I felt growing inside me. But it wasn't only about her, I was angry at a lot of things. My career had suffered in the previous year, several kids had gone missing, run away from home in search of the *underground*—the fictional place I had written about in my books. My stories were too dark, many said. And they were inspiring children to trek into forests and backwoods, hoping they might find the place where Eloise had followed the fox and become the monster. But the worst had happened only a month before I stood on the wharf with my mom—a boy had died. Markus Sorenson was only fourteen years old when he walked into the Alaskan wilderness not far from his home, the first book in the *Foxtail* series tucked into his backpack along with a thermos of hot apple cider, a flashlight, a small shovel, and an extra pair of socks. His body wasn't found until a week later; hypothermia had taken his life only a couple days after he vanished. And the guilt that tore through me was enough to make me start drinking at a rate that began to drown out the days.

When I came to Whidbey Island to see my parents, I wasn't in good shape. I hadn't had a sober day in a month, and hearing my mom say that my father was not my real father felt like a brick slamming against my bones. I hated her for it, hated her for the lies she had told me my entire life. And I hated her for finally telling me the truth.

She told me how she had married too young, how she had had an affair with a man who had only been visiting friends on Whidbey Island, a few houses down from my parents' home. How when she learned she was pregnant, the man told her she could come live in a community where they would care for her and the child after it was born. So she left her husband, packed her things, and went to Pastoral. But after I was born, she began to realize she couldn't stay there—it wasn't the kind of life she wanted for herself, or her child. She fled Pastoral and retreated back to her husband. She lied and told him that the baby was his, and he believed her—or at least pretended to. And I was raised by a man who I thought was my father.

My mother told me all this that day, waiting for the ferry, and I understood why she had always treated me like she did—kept me at arm's length—I held her secrets inside my very existence. When she looked at me, she saw my real father, she saw the mistake she'd made, and she feared that someday her husband would look at me and see it too. I was a bomb waiting to go off—to break apart her entire world. I could ruin everything.

With the rain streaming over us, I asked her the name of my real father. I asked her about the place where I was born. *His name was Cooper,* she had said.

I need to see it, I told her. I pleaded with her. *I need to go there.*

She refused at first, but she also must have known that there was no turning back now. She had given up her secrets, and I deserved to see the place where I took my first breath, to know if my real father was still alive. So she told me how to get there: the route into the mountains and the old red barn and the path through the woods.

Now, facing my mother in this hotel room, a new betrayal begins to surface. "You knew where I was this whole time?"

Her head moves slowly, nodding.

"You could have told someone, said something."

I think of my father who raised me, waking each morning for the last seven years, not knowing where I was. His only daughter.

"I couldn't," she answers.

I press a hand to my side where the incision has started to throb, the pain meds wearing off. I need to sit down, but I don't—not yet. "You wanted to protect yourself, you mean," I say. "You didn't want my dad to know the lie you've kept from him after all these years." She would rather let him suffer, than tell him the truth—than tell him how she had had an affair, how I wasn't his real daughter.

I bite down on all the things I want to say to her, all the vile thoughts swirling inside me.

"Is he still alive?" she asks.

"Cooper's dead," I tell her bluntly. "He died before I arrived. I never got to meet my real father."

"But you stayed there all these years. There must have been some reason you never left."

"I didn't have a choice." Pastoral is not the same place it was when my mother lived there, when Cooper was still alive—when members came and went as they liked. The borders were open then, and there was nothing to fear.

"I told Travis how to find you," she says, as if this makes it all okay.

"Theo," I correct her.

"What?"

"His name is Theo."

She wipes at her cheeks, the tears dried up now. "Theo," she amends.

"And my name is Calla."

Her eyes have stopped blinking, her mouth drooping at the corners. "I'm sorry," she says. "I'm sorry for all of it."

I don't know what to say, how to piece together seven years of being trapped in a place, forgetting who I used to be, when my mother knew exactly where I was. I feel angry and sorry for her, I want to blame her for it all—but I know that I can't. I have my own festering regret, my own responsibility for the things that have happened.

She lowers her head, gathering more words together in her mind. "I loved it there, for a time. I thought maybe you stayed because you loved it too."

I touch the necklace against my shirt, counting through each tiny silver book, trying to dig through the cluttered mess of my mind, pinpointing all the moments that felt real inside Pastoral. "It was my home," I admit. The truth. Even if I never intended to stay in Pastoral, even if the lies Levi told us kept me there longer than I should have been, it did become my home. And in some ways, it was a balm for my broken soul, forgetting everything I left behind in this world: my mother, the boy who died while searching for a place that only existed in my mind, and even the reason I came to Pastoral in the first place—to find Cooper, a man who was already long dead when I arrived.

"When you were little, I used to tell you stories," Mom says now. "They were fairy tales about a forest and a girl who vanished inside it. They were tales I remembered from Pastoral." Her mouth quirks to the side, almost a smile. "I think it's why you wrote your Foxtail books. They were based on the stories I told you as a child. You were writing about the forests of Pastoral, you just didn't know it."

"You told me those stories?" It feels like a riddle finally stitching itself back together, the thread made of my mother's words. When I was young, she told me the tales of the wheat farmer's daughter—the girl who lived in the woods when the town was first built. A story I would later grow up to write about in my books.

But Levi had used that same story to make his lies true, to convince us the forest was infected with an illness. When in truth, perhaps that young girl merely wandered into the woods and got lost, never to return.

It was a tale that grew and became something different each time—as stories tend to do.

I let my gaze settle on my mom, the warmth in her face, the distant look in her eyes like she too is recalling her time in those woods. "The Pastoral you remember is not what it is now," I say. "The people who live there are afraid."

Her expression drops, turns cold. "Afraid of what?"

"Disease. A sickness that we've feared for years—but it was never real."

"I don't understand."

If I wasn't so exhausted, so lost in a sea of my own thoughts, I might cry. I might scream. But instead I stand mute, staring at my mother in a hotel room that feels like a midway place between an old life and an unknown one I haven't figured out yet. "I know you don't understand," I say. "You've never understood. But I am not the daughter you raised; I'm someone different. And I think, for the first time, I know who I am."

"Maggie," she says, and now she reaches out for me, touching my arm. Growing up, she rarely placed her arms around me unless I was sick, rarely brushed my hair away from my face. She kept her distance. And now I understand why: She saw in me the man, and the place, she was trying to forget. A past she was trying to rid from her mind.

I was an outsider in my own home.

I meet my mother's ivory-blue eyes, unblinking, and I feel sad for her: this awful secret she's kept, the thing she's held on to all these years, only ever revealing small clues to me as a kid—stories that rooted themselves inside me. As if those woods, as if Pastoral had been calling to me all my life, urging me to come back.

"Come home with us," she says at last. "You can start your life again."

I smile at her, but it feels like a wince. "My life didn't stop just because I was gone. I have another life now, and a husband."

She lowers her hand from my arm. "You don't believe that, do you? That he's really your husband?"

White spots of anger burn against my eyes. "I forgive you, Mom," I say, instead of the thing I want to say. "I forgive you for not knowing how to fit me into your life when I was younger, and for still not knowing how. But thank you for telling me the truth that day at the ferry, and thank you for sending Theo to find me. But I can't go back home with you and Dad. I can't go back to my life in Seattle, either." Although I suspect my home in Seattle is long gone. After seven years, my parents have surely boxed up my things and sold off the old house where I once lived alone.

My mother lets out a long, labored exhale, as if she's been holding it in for seven years, and I let her pull me into a hug. She holds me like that, not letting go, like she could make up for all the times she didn't draw me to her and tell me everything would be okay.

I thought my life inside Pastoral was an illusion, a shell formed over the person I used to be, but maybe my life out here is just as scarred and scabbed over.

Just as broken.

No matter where you go, there are cracks in the plaster, nails coming loose, you just have to decide *where* you want to piece yourself back together. Where the ground feels sturdiest beneath your feet.

I forgive her for the secrets she's kept: for not coming to look for me when I disappeared.

But maybe I also understand why she didn't. Pastoral was never a place she feared; it was where she ran away to; it was an escape. And maybe she thought I wanted to stay lost, stay gone—she was only protecting me.

After all, Pastoral is where I was born—I was never an outsider in that secluded stretch of forest.

I was an original. Born within the boundary.

THEO

I sit up in bed, sweat pricking my forehead, eyes struggling to make sense of the room—I search for the bedside table, the old dresser, the tall window and the curtains letting in the moonlight. But I'm not in the farmhouse, I'm in a hotel room in a town I've never heard of.

Calla touches my shoulder. "Nightmare?"

"A memory."

"Of what?"

I dig my hands along my scalp to the back of my neck. "My sister."

Calla sits up beside me, placing her hands gently against my arm. "You have a sister?"

"I used to."

I close my eyes and I can see her: Ruth. She'd blow bubbles from her bedroom out into the narrow hall that separated our two rooms, then she'd squeal, *Did you see it, Travis?* And if I didn't answer right away, she'd stomp her small, eight-year-old feet on the floor to get my attention. *Bubble wishes, Travis! If you catch one, you get to make a wish.* But this memory of her is quickly replaced by a worse one: finding her in that shitty motel room. Arriving a few minutes too late.

But more painful than the memory is realizing that I had forgotten about her. For the last two years, I forgot that my sister had ever existed, ever lived and then died. It feels like a gut punch.

"She died," I say to Calla. "Suicide."

"Theo." She squeezes her hand against my arm. "I didn't know."

"Neither did I. I couldn't remember her until now."

"I'm so sorry." Calla's eyes look glassy, the faint light from the streetlamps outside reflecting across her dark skin. "It was cruel, taking our memories from us. But even crueler now that we remember them."

My old life is only scraps. Everyone I cared about, my parents, my sister, are all long gone. I didn't have much more than what I do right now: a hotel room and an old truck. I dropped off the map long ago, before I ever found Pastoral. Even my talent has slipped away from me, a thing I'm afraid to let come rushing back: afraid of what it will show me, what it will mean.

"My sister is still out there," Calla says now.

I know she's been thinking of Bee; I can see the worry tunneling through her, making her hollow. But it's not only Bee we left behind. The others are still trapped inside the border that Levi created, frightened of an illness that isn't real.

I touch my wife's hand, winding my fingers through hers. Palm to palm. Even here, in this hotel room, she seems grown from the forest, a wild creature not meant for cityscapes. She rests her head against my shoulder. *I'm sorry*, I want to tell her. *For the time we lost, for the people we really are.* But this thought is cut through by another: Maybe those two years spent in the woods together were the only time that mattered.

Maybe we only believed Levi's lies so completely because we wanted to, because we needed to forget the pains of our past. We all have something we'd like to forget, some broken piece of ourselves we'd like to bury in the grave of our minds, and living in Pastoral allowed us this small gesture. A part of me healed while inside that farmhouse—the awful wrenching pain of losing my sister fell away. The hurt and anger shed from my bones, and now, thinking of her, I feel a sadness that doesn't suffocate quite so bad. I can think of her and still take a breath. I can think of her and remember more than just the last time I found her.

The *forgetting* healed old wounds.

The forgetting wasn't all bad.

"We can't stay here," Calla says, releasing my hand.

"I know." I turn to face her. "In the morning, we'll leave. We can go with your parents, if that's what you want; we'll figure things out from there."

"No." She touches her fingertips to my forehead, then winds them through my hair, following the motion with her eyes. "These aren't our lives, Theo." She smiles. "We have to go back."

"Where?" I ask dumbly, like I'm afraid to hear her say it, admit what I've already been thinking.

"You know where."

I trace the line of my wife's shoulder to where her hair falls down her back. I try to imagine her sitting in a coffee shop, talking on a cell phone. I try to imagine her in rush-hour traffic. But I don't know who that woman is, the person she was before.

"I can't live here, can you?" she asks.

"I was barely *living* here before."

"Neither was I," she says.

I shake my head, certain that's not true.

"We left the others behind," she adds, her eyelashes flicking, reminding me of feathers falling from a sad winter sky.

We fought so hard to get out of those woods, I can't believe we're talking about returning to the place that held us captive. Going back into the dark of that forest.

"Theo," she says, pulling my focus back to her. "Maybe we only get a few chances to choose our own lives." Her eyes skip to the door, wavering, before finding me again. "And this is one of them. This is ours."

She lowers her palm to place it against my chest; my heart beats wildly, my head feeling suddenly loose and alive, a fever threading through me. "I'll go wherever you want," I tell her. "I'll go back to Pastoral."

Calla's eyes are like full moons, and she leans forward, kissing me on the lips, running her hand up my chest to my neck. "I love you still," she whispers against my mouth.

She slips from bed and walks to the small chair beside the window, pulling a sweater over her head.

"Now?" I ask.

She nods back at me, grinning. "I need to go home."

"What about your parents?"

"I'll leave them a note—they'll understand or they won't. I don't really care."

We have nothing to pack, only the few supplies given to us by the hospital, so we leave our room without a suitcase, without things to weigh us down.

All we have now are our memories.

And we will go back to the place where we first forgot, to pick up the pieces. To make the wrongs right.

EPILOGUE

CALLA

Bee has her baby in the spring.

It rains against the farmhouse, a deep welcoming rain, coaxing the baby into the world. Faye stands at the foot of the bed, murmuring to Bee softly, calming her. "We're close," she says.

I heat water on the woodstove and bring up clean washcloths, anything to keep my hands busy, to feel useful while nerves clack up and down my spine.

"Open a window," Bee says to me.

"But it's raining."

"I know." Her lips curl up into a gentle smile. She's always loved the rain—even when we feared it, she longed to stand out in the meadow and catch the drops on her tongue. It rained the day she was born, she tells me. A good omen.

I slide the window up into the frame, drops of water pelting the bedroom floor. Bee stretches her hand away from the bed, toward the open window, palm wide. She smiles when she feels the drops on her skin. "Thank you," she says, closing her eyes.

Another contraction drives through her and she clamps her teeth shut, moaning against the pain, seizing my hand in hers. *My sister.* We might have been born to different parents, but we were both born in these woods, in Pastoral. And she is my sister—a truth that cannot be undone.

Downstairs I hear Theo pacing across the living room floor, Henry is there too, speaking in low, anxious tones. The community has been awaiting this birth—a child born to the woman who has become our new leader.

Bee has taken the place of the man who lied to us.

She told the others the truth: about the border, about the pox, and how she killed Levi to save her own life. All decisions are now made together, for the common good—governed by all—the same principles that Cooper believed in when he founded Pastoral.

The road is open now too, our fear subsiding.

Members come and go as they like, but mostly they stay—the outside world not how they remember it. *Or how they want to remember it.*

Outsiders come too, visiting those they thought were lost. Even my parents have come—my mother finally admitting to my father the truth— and she walks through the garden, recalling a time long ago when she lived in these woods, when she gave birth to a little girl who found her way back.

Parker and Theo still guard the gate, they keep the outside from spilling in too quickly—they keep reporters and TV crews from converging on our quiet life.

We're building something new.

The kind of place the founders had set out to make. A slower life, a return to something lost. And sometimes, I wonder if Levi wasn't entirely to blame for what happened to us—perhaps we allowed ourselves to be fooled, because we wanted to be someone else.

The sound of footsteps on the stairs echo down the hall, and the bedroom door swings open. It's Netta, carrying a glass bottle. "It's all Roona had," she says, handing the bottle to Faye.

"It'll be enough," Faye answers, taking the bottle of neroli oil and pouring some into her palms. "The baby is ready," she says, touching Bee's stomach with her hands. "It's time to push."

I brush Bee's hair back from her face, last summer's freckles dotting her cheeks and forehead. I will tell the story of Bee in my book—if there are still stories inside me—I will tell how she lost her eyesight then gained it back; I will tell how a man named Travis came in search of me, how if we had met *before*, in the outside, we might never have fallen in love. But here, in Pastoral, we became who we were always meant to be.

The story will begin with a man driving down a snow-covered road in search of a barn. In search of a woman who would become his wife.

There is no history in a place until we make it, until you live a life worth remembering. We have made a history here—some of it was more folklore than truth, more fear than anything else. But some of it was good. Some of it lives inside each of us, the history of this wild, wild land.

Bee lets out a low cry and her chin tilts to the ceiling. It will be a long delivery, several more hours until the baby finally wails into the night sky and feels the first drops of rain against her skin through the open window. And I wonder if she will love this place as I do. If she will feel rooted here at birth.

If she will look up at the stars and know, we're all just trying to find our way home.

ACKNOWLEDGMENTS

Pastoral was not always as idyllic as it seemed, but I hope you found some quiet solitude within its pages. As I know I did while writing it.

There are many people to thank for bringing this book to life. My agent, Jess Regel, has been by my side for the last ten years, and I couldn't imagine a better partner to help usher my books into the world. Thank you, Jess, for all the countless revisions, phone calls, and encouragement. This one is for you.

Loan Le, my magnificent editor (and also a brilliant writer herself), dove headfirst into this story with me, and we found the heart of this book together. Loan, I feel so lucky that this book found its way into your hands.

To everyone at Atria Books who has worked behind the scenes to bring this story to life: THANK YOU from the bottom of my heart. Libby McGuire, Lindsay Sagnette, Dana Trocker, Lisa Sciambra, Suzanne Donahue, James Iacobelli, Danielle Mazzella di Bosco—who crafted a stunning cover—Gena Lanzi, Maudee Genao, Paige Lytle, Jessie McNiel, Fausto Bozza, Jill Putorti, Sara Kitchen, Nicole Bond, Lauren Castner, and Elizabeth Mims—for your brilliant copyediting.

Thank you Jenny Meyer and Heidi Gall for all your hustle in foreign rights. Leo Teti—thank you for believing in my books, and for all your ongoing support. To Tara Hart, thank you for reading the very first book when I signed with Jess, and for loving it. A BIG thanks to Jody Hotchkiss for finding ways to turn my books into even larger stories—I'm beyond grateful to have you in my corner!

Cassie and all the hardworking humans at Roundabout Books, thank you for always shelving my books face out, and for being my home away from home. Thank you to the reviewers, bloggers, booksellers, booksta-grammers, and authors who read early copies and said nice things. You are the true magic that helps a book find the right readers.

To my talented, kind, unstoppable writer friends: You inspire me every day with the stories you create. You know who you are.

To my parents, thank you for being the first storytellers in my life. And for letting me read Stephen King and Dean Koontz when I was much too young. To Sky, thank you for reminding me to trust the story inside me. It's always there if you choose to listen.

To the readers: We have gone on many adventures together. Thank you for going on one more.

ABOUT THE AUTHOR

Shea Ernshaw is a *New York Times* bestselling author and winner of the Oregon Book Award. Her books have been published in more than twelve countries, and her novels *The Wicked Deep* and *Winterwood* were Indie Next Picks. She lives in a small mountain town in Oregon and is happiest when lost in a good book, lost in the woods, or writing her next novel.